Dennis O'Sullivan

The Loves and Intrigues of Kings and Queens

Embracing the romantic adventures of the most remarkable heroes, rulers

etc.

Dennis O'Sullivan

The Loves and Intrigues of Kings and Queens
Embracing the romantic adventures of the most remarkable heroes, rulers etc.

ISBN/EAN: 9783337195533

Printed in Europe, USA, Canada, Australia, Japan

Cover: Foto ©Andreas Hilbeck / pixelio.de

More available books at **www.hansebooks.com**

THE

ves and Intrigues

OF

NGS and QUEENS

EMBRACING

The Romantic Adventures

OF THE

emarkable Heroes, Rulers, Statesmen and Prelates
ho have figured in the History of the World.

AS WELL AS

THE AMOURS

OF THE

PRESSES, QUEENS and PRINCESSES

FRANK TOUSEY,

in the Office of the Librarian of Congress at Washington, D. C.

CONTENTS.

pathriot-m

AN INTRODUCTION.

With Some Pertinent Remarks and Facts as to the Loves and Intrigues of Kings, Queens, and other Favored Mortals.

> " The king can drink the best of wine ;
> No can I,
> He cannot order rain or shine ;
> Nor can I,
> Then what's the difference, and tell me why
> Betwixt my lord the king, and I?"

This was the question propounded by Charles Mackay, a popular English poet, some thirty years ago. As we quote from memory, the words may not be given exactly as the poet wrote them, but the meaning of the democratic writer is very plain for all that.

He intends to convey the idea that the king may be no happier than any humble subject who is able to enjoy the good things of this life without aspiring to the performance of the impossibilities.

The rulers of nations may not recline on beds of roses at all times, while the paths of many have been full of very sharp briers; yet the average citizen is apt to regard them as favored beings, more especially when he reads of their pleasures and pastimes, and of their tender amours.

A certain Irish friend of ours tells a story about the celebrated Daniel O'Connell, who was, by the way, a great favorite with the gentler sex.

At a time when the poor people of Ireland were suffering from a famine, the great liberator was arrested by the British government, and consigned to prison as a patriot-martyr.

O'Connell was adored by the people; and the national press of the country made much ado about consigning the stalwart leader to the cell as a common felon.

One evening a group of citizens assembled at a tavern in a southern town, when the school-master began to read aloud the weekly newspaper account of the arrest, imprisonment and sufferings of the great martyr in the cause of freedom.

Among the eager listeners was a poor, half-witted shoemaker, named Teddy O'Ryan, who had not enjoyed a substantial meal during the year, and who had scarcely a pound of flesh on his miserable body.

Teddy listened to the story of the sufferings of the great patriot without betraying the least emotion, although there was not another dry eye in the audience; but the schoolmaster soon touched on a point that arrested the poor shoemaker's attention and caused him to become unduly excited.

" A delegation composed of some of the noblest ladies in Dublin," said the local orator, " waited on the great liberator in his martyr cell yesterday and, after saluting him with kindly tokens of their love and esteem, they presented him with a splendid turkey and a magnificent pound-cake prepared with their own fair hands, for——"

" Oh, Jaycus!" exclaimed poor Teddy, in tones that could be heard all over the house.

" What ails ye, Teddy, you goose!" cried the indignant schoolmaster, while all the others greeted the poor fellow with angry frowns.

Teddy placed both hands on his empty stomach and turned his eyes aloft, as he exclaimed, in heart-rending tones:

" Oh, Jaycus—Jaycus! Wouldn't I like to become a grate pathriot-murther!"

The half-starved Irishman had no pity for the patriot while he could enjoy fat turkeys and fine pound-cakes, and he wished himself in Daniel O'Connell's place, even though that place was a prison cell.

And so it has been with many who are famishing for the pleasures and allurements enjoyed by the rulers of the earth.

Historians and moralists may preach until Doomsday about the sufferings, sorrows and the anxieties of kings and queens, yet the average mortal will be apt to exclaim, when hearing of their enjoyments:

" Oh, Jaycus, Jaycus! but I'd like to be a great ruler."

It would be all in vain for the philosopher to tell an ardent lover of the many trials, disasters and great wars brought about by love intrigues, as the latter would only say, with one of our popular poets:

> " Love came, and brought sorrow too soon to his train;
> Yet so sweet that to-morrow 'twere welcome again.
> Though misery's full measure my portion shall be,
> I would drain it with pleasure if pour'd out by thee."

While perusing the histories of nations, we have found some very strange facts and incidents connected with the adventures of those who devoted their lives and their fortunes to love intrigues.

A celebrated French historian, in speaking of the manners of the thirteenth century, mentions a very extravagant society of fanatics, which went by the name of La Ligue des Amans, that is to say, the Amorous, or the Lovers' League. Their scheme was to prove the excess of their love, by their invincible obstinacy in withstanding the seasons.

The knights, the equerries, the married and single ladies who were initiated into that order, were bound, according to the rules of the institution, to cover themselves very scantily in the most frosty weather, and very warmly in the hottest days of summer. In this last season they lighted great fires, with which they warmed themselves, as if they stood in the greatest want of it. In the winter, it would have been a shame and a sin to find the least spark of fire in their houses. Their chimneys, in that cold season, were trimmed with green foliage.

As soon as one of them entered a house, the husband took great care that his guest's horse should want for nothing, and left him master over everything in the house, to which he never returned till he was gone. Then, if he were of the same brotherhood, he met likewise with the same treatment and the same complacency from the husband, whose wife was the object of his cares and his visits.

This ridiculous society existed till the greatest part of those chilled lovers starved with cold, or died one after another, with the lie in their mouth, by protesting how ardent were the flames which burned in their hearts.

The same historian writes of another band of distinguished gallants which existed in a portion of France in the days of chivalry.

These chivalrous lovers lived under a regular code of laws, and they were sworn to obey the rules thus laid down. Among the maxims thus presented were the following:

Marriage is not a lawful excuse for not falling in love.

A man who cannot be silent cannot love.

No one can love two persons at the same time.

Love must ever be increasing or diminishing.

A widowhood of two years must be undergone for a dead lover.

Every lover is bound to grow pale at the sight of his mistress.

A new love expels the old.

A true lover is bound to be sparing in sleep and food.

Love can deny nothing to love.

A certain cavalier, who was a member of this society, loved a fair lady, and as he did not enjoy a frequent opportunity of conversing with her, it was agreed between them that they should communicate by the intervention of a secretary, by which means their passion might be the better concealed.

Their secretary, however, forgetting the confidence reposed in him, pleaded his own cause, and was heard with a favorable ear.

The cavalier then denounced him to the leading lady of the court, and humbly demanded that the offense should be judged by her and other ladies; to which the criminal himself assented. The countess having convoked sixty ladies, pronounced the following judgment:

" Let this fraudulent lover, who has met with a lady worthy of him, that has not blushed to become an accomplice in so shameful an offense, enjoy his ill-bought pleasure, and let her pride herself in her lover. But let them both be excluded from all other attachments; and let them never be invited to the assemblies of the ladies or the courts of the knights, since he has offended against the knightly oath, and she contrary to womanly modesty has yielded to the love of a secretary."

Whatever may have been the rules of the chivalrous knights and ladies of old as to herding with folks of low degree, we find that the kings and queens of later days were not so particular in their amours.

The old King of Bavaria became enamored of Lola Montez, a fascinating woman who made a living by dancing on the stage, and was the cause of inciting his people to an outbreak.

The great Catharine of Russia, as will be seen in the following pages, selected her lovers from among her own stalwart soldiers.

The late Victor Emanuel of Italy had mistresses who were in league with the most desperate secret societies formed by the discontented people of Europe; and some of these same fair creatures were also employed to entice Louis Napoleon into dangerous snares and pitfalls.

The late Emperor of Russia, who was assassinated by the Nihilists, had a favored mistress who was selected by him from a peasant home and placed in a palace, where she bore him several promising children.

The wife of Peter the Great of Russia was a woman of unknown origin; while one of his favored mistresses was the daughter of a German brewer.

The great Napoleon was paying court to two actresses at one time, and it was said that the woman he favored most was not at all prepossessing when off the stage.

George the Fourth of England led a disgraceful life, even in

his old age. The flunkies who thronged the court of London called him the first gentleman of Europe; but Thackeray informs us that the English sovereign merited the title of the greatest blackguard in Great Britain. Lord Byron, who was not an admirer of kings, called him an old profligate.

The marriage of George the Fourth was especially unfortunate. He married on April the 8th, 1794, his cousin, Caroline Amelia Elizabeth, second daughter of the Duke of Brunswick, under the pressure of debt, and of his father. Their conjugal happiness, if it ever existed, did not last many weeks. The Princess Charlotte Augusta was born of the marriage, on the 9th of January, 1796, and shortly after her parents separated, having ceased to speak to each other months before.

We also find that, while love inspired great conquerors and rulers, it also affected a great many of the leading prelates of the olden time, and that it even brought about divisions in religious communities.

The sect of the Mammilaries, which is a branch of the Anabaptists, owes its origin to love. A young Anabaptist was deeply enamored of a lady, whom he proposed to marry. In a tete-a-tete with her, infatuated by the violence of his love, he believed he might take any liberties, and he ventured too far. This action came to the knowledge of the doctors of the sect, and they soon convened an assembly to deliberate upon the punishment they should inflict upon the young lover. Some declared for excommunication, others, more indulgent for the impulses of nature, maintained that the fault was pardonable. This raised a dispute among the two parties. As is general in such cases, neither would yield, and it occasioned a schism. Those who were for the pardon were called Mammilaries.

Cardinal Richelieu aspired to win the love of the queen, and he stooped to receive the smiles of a fair maid of honour.

The late celebrated Cardinal Antonelli was reported to have carried on an intrigue with a lady of Rome, and when he died a certain young woman claimed to be his daughter.

The famous Dean Swift, who was pastor of a leading Episcopalian Church in Dublin, and who was noted as a humorist and a satirical writer of great power, had a faithful mistress who was devoted to him until she died.

Indeed, lovely damsels have bewitched the leading men of the world in all ages. Some of the greatest heroes have fallen victims to their passions, as did Marc Antony; while many others have been inspired to heroic deeds of valor by their attachments.

The brave Lord Nelson was not regarded as an outcast from society by the fiendish dames of England, though his intrigue with a certain fair lady was almost as well known as his famous victory in Trafalgar Bay.

The present Prince of Wales bears the reputation of being a regular Don Juan, yet he is welcomed and feasted in the stateliest homes of Great Britian; and on the morrow or next day, when he is crowned king, the poet laureate will sing his praises in choice verse.

The immortal Shakespeare refers to the "divinity that doth hedge a king;" but then simple citizens of our republic, when reading about the loves and intrigues of courts, will be apt to imagine that the monarchs of the world were more favored by the demons of their evil passions than by any protecting angels from the regions above.

THE
LOVES AND INTRIGUES
OF
KINGS AND QUEENS.

THE LOVES AND WICKED DEEDS OF CLEOPATRA, THE FAMED QUEEN OF EGYPT.

THE EARLY LIFE OF A WICKED WOMAN—ENTRAPPING THE GREAT CÆSAR—MARC ANTONY IN THE WEB—REVELING IN A GUILTY LOVE—THE AVENGER ON THE MARCH—DESPAIR, MADNESS AND DEATH.

Who has not heard of Cleopatra, the sinful, voluptuous, wicked Queen of Egypt.

The story of her life is a romance of murder, of licentiousness, and of vile intrigue. In her strange and romantic history we see that unlawful love controlled her and kept her enslaved during a life of adventure and of crime, and that her beauty and her blandishments affected the destinies of some of the greatest characters in the world's history.

The famous queen was born in Egypt, but she was of Greek descent. The ancient blood of Macedon flowed in her veins, and her character was marked by the genius, the courage, and the impulsiveness common to the proud stock from whence she sprung.

About two hundred and fifty years before Cleopatra's time, Alexander the Great, after he had conquered Persia, took possession of Egypt and annexed it to his own dominions.

After the death of Alexander Egypt fell into the hands of one of his generals named Ptolemy. This soldier made it his kingdom, and on his death he left it to his heirs.

A long line of sovereigns succeeded the founder of the kingdom, and they are known in history as the Ptolemys. Cleopatra was the daughter of the eleventh of that line.

Alexander the Great founded the great city which bears his name to this day, and which continues to be, after the lapse of twenty centuries of change, warfare, and revolution, one of the principal commercial emporiums of the East.

At the time when Cleopatra appeared on the world's stage Rome was in the zenith of her power, and her all-conquering armies were making conquests throughout the civilized world.

Up to this time Egypt had been too remote from Rome to be directly reached by her great armies, but circumstances at length brought the conquerors to the banks of the Nile.

Cleopatra's father was a degraded, dissipated wretch, who spent most of his time in vile debauchery. The only accomplishment of which he could boast was his skill in playing on the flute. He was hated and despised by the people of Alexandria, who felt that he was a degenerate son of a glorious race.

Rome was a sort of a republic at the time, and the most powerful men in the great state were Cæsar and Pompey. The former was a very extravagant man, who was always in need of large sums of money, wherewith to prosecute his ambitious designs, as well as to lavish presents on his numerous favorites.

As the people of Egypt were becoming dissatisfied with the reign of Ptolemy, whose birth on the mother's side was considered irregular and ignoble, that degraded monarch conceived the idea of getting himself recognized at Rome as one of the allies of the Roman people. If this was once accomplished, Ptolemy felt that he could have the support of the Roman government in the event of a revolution.

After many negotiations and delays Cæsar agreed to exert his powerful influence in order to secure an alliance between the Roman people and Ptolemy. The latter was to pay Cæsar a sum equal to about six millions of dollars for the service, a portion of which was to be given to Pompey, who was then prosecuting a war in Asia Minor.

When the negotiations were concluded, Ptolemy undertook to raise the money by taxing his dissatisfied people, who could not endure to see their country sold to Rome, and then pay a tremendous sum for the treachery of their degraded and debauched king.

A revolution was commenced in Alexandria, and Ptolemy was compelled to fly. Hastening to Rome, he demanded succor in the putting down of his rebellious subjects.

The banished king left five children behind him in his flight.

The eldest of these was the Princess Berenice, who had already reached the age of maturity, and who was an ambitious creature.

The second child was the famous Cleopatra, who was destined to occupy such a prominent place in the history of the period.

There were two sons, also, but they were very young at the time of the revolution.

The revolted citizens determined on placing Berenice on her father's throne after he had fled to Rome, as they thought that the boys were too young to reign in trying times.

Berenice was only too glad to accept the honor conferred on her, and she at once established herself in her father's palace, beginning her reign in great magnificence and splendor, while she commenced to look out for a suitable husband at the same time.

After a time her choice fell on a prince of Syria, named Seleucus. The young prince hastened to Alexandria, and he and Berenice were married in great state.

The young Syrian prince, however, did not enjoy the delights of wedded life for any great length of time. Berenice, for reasons only known to herself, soon grew tired of him, and she caused him to be strangled.

After various other intrigues and secret negotiations, Berenice married a prince from Asia Minor, named Archelaus. The man pleased the Egyptian queen better than her first husband; and she felt that he would be of great assistance to her in maintaining the throne against her father, should that degraded despot ever attempt to regain his lost power.

It was in such scenes of revolution, crime, and debauchery that Cleopatra spent the opening years of her life, and at a time when one's character is formed for good or ill.

In the meantime, the deposed king arrived at Rome. Before flying from Alexandria he had caused a report of his death to be spread, in order to effect his escape in safety.

When Ptolemy reached Rome, Julius Cæsar was absent in Gaul

with his conquering armies; but Pompey, who had received a portion of the Egyptian gold, had just returned from his conquests in Asia Minor.

On hearing of her father's arrival in Rome, Berenice became aware of his object, and she adopted measures for frustrating him. She appointed a large deputation, supplied the members thereof with valuable presents for the Romans, and dispatched them to the imperial city, in order that they might present her side of the question to the Roman people.

Ptolemy contrived, however, with the aid of his partisans in Rome, to waylay the delegation on its way to Rome. Some of the company were assassinated, others were poisoned, and the remainder were either bribed or terrified from pursuing their mission.

The people of Rome were very much divided on the question of giving military aid to the banished king in his project for regaining his lost throne. Pompey supported the claims of Ptolemy with great vigor, but other leading Romans opposed him with great force and eloquence, contending that they had no right to interfere in the internal affairs of a friendly nation.

At length the party opposed to Ptolemy consulted the several oracles which were in the custody of the priests, and they pretended to have found the following prophetic passage:

"If a king of Egypt shall apply to you for aid, treat him in a friendly manner, but do not furnish him with troops; for, if you do, you will incur great danger."

The finding of this passage confounded Ptolemy and his friends for a time, but Pompey did not hesitate to uphold the treacherous king with all his power and eloquence.

At length Gambinius, the Roman lieutenant who commanded in Syria, was induced to take command of an Egyptian expedition for the purpose of replacing the deposed king on his throne.

In the prosecution of this very hazardous enterprise Gambinius placed great reliance on the assistance of a very remarkable man, then his second in command, who was afterwards destined to play an important part in the tragic life of Cleopatra. This man was Marc Antony.

Antony was a Roman, born of distinguished parents, whose father died when he was very young, and who became a wild and dissolute youth. He wasted all his father's money in vice and folly, and soon incurred enormous debts, which placed him in extreme difficulties.

Being pursued by the hostility of his creditors and enemies, and having committed many crimes, Marc Antony was compelled to fly to Greece.

When Gambinius was on his way to Syria he met Marc Antony, and he invited him to join the invading army.

Marc Antony was as proud and as ambitious as he was reckless and wicked, and he refused to join Gambinius unless that general would give him an important command.

Gambinius saw that the young Roman was possessed of courage, daring and energy; that he had all the qualities requisite for a successful soldier of the time, and he gave him command of his cavalry.

The daring exile distinguished himself in the Syrian campaigns. He won great honor and renown; and when he returned to Rome he placed himself under the protection of the all-powerful Cæsar, to whom he remained faithful in life and in death.

Marc Antony entered into the Egyptian expedition with great enthusiasm, making light of the difficulties presented to him by those who opposed the hazardous undertaking.

In order to reach Egypt it was necessary to march the troops across trackless deserts, wholly destitute of water, through which peaceful caravans could only pass with great difficulty, and often encountering many dangers.

Placing himself at the head of his cavalry, Marc Antony set out on his perilous march across the desert, leaving Gambinius to follow him. The deposed king accompanied Antony.

While the renowned soldier was noted for his many faults of character, he also possessed many excellent qualities of mind and heart.

In danger he was cool, collected and sagacious; he was frank and manly in his dealings with his men, with whom he was an especial favorite; and he never assumed the manners of a leader during the hours of recreation and amusement, as he joined in all the sports and merry-makings of the camp with perfect freedom.

Marc Antony at this time was just twenty-eight years old. He possessed a tall and manly form; he had an expressive and intelligent cast of countenance, and his eyes were full of life and vivacity.

Pushing along over the desert with great speed, and without incurring any loss, Marc Antony soon reached the city of Pelusium, which was held by Berenice's adherents. Antony surprised and captured the city.

The deposed king wished to put the garrison to death, declaring that they were rebels, but Antony would not consent to such barbarity.

Berenice and her people were struck with dismay when they heard of the fall of Pelusium, and the approach of the Roman army under Gambinius; but, soon overcoming their first alarm, they proceeded to raise a large army to encounter the invaders.

This Egyptian army was placed under the command of Archelaus, Berenice's husband, who was Antony's friend in former days.

Several battles were then fought, in all of which the Romans were victorious. At length a decisive engagement ensued, which settled the controversy. Berenice was taken prisoner, her husband was slain, and the Roman armies marched to the city of Alexandria.

One of Ptolemy's first acts on regaining his throne was to have his daughter beheaded.

There were great rejoicings in Alexandria when the Roman troops entered that city, and Marc Antony was the subject of especial admiration and regard.

It was at that time that Antony first encountered Cleopatra. It does not appear that she was especially attracted to the handsome Roman, with whom she afterwards became so intimate, but it is certain that Antony was attracted to her, and that he admired her blooming beauty, her beautiful form, and her wit and spirit.

Cleopatra was then but fifteen years of age, while Antony was verging on thirty. Antony went back to Rome soon after the capture of Alexandria, and he did not see his fatal charmer again for many years.

The results of these campaigns raised Antony from the position of a homeless wanderer to that of a wealthy and powerful leader. On his return to Rome a civil war broke out between Cæsar and Pompey, and Antony espoused the cause of Cæsar.

In the meantime Ptolemy maintained himself in Alexandria by aid of the Roman soldiers left him by Gambinius. When he found death drawing near, he ordained that Cleopatra and one of her younger brothers should succeed him, and that they should be married according to the unnatural custom of the Ptolemy family.

Having made his will, Ptolemy intrusted the guardianship of his children to the Roman Senate. The Roman Senate accepted the responsibility, and intrusted Pompey as an agent to perform the duties of this trust.

But Pompey was busily engaged in the civil war against Cæsar, and he had no time to bestow on the affairs of Egypt.

On the death of Ptolemy, Cleopatra and her brother were married, and they were placed on the throne. The young queen was then eighteen years of age, while her young brother was only eight. Of course they were both too young to govern the nation, and the marriage was merely a nominal affair. The affairs of the kingdom were regulated by ten ministers.

One of these ministers was a eunuch named Pothinus, a proud, domineering, and ambitious man, who soon conceived a jealousy and a hatred for the beautiful young queen.

Cleopatra soon became very popular with the people, and more especially with the young men of the nation, who could not shut their eyes to her charms and accomplishments. The eunuch became alarmed at the young queen's increasing popularity, and her disposition to throw off the restraints of his guardianship. He intrigued with the young king, a conspiracy was formed, and Cleopatra was expelled from the kingdom.

Cleopatra sought refuge in Syria, where she appealed for aid against her usurping minister. Her appeal was heard and applauded, and she was soon on the march for Alexandria at the head of an army.

The usurping minister raised another army and marched out towards Pelusium to give battle to the adventurous Cleopatra. The armies met near the city, and all preparations were made for a decisive battle, when an event occurred which not only prevented the conflict, but was the means of opening a new epoch in the career of Cleopatra.

The armies of Cæsar and Pompey had met on the Plains of Pharsalia, and Pompey suffered a crushing defeat. The defeated general fled to the seashore with a small number of followers and put out to sea in a few ships.

The impetuous Cæsar followed him in eager pursuit, having at his command a small fleet of galleys, on which he embarked a small army of about three thousand men.

Pompey thought of Ptolemy in his hour of danger, and of the great services he had rendered the Egyptian king in regaining his throne, and he sailed directly for Pelusium, where Cleopatra's guardian was in power.

When the little fleet anchored, Pompey asked for aid and protection. He was invited on shore by Pothinus. As soon as he landed he was set on by the treacherous Egyptians, who stabbed him and beheaded him on the sand, while his wife watched the bloody work from the deck of one of the vessels.

Cæsar, in the meantime, pressed on to Alexandria in pursuit of his flying foe, landed his troops, and established himself in the city.

The assassination of Pompey and the landing of Cæsar in their capital filled the Egyptians with great astonishment; and, instead of thinking of battle, both parties commenced to speculate on turning the events for their own benefit.

Pothinus and the young king returned to Alexandria with the head of Pompey, which they sent to Cæsar as an offering, hoping thereby to conciliate the great conqueror in their favor. But the noble Roman general was shocked and disgusted at the bloody sight, and he denounced the assassins in unmeasured terms of reproach.

Pompey and Cæsar had been warm friends in happier days; and when the victor beheld the head of his great rival, all the tender feelings of the past were recalled. He caused the head to be buried with imposing funeral ceremonies, and it is recorded that he wept over the face of his ancient friend.

While Cleopatra remained at Pelusium with her army, her young brother and his cunning guardian endeavored to conciliate the great Cæsar. The Roman general made demands on Pothinus, and the eunuch resisted them in secret, while he made every open profession of friendship for the Romans.

At length the invader and the eunuch came to an open rupture. Cæsar, with his small army, held the principal strongholds of the city, while Pothinus had a large army at Pelusium.

While these contentions were taking place, Cleopatra remained in her camp near Pelusium. Knowing full well the power of the great Cæsar, the deposed queen was anxious to fly to his aid, and claim his assistance and protection; but the army of the enemy was strongly intrenched before her, and she could not proceed to Alexandria without dispersing it, or cutting her way through the lines.

The daring Cleopatra was destined, however, to seek Cæsar at all hazards. As she had no fleet at her command, she could not proceed to the city by sea. Besides, if she did succeed in reaching the gates of Alexandria, she would run the risk of being seized and slain by her merciless enemies.

Under these circumstances, Cleopatra resolved to employ stratagem in order to accomplish the great object in view.

Having sent a message to Cæsar, requesting permission to appear before him, she received an answer, in which she was urged to go to him by all means. Cleopatra prepared to put her stratagem into play.

Taking a small boat, and accompanied by a few attendants, she made her way along the coast to Alexandria. The person on whom the queen principally depended in this hazardous expedition was one of her most faithful male attendants named Apollodorus.

On reaching Alexandria, the little party rested until night, and then they advanced to the front of the walls of the citadel. Then the faithful attendant rolled the daring queen up in a piece of common carpet, tied each end so as to give it the appearance of a bale of merchandise, raised the precious load on his shoulders, and advanced with it into the heart of the city.

When the pretended porter arrived at the palace where Cæsar was residing, he was stopped by the guards, who demanded to know what it was he carried. The man replied that it was a present for the noble Cæsar. He was allowed to pass, and he bore his burden along in safety.

When the packet was unrolled before the astonished Cæsar, and the beautiful woman appeared to his view, he was completely charmed.

Cleopatra at that time was about twenty-one years of age, and while she was graceful and in the full bloom of womanhood, she was not very heavy.

When she stood before the great Roman general, blushing with excitement and hope, and still abashed at her situation, she presented a picture on which the eye and the soul of a susceptible man could feast forever—almost.

Her beautiful face was glowing with a rosy tinge, her expressive eyes flashed with all the fire of her warm race, and her very form seemed animated by the impulse that prompted her to throw herself at the feet of the great man, and trust to her eloquence, as well as to her resistless charms, in gaining him as her ally against her enemies.

And Cleopatra did not pass through the trying ordeal without receiving her looked-for recompense. From that moment the great Cæsar became her devoted admirer, her earnest advocate, and her valiant champion. The great man caressed Cleopatra, he kissed her red, voluptuous lips over and over again, and he seemed to live for her, and for her alone.

And Cleopatra seemed to be proud of her conquest, and to take great delight in the caresses of the renowned Cæsar. She had enjoyed other loves and other embraces, but what were the tawny sons of Egypt as compared with the great man who was now smitten with her glowing charms?

Cæsar at the time was about fifty years of age, and he was a splendid specimen of manly beauty and elegance.

To be sure, he had a good wife, who was living in retirement in Rome, and one who was most devotedly attached to him; but if he ever thought of the absent one while dallying with the Egyptian enchantress, it was only to arouse comparisons not at all favorable to the former partner of his love.

When Cæsar had enjoyed the pleasures of Cleopatra's company for some time, he commenced to take a very strong interest in her cause. Feeling that he was not fully able to cope with her enemies, while commanding the small force with him he dispatched messengers to Syria, the nearest country under the Roman sway, for reinforcements.

He endeavored to bring about a reconciliation between Cleopatra and her young husband and brother; but failing in that object, he denounced the young king, and commenced to make war on him.

Then followed what is known in history as the great Alexandrine war, in which, while Cæsar was eventually the conqueror, he incurred the displeasure of many of the Roman people.

During the war Cæsar encountered and overcame many great dangers; he was incessantly engaged in fighting the enemies of his mistress, who often beheld him in battle and in single combat, and who always received him in the palace, which they occupied together, with open arms and caressing smiles.

At length, Cæsar having received reinforcements, the Egyptian forces were totally routed, young Ptolemy and his leading generals were slain, Cleopatra's sister, a young girl named Arsinoe, was taken prisoner, and led captive to Rome, and the fair charmer of his heart was placed on the throne.

Although the conqueror's work was fully accomplished, he could not tear himself away from Cleopatra.

It was all in vain that his wife and his friends in Rome urged his return, and remonstrated with him for his guilty attachment to the Egyptian queen. The great general was so fascinated by Cleopatra's charms, and by the mysterious influence which she exercised over him, that he was deaf to all entreaties and remonstrances.

After the war was ended he remained some months enjoying his favorite's caresses. He would spend whole nights with her in feasting and revelry. He traveled with her through Egypt, attended by a numerous train; and he even formed the design of taking her with him to Rome and marrying her there, having taken measures to have the laws so altered as to enable him to do so, although his faithful and lawful wife was still living.

About this time Cleopatra gave birth to a son, whom the Alexandrians named Cæsarian, after his father. The birth of this son caused the guilty Cleopatra to be regarded by the people with great reproach, but she braved it all in her love for Cæsar.

All this time Cleopatra was growing more and more beautiful and accomplished. She lost, however, all the simple manners of her youth, and she became bold and forward. Perfectly indifferent as she was to the opinions of her subjects, her only object seemed to be the maintenance of her guilty ascendancy over the heart of the love-stricken Cæsar.

Cæsar determined, however, to return to Rome. Leaving Cleopatra a sufficient force to secure herself on the throne, he embraced her tenderly, promised to meet her soon again, and sailed away with his transports and his galleys. He took Cleopatra's young sister with him, intending to exhibit her in Rome as a trophy of his Egyptian victories.

After the war was ended. Cæsar decreed that she should marry her younger brother, a boy of eleven, who was also named Ptolemy. A marriage of the guilty queen with one so young was, of course, a mere form.

After the departure of Cæsar, Cleopatra led a life of sensual luxury, indulging in all kinds of extravagant pastimes and pleasures.

Although she retained all her beauty and fascination, she became heartless, selfish and designing. Her little brother soon became an object of jealousy to her, as she feared that he would give her trouble when he arrived at the years of manhood, which period he would attain, according to the usages of the Egyptian kingdom, at the age of fifteen.

To free herself of this dread the wicked woman had her brother put to death by poison, and then she gave free rein to all her luxurious and amorous propensities, paying no attention to the laws of God or of nature in pursuing her pleasures.

While Cleopatra was enjoying the fleeting pleasures of a guilty life, Julius Cæsar was pressing his glorious conquests in Asia Minor, in Spain, in Africa, and in Italy. He conducted all his campaigns with an energy and a skill that astonished the natives, and when he returned to Rome in triumph he was the acknowledged master of the world.

Cleopatra had watched her lover's career with pride and pleasure, and when she heard that he had returned to Rome she determined to set out for that city to make him a visit.

Cleopatra's young sister, who had taken sides against her in the war, was then held as a prisoner in Rome, where she had excited the sympathies of the people in her behalf.

The witching queen proceeded to Rome in great splendor, and she was received by Cæsar with open arms, while the people of the city, notwithstanding her beauty and her many charms, looked coldly upon her. During her visit to Rome the guilty creature

lived with Cæsar, enjoying his entertainments and his feasts, and sharing with him in all the guilty pleasures of the hour.

About this time the famous conspiracy was formed by Brutus and Cassius, which culminated in the assassination of Cæsar in the Senate Chamber.

On hearing of this dreadful tragedy, Cleopatra fled from Rome and returned to Egypt. Her sister had left the city some time before.

Marc Antony beheld the murder of his best-loved friend, but he was unable to resist. He was enabled to avenge him, however.

Marc Antony, Octavius Cæsar, a nephew of the great emperor, and an officer named Lepidus, formed a league against Cassius and Brutus, and they marched to meet the assassins at Philippi, where a terrible battle was fought. Brutus and Cassius were slain in this battle, their armies were defeated, and Antony and his friends returned to Rome in triumph, having avenged the death of the great Cæsar.

The result of this great battle established the ascendancy of Marc Antony, and he was regarded as one of the most conspicuous men in the civilized world. Cleopatra, the beautiful queen of Egypt, was regarded as the most conspicuous woman. Fate destined that they should soon meet again, and live and love for themselves alone.

While Antony had made a great name for himself in the world, he was as utterly abandoned and depraved as was possible for a human being to become. All the spoils that he obtained during his campaigns were squandered in a reckless manner, or bestowed upon his soldiers with a free and reckless hand.

In the height of his prosperity, Marc Antony lived among his soldiers in the most immoral manner. He prided himself on being descended from Hercules, and he affected a style of dress and manner in keeping with the savage character of his ancestor. He had always around him a set of dissolute characters, composed of frail and beautiful dancing girls, play-actors and jesters, with whom he reveled, and drank, and sported for days at a time.

Soon after Cæsar's death Antony married a widow named Fulvia. This woman had led a wild and irregular life previous to her union with the famous general; but she conceived a very strong attachment for her new husband, and she devoted herself to him with constant fidelity.

This woman possessed a stern character; she was ambitious and bold; and she soon exercised a decided influence over her wild and reckless husband, whom she persuaded into a mode of life suitable to his rank and fortune.

After remaining in Rome for some time, Antony proceeded to take command of the armies in Asia Minor, and in the course of the following year arrived at Cilicia.

From that place he sent a messenger to Egypt summoning Cleopatra to appear before him, and asserting that there were charges against her of having aided Cassius and Brutus during the late war, instead of sending assistance to her old lover's avengers. These charges had no foundation in fact, as Cleopatra had endeavored to aid Antony and his friends.

It is supposed that Antony fabricated this story, in order to draw Cleopatra towards him, as he did not forget her early charms, while the fame of her matured beauty was a matter of very wide report. Antony's wife was not with him at this time, as he had left her behind him in Rome.

The name of the messenger thus dispatched to Cleopatra was Dellius. When he arrived at her court he was struck with her fascinating beauty, as well as by the magic of her enchanting conversation, which has been described by the ancient biographers as perfectly irresistible.

Cleopatra was then in her twenty-eighth year, and time had only served to increase her beauty and her numerous charms.

Dellius delivered his message in the most courteous tones, begged of Cleopatra to accept Antony's invitation without fear, and assured her that she had only to present herself before him in all her beauty; no matter how grave the charges against her, to acquire an unbounded ascendancy over the susceptible Roman leader.

Cleopatra was not slow in profiting by the advice thus tendered. Indeed, her glowing imagination was aroused at the thought of encountering the proud Antony, and of once more making conquest of the greatest general and the most powerful man of the age.

She began at once to make extensive preparations for the voyage, and to collect stores of plate, diamonds and gold, as presents for Antony, who was pressing her to appear before him by frequent communications.

All being prepared, Cleopatra set sail to meet the man who was destined to share her fortunes and her favors in the future. She crossed the Mediterranean Sea, and entered the mouth of the river Cydnus. Antony was at Tarsus at the time, awaiting her arrival. Tarsus was a city near the mouth of the Cydnus.

When Cleopatra's fleet entered the river she embarked on a magnificent barge, the sails of which were purple, and the oars were inlaid and tipped with gold. On the deck of this gorgeous barge Cleopatra reclined under a canopy of cloth-of-gold.

She was dressed in a magnificent costume, in which she represented Venus, the goddess of Love and Beauty, and she was surrounded by a company of beautiful boys, who attended upon her in the form of Cupids, and fanned her with their wings, while a company of charming young girls were arrayed as the Nymphs and Graces.

A band of chosen musicians were stationed on the deck of the royal barge, who kept time to the movements of the oars, and the sounds of whose instruments could be heard far and wide over the waters and along the shore.

The whole spectacle appeared like a vision of an enchanted land, and it was well calculated to impress the beholders with the magnificence and wealth of the voluptuous queen, on her mission to enslave the heart of a warm and susceptible soldier.

When Cleopatra's splendid escort arrived at Tarsus Marc Antony was giving public audience to a large assemblage at his palace. On hearing of the arrival of the beautiful queen, the whole audience hastened to the banks of the river to witness the great display, leaving the great soldier alone with a few attendants.

Cleopatra landed on the shore, and commenced to pitch her tents, when she received a message from Antony inviting her to come and sup with him.

The designing queen declined the invitation, saying that it was more becoming of him to come and sup with her; and added that she would be happy to receive him at her proper hour.

Antony complied with the proposal, and went to the grand entertainment prepared for him. He was received with a magnificence and a splendor that fairly amazed him. It surpassed anything that could be imagined even in that land of luxury and wealth.

The rough Roman soldier was fairly enchanted by the gorgeous scene; he was bewitched by Cleopatra; and he became her slave from that moment until the hour of his death.

On the following day Antony invited Cleopatra to return his visit; but he could not rival her in display, although he made every possible effort to entertain her in a sumptuous manner.

During their interviews Cleopatra commenced to weave her webs around the great soldier. He was at once attracted by her wit, her thousand accomplishments, and by the adroitness and the tact which she at once displayed in assuming a social superiority over him. She beguiled him into security with smiles and caresses, while she was only toying with him for the gratification of her own amorous and ambitious designs.

Just as soon as Cleopatra gained her lover's favors, she asked him, for the sake of her own security, to destroy her sister Arsinoe, who had been her enemy, and who had been liberated at Rome by Julius Cæsar. That unfortunate creature was living in retirement in Asia Minor.

Antony, only too glad of the opportunity to please his charmer, dispatched an officer in quest of the young girl. The ruthless officer slew the poor maiden in a sanctuary, whither she had fled for protection on hearing of his approach.

Cleopatra remained at Tarsus with Antony for some time, with whom she lived on terms of open intimacy, and indulging in scenes of the wildest revelry and debauchery. The guilty creature loaded her lover with gold and costly gems; she distributed presents among his officers, with a lavish hand; and she gave entertainments that could not be surpassed, except in the imagination of the author of the "Arabian Nights."

While Antony was basking in the smiles or receiving the warm caresses of his Egyptian charmer, he was neglecting his public duties. His wife, who was apprised of his connection with the degraded Cleopatra, wrote to him and insisted on his return to Rome, where she had to fight the battle against his powerful enemies.

At length Antony made up his mind to tear himself away from the vile enchantress. He broke his quarters at Tarsus and moved south towards Tyre, with the purpose of taking a ship for Rome.

Cleopatra accompanied him on the march towards Tyre, where he intended to leave her. The bold woman was determined that he should accompany her to Alexandria.

A brief struggle followed between the two guilty lovers. Antony thought of home and of duty, and he endeavored to throw off the tender chains that bound him, but he could not contend against the wiles and the blandishments of this enchanting queen.

Cleopatra carried her point. Antony was seduced from the homeward path, and he was borne away to Alexandria by the queen. There he spent the winter with her, and there they gave themselves up to every sensual indulgence that the most remorseless license could tolerate and the most unbounded wealth provide.

There was no limit to their wild excesses and debasing practices. Sometimes, at midnight, after having spent many hours together in mirth and revelry, Antony and Cleopatra would sally out from the palace in disguise, mingle with the common people, and indulge in brawls, riots, and desperate quarrels with the police.

At last, and to Cleopatra's great chagrin and disappointment, Antony was compelled to return to his duties. Great disasters had befallen the Roman armies in Asia Minor, and the love-lorn general was called on to retrieve the disgrace.

During Antony's absence from Rome, his wife, Fulvia, who was a strong-minded woman, became engaged in a war with Octavius Cæsar, the nephew of the great Cæsar, and one of the generals who had fought against Cassius and Brutus at the battle of Philippi.

Marc Antony was incensed at his wife for making war with Octavius, and he upbraided her in unmeasured terms. He then left her, swearing that he would never see her again. Fulvia died a short time after, crushed with sorrow and chagrin.

Then Antony became reconciled to Octavius; and he soon after married Octavia, the sister of Octavius, who was the widow of a celebrated Roman general named Marcellus. Octavia was a beautiful, intelligent woman, who was as kind and as gentle as she was fair to look upon; and she was most devotedly attached to her brave husband, notwithstanding the fact that she was aware of his infatuation for the guilty Cleopatra. Alas! that same Cleopatra was destined to break the peace of another worthy wife.

Marc Antony and Octavius Cæsar ruled the Roman provinces together. They had many quarrels and many rivalries; but the sweet Octavia exerted a peaceful influence over her husband and her brother, and she was the means of reconciling them in their disputes.

The wayward husband was well pleased with his good wife for a time, but it was for a very short period only. The distant charmer was ever in his mind: Cleopatra's glorious eyes and her voluptuous form appeared to him in his dreams as well as in his wakeful hours. Her jewel-covered hand seemed to be ever beckoning him back to Alexandria, and to the several pleasures of that corrupt city.

Leaving his wife at Rome, Marc Antony proceeded to the East, under the pretense of settling some disputes in that portion of the Roman empire; but instead of following out his pretended designs, he hurried away to Alexandria, and flung himself once more into the arms of the enchanting Queen of Egypt. The great soldier fled to his own destruction.

The good wife was very indignant at this base desertion. Octavius, who was devotedly attached to his sister, became furious in his resentment at Antony's outrageous conduct. Cleopatra gloried in her own triumph, for she loved Antony with all the power of a guilty passion; and she laughed in scorn at the tender appeals of the loving wife in Rome.

Antony's infatuation for Cleopatra, and the continued indulgence in guilty pleasures, had a fearful effect on the great soldier. He became indolent, weak, vacillating. He was no longer the impetuous, hardy, courage-inspiring general who had so often led his troops to victory.

During his subsequent campaigns in Asia he lost the confidence of his men, his armies were destroyed, and he would have been compelled to retreat before his enemies, were it not that his faithful wife hastened to him with reinforcements.

Again and again Octavia appealed to her husband to desert his mistress, and to return to his home and to his faithful love; but all these appeals were in vain. Cleopatra had woven her webs around him, and the strong warrior of other days had not the power to burst them asunder.

Then Octavius became determined to avenge the continued insults offered to his beloved sister. He raised a powerful army, he organized a splendid fleet, and he set out to invade Egypt.

Antony and Cleopatra collected their forces and their ships, and they sailed from Alexandria to oppose the young avenger. The hostile fleets and the armies met at a place called Actium, on the western coast of Epirus, north of Greece. A naval combat ensued, and the guilty lovers were defeated in a disgraceful manner.

During the battle, save in one affair, Marc Antony played the part of an imbecile. His guilty love appeared to have quenched all the former fire and manhood of the great soul; and he fled back to Alexandria, where he acted as one who was bereft of sense, reason, and manhood.

Cleopatra was disgusted with Antony's conduct on that occasion, and the lovers became estranged for a time. The hero became a moody misanthrope, and retired to an island to ponder over the errors of his life. The guilty queen, in the meantime, took measures for securing her treasures and preparing for flight.

After a time Antony returned to Alexandria, and he became reconciled to Cleopatra. The guilty pair renewed their life of debauchery and wild revelry, while the avenging hand appeared before them at all hours and in all places.

After the battle of Actium, Octavius marched into Asia Minor, and from thence into Syria. Even while the guilty pair were enjoying themselves in the palaces of Alexandria, the stern Roman avenger was pushing his arms across the deserts of Syria, and he was soon thundering at the walls of the Egyptian capital.

During the siege that followed Antony acted the part of a madman. At one time he would sally out and perform great deeds of valor, at other times he would wander around the city, crying out that he was betrayed by Cleopatra, and then again he would shut himself up in his chambers, and give way to his despair in the most cowardly manner.

Cleopatra, fearing that Antony would slay her in one of his furious fits of jealousy, gave out that she was dead. She caused herself to be laid in a tomb, and bade her ministers inform her lover of the event.

Antony rushed to the tomb, and on beholding the form of the guilty loved one lying there in all the semblance of death, he called on one of his faithful officers to slay him. The officer drew his sword, but, instead of plunging it into Antony's breast, he pierced his own body with the weapon, and fell dead at the feet of his master.

Antony gazed at the dead man for a moment, and then, drawing his own sword, he said:

"I thank thee for this, noble Eros. Thou hast set me an example. I must do for myself what thou couldst not do for me."

So speaking, he took the bloody sword from the dead man's hand, and plunged it into his own breast. He had inflicted a mortal wound, but death did not occur at the moment.

While reeling in mortal agony, he learned that the report of Cleopatra's death was not true, and he begged of his assistants to bear him to the monument, where the queen still remained. He was borne along the streets in a dying state, but when his assistants arrived at the monument, Cleopatra, fearing the treachery of her enemies in the city, refused to open the gates. She went to a window above, however, and causing her attendants to lower ropes, the dying Antony was raised and borne into the monument. He died soon after, in the arms of Cleopatra, who was overwhelmed with anguish and remorse.

Octavius entered the city on hearing of the death of Antony, and Cleopatra was taken prisoner. But she did not survive long after the death of her famous lover. Fearing that she would be borne away to Rome as a captive, it is reported that she applied a deadly wasp to her arm, and that the sting of the poisonous insect caused her death.

Thus perished the great Marc Antony and the famed Queen of Egypt.

THE DISASTROUS LOVE OF A FAITHLESS IRISH PRINCESS.

THE MEETING IN THE ARBOR—THE SUSPICIOUS FATHER—THE SICK WIFE AND THE PRETENDED DOCTOR—THE FLIGHT AND THE DISCOVERY—THE DISASTROUS CONSEQUENCES OF A GUILTY LOVE.

The daughters of green Erin are noted for their virtue as well as for their beauty; but yet it is recorded that one fair damsel in that fertile island was frail enough to follow the example of Helen of Troy, and bestow a guilty love on one who proved to be a traitor alike to friend and to native land.

Many years ago there dwelt in one of Ireland's pleasant valleys a prince who was known and loved by all his neighbors as O'Rourk, Prince of Breffni. This prince was valiant in war, right faithful in his friendships; and he was devotedly attached to his beautiful young wife, who was called Deborah, and who was the daughter of the King of Meath.

One pleasant evening in the spring time of the year, a young woman, attended by a female servant, was strolling through the woods near the Castle of Breffni, when she was attracted by a peculiar noise that resembled the cry of an owl.

The young woman paused on the instant, and, turning to her female attendant, said:

"Go back and watch, Norah. Give me the two warning signals, should any one approach."

The confidante retired on the instant, muttering to herself, in a mischievous manner:

"It will all come to ill, I know; but what is that to me? I am making a rich harvest out of the pair, and I will serve them to the end right faithfully, indeed."

The young woman advanced into the depths of the dark wood, repeating the cry of the owl as she advanced; and she soon reached a natural arbor, beneath which a rustic seat was formed by the twining limbs of some small dead trees.

She had scarcely reached the entrance to the arbor, when a man in the prime of life, and who was dressed in very humble garments, sprang out to meet her with extended arms, as he said, in joyous tones:

"Once more, my beloved one! Oh, how I have been counting the moments since the sun went down!"

"Once more, dear Murrough, and for the last time," said the young woman, as she kissed her lover over and over again—"the very last time." *

"The last time, say you, Deborah? Do you want to drive me out of my mind, dear one!"

"It must be, Murrough. These guilty meetings of ours cannot last forever. We will be discovered, and then what will follow? Disgrace, death, and perdition in the life to come. Oh, my loved one, we must never meet again."

The man had drawn her into the arbor; his arm was entwined around her waist, and he was showering kisses on her red lips, while she was declaring her intention of never meeting him again.

"Never meet again!" he said. "Tell me to die, Deborah, and death will be most welcome. But do not speak of parting forever. We will live, and we will live for love and happiness. I have found a plan for the destruction of your confiding husband. I will declare war against him, and slay him in battle, and then——"

"You will be defeated, dear Murrough, as you were defeated before. King Roderic will aid my husband. You may be slain; and then I would die of a broken heart. Oh, no, no! Better to even live as we do, tasting the sweets of a guilty love for a time, than to risk your precious life in that way."

"But you said you could never meet me again, sweet Deborah; and——"

"I fear that we are watched, Murrough."

"Who watches us, my darling? Your sleeping husband has not the least suspicion."

"I fear that my father suspects me, dear Murrough. I have caught his stern eye fixed on me more than once, when I returned from enjoying our sweet, stolen interviews. He would slay me on the instant, if he were assured of my guilt, and he could then hide my disgrace from the world. This very night, as I was leaving the castle, he questioned me as to where I was strolling to."

"The suspicious old fool! Why should he interfere with our pleasures? Would that I could crush him with my good sword. But away with all forebodings, dear Deborah. The moments are too precious to be wasted in that way; let us forget all future dangers in the sweet bliss of the present. Let us——"

Before the amorous lover could utter another endearing word a shrill cry was heard in the wood, as if it came from an alarmed owl, and it was repeated over and over again in quick succession.

"Fly, fly, dearest," cried Deborah, as she pressed a kiss on her lover's lips. "Some one comes this way. That is Norah's warning."

"When will we meet again, Deborah?"

"This night week, if possible. There's the cry again. Fly, fly, on your life."

The young woman ran out in the woods, and the guilty lover dashed into the bushes behind.

"Who is it, Norah?" inquired the guilty creature, as she met her maiden on the path.

"Your father, lady. Beware how you act after he meets you. Your face is all flushed, and your hair is in disorder. Fly along the path with me, and we will seek to avoid him."

"Stay, Deborah," rang out a stern voice, as a noble-looking old man ran down the path leading from the castle. "Away with you, maiden. I would speak to my daughter."

Norah ran along the path on the instant, leaving her mistress with the stern old king.

"Where have you been loitering, Deborah?" demanded the stern old king, in angry tones.

"Beyond in the wood, father."

"Whom did you meet there?"

"No one, father."

"Your flushed cheeks and your disordered hair tell a different story, false one. Woe to me that I should give being to such a child. I am aware of your guilty passion. But I will hide your shame for the sake of the honor of our house. Go back to your chamber. I will see that you do not meet your false-hearted lover again. Go and pray, and be penitent."

On the following morning it was announced in the castle that the Princess of Breffni was dangerously ill. Her doting husband was fearfully alarmed, and he sent for the ablest doctors in the land to give her comfort.

The stern old father, who was on a visit to the castle of his son-in-law, did not appear to be much alarmed for his child, although it was remarked that he kept strict watch and guard at the door of her chamber.

A week passed away, and Deborah appeared to be growing weaker and weaker, despite the attentions of her doting husband and the medicines of the great doctors.

"Oh, what can I do to save you, my loved one?" cried the fond husband, as he bent over her pillow one night. "The doctors say that a miracle alone can save you."

"Then you should go on a pilgrimage to the shrine of St. Patrick, good Breffni," responded the deceitful one, "and pray there for my happy recovery."

"I will set out on the morrow, Deborah. I was to have marched under the standard of good King Roderic, but the great monarch will pardon me when he is informed of my mission. My dear one, you will be saved, if my prayers will avail you."

"Go, dear Breffni. I will keep that lamp burning at my chamber window until the night of your return. When you reach yonder hill and see the light in the window, you will know that I live. If you do not see the light, you will know that I am lost to you forever."

"Heaven forbid!" exclaimed O'Ruark, as he kissed the pale lips; and then hastened from the chamber to prepare for his journey.

The Prince of Breffni, arrayed in the humblest garments, and bearing a pilgrim's staff in his hand, departed on his pilgrimage at daylight on the following morning.

The old king, who was now becoming alarmed about his daughter, remained in the castle with her, while his confidential guards kept watch in the neighborhood, to see that her guilty lover did not approach the castle. On the night following the day of Breffni's departure, Norah, the confidante, stole out from the castle, and took her way toward the city of Ferns. She was back again in the morning, and her absence had not been noticed by the watchful old king.

Three days passed away, and the sick woman did not improve in health, while her father grew more and more anxious about her.

The time was drawing near for the return of Prince Breffni from his pilgrimage, and the old king saw that the signal lamp was suspended at the window every evening. His daughter appeared to be so anxious about the absent husband that the suspicious father commenced to upbraid himself for doubting her love for him.

One evening, as the castle gates were about to be closed for the night, a stranger applied for admittance; and he was hospitably received and welcomed, according to the good old custom then prevailing in the land, and which custom still prevails in portions of Ireland, despite of oppression and misery.

The stranger appeared to be an old man, and he was dressed in the costume worn by the doctors or leeches of the age.

When the old stranger had partaken of some refreshments, the old king addressed him, saying:

"I believe you are a doctor, sir?"

"I am, good king."

"Would that you would cure my daughter, stranger."

"If it is possible for a human being to cure the famed Deborah, I can effect a cure, sire."

"Then come with me to my daughter's chamber," continued the old king, leading the way.

The old doctor approached the bedside of the sick princess, took her hand within his own, and commenced to count the beatings of her pulse, without uttering a single word.

Laying the hand down on the pillow again, he approached the old king, saying:

"Your fair daughter is very ill indeed, but hers is not a hopeless case. If you would have me cure her, let all withdraw save her chosen female attendant. She is troubled with the disease of the heart. This magical medicine must be applied to her heart by careful and skilled hands."

As the old man spoke these words, he drew a bottle from his pocket, and held it up before the unsuspecting old king.

"Of a certainty," replied the king, as he motioned to the others to withdraw. "I will await you in the anteroom, good leech, and I will pray that Heaven may assist you in the cure of my child."

The old father withdrew. Norah returned to the recess of the window, and looked out on the valley beyond, and the doctor advanced to the bedside of the dying patient.

Bending down, he whispered some words into the sick one's ear, and their effect was magical indeed.

Deborah uttered a low cry of joy; she clasped the hand held out to her, and she raised the flushed face to meet the lips of the old doctor, while she clasped his neck in a fond embrace.

"You have come, Murrough," she whispered, in joyous tones. "Oh, if you are discovered!"

"Fear not, dear Deborah," was the disguised man's reply. "I have come to you, and we will never part again. To-morrow you will fly with me. To-night we will renew our fond embraces. You are much better, are you not, my sweet Deborah?"

"Much better," responded the guilty one. "I feel that I have strength enough to sup and eat at the festive board this very night."

"As you will, dear Deborah. But a perfect cure will not be effected until you have partaken freely of the waters of St. Bridget's holy well. You must drink of the water fresh from the fountain; and I would be with you to see that you do not drink too much. You understand me, my adored one?"

"I do! I do! I will do as you suggest. Life with you will be paradise; without you, I am in eternal misery. Oh, how I long for the moment when I can clasp you in my arms again."

When the old king was admitted to the room, and beheld the wonderful change in his daughter, he turned to the doctor, saying:

"In the name of all that is wonderful, how did you effect the magic cure, good leech?"

"By very simple means, good king. This bottle contains some water from the holy well of St. Bridget, in the valley near Clontarf. One small draught and one application outside the heart has improved her, as you see."

"But will she continue to improve, sir?"

"She will relapse again, unless she drinks of the water fresh from the fountain, and procures, at the same time, a supply for the future."

"We will set out on the morrow," said the old king, joyously. "We will——"

"Pardon me, sire," interrupted the wily lover; "but it is necessary that your daughter should be accompanied by only a single female attendant, and a skilled physician only, or there will be no virtue in the water. On the contrary, it may increase her malady. She must be also very careful about partaking too freely of the water. An overdose may, and it is very likely, to cause instant death."

"How is that to be avoided, good leech?"

"Were it not that I am bound to visit and administer to the monarch Roderic before he sets out for the war against Tyrone, I would be most happy to proceed to the holy well with her."

"I will dispatch a messenger to the good King Roderic on the instant, and inform him that you are waiting on my daughter, sir. Accompany her to the holy well, and I will reward you richly."

After many objections were offered by the pretended physician, he consented, at length, to accompany the princess on her journey.

The princess was seated at the festive board during the evening's entertainment, and the physician was placed at the seat of honor beside her.

When the people of the castle had all retired to rest, the guilty princess received her disguised lover in her chamber, where they made final arrangements for their flight on the morrow.

On the following day, while the sun was peeping up over the distant hills, the old physician and the intriguing Norah, and they rode the best horses in the Prince of Breffni's stables.

They rode along demurely enough until they reached the brow of a hill overlooking the castle of Breffni; but just as they were descending into the valley beyond, and when they were lost to the view of the watchers on the battlements, the disguised lover clasped the guilty woman in his arms, and kissed her in the most rapturous manner, as he cried:

"You are mine now, and mine forever, Deborah. I will defy all Ireland for your sake."

These passionate caresses were witnessed by an astonished shepherd who was tending his flocks on a neighboring hill. The man knew the faithless princess right well, but he did not know the disguised lover.

Dashing over the hill as fast as his active feet would bear him, the shepherd rushed into Breffni Castle, sought out the old king, and cried, in alarmed tones:

"Murder alive, good king, but there's a strange old man hugging and kissing your daughter like mad on the hills beyond there."

The old king's eyes were opened on the instant.

Calling out a body of mounted men, he started off in pursuit; but the guilty lovers rode the swiftest horses in the stables, and they were well able to defy their pursuers.

It was growing dark on the hills of Breffni, when a weary pilgrim reached a spot overlooking the castle in the valley.

It was the Prince of Breffni returning from his pilgrimage; and long and anxious were the looks that he cast at the casement, where he expected to see the promised beacon.

The betrayed prince looked in vain.

Fully expecting to find the loved one lying in the arms of death, he flew to the castle, only to learn that she had fled with his hated rival, MacMurrough, King of Leinster.

When the betrayed prince recovered from the first outbursts of grief, he turned his thoughts on vengeance. He immediately made preparations for invading the country of his rival, and he was ably assisted by the disgraced old king.

MacMurrough and the faithless wife fled to the city of Ferns, the capital of the province which he ruled over, and while they lived in guilty intercourse, they proposed to resist the betrayed husband.

At the same time O'Ruark sent a message to Roderic, Monarch of Ireland, calling on him to aid him in punishing a wretch who had so wantonly betrayed the most sacred rights of friendship and humanity.

On receipt of the express, the monarch held a council; and the result was, that MacMurrough was pronounced unworthy to govern, and therefore must be deposed and banished. He immediately dispatched a body of his troops, and sent with them orders to the King of Meath, and to the people of Dublin and Ossory, to join O'Ruark, whom he nominated general in this expedition. MacMurrough endeavored to oppose their passage into Leinster, but on this occasion found himself deserted by the nobility, the military, and even by his principal favorites and dependents, so horrible did the crime he was charged with appear in their eyes.

Thus circumstanced, he retired to Ferns, and not daring to stand a siege, he fled from thence, and had himself and about sixty persons in his suite conveyed to Bristol. The castle of Ferns soon surrendered; his country was divided between the

Prince of Ossory and Murcha, a prince of his blood; and seventeen hostages were brought to the monarch.

When MacMurrough found that he was deserted and detested by every one, he fled to England, hoping that, in a strange country, where his tyranny and crimes were not so well known, he might procure friends and followers to assist him. After remaining some time at Bristol, he proceeded to Normandy to claim the protection of Henry, King of England. Henry gave him a favorable reception, heard his tale, but excused himself from at present engaging in his cause. MacMurrough requested at least his permission to convey to Ireland such volunteers as he could procure in England, which Henry agreed to, and sent with him the following proclamation:

"*Henry, King of England, Duke of Normandy and Aquitaine, Earl of Anjou, etc., unto all his subjects, English, Normans, Welsh and Scots, and to all nations and people, being his subjects, greeting:*

"*Whereas* Dermod, King of Leinster, most wrongfully (as he informeth) banished out of his own country, hath craved our aid; therefore, forasmuch as we have received him into our protection, grace, and favor, whoever within our realms, subject onto our command, will aid and help him, whom we have embraced as our trusty friend, for the recovery of his land, let him be assured of our grace and favor."

MacMurrough, by sound of trumpet, had this proclamation frequently read in Bristol, and some adjoining cities. He offered great rewards in money and lands to such as would enlist under his banners; but his success was not great. After a month's stay at Bristol he retired to Wales. He applied to Richard, Earl of Strigul, commonly called Strongbow, a powerful and popular chief in Wales. He made him considerable offers to attach him to his service. He went so far as, at last, to promise him his daughter in marriage, and the reversion of his kingdom after his death, if by his means, and those of his friends and associates, he should be restored to his dominions. So tempting an offer could not be resisted.

Strongbow immediately entered deep into all the schemes of the exile. The treaty was signed and sworn to on both sides; and MacMurrough bound himself by oath to give him, at a proper time, his daughter in marriage, and to settle the reversion of his kingdom on him; though this last he knew was contrary to the fundamentals of the constitution, for the right of election was vested in the chiefs of the country, and none could be put

in nomination for the crown of Leinster who were not of the line of Cathoir the Great.

And thus we find that the love of a guilty Irish princess was the cause of the first invasion of the Normans in that land.

With the assistance of the English invaders, MacMurrough waged a relentless war on O'Ruark and his confederates, and the green fields of the unhappy isle were stained with the blood of thousands before the invaders gained a firm footing on the shores.

It is recorded that Deborah retired into a convent after her lover was banished, where she soon died of a broken heart.

This romantic and disastrous adventure inspired Tom Moore, the great poet of Erin, in the production of one of his most tender and soul-stirring Irish melodies. The words of this beautiful song will be recognized by all who are familiar with the works of the well-known bard:

The valley lay smiling before me,
　Where lately I left her behind,
Yet I trembled, and something hung o'er me
　That saddened the joy of my mind.
I looked for the lamp which she told me
　Should shine when her pilgrim returned;
But though darkness began to enfold me,
　No lamp from her battlements burned.

I flew to her chamber—'twas lonely,
　As if the loved tenant lay dead;
Ah, would it were death, and death only!
　But no, the young false one had fled.
And there hung the lute that could soften
　My very worst pains into bliss;
While the hand that had waked it so often
　Now throbbed to a proud rival's kiss.

There was a time, fairest of women,
　When Ireful's good sword would have sought
That man, thro' a million of foemen,
　Who dared but to wrong thee in thought.
While now,—oh, degenerate daughter
　Of Erin, how fall'n is thy fame !
And through ages of bondage and slaughter
　Our country shall bleed for thy shame.

Already the curse is upon her,
　And strangers her valleys profane;
They come to divide, to dishonor,
　And tyrants they long will remain.
Not onward—the green banner rearing,
　Go, flesh every sword to the hilt,
On our side is Virtue and Erin,
　On theirs is the Saxon and guilt.

THE FATAL AMOUR OF AN EAST INDIAN KING.

THE YOUNG PRIEST AND THE LADY—A BOAR HUNT AND ITS CONSEQUENCES—LOVE'S FIRST CARESSES—THE SECRET MEETINGS—A FALSE FRIEND'S TREACHERY—THE FRUITS OF A GUILTY LOVE—A TERRIBLE VENGEANCE.

The celebration of the august and imposing rite of admission to the priesthood of the ancient and venerable order of Seva, had drawn together a crowd of persons from various parts of the southern district of India, to witness the scene in the great temple of the God, in the river-island of Iswara. The ceremony was now over, and the multitude had dispersed. One person still lingered near the altar; it was he who had just assumed the vows of a priest.

Godari was the younger son of a powerful and distinguished officer of the state. If abundant wealth, worldly honor, and high mental endowments could have secured the happiness of their possessor, there had been few whose blessedness had equaled his; but it was the misfortune of Godari to be born with that morbidness of feeling and susceptibility of passion which are the bane of comfort in every condition of existence.

In addition to the sufficient curse of an over-sensitive heart, it happened, unfortunately, that the elder brother of Godari was a

person of a nature and disposition the very opposite of his own. Cold, callous, and unfeeling, he took a savage pleasure in tyrannizing over the tenderness of his brother; he hourly vexed his soul with deep and aching insults, and stung him into madness by cruel irritation. The very presence of so uncongenial a spirit stirred up by a species of magnetic influence a dark strife of struggling passions.

His father, also, though kindly natured, was of the world, worldly; he had breathed the petrifying air of a court until his temper had become stern, hard, and inflexible. His son found in his forceful spirit nothing cognate to his gentle wishings. His father put down all romantic and dreamy sentiments as false and noxious; and ardent minds, when they despise or condemn a passion or a principle, often forget to allow for its existence. Under such circumstances, it is not surprising if Godari looked back upon his past life as a dark and distressful memory of woe.

The ceremony of his entrance on the priesthood was completed; and none remained in the temple, except the young devotee. There was a gloom and weight upon his spirit which he could neither conquer nor account for; it was not that instinctive foreboding of ill which we sometimes feel, but merely a dullness and ungeniality of feeling.

Perhaps it was the natural effect of the fatiguing pomp which he had just passed through; perhaps it was an uneasy feeling produced by the want of sympathy from his family in the course which he had adopted; perhaps it was a shade cast upon the glass of his spirit by the breath of some passing dream—for so small a thing as a forgotten vision of the night has power to color the substance of our being.

He presently rose and turned to a room joining the main temple, and separated from it by a hanging curtain. As he approached it he thought he saw the figure of some one standing upon the other side. He withdrew the folds a little, without noise, and felt breathed upon his face a soft, warm and delicious air, "so sweet that the sense ached at it."

He paused a moment to inhale the ambrosial smell, and then moving the curtain, beheld the loveliest woman he had ever seen, standing and looking attentively upon a picture hung upon the wall above the curtain. Her countenance was all roseate with the bloom of splendid intelligence; her complexion was as freshly soft and brightly pure as the dewy tints of a new-born flower; her features were gently proud with the high-born grace of purity and fine recession of a queenly innocence; and with a swan-like majesty,

The mantling spirit of reserve
Fashion'd her neck into a goodly curve.

Her startled glance fell upon the intruder, and then fluctuated with a painful timidity. It was a dove-like eye that seemed a sphered soul; you might have loved and worshiped it apart from its possessor. In the breast of young Godari the bright conflagration of love was kindled in a moment.

It would be difficult to determine which party was the most embarrassed. They both stood bowing towards one another for some time, blushing deeply, and looking on the ground. At length the lady spoke.

"My brother left me here," she said, with an agitated voice, "while he has gone to see if we could be permitted to look at the curiosities of the temple." And what a voice! There was a spirit in the sound; the gushing tones seemed angels uttered into immortality: there was a breathing life upon the words that pierced and played upon the hearer's heart.

"Certainly," said Godari, "on any day that the rooms shall be open, they will be infinitely honored by your presence. To-day, however, they are closed, and no exception of persons is made. Yet to you, I am sure, that even now they will be open. To you I am sure that neither that nor anything else will be denied."

"O, no." said the strange lady. "I cannot think of opposing any of the usual laws. It is not a matter of any consequence," and she was moving away.

"Will you suffer me to bring you word," said Godari, "of the time when the rooms are open?"

The lady bowed.

"And will you promise me to come?" said Godari, taking hold of her hand, and looking into her eyes with a supplicating impression, which it was impossible to resist. The lady smiled with an embarrassed air, and looked sideways at him.

"Promise me," continued the lover with the most persuasive accent.

"I will," said the other, half unwillingly, and making her escape at the same time from the room.

Like the dazzling blaze of sunlight, through a cloudy day, making an unconsuming flame of all the air, was the infinite illumination of the passion that blazed forth in the darkling mind of young Godari.

He was panting with the agitation of this exciting interview. Whether accident had hitherto prevented his meeting with one whose presence was fitted to disturb his soul with the might of

quivering feelings, or whether his proud and jealous temper had felt a lonely joy in turning softness into scorn, certainly never till now had masterless love possessed his being.

Godari had taken the precaution of sending an attendant after the lady to ascertain where she resided, and had resolved on visiting her on the following day. The night was passed by him in tasting the sweetest thing the mental sense can ever know—a lover's fragrant fancies and nectared hopes.

The summer shadows were beginning to lengthen through the ancient forest which was skirted by the deep and rapid river Caveri, when the young king Goroyen rode through the wood to enjoy the freshness of the rising breezes. This monarch, while yet a boy, had been called to assume the throne of the southern district of India; and was in the habit of compensating himself for the annoying absorptions of business in the morning, by long and solitary rides through the royal forest in the afternoon. It was on the same day that Godari had taken his vows, that the king, after being present at the ceremony, and having returned to his palace to dine, mounted his horse and set out on his usual excursion. The father of Goroyen, who was a man of solitary and meditative disposition, had built a lodge in the heart of the forest and furnished it with the utmost luxury and elegance, as a place of retreat and privacy from the business and bustle of his court. The rooms were arranged every morning by a confidential servant from the palace, but no attendant resided at the house and no one was intrusted by the king with the key. Goroyen visited this place almost every afternoon, and its silence and solitude rendered it a delightful spot for reading or for thought.

The king was riding leisurely along, within sight of this lodge, when he was startled by a wild cry of terror and distress, issuing from beyond a thicket of underwood which concealed the view. The cry was followed by a loud crashing of limbs and rustling of leaves, and the king spurring his horse quickly around the obstructing bushes, beheld with consternation a young and delicate woman flying with breathless rapidity, and closely pursued by a terrible wild boar. The lady in a few moments sank to the earth, in horror and affright, and the ferocious animal was about to spring upon her, when Goroyen threw himself from his horse, and drawing his sword with inconceivable swiftness, confronted the monster in the full rush of his violence. The boar, suddenly jerking his tusks sideways, inflicted a wound upon Goroyen, and brought him to his knee; then, drawing back, lowered his front and dashed with all his vehemence at his bending foe. Goroyen planted himself firmly upon one knee, threw out his other foot and fixed it against a root, then supporting one end of his sword against his breast with one hand, and directing the blade with the other, was prepared to receive the assailant on the point of his weapon. The animal made one spring; the steel met and clove the center of his skull; in a moment, he lay dead upon the body of the king.

Goroyen was stunned by the violence with which the enormous creature had leaped upon him; but, soon recovering, extricated himself from the lifeless load that rested upon him, and turned towards the lady whose safety had urged him to this contest, and who still lay where she had fallen, pale and insensible. The first conviction of Goroyen was that she was dead.

Without a moment's delay he raised her lifeless form in his arms, carried her to the lodge which was close at hand, and laid her upon a rich velvet sofa in one of its rooms. He resorted at once to all the modes of restoration which he could think of; he called her, shook her, begged her to come to life; then threw water in her face, and loosened her dress behind, that her returning breath might not be obstructed. Finding that none of these appliances were effectual, he knelt down and looked intently in her face; partly fascinated by her wondrous and peculiar beauty, and partly to see if no signs of vitality were discovered in her countenance. He then threw himself beside her on the sofa, and clasped her to his bosom in the hope that the warmth of his person might quicken the coldness of her frame. In a little while she heaved a deep sigh, and presently after opened her eyes, and closed them again; she then drew a long and difficult breath, folded Goroyen to her bosom, and muttered—"My brother."

The king, delighted with her restoration, imprinted eager kisses on her cheek. The lady again opened her eyes, and fixed them upon him.

"It is not my brother," she said, but without any surprise or agitation.

"It is one who loves you," replied the other, "with more than a brother's love."

"Are we quite safe?" she asked, gazing intently in the air.

"Entirely."

"Oh, what a horrid scene a few minutes after you left me I was hastening home, when a horrid animal sprang out of a thicket, and ran directly towards me. I thought I should have died with terror. I tried to run, but I felt so weak that I could scarcely move. The animal was just upon me, when you, my brother, appeared. Oh! oh! what I felt when I saw you," and she burst into a flood of burning tears.

Goroyen rose from the couch, and kneeling on one knee, watched her blind emotion, without interrupting the natural course of her feelings. He was deeply touched, as well by her beauty as by the interesting exhibition of uncontrollable disturbance. As the violence of her sobs abated, and she grew more composed, he took her hand in his with kindness, and said in an affectionate tone:

"Well, the danger is now passed; you are entirely safe now."

The lady started, and fixed her eyes in astonishment upon the speaker. The indulgence of her excited feelings in tears had calmed her agitation and recalled her wandering thoughts to the reality of her position. She raised herself upon the sofa, and looking wildly round upon the gorgeous furniture of the apartment, exclaimed: "Where am I? Who are you? What place is this?" Then looking down to where her falling dress had exposed the exquisite fairness of her bosom, she raised her hand hurriedly to conceal her breast, and blushed like scarlet.

Goroyen was enchanted by the graceful confusion and maiden delicacy of the lovely girl; and pressing her hand gently to his lips, said in a tone of profound respect: "Be assured, madam, that nothing but the eye of the purest and sincerest love has looked upon those charms." The lady blushed more deeply than before.

Goroyen was silent. The stranger, after struggling with her embarrassment, and essaying in vain several times to speak, said in a broken voice, looking upon the ground, "I—I thought it was my brother. I am indebted to you, I suppose, for my life. How shall I display my gratitude and—and regard?" Then fearing that she had said what she ought not to have done, she hung her head and trembled with perplexity.

"Chiefly," replied the royal wooer, "by assuring me that you are not hurt in the least."

"I am not hurt at all; but—but, cannot I go home?'

"At any moment that you please; yet I shall be most honored and delighted if you will remain. Listen to me. This place is sacred from all intrusion. Your presence will give me pleasure. If you will stay here a little while, I pledge you my stainless honor that nothing shall occur that can possibly embarrass or offend you, and that I will obey your directions in everything. And, that you may feel yourself protected, put this little dagger in your belt."

As she was extending her hand to receive the weapon, her eye fell upon a little stream of blood creeping slowly along the carpet. She started up, exclaiming with alarm, "You are wounded."

"Not the least; the merest scratch," said Goroyen, who, in the warmth of interest, had forgotten his wound.

But in attempting to raise himself from his knee, the necessary strain upon the sinews of his limb caused him such acute suffering that he cried out, in spite of himself. Forgetful of his boast, he was fain to crawl to the sofa and stretch himself upon it, with a countenance expressive of extreme pain.

"Does it give you much pain?" said his companion with solicitude.

"Not much, my love," said Goroyen in a kindly tone, at the same time frowning with anguish.

"I will dress it for you," said she.

"My darling!" said Goroyen, in an incredulous tone, "what should you know about dressing wounds? You had better let it alone."

"No, indeed, I can dress it very well. Will you not let me?"

"You may try it, if you like. But you will kill me, I am sure."

The lovely chirurgeon began her operations. The congealing blood had caused the dress of the king to be stuck to the flesh, and the removal of it inflicted severe pangs upon the patient. "Ouch! my sweetest!" was the exclamation which the first motion elicited: "Booh! my dearest cherub!" marked the second: "Bah! you loveliest dear!" was roared at the third.

At length the operation was completed. "Do you find yourself better?" asked the successful surgeon.

"Much," replied the king, "and shall be still better if you will do one thing more."

"What is that?"

"Kiss me," said the modest patient.

There was something so frank yet so delicate about the countenance of Goroyen, that he inspired confidence and ease in all who came near him. Though the lineaments of his face could not have disclosed his rank, they would have told you at once that he was a thorough gentleman. The lovely lady seemed to understand in a moment the playful refinement, and unpresuming familiarity of his manner; she only pouted with her pretty lips, and said "I shan't."

"By the bye," said she, "I wonder whereabouts we are. Do you know?" And she looked with curiosity about the room. She then walked to the window and looked out. "Good gracious! this is the king's lodge. There is no other building in the forest. I tell you what, the king often rides at this hour, and if he comes and finds us here he will be terribly angry. What shall we do? We had better get out as soon as possible. How in the name of goodness did you get in?"

"There is the key," said Goroyen.

"There are but two persons who ever have that key," said she, looking at him with a certain queerness; "the king and his private servant."

"Might it never occur to you, you perverse little angel! that I was the private servant of the king?"

She paused a moment, and looking keenly at him. "No, no," said she, shaking her head, "you have not the appearance of a servant."

"Then," said Goroyen, smiling kindly towards her, "I must be——"

He stopped and looked inquiringly at her.

"The king!" she exclaimed with surprise and awe. An Indian monarch is looked upon as belonging to a superior order of mortals. The color fled from the lady's cheek, and she bowed with the deepest reverence.

"Nay, nay, my darling," said Goroyen, "do not tremble at having conquered a king. By my faith, I must renounce my rank, if it deprives me of the privilege of your affections. Come to me," said he. "I told you that you would be no unskillful surgeon; for while you cured one wound, you inflicted a deeper. That wound," he continued, pressing her to his bosom, "only yourself can heal."

Leaving the lovers in the solitude of sacred feeling, let us return to the history of young Godori. The servant whom he had sent after the lady whom he had met so suddenly, and whom the reader has doubtless discovered to be the same whom the king had rescued in the forest, returned with the intelligence that her name was Chatryn—that she resided a little beyond the termination of the forest, and that she belonged to the ancient and honorable tribe of the Samides, the descendants of an old dynasty of kings who had been dethroned ages before by the founder of the present reigning family, and had since lived in entire seclusion, within a separate district, totally disconnected with every other family in the kingdom. Besides the interest of such pure and illustrious blood, there floated around the history and position of this tribe, or family, an air of romance, which further enfettered the fancy of Godari and made him still more anxious to meet her again.

Two or three days elapsed before the engagements of his office allowed him leisure to leave the temple long enough to visit her. At length, an unoccupied afternoon occurred, and mounting his horse, and obtaining a very precise direction from his servant, he set out towards her residence. In front of the house, above the door, was a little terrace of flowers, upon which a large window opened from the second story. As Godari drew near he recognized the form of Chatrya stooping down to examine one of the flowers. She raised her head and saw him, and instantly retreated within the window. The heart of Godari beat with strange and painful quickness. He almost repented of his enterprise, and actually slackened his pace considerably, to protract the period of meeting. He pictured to himself so vividly the first encounter with the lady, that the scene, with all its pleasing terrors, seemed present before him.

He at length gained the porch, and asked if Chatrya was at home. The inquiry was a mere matter of form; without thinking about an answer he was about to enter, when the servant replied that she was not. Godari was thunderstruck. He had seen her himself at the window; and he stood for a moment balancing in his mind between the fact and reply, in confused surprise, and then turned from the door.

A man does not feel while he fancies. The young priest had nearly finished his homeward journey, before his senses had so far pierced the thick mists of imagination as to receive from beyond them the impressions of disappointment. Still he did not feel aggrieved or vexed; hopes, such as he had scaffolded about his being, were not to be dashed down by so slight a repulse. He imputed the denial to some mistake or accident, and looked forward to his next visit as assuredly successful. That second visit he made a few days after, and met with the same cold refusal. This time he was stung and irritated. He was convinced that Chatrya must be resolved not to meet him again, for certainly, she might either have appeared or offered some explanation. He rode home in a savage humor, and felt mad and desperate all the evening. From these annoyances of "reality's dark dream" he took refuge in airy visions of success; he imagined himself in her company, happy and beloved, and thus his equanimity was soon restored. Pleasing fancies soon renewed pleasing hopes. He began to think that he had been hasty in his conclusion of failure.

Accordingly, after some days, he again took his way through the forest, which afforded the only approach from the temple to the residence of Chatrya. After riding a little way, he fell in with the king. By the established law no one was allowed to pass through that wood except the king, and though the prohibition was not penally enforced, yet as it was known that the king loved to be there alone, all who went through it took care to keep as much as possible out of his way; Godari therefore felt a little awkward in intruding upon him. The priesthood, however, constituted a high elevation in the rank, and the family of Godari was so much connected with the court, that there had always existed as much familiarity between himself and the king as was practicable between a subject and his sovereign; these considerations and the affable bearing of the monarch soon set him at ease, and they rode on together in familiar conversation. After a little while the king turned to him and said that he had an appointment at his lodge at that hour which would render it necessary for him to leave his companion, and, smiling with a peculiar expression, rode off through a narrow path and left Godari alone. The latter suspected the nature of the engagement, but his own thoughts were too much interested in a similar manner to suffer him to blame the conduct of the king.

A brisk canter soon brought him to the brow of a hill from which there issued a fine spring of water. He stopped his horse to let him drink, and in the silence of the breezeless air, he presently heard a sound of motion among the leaves and branches

at a little distance which he at first imputed to a playful squirrel. In a moment, however, he heard the low humming of a sweet human voice, that floated, flake-like, on the yellow air, and seemed the vocal incense of a happy heart. He raised his eyes, and at the bottom of the hill saw his own Chatrya. With one hand she was swinging her bonnet by its string and carrying in the other a choice bunch of flowers. The first impulse of Godari's gladness to spring forward and embrace her was arrested by a feeling of wonder at her presence in this place, and curiosity to discover the object of her walk. A vague feeling of suspicion, too shadowy to be combated, and too dark to be forgotten, crept over his mind. He stood motionless till she was out of sight, and then dismounting walked quickly in the direction which she had taken, until he again came up with her. He followed her till they came within view of the royal lodge. The heart of Godari sank within him, and a sense of inexpressible mortification came upon him, as he saw that her steps were directed towards it. She tripped gayly along, as soon as she saw the house, and running up the steps, the door opened to her as to one expected.

Godari leaned against a tree, breathless with dismay. His frame grew rigid with the force of unutterable feelings. Scarcely master of his actions, he walked towards the lodge, and observing a window in one end, accessible by a little effort, he climbed noiselessly up, and looked within. In the midst of a room, furnished as became the secret place of royal luxury, on a couch of richest crimson, he saw Goroyen and Chatrya lying in the tenderest embraces of love. He looked for one moment; and in that moment the curdling coldness of a demon's temper crept over his spirit and froze his soul to adamant. It was one of those instants that are epochs in the calendar of the soul, transforming it thenceafter ever. Godari sprang to the ground, another creature. He cursed himself for having been the bubble of a week and womanish feeling, and the dupe of what now seemed the most trivial passion in the world. Till this moment he had been a boy, begirt with boyhood's self-forming atmosphere of tenderness; but now he waved and whistled down the wind all gentleness of thought, and thrilled with unblenching manhood's steel-nerved force.

Godari felt that he had staked his destiny on a single cast, and that had gone against him. Henceforth his portion was such selfish gain as, by the onward might of abandoned fury, he could work out for himself. He rode home calm and composed—one might almost say, happy. Feeling in him was crushed and swept away; and feeling is, to a man of sensibility, a source of more misery than joy.

Days passed on, and the young priest grew sterner and more relentless; for the sources of moral vitality were dried up within him.

To detach the king from Chatrya revenge as well as restlessness suggested; to marry the king to his own sister, was a purpose following close upon. The first of these objects he saw an easy manner of accomplishing.

To the sect of Seva, of which Godari was a priest, it was usual for the king and nobles of the country to be at some time admitted; for the order was honorable, and held forth high promise of favor in a world to come. This was the religion professed by the ancestral family of Goroyen, who had vanquished and exiled the race of Samide kings; and in the oath taken by the king at his admission, there was inserted a promise never to speak to, or sit or eat with, any of the tribe of the Samides. It was not usual for the lay members of this sect to take the vows 'till late in life, for they imposed a greater strictness in life and austerity of conduct than was usually agreeable to the eagerness of youth; some solicitation and management on the part of Godari was therefore necessary to prevail upon the king to be initiated into this sect. His consent, however, was at length obtained, and he yielded to the wishes of his friend, profoundly ignorant of the existence of the prohibitory clause, which we have spoken of, in the oath.

A day was accordingly appointed for the ceremony to take

place, and at the appointed time there assembled in the temple all that the country held of distinguished, beautiful and great. By the private order of the king, a favorable place for viewing the scene was reserved for Chatrya, who, being informed of all the proceedings by Goroyen, looked forward to the event with great curiosity and interest. Goroyen, meanwhile, went through the successive ceremonies with grace and dignity, and at length arrived at the solemn oath. The high-priest recited the successive clauses, and Goroyen pronounced them after him. When he came to that part in which it was necessary to renounce all connection and communication with the Sainides, the king started with surprise and embarrassment. To repeat those words with that sincerity with which he was performing the entire service was utterly inconsistent with that relation to Chatrya, which nothing would induce him to renounce; to mar the order of the solemn ceremonies, and break up the assembly by refusing to continue his part, was not to be thought of. His brain grew dizzy with the perplexity; the clearness of his thoughts was confused by the influence of the observant multitude, and the holy and venerable countenance of the officiating hierarch; his head swam round with overpowering disturbance, and he insensibly pronounced the words that divorced his lover from Chatrya.

The disorder and agitation of mind with which Goroyen sought his chamber, when the services were over, cannot be easily described. Bred in the strictest integrity of principle, he could not tolerate the idea of violating so sacred an oath; yet, on the other hand, honor and affection, and every impulse of piety, duty and desire, forbade him to desert one upon whom his love would soon entail the cares and sorrows of a mother. He paced his room in distraction of thought and distress of heart during the remainder of the day, and meeting with no suggestion that afforded him light or consolation, finally resolved on sending for his friend Godari, to obtain the benefit of his counsel in this difficulty.

Godari listened to his disclosures with gratifying interest; sympathized with him in his distress; pitied his unfortunate position; and pondered profoundly upon the best course to pursue. He showed him that this was a case in which inclination and duty were opposed to one another, and pointed out to him the necessity which always existed of disregarding one's own feelings whenever they were at variance with the dictates of duty. To this principle the well-regulated mind of Goroyen cordially assented; but between the obligation of his oath and that of his connection with Chatrya there arose apparently a conflict of equivalent duties.

Godari went on to say that as far as the king himself was concerned, the paramount force of his vow was manifest; and that as respected Chatrya, every obligation was performed if by any means her happiness was secured. If, therefore, the king would provide for her all those things which would promote her comfort and enjoyment, he might fairly consider himself as absolved from the duty which rested upon him. This seemed to clear the difficulty very well, and Goroyen was delighted with this satisfactory exposition of the case.

He gave directions to Godari to assign the lodge as the residence and property of Chatrya, determining himself never to visit it again; and he placed in his hands a liberal sum of money for her use. Satisfied by his own judgment, and the assurance of the priest that he had performed his duty, he determined to conquer the feelings of attachment which had held him to Chatrya, and as a means of succeeding more fully in this, to fix them, if possible, on some other object. This state of inclination was exactly that which was required for the effecting of Godari's ambitious intentions. While the affections of the king were hovering, as it were, at large, doubtful upon what to alight, and willing to adopt any object that should present itself, Godari directed one of his creatures to represent to Goroyen that the sister of the former cherished an ardent but concealed attachment for him. Such a representation, when made to a man of kind nature, will almost invariably accomplish its purpose; with one of Goroyen's refined sense of honor, and especially at a time when he was peculiarly susceptible, it was certain of success.

Goroyen was deeply touched by the statement which was made to him, and lost no time in presenting himself to the lady, and offering his hand. The wish to forget Chatrya in the ardor of another pursuit, united with the attractions of the person herself; and in a short period the approaching nuptials of the king were publicly announced.

Let us turn now to the gentle victim of these priestly machinations. Chatrya, with her eyes intently fixed upon the king, sat listening to the oath which he was repeating. The fatal words of separation from herself fell upon her ear without, at first, producing any surprise or emotion. She concluded that she had not heard the words aright, or that something would presently follow to explain or qualify them. She had seen Goroyen the very evening before, and his manner at that time suggested nothing less than an intention of parting from her. As the oath, however, concluded without anything which could relieve her alarm, her heart gradually sank within her; a heaviness crept over her feelings which she could not dissipate. The mere imagination of being alienated from her lover, her only support and comfort, made her sick in spirit. She sank into a dreary reverie, till the heartless noise of the dispersing assembly aroused her to her lonely fears; she had nothing else to do but make her way home, and wait until some intelligence reached her from the king. She then set out, with something of hope but none of dread, to take that path she had so often trod in gayety and joy; one who had seen her hasty step would not have thought "how ill was about her heart." She gained the lodge, but it was closed and silent. While she was standing upon the steps in the deep disquietude of her heavy disappointment, she heard a sound of footsteps on the adjoining path, and her bosom heaved with anxious expectation; but a carelessly-whistled song which presently smote upon her ears, showed that it was only a passing plowman. How that whistling jarred upon her feelings! She walked down from the door, and paused in front of the lodge. As she looked up at the building she was sure she saw Goroyen peeping at her from behind one of the curtains. She threw out her hand with delight, and called to him that she saw him plainly enough; but the object did not move, and upon changing her position she perceived that she had been deceived by the shadow cast by one of the trees. The iron of cruel anguish entered into her soul. She walked around the lodge, and into the road which was near it, feeling as if she should fall to the earth. She listened to the dropping of twigs among the leaves, till she seemed as solitary as if she were standing in a desert. Occasionally a dog ran contentedly along, engaging attention as he passed by, and then leaving her more hopelessly alone. But to the griefs and joys of life Time is alike relentless; and the "cloud of night" descended drearily around her path, "as if she had not sought a lover." She resolved to wait just so many minutes longer, and then, if Goroyen did not appear, to retrace her steps as she had come. The time was nearly past when a flash of hope was again kindled in her breast. She distinctly heard the tread of a rapid horseman in the forest; she was sure it was the king, and I was almost resolved to go home before he came, in order to punish him for his neglect. The sound grew louder and louder, and not a doubt remained in her heart. She walked back to the door of the lodge, sighing for very excess of joy, and picturing the pleasure that soon awaited her. Tracing, in fancy, the scene of their first meeting, she forgot for awhile to observe that the sound of footsteps was no longer audible. Surprised, at length, at the long delay, she paused her breath in sudden alarm to listen for the noise—but nothing was to be heard. She ran back to the road, and "e'en with the very scrutiny of her soul," she listened for his coming. She heard in a moment the faint sound of a horse's hoofs upon the hill which wound along the edge of the forest. It was manifest that the horseman had passed round the wood. She heaved one long and burdened breath, and sank into deep and utter despair. A stone seemed to lie upon her heart. She tried to weep, but could not. Sorrow rested on her spirit with the hopeless weight of guilt.

On the following day Chatrya again came to the lodge, and

again returned home, but on the third her strength was not sufficient to bear her from her door. She was soon seized with a violent, malignant fever; she became delirious, and her ravings disclosed the dishonorable connection with Goroyen.

Chastity, among the Samides, was the first of virtues; no pardon was granted, or allowance made for any who erred. The father of Chatrya, a stern and proud-hearted man, renounced his daughter at once; the moment that she was sufficiently recovered to walk, he gave her a purse of gold, and turned her from his house. Destroyed in character, ruined in health, broken in spirit, without anything to vary the dull desolation of unpitied desertion, except the stings of regret and the pangs of conscience, Chatrya went forth from the house of her childhood. Incapable of judging of her course, she wandered on till she reached a cottage, inhabited by a woman, who bore the reputation of a sorceress. She tottered into the house, and sank upon the floor. The hag, who perceived her condition, poured forth a torrent of abusive and irritating language, which wrung Chatrya to the very soul. The old woman was, however, pacified by the sight of gold, and consented to receive the unhappy girl as a lodger. Before long she gave birth to a child, and the companionship of the little creature relieved her sorrows. From him she might hope for sympathy and kindness; she would have something to love, and some one she might care for.

She was one night pressing her infant to her bosom, and shaping some faint plans of future comfort, when her child was seized with one of those sudden difficulties of breathing which so often assail their tender lives. The mother rose to procure something from another part of the room, and when she again laid her hand upon her child, it no longer breathed. In the silent solitude of midnight she stood a childless woman.

For Chatrya there remained no further hope; she was stripped of the last promise of consolation; her health forbade her to leave her bed; and she was doomed to lie daily exposed to the taunts of the harsh woman who attended her, and to the goadings of her own tortured mind. There seemed to remain nothing for her but "to curse God and die." From the weary load of despair her only relief was—hate.

Meanwhile, to her road of suffering and shame Godari had been running his parallel courses of villainy and deceit. He had converted the lodge to his own use, and put the money of the king in his pocket. Farther than to desert her, he cared not to persecute her; leaving it to the ban-dogs of Poverty and Infamy to hunt her down the precipice of woe. Well knowing that to one of her condition life was agony and circumstance was grief, he dismissed his revengeful thoughts toward her from his memory, and thought no more about her. But his malignant spirit towards the king was not yet exhausted, nor was his ambition yet sufficiently gratified. By the laws of the country none but males were allowed to ascend the throne, and on failure of the blood relations of the reigning king, his male connections by marriage succeeded. No male relations of Goroyen survived; and it was manifest to Godari that if the queen were now dead without issue, he would himself be the heir presumptive of the throne. To place upon his brow the envied coronet of sovereignty it was only necessary that the king and queen should cease to live. Accordingly, this remorseless friend and brother resolved speedily to destroy both of them. An accident, ere long, presented a means which promised success.

The king was one day riding alone some distance from the city, when he met a woman on the road, whose miserable appearance so much affected him that he stopped to make some inquiries as to her condition. She was sallow and wrinkled, though apparently not with age; her hair was floating carelessly in the wind; and her tattered garments barely protected her from the cold. Goroyen addressed some questions to her, and his penetrating eye discovered, as he looked more closely at her, that this abject person was no other than the object of his former love—Chatrya.

Shocked at such a result of misery to others from his own conduct, he demanded if she had not received the benefits of the provision which he had directed Godari to make for her, and

learned with inexpressible indignation that the malignant priest had intercepted his intended kindness, and left the object of it to perish in desertion. Goroyen explained to Chatrya all the circumstances of the case—spoke to her with kindness and regard—a language that had long ceased to greet her ears—declared to her that his love had never failed, and assured her that nothing should hereafter be wanting that should contribute to her happiness.

"It is too late," said Chatrya. "There remains no happiness, and but little time, for me on earth. It is a comfort for me to know that you did not purposely turn me over to neglect and want. The things of earth no longer interest me, but I will not die until that cold and selfish priest has tasted the dregs of the cup of vengeance."

When Goroyen reached the palace he sent for Godari.

"I have seen Chatrya," said he, pale with excessive rage. "What have you to say?"

"Simply to inquire," said Godari, coldly, "whether she was as miserable as she deserves to be?"

"You admit, then, the villainy which stands charged against you?" said Goroyen, gasping for breath.

"And only regret," said Godari, "that part of the suffering it produced did not light upon her accursed lover."

"Leave me," roared the king.

The instant that the king had mentioned his having seen Chatrya, Godari knew that he had him in his power. He might defy his vengeance, for an easy calculation of time assured him that he could destroy the king sooner than the king could punish him. The mode which he proposed was briefly this: In the river of Cavery, near to the temple in which he officiated, there was a fall of water above sixty feet in height. On one side of the cascade there rose a huge lip of rock, about eighty feet above the upper bed of the stream.

It happened that Godari, in rambling recently among the rocks that stood piled around this eminence, had clambered up to the very summit of the ridge. On the top of the great rock he discovered a crevice or niche, which was open towards the direction in which the stream was flowing, but hidden for a long distance by higher projections, from any observer on the shores. He was standing in this niche and looking down upon the horrid chasm of waters below, when he observed that a little platform of stone, which had been carved out ages before by a superstitionist, upon the lowest level of the water, was directly below a huge piece of rock that lay loose upon the top of the eminence where he stood, and so singularly balanced that a very slight motion would suffice to cast it down. This platform had been used for a long time as a standing place for persons who were required to bathe their heads in the falling waters of the sacred river Cavery, in expiation of certain crimes, as required by the sect of Seva.

The strictness of the order had been so much relaxed of late, that an instance of this sort of purification had not occurred for many years; but Godari as he examined the place could not help remarking, with the fertile invention of a scheming villain, that if any one were standing on that platform, the precipitation of this great stone upon their heads would be a mode of destroying them as beautiful as it would be safe and efficacious. Of this "gained knowledge" he now determined to make use for the removal of the king.

As soon, therefore, as he went from his presence, he hastened to the archives of the temple, and took down a volume of the institutes of the religion of Seva. He turned over the leaves until he found a blank space opposite of the places large enough to contain a couple of written sentences. Imitating with admirable skill the chirography, in which the rest of the book was written, he inserted a paragraph to this effect among the rules of the order: That if any King, after taking the oath to abstain from holding any verbal communication with a Samide, should by accident or design hold any conversation with one, he should, the moment the fault was discovered, burn incense in the temple for two days, and then, together with his queen, perform the usual ablution on the platform on the Cavery, before transacting any other business. As soon as Godari had finished the writing he took the book, and proceeded to the room of the high priest, and laid the passage before him. He informed him that the king had been holding communication with a woman of the forbidden race; and calling his attention to the peculiarly strong language of the injunction in question, suggested to him the propriety of now putting it in force.

The venerable priest, with a placid smile, read the sentence alluded to by Godari, and applauding the learning of his young friend for discovering a passage in the sacred institutes which he confessed had escaped him, he directed the usual deputation to wait upon the king with an order to appear at the temple. This direction Godari obeyed, with the substitution of sending for 'going; and having done all that was required, retired to his chamber to make his reflections.

"A most fortunate thing, this of the king's meeting with Chatrya!" said he to himself when he was alone. "In the first place it enables me to disappoint both of them in their plan of taking vengeance upon me. In the second place, it gives me a much earlier chance than I should otherwise have had of sweeping the throne and placing myself upon it. This deputation will soon reach the palace, and from its arrival, all business there is suspended. The only precaution I have to take is to keep clear of all the services of this occasion."

Goroyen gave a respectful reception to the officers, and consented at once to the course which was proposed. He laid aside the intention of proceeding against Godari until the ceremony was over, and went at once to the temple to commence the burning of incense.

The crisis was now approaching. The third day of the ceremonies, the day appointed for the purification of the king and queen on the platform in the river, had arrived. Before the earliest dawn, Godari had risen and gained the rock which was to be the scene of his operations. He ascertained that the stone, which he was to cast down, would alight directly upon the platform, and that even after it had fallen he would be entirely invisible from all those spots that would probably be occupied by spectators. There was no danger of his being interrupted or discovered, for the elevation in which he was hidden was usually called "The Inaccessible;" and, as it was directly above the place where the king and queen were to stand, no one would think of occupying it on this occasion. The niche or step on which he

stood was pretty narrow, and hung directly over the deepest part of the stream, at a height of an hundred and forty feet. As he supported himself against the sides of the rocks which rose around him, he could just discern, under the bubbled surface of the pool beneath, the sharp top of a yellow rock.

Godari counted the hours in his perilous situation, until the time appointed for the ceremony arrived. At an early period in the day numbers began to collect along the contiguous shores; he heard their movements and their voices. At length a shout from the multitude announced the coming of the royal couple. Godari, by leaning over a little, saw them pass directly under his feet, and gain the platform, where they were again hidden from his view. The time had arrived for the execution of his scheme. He raised his hand to push the huge stone, which was to accomplish his object, when he felt his hair griped by a steel-like hand, that scraped his skull as it gathered his hair in its grasp.

His blood ran cold within him. To bend back his neck sufficiently to see the person who had seized him was impossible, with the certainty of his being precipitated from the ledge. He stood, therefore, motionless.

"It is Chatrya," said a shrill voice above him; and the arm which held him was drawn forward, so as to compel him to look into the abyss beneath. The mind of Godari tottered as he gazed, and his breast seemed to collapse with horror. At that moment the multitude perceived the woman, and all eyes were directed towards her.

"Let the king and the queen leave the platform, and go upon the shore," cried Chatrya; and she was instantly obeyed.

"The priest Godari placed himself here," she continued in a loud voice, while the deepest silence reigned over the crowd, "for the purpose of throwing this rock upon the king," and as she spoke she touched the stone, and it thundered down, and swept the platform away in an instant.

A deeper silence ensued among the multitude—the silence of horror and expectation. It was broken by the voice from the summit of the rock.

"Upon the neglectful lover and the perfidious priest, Chatrya is alike avenged."

Clenching the hair of her victim more firmly in her grasp, she sprang from the rock, and in a moment the ruined pair were buried beneath the waves.

THE SCANDALS OF THE COURT OF MARY, QUEEN OF SCOTS.

THE YOUNG BEAUTY IN FRANCE—THE DEATH OF A CRAZY LOVER—THE ASSASSINATION OF RIZZIO—HER HUSBAND KING—BOTHWELL THE CORSAIR—THE DEATH OF DARNLEY—MARRIAGE WITH BOTHWELL—DEFEAT AND IMPRISONMENT—THE TREACHERY OF ELIZABETH OF ENGLAND—THE EXECUTION OF THE UNFORTUNATE MARY.

MARY, Queen of Scots, was undoubtedly one of the most beautiful of women, and she was as charming and attractive as she was fair to behold.

Lamartine, one of the most eloquent of her historians, while at the same time one of the severest critics of her reign, tells us that, if another Homer were to arise, and if the poet were to seek another Helen for the subject of a modern epic of war, religion, and love, he would beyond all find her in Mary Stuart, the most beautiful, the weakest, the meekest and most attracted of women, raising around her, by her irresistible fascinations, a whirlwind of love, ambition, and jealousy, in which her lovers became, each in his turn, the motive, the instrument, and the victim of a crime.

Mary Stuart was the only daughter of James V., King of Scotland, and of Marie de Lorraine, daughter of the Duke of Guise. She was born in Scotland on the 7th December, 1542. Her father was one of those adventurous, romantic, gallant, and poetic characters who leave behind them popular traditions of bravery and

of licentiousness in the imagination of their country, like Francis I. and Henry IV. of France.

James V. died young, prophesying a mournful destiny for his daughter, yet in her cradle. This prophecy was suggested by his misgivings regarding the fate of a child.

His widow, Mary of Lorraine, deposed from the regency by the jealousy of the nobles, reconquered it by her ability, and allowed the cardinals—the usual supporters of thrones at that period—to govern the kingdom under her. Her daughter was sought after by all the courts of Europe, not only because of her precious renown for genius and beauty, but also, and principally, for the purpose of acquiring, by marriage with her, a right to the Scottish crown—an acquisition strongly coveted by the wearers of other crowns.

After a journey to Lorraine and France to pay a visit to her uncles, the Guises, the queen determined, by their advice, to marry her daughter to the Dauphin, son of Henry II.

The Queen-Regent of Scotland left her child-daughter in the

château of St. Germain, to grow up under their protection in the atmosphere of that France over which she was destined one day to reign.

The learned and Italian education of the young Scottish woman developed the natural gifts she possessed. French, Italian, Greek, Latin, history, theology, poetry, music, and dancing, were all learned and studied under the wisest masters and greatest artists. In the refined and voluptuous court of the Valois, governed by a favorite, she was brought up rather as an accomplished court lady than as a future queen; and her education rather seemed to fit her for becoming the mistress than the wife of the Dauphin. The Valois were the Medici of France.

The poets of the courts soon began to celebrate in their verses the marvels of her beauty and the treasures of her mind—

" The gods themselves excelled, in framing thy fair mind,
Nature and art in thy young form their highest powers combined,
All beauty of the beautiful to concentrate in thee,"

writes du Bellay, the Petrarch of the time.

Ronsard, who was the Virgil of the age, expresses himself, whenever he speaks of her, in such images and with such deficiency and polish of accent, as prove that his praise sprang from his love—that his heart had subjugated his genius. Mary was evidently the Beatrix of the poet.

" In fullness of the springtide, from among the lilies fair,
Sprang forth that form of whiteness, fairer than the lilies there,
Though stained with Adonis' blood, the gentle summer rose
Lies vanquished by the ruby tint her cheeks and lips disclose.
Young Love himself with arrows keen hath armed her peerless eye,
The Graces too, those fairest three, bright daughters of the sky
With all their richest, rarest gifts my princess have endowed,
And evermore to serve her well have left their high abode."

The sudden death of Henry II., killed in a tournament by Montgomery, sent Diana to the solitary Château of Anet, where she had prepared her retreat, and where she grew old in tears. The young Mary of Scotland was crowned with her husband, Francis II., who was even more of a child in mind and in weakness than in age. The Guises reaped what they had sown in advising this marriage; they reigned through their niece over her husband, and through him the king over France.

This reign only lasted eleven months; France lost the phantom of a king rather than a master, and barely granted him royal obsequies. Mary alone sincerely mourned him as the mild and agreeable companion of her youth rather than as a husband. The verses which she composed in the first months of her widowhood neither exaggerate nor lessen the sentiment of her grief; they are sweet, sad, but lukewarm as the first melancholy of the soul before the age of passionate despair.

" All that once in pleasure met
New is pain and sorrow;
The brilliant day hath quickly set
In night with dreary morrow.

" Where'er I sojourn, sad, forlorn,
In forest, mead, or hill ;
Whether at the dawn of morn,
Or vesper hour so still—
My sorrowing heart shall beat for thee,
This absent one I ne'er shall see !

" When slumbering on my conch I lie,
And dreams the past reveal,
Thy form, beloved, seems ever nigh,
Thy fond caress I feel."

It was in a convent at Rheims, where she had retired to enjoy the society of the Abbess Renee of Lorraine, that she lamented so sweetly, not the loss of a throne, but the loss of love. Soon after she heard of the death of her mother, the Queen of Scotland. A new throne awaited her at Edinburgh, and she prepared for her departure.

"Ah!" cries her poet and adorer, the great Ronsard, on learning the approaching return of the young queen to Scotland—

" Like to the heaven when starless, dark,
Like seas dried up or sailless bark,
Like ring its precious pearl gone,
Mourns France, without thee sad and lone.
Thou wert her gem, her flower, her pride,
Her young and beauteous royal bride."

" Scotland," continues the poet, " which is about to snatch her from us, becomes so dim in the mist of its seas that her ship will never reach its shores."

" But she I've sought long time in vain
May soon to France return again,
To dwell in castle of Touraine !
Then, full of song, my lips would try
To swell her praise, and sing till I,
Like fabled swan, might singing die !"

The same poet, when contemplating her dressed in mourning in the park of Fontainbleau some days before her departure, thus with a loving pen traces her image, blending it forever with the beautiful shades of Diana of Poitiers and of Lavalliere, which people, in imagination, the waters and woods of that exquisite spot :

" A long and slender veil of sable crape;
Its folds unfolding, ever folds anew;
The mourning symbol that enwraps thy shape
From head to girdle falls;
Now swelling to the wind, even as the sail
Of bark urged onward by the passing gale;
(Leaving, alas ! this ever beauteous land,
Whose sceptre once was borne by thy fair hand;)
Thus wert thou clad, when thou didst pensive stray
Along the royal garden's paths that day,
Bathing thy bosom with the crystal tears."

A cortege of regret, rather than of more honor, accompanied her to the vessel which was to bear her to Scotland. He who appeared most grieved among the courtiers was the Maréchal de Damville, son of the Great Constable de Montmorency; being unable to follow her to Scotland, on account of his official duties, he resolved to have a constant representative there in the person of a young gentleman of his household, Du Chatelard, by whom he might be daily gratified with a narrative of the slightest events, and, so to speak, of every breath drawn by his idol.

Du Chatelard, unhappily for himself, fell madly in love with her to whom he was the accredited ambassador of another's love. He was a descendant of the Chevalier Bayard, brave and adventurous as his ancestor, a scholar and a poet like Ronsard, with a tender soul ready to be speedily scorched by such a flame. Everybody knows the touching verse written by Mary, through her tears, on the deck of the vessel, while the coast of France faded in the distance:

" Farewell, thou ever pleasant soil of France,
Beloved land of childhood's early day!
Farewell, my France ; farewell, my happy years!
Though from thy shores I now am snatched away,
Thou still remainest half my loving heart,
The rest will ne'er forget thee though we part!"

On the 19th of August, 1561—the very day on which she completed her nineteenth year—Mary landed on Scottish ground.

She confided the direction of the government to a natural son of her father, James V., who bore the name of the "Lord James," whom she treated as a brother, and elevated to the rank of Earl of Murray. Murray was, by character and spirit, worthy of the confidence of his sister; young, handsome, eloquent like her, he was better acquainted with the country than she was; he had the friendship of the nobles, wisely managed the Presbyterians, had acquired the esteem of the people, and possessed that loyal ability, that skilful uprightness, which is the gift of great statesmen. Such a brother was a favorite given by nature to the young queen, and so long as he remained the only favorite he made his sister popular by his government as by his arms. He led her into the midst of the camps, and she fascinated all by her charms and her courage; her address in horsemanship astonished her subjects; she was present at the battle of Corrichie, in which Murray vanquished the rebels and killed the Earl of Huntly, their leader.

Everything promised Mary Stuart a happy reign for herself and her kingdom, had her heart been devoted to nothing but state policy; but hers was the heart not merely of a queen, but of a woman accustomed to the court of France, and to the idolatry of her beauty professed by an entire kingdom.

The Scottish nobles were not less enthusiastic than were those of France in this chivalric worship; yet to declare herself sensible to the homage of any one of her subjects would only have been to alienate all the rest by exciting their jealousy; but the politic watchfulness over herself with relation to the Scottish lords, which had been recommended by Murray, her brother and minister, was precisely that which ruined her.

Unconsciously to herself, an obscure favorite insinuated himself into her heart; this favorite, so celebrated afterward for his sudden elevation and tragical death, was named David Rizzio. Rizzio was an Italian of low birth and menial station. Gifted with a touching voice, a pliant spirit, which enabled him to bow before the great; possessing a talent for playing the lute, and for composing and for singing that languishing music which is one of the effeminacies of Italy, Rizzio had been attached at Turin to the household of the French ambassador at the court of Piedmont in the capacity of musical attendant. On his return to France, the ambassador had brought Rizzio with him to the court of Francis II., and he entered the suite of one of the French nobles who had escorted Mary to Scotland.

The young queen had begged him of this nobleman, that she might retain in the country where she was less a queen than an exile one who would be to her as a living memory of the arts, leisure, and delights of France and Italy, those lands of her soul. A musician herself, as she was also a poet—charming frequently her sadness by composing words and airs in which she exhaled her sighs—the society of the Piedmontese musician became habitual and dear to her. The study of his art and even the inferiority of Rizzio's condition concealed for some time the assiduity and familiarity of this intimacy from the observation of the court of Holyrood.

Rumors in the palace regarding this preference of the queen for the Italian were not slow to find an echo in the city, and from thence they spread all over Scotland.

Du Chatelard, treated as a child by the playful indulgence of the queen, had conceived for his mistress a passion bordering on madness. The queen had encouraged him too much to retain the right of punishing him. Du Chatelard, constantly admitted to the most intimate familiarity with his mistress, ended by mistaking sport for earnest, persuading himself that she only desired a pretext for yielding to his audacity.

The ladies of the palace discovered him one night hidden under the queen's bed; he was expelled with indignation, but his boldness was placed to the account of the thoughtlessness of his age and character. Raillery was his only punishment. He continued to profess at court an adoring worship for Mary, filling the palace with his amorous verses, and reciting to the courtiers those lines which Ronsard, possessed with the same image, had addressed to her in Paris.

> "The ivory whiteness of thy bosom fair;
> Thy long and slender hand so soft and rare,
> Thy all-surpassing look and form of love,
> Enchanting as a vision from above;
> Then thy sweet voice and music of thy speech,
> That rocks and woods might move, nor art could reach,
> When these are lost, fled to a foreign shore,
> With loves and graces, France beholds no more.
> How shall the poet sing now thou art gone?
> For silent is the muse since thou hast flown;
> All that is beauteous short time doth abide,
> The rose and lily only bloom while lasteth the spring-tide.
>
> "Thus here, in France, thy beauty only shone,
> For thrice five years, and suddenly is gone;
> Like to the lightning-flash, a moment bright,
> To leave but darkness and regret like night;

> To leave a deathless memory behind,
> Of that fair princess, in my heart enshrined,
> My winged thoughts, like birds, now fly to thee,
> My beauteous princess, and her home I see,
> And there for evermore I fain would stay,
> Nor from that sweetest dwelling ever stray.
>
> "Nature hath ever in her deepest floods,
> On loftiest hills, in lonely rocks and woods,
> Her choicest treasures hid from mortal ken,
> With rich and precious gems unseen of men.
> The pearl and ruby sleep in secret stores,
> And softest perfumes spring on wildest shores,
> Thus God, who over thee his watch doth keep,
> Hath borne thy beauty safe across the deep
> On foreign shore, in regal pride to rest,
> Far from inine eyes, but hidden in my breast."

These beautiful verses of Ronsard were doubtless esteemed an excuse for the passion of a poet equally fascinated, but less discreet.

Du Chatelard, surprised a second time hidden behind the curtains of the queen's bed, was sent to trial and condemned to death by the judges of Edinburgh for a meditated treason. With a single word Mary might have commuted his punishment or granted him pardon, but she ungenerously abandoned him to the executioner. Ascending the scaffold erected before the windows of Holyrood palace, the theater of his madness and the dwelling of the queen, he faced death like a hero and a poet.

"If," said he, "I die not *without reproach*, like the Chevalier Bayard, my ancestor, like him, I die, at least, *without fear*."

For his last prayer he recited Ronsard's beautiful Ode on Death. Then casting his last looks and thoughts towards the windows of the palace, inhabited by the charm of his life and the cause of his death:

"Farewell!" he cried, "thou who art so beautiful and so cruel; who killest me, and whom I cannot cease to love!"

This tragedy was only the prelude to others which were soon after to fill the palace with consternation and bloodshed.

But already state politics began to intermingle with love, and to invade the happiness of the young queen. England, by right of kindred, had always exercised, partly by habit, partly by force, a sort of recognized mediation over Scotland.

Elizabeth, the daughter of Henry VIII., less woman than statesman, was not of a character likely to forego this right of mediation. Public and personal policy alike prompted her to retain it, the more so that Mary Stuart possessed eventual rights to the crown of England—rights even more legitimate than her own. In the case of Elizabeth—who gloried in the title of virgin queen—dying without issue, Mary might be called to succeed her on the English throne. The marriage of the Queen of Scots was therefore a question which essentially interested Elizabeth, for, according as the Scottish princess should marry a foreign, a Scottish, or an English prince, the fate of England would not fail to be powerfully influenced by the king, with whom Mary should divide her two crowns.

Elizabeth had begun by supporting the pretensions of her own favorite, the handsome Leicester, to the hand of Mary; then jealousy restrained her, and she transferred her favor to a young Scot of the almost royal house of Lennox, whose father was devoted to her, and lived at court. She indirectly intimated to Mary that such a marriage would cement an eternal friendship between them, and would be agreeable to both nations.

This advice, moreover, could not fail to be well received by a young queen, whose heart should naturally take precedence of her hand, for Darnley, then in the flower of his youth, was one of the handsomest of men, and the most likely to captivate the eyes and heart of a young queen by the graces of his person.

Rizzio might perhaps have made himself the sole obstacle to the marriage of Mary; but whether it arose from womanly caprice or from the refined policy of Rizzio, which prompted him to concede a throne in order to retain his influence, he favored the idea of Elizabeth by every means, thinking, doubtless, that he might be unable to resist alone, or for a length of time, the enmity of the Scottish nobles leagued against him; that a king was necessary to reduce them to obedience, and that Darnley, who, though possessing a charming exterior, had only an inferior mind, would be very grateful to him for placing him on the throne, and would leave him to reign in reality, sheltered from public envy under the protection of the king.

Darnley appeared at Holyrood, and charmed all eyes by his incomparable beauty, but it was that incomplete kind of beauty wanting in the manliness bestowed by years. He had youth in his face, and something of a woman in his shape, which was too slender and unsteady for a king. A change, however, seemed to come over Mary's heart on seeing him, and she bestowed upon him her whole soul with her crown.

The recitals of the French ambassador at the Scottish court represent this marriage as the perfect union of two lovers, having but one heart, and ardently enjoying the prolonged revelries of this first bliss of their lives.

Murray, the brother of Mary, who had firmly established the kingdom under her rule by his spirited and wise administration, was soon dismissed by the new king.

Mary had, after a few days of marriage, abandoned her transient fondness for the youth she imagined she had loved, conceived a coolness for Darnley, and became again prodigal of everything toward Rizzio, on whom she lavished power and honors, violating the almost sacred etiquette of the times by admitting him to her table in her private apartments, and, suppressing the name of the king in public papers, substituted that of Rizzio.

Darnley, a prey at once to shame and to jealousy, bore all this like a child, dreaming of the vengeance which he had not the strength to accomplish. The Scottish nobles, feeling themselves humbled in his person, secretly excited in him this ferment of hatred, and offered to rid him at once from the worthless parasite who had palmed on the kingdom as its ruler. What may be called a national plot was formed between them and Darnley, whose objects were the death of the favorite, the imprisonment of the queen, and the restoration of the outraged royal power into the hands of the king.

The Earl of Murray, brother of the queen, whom she had so imprudently driven away to deliver herself up to the ascendancy of Rizzio, was consulted, and listened with caution to the incomplete revelations of the plotters. Too honest to participate by his consent in an assassination, he gave his approbation, or at least his silence, to the enterprise for the delivery of Scotland. He promised to return to Holyrood at the call of the lords, and to resume the reins of government in the interest of the heir to the throne, whom Mary already carried in her bosom. Rizzio, defeated and captured, might be embarked and thrown upon the coast of France.

The queen and the favorite, ill-served by a disaffected court, suspected nothing of the plot, though the conspirators, flocking from the most distant castles in Scotland, were already armed and assembled in her ante-chamber.

On the night of the 9th or 10th of March, 1566, Darnley, the Earl of Lennox, his father, Lord Ruthven, George Douglas, Lindsay, Andrew Ker, and some other lords of the party, awaited the hour in the king's chamber; three hundred men-at-arms, furnished by the different counties, glided silently into Edinburgh one by one, under the shade of the walls, by the street leading from the city to the palace, ready to succor the conspirators if the queen's guards should attempt to defend her.

According to the French ambassador, the murderers had a still more flagrant and justifiable pretext for the assassination of the favorite than historians relate.

"The king," we read in the dispatches of Paul de Foix to Catherine of Medici, "a few days before had gone to the door of the queen's chamber, which was immediately above his own, about an hour after midnight. After having knocked frequently, and no one replying, he called the queen several times, praying her to open the door, and finally threatening to break it open, upon which she admitted him. The king supposed her to be alone in the chamber, till, after having searched everywhere, he discovered David in the cabinet, his only garment being a furred robe."

This was probably the official version given by the king and his accomplices, but the witnesses, and even the actors in the murder, gave a more truthful one of it afterward. The following is the account given by Lord Ruthven, one of the conspirators, after his flight to England, confirmed by unanimous testimony and by documentary evidence.

The queen had unsuspectingly prolonged a nocturnal supper with her favorite, in company with a single female confidante, in a small room of the palace next to her bed-chamber. Here let us quote the French writer, who has studied on the spot the most minute circumstances of this event, and who engraves them in our memory as he relates them:

"The king had supped in his own apartment in company with the Earls of Morton, Ruthven, and Lindsay; the king's rooms were on the ground floor, elevated by a few steps, and were situated under the apartments of the queen in the same tower. During the dessert he sent to see who was with the queen. He was told that the queen had finished her supper in her little cabinet, with Rizzio and her natural sister, the Duchess of Argyle. Their conversation had been joyous and brilliant. The king went up by a back stair, while Morton, Lindsay, and a troop of their bravest vassals occupied the great staircase, and dispersed in their passage some of the queen's friends and servants.

"The king passed from the chamber into Mary's cabinet. Rizzio, dressed in a short mantle, a satin vest, and lower clothes of purple velvet, was seated, with his head covered. He wore a cap decorated with a feather. The queen said to the king: 'My lord, have you supped? I thought you were supping now.' The king leaned on the back of the queen's chair, who turned round toward him; they embraced, and Darnley took a share in the conversation. His voice trembled, his face was inflamed, and from time to time he cast anxious glances toward a little door he had left ajar. Soon after a man issued from under the fringes of the curtain which covered it—Ruthven, still pale and shaking with fever, who, in spite of his extreme weakness, had determined to join in the undertaking. He wore a damask doublet lined with fur, a brass helmet, and iron gauntlets; was armed as if for battle, and accompanied by Douglas, Ker, Ballantyne, and Ormiston. At this moment Morton and Lindsay violently burst into the bedchamber of the queen, and, pushing toward the cabinet, rushed into that small room.

"Ruthven threw himself forward with such impetuosity that the floor groaned beneath his weight. Mary and her guests were terrified; his livid, fierce aspect, distorted by illness and wrath, froze them with terror.

"'Why are you here, and who gave you permission to enter?' cried the queen.

"'I have a matter to settle with David,' replied Ruthven, in a deep voice.

"Another of the conspirators coming forward, Mary said to him, 'If David be guilty, I am ready to deliver him up to justice.' 'This is justice?' replied the conspirator, taking a rope from under his mantle.

"Haggard with fear, Rizzio retreated to a corner of the chamber. He was followed, and the poor Italian, approaching the queen, took hold of her dress, crying, 'I am a dead man! giustizia! giustizia! save me, madame! save me!' Mary threw herself between Rizzio and the assassins. She tried to stay their hands. All were crowded and pressed together in that narrow space in one confused mass. Ruthven and Lindsay, brandishing their naked dirks, spoke roughly to the queen; Andrew Ker placed a pistol to her breast and threatened to fire, and Mary, throwing upon her bosom, cried,

"'Fire, if you do not respect the infant I bear!'

"The table was overturned during this tumult. The queen still struggling, Darnley threw his arms round her and pressed her into a chair, in which he held her down; while the others, taking Rizzio by the neck, dragged him from the cabinet. Doughas seized Darnley's dirk, struck the favorite with it, and leaving the dagger in his back, cried, 'That is the king's stroke!' Rizzio still struggled desperately. He wept, prayed, and supplicated with lamentable groans. He at first clung to the door of the cabinet, and afterward crept to the fire-place; then he grasped the bed-posts of the queen's bed; the conspirators threatened, struck, insulted him, and forced him to let go by pricking his hands with their dirks. Having at last been dragged from the queen's chamber into the anteroom, Rizzio fell, pierced with fifty-five dagger wounds.

"The queen made almost superhuman efforts to fly to the succor of the unhappy man. The king could scarcely restrain her. Placing her in other hands, he hastened to the room where Rizzio lay expiring. He asked if there yet remained anything to do, and plunged his dagger into the poor corpse. After the Rizzio was tied by the feet with the rope brought by one of the party, and was then dragged down the stairs of the palace.

"Lord Ruthven then returned to the queen's cabinet, where the table had been replaced. He then sat down and asked for a little wine. The queen was enraged at his insolence. He said he was sick, and pouring out some wine with his own hand into an empty cup (Rizzio's perhaps), he added that 'he could not submit to be governed by a servant. Your husband is here; he is our chief!'

"'Is it so?' replied the queen, still doubtful of Rizzio's death. 'For some time,' said Darnley, 'you have been more devoted to him than to me.' The queen was about to reply, when one of her officers entered, of whom she asked whether David had been taken to prison, and where? 'Madam,' replied he, 'we must speak no more about Rizzio; he is dead.'

"The queen uttered a cry, and then turning to the king, exclaimed: 'Ah, traitor and son of a traitor! is this the reward you have reserved for him who has done so much for your good and for your honor? Is this my reward for having by his advice elevated you to so high a dignity? Ah! no more tears, but revenge! No more joy for me till your heart shall be as desolate as mine is this day!' Saying these words, she fainted away.

"All her friends at Holyrood immediately fled in disorder. The Earl of Athol, the Flemings, and Livingstone escaped by a dark passage; the Earls of Bothwell and Huntly slid down a pillar into the garden.

"Meantime a shudder ran through the city. The bells were rung; the burgesses of Edinburgh, with the Lord Provost at their head, assembled instantly around the palace. They asked for the queen, who had now recovered her senses. While some of the conspirators threatened that if she called out she would be slain and thrown over the walls, others assured the burgesses that all went well.

"Darnley himself opened a window of the fatal tower and begged the people to retire, with the assurance that all was done by order of the queen, and that instructions would be given next day.

"Guarded as a prisoner in her own palace, and even in her bedchamber, without a single female attendant, Mary remained alone all night, delivered up to the horrors of despair. She had been pregnant for seven months, and her emotions were so powerful that the infant she afterward bore, and who became James I. of England, could never look upon a naked sword without a shudder of fear."

With astonishing promptitude Mary charmed, reconquered, and again drew toward herself more than ever the eyes and the heart of her young husband.

"From the 12th of March, while the blood of Rizzio was still reeking on the floor of the chamber and on the king's hands," writes the French envoy, "the queen resumed all her empire over Darnley; the fascination was so rapid and complete that people believed in the influence of witchcraft on the part of the queen over her husband."

The real witchcraft was the beauty of the one, the ardent youth of the other, and the intellectual superiority of a woman who now employed her genius and her charms in apparent submission, as she had formerly employed them in offense.

This reconciliation entirely concealed the new conspiracy between the king and queen against Darnley's own accomplices in the murder of the favorite, but which suddenly became apparent on the 15th of March, six days after the assassination, by the flight of the king and queen to the castle of Dunbar, a fortress whence the king could brave his accomplices and the queen her enemies. From thence Mary wrote to her sister, Queen Elizabeth of England, recounting her misfortunes in her own way, and demanding succor against her revolted subjects. She then summoned to Dunbar those nobles who were innocent of the conspiracy against her, and eight thousand faithful Scots obeyed her call.

Placing herself with the king at the head of these troops, she marched upon Edinburgh; astonishment and terror went before her; the presence of the king disconcerted the insurgent nobles, clergy, and people, and, without striking a blow, she entered Holyrood. A proclamation was issued forbidding any mention of Darnley as a participator in Rizzio's murder, and all the accomplices in that deed who fell into the queen's hands were beheaded; Ruthven, Douglas, and Morton fled beyond the frontiers; she recalled, as chief of her council, the able and upright Murray, who had been sufficiently mixed up with the conspiracy to insure his popularity, though sufficiently guarded to preserve his honor.

Finally, to gratify her affection, after having attained the object of her ambition, she threw aside the mask, bewailed the fate of Rizzio, ordered his body to be exhumed, and buried it with regal obsequies in the sepulcher of the kings in Holyrood chapel.

Reconciled with Darnley, whom she more and more despised; well served by Murray, who brought back to her the affections of the nation, on the 19th of the following June Mary gave birth to a son, destined one day to reign over England. An amnesty, ably counseled by Murray, granted a pardon to the conspirators on the occasion of the auspicious event, and allowed those who had been proscribed to return to their country and homes.

The hour of vengeance on her husband had, however, come; her aversion for him made their lives miserable, and she no longer took any pains to conceal it. Melvil, one of her most intimate confidants, says, in his memoirs of the reign of his mistress, "I constantly found her, from the time of Rizzio's murder, with her heart full of rancor, and the worst way to pay court to her was to speak of her reconciliation with the king."

The secret cause of this growing aversion was a new love, more resembling a fatality of heart in the career of a modern Phedra than the aberration of a woman and a queen in an age enjoying the light of civilization.

The object of this love was as extraordinary as the passion itself was inexplicable, unless, indeed, we attribute it to the effect of magic, or of *possession*, a supernatural explanation of the phenomena of the heart which was common in those superstitious times. But the female heart contains within itself greater mysteries than even magic can explain. The man now beloved by Mary Stuart was Bothwell.

The Earl of Bothwell was a Scottish noble of a powerful and illustrious house, whose principal stronghold was Hermitage Castle, in Roxburghshire. He was born with those perverse and unruly instincts which indifferently drive men from exploit to exploit, or from crime to crime—to a throne or to a scaffold. Impetuous in every impulse, in ambition, and in enterprise, Bothwell was one of those adventurers gifted with superhuman daring, who, in their development and as their desires expand, seek to burst the social bounds within which they exist, to make room for themselves or perish in the attempt.

Some men seem born to madness, and Bothwell was one of those. Byron, whose mother's ancestry was connected with Lady Jean Gordon, Bothwell's wife, has depicted him in the romantic and somber "Corsair;" but the poem is far behind historic truth, for the sovereign poet, Nature, outvies fiction by reality.

We know not whether precocious crime, parental severity, or voluntary flight exiled him from the paternal home; but in his early youth he became enrolled among those corsairs of the ocean who stained the coasts, the islands, and the waves of the North Sea with blood. His name, his rank, his courage, had speedily promoted him to the command of one of those squadrons of criminals who had a den wherein to stow their spoils and an arsenal for their vessels, in a rock-fortress on the coast of Denmark. The crimes of Bothwell, and his exploits among those pirates, lie hidden in the shadow of the past; but his name inspired terror along the shores of the North Sea.

After this stormy youth the death of his father recalled him to his Scottish domains and wild vassals. The troubles of the court of Edinburgh had attracted him to Holyrood, where he discovered a wider field for ambition and crime.

He was among those Scottish chiefs who, at the appeal of the king to his subjects while in the castle of Dunbar, hastened thither with their vassals, in the hope of seizing and pillaging Edinburgh. Since the return of the court to Holyrood, he had distinguished himself among the foremost partisans of the queen. Whether inspired by ambition or spurred on by an indefinite hope of subjugating the heart of a woman by striking her imagination, he at all events succeeded in his enterprise; perhaps he knew that the surest way to conquer feminine pride is to appear indifferent to it.

Bothwell was no longer in the flower of his youth; but although he had lost an eye by a wound received in one of his sea-fights, he was still handsome. His beauty was not effeminate like Darnley's, nor melancholy and pensive like Rizzio's, but of that rude and manly order which gives to passion the energy of heroism. The licentiousness of his manners and the victims of his libertinage had made him well known at the court of Holyrood. He had many attachments among the women of that court, less for their love than their dishonor. One of those mistresses, Lady Reves, a dissipated woman, celebrated by Brantôme for the notoriety of her adventures, was the confidante of the queen. She had retained for Bothwell an admiration which survived their intimacy. The queen, who amused herself by interrogating her confidante regarding the exploits and amours of her old favorite, allowed herself to be gradually attracted toward him by a sentiment which, at first, assumed the appearance of a good-natured curiosity. The confidante, divining, or believing she divined, the yet unexpressed desires of the queen, introduced Bothwell some evening into the garden, and even to the apartment of her mistress. This secret meeting forever sealed the ascendancy of Bothwell over the queen.

Her passion, though hidden, was, for that reason, still more commanding, and became for the first time apparent to all some weeks after this interview, on the occasion of a wound Bothwell had received in a border feud, on the marches of which he had command. On hearing of this, Mary mounted on horseback, and rode, without resting by the way, to the Hermitage where he had been carried, assured herself with her own eyes of the danger he had run, and returned the same day to Holyrood.

"The Earl of Bothwell," writes at this time the French ambassador to Catherine of Medici, "is out of danger, at which the queen is well pleased. To have lost him would have been no small loss indeed to her."

She herself avows her anxiety in verses composed on the occasion:

"When first my master he became,
For him I shed full many a tear;
But now this new and dire alarm
Destroys in me both life and fear!"

After his cure, Bothwell became master of the kingdom. Everything was lavished on him as previously on Rizzio, and he accepted all, not as a subject, but as a master. The king, shut out from the councils of the queen, and even from her society as his wife, "walked about alone," says Melvil, "from place to place, and it was evident to all that she regarded it as a crime that any one should keep company with him."

"The Queen of Scots and her husband," writes the Duke of Bedford, envoy of Elizabeth at the court of Scotland, "live together as before, and even worse; she rarely sits at table, and never sleeps with him; she in no wise esteems his society, and loves not those who entertain friendship for him. To such an extent does she exclude him from business, that when she leaves the palace to go out, he knows nothing. Modesty forbids me to repeat what she has said of him, and which would not be honorable to the queen."

The insolence of the new favorite partook of the ferocity of his former life; he once drew his dagger in full council before the queen to strike Lethington, another member of the council, for having objected to his advice.

The king, outraged every day by Bothwell's contempt, and something by his insults, retired to Glasgow, where he lived in the house of his father, the Earl of Lennox. The queen and Bothwell became alarmed lest he should make public complaint against the humiliation and neglect to which he was condemned, appeal to the discontented among the nobility, and in his turn march against Edinburgh. It is to this motive and to Bothwell's fear, rather than to his desire to become the husband of the queen, that we must attribute the odious crime which soon after threw the world into consternation.

The queen, on hearing of the flight of Darnley to the house of his father, the Earl of Lennox, suddenly left her favorite Bothwell, and repairing to one of her pleasure castles called Craigmillar, near Edinburgh, secretly convoked the confederate lords of her own and Bothwell's party. The French ambassador remarks on her sadness and anxiety; her torment between the fears of her husband and the demands of her favorite was such as to make her cry out in presence of the ambassador, "I wish I were dead!"

She then leaves the conspirators at Craigmillar, and against all propriety or expectation, she proceeds to Glasgow, where she finds Darnley recovering from the small-pox, overwhelms him with tenderness, passes days and nights by his pillow, renews the scenes of Holyrood after the murder of Rizzio, and finally consents to the conjugal conditions implored by Darnley. In vain is Darnley warned of the danger he incurs in following the queen to Craigmillar into the midst of his enemies; he replies that though it may appear strange, he will follow the queen he adores even to death. The queen leaves Glasgow before him, to await his restoration to health, prolongs with him the tenderest farewells, and places on his finger a ring, as a precious pledge of reconciliation and love.

Darnley followed her shortly after. Under pretext of promoting his recovery, apartments were prepared for him in a solitary country-house in the neighborhood, called Kirk o' Field, with no other attendants than five or six servants, underlings sold to Bothwell, and whom he ironically called his lambs. Only a favorite page, named Taylor, slept in Darnley's chamber. The queen came to visit him with the same demonstrations of tenderness as she exhibited at Glasgow, but refused to live with him yet. Darnley, astonished at this isolation, fell into deep melancholy, from which he sought relief by praying and weeping with his page. An inward presentiment seemed to warn him of approaching death.

Meantime the festivities at Holyrood continued. At the close of one of these feasts, during which Bothwell had conversed much and alone with the queen, the favorite (according to the testimony of his valet, Dalgliesh) came home and retired to bed; soon after he calls his valet and dresses; one of his agents enters and whispers something in his ear; he takes his riding-cloak and sword, covers his face with a mask, puts on a hat with a broad brim, and proceeds, at one o'clock in the morning, to the king's solitary dwelling.

What happened on that mysterious night? We know not; the only thing known is that before the morning twilight a terrible explosion was heard at Holyrood and in Edinburgh. The house of Kirk o' Field was blown to atoms, and its ruins would have buried the victim, but owing to a strange forgetfulness on the part of the assassins, the bodies of Darnley and his page had been left lying in an orchard attached to the garden, where they were found next morning, bearing on their bodies, not the marks of gunpowder, but those of a deadly struggle and of strangulation.

It was supposed that the king and his page, hearing the steps of the murderers early in the night, had tried to escape by the orchard, but had been overtaken and strangled by Bothwell's assassins, and their bodies left on the scene of the murder by negligence, or in ignorance of the explosion which was to have destroyed the murderers with their victims. It is added that Bothwell, believing that the corpses of Darnley and the page were in the house, had needlessly fired the mine, and had returned to Holyrood after the explosion, believing that no vestiges of the murder remained, and hoping that Darnley's death would be attributed to the accidental explosion of a store of gunpowder fired by his own imprudence.

However that might be, Bothwell went home without betraying any agitation; again went to rest before the end of the night, and when his attendants awoke him and told him of what had occurred, manifested all the surprise and grief of perfect innocence, and, leaping from his bed, cried "Treason!"

The two bodies were not discovered in the orchard till daylight.

Morning spread horror with the rumor of this murder among the people of Edinburgh. The emotion was so great that the queen was forced to leave Holyrood and take refuge in the castle. She was insulted by the women as she passed along the streets; avenging placards covered the walls, invoking peace to the soul of Darnley, and the vengeance of Heaven on his guilty wife. Bothwell mounted on horseback, and sword in hand, galloped through the streets, crying, " Death to the rebels, and to all who speak against the queen!"

Sedition being calmed for a time, the queen proclaimed her grief at Holyrood by assuming the garb of a mourning widow, and remained for some days shut up in her apartments, with no other light than the dim glimmering of lamps. Bothwell was accused of regicide before the judges of Edinburgh, at the instance of the Earl of Lennox, the king's father. The favorite, with undaunted audacity, supported by the queen and by the troops, devoted, as usual, to the reigning power, appeared in arms before the judges, and insolently exacted from them an acquittal. The same day he rode forth, mounted on one of Darnley's favorite horses, which the people recognized with horror bearing his murderer. The queen saluted him from her balcony with a gesture of encouragement and tenderness.

Some days after the 24th of April, while returning from Stirling, where she had been visiting her son, Bothwell, with a body of his friends, awaited her at Almond Bridge, six miles from Edinburgh. He dismounted from his horse, respectfully took hold of the bridle of the queen's palfrey, feigned a slight compulsion, and conducted his voluntary captive to the castle of Dunbar, of which he was governor, as warden of the borders. There she passed with him eight days, as if suffering violence, and returned on the 8th of May with him to Edinburgh, " resigned," she said, " to marry with her consent him who had disposed of her by force."

Bothwell, besides the blood which stained his hands, had three other wives living. By gold or threats he rid himself of two, and he divorced the third, Lady Gordon, sister of the Earl of Huntly. In order to secure this divorce, he consented to be found guilty of adultery. The verses written by Mary at this period and addressed to Bothwell prove the jealousy with which she regarded this repudiated but still loved wife.

" Her painted words, complaints, and tears,
Her cries, her loud laments, her fears,
Though feigned, deceitful, every art,
Are cherished still within thy heart.
To all she writes full faith thou givest,
In her love more than mine thou livest.
Still, still thou trustest her too well, I see,
And doubted ever my firm constancy.

O my sole hope! My solitary bliss!
Could I but show thee my true faithfulness,
Too lightly thou esteem st my love, my pain,
Nor of my faith can full assurance gain.
With dark suspicion thou dost wrong my heart,
As if another in my love had part;
My words and vows seem but a fleeting wind,
Bereft of wit, a woman's idle mind!
Alas! all this increases but the flame
That burns for thee forever and the same.
        *   *   *   *   *
My love still grows, and evermore will grow,
So long as life shall in this bosom glow"

She only refused Bothwell one thing—the tutelage and guardianship of her son, who was kept at Stirling. Violent and noisy quarrels took place about this at Holyrood, even on the evening before the marriage of the widow and her husband's assassin. The French ambassador heard the turmoil. Bothwell insisted, and the queen, determined to resist, called loudly for a dagger wherewith to kill herself.

" On the day after the ceremony," writes the ambassador, " I perceived strange clouds on the countenances both of the queen and her husband, which she tried to excuse, saying that if I saw her and it was because she had no reason to rejoice, desiring nothing but death."

The expiation had begun. A league was formed by the Scottish lords against her and Bothwell. Thus confederated to avenge the blood-stained throne, they, on the 13th of June, 1567, met the troops of the queen and Bothwell at Carberry Hill. Courage deserted their partisans before the battle—they were defeated.

Bothwell, covered with blood, rode up to the queen, when all hope of safety from flight was already lost. " Save your life," cried he, " for my sake; we shall meet in happier times!" Bothwell seemed to desire death. The queen burst into tears. " Will you keep faithful to me, madam," said he, in a doubtful accent, " as to a husband and king?" " Yes," she replied, " and in token of my promise I give you my hand." Bothwell carried her hand to his lips, kissed it, and fled to Dunbar, followed by only a dozen horsemen.

The lords conducted the queen as a prisoner to Edinburgh Castle. In passing through the army she was assailed with the imprecations of the military and the populace. The soldiers waved before her horse a banner, on which was represented the dead body of Darnley lying beside his page in the orchard of Kirk o' Field, and the little King James on his knees invoking the vengeance of Heaven against his mother and the murderer of his unhappy father, in these words of the royal poet of Israel, " Judge and avenge my cause, O Lord!"

" By this royal hand," she said to Lord Lindsay, who had aided in the murder of her first favorite, Rizzio, " I'll have your heads for this!"

On her arrival in Edinburgh she took courage even in the excess of her humiliation. She appeared, says a chronicle of Edinburgh, at the window fronting the High Street, and addressing the people in a firm voice told them how she had been thrown into prison by her own traitorous subjects; she showed herself many times at the same window in miserable plight, her dishevelled hair flowing over her shoulders and bosom, her body uncovered to the girdle.

At other times she became softened, and assuming the accents of a suppliant,

" Dear Lethington," she said, " you, who have the gift of persuasion, speak to these lords; tell them I pardon all who will consent to place me in a vessel with Bothwell, whom I espoused with their approbation at Holyrood, and leave us to the mercy of the winds and waves."

She wrote the most impassioned letters to Bothwell, which were intercepted by her jailers at the gates of her prison. Finally she was conducted with a small escort through a hostile country to the castle of Lochleven, belonging to the Douglases.

Lady Douglas, who inhabited this stronghold, had been the

mistress of King James V., the queen's father, and was the mother of Lord James Murray.

"Of a proud and imperious spirit," says a Scottish historian, "she was accustomed to boast that she was the lawful wife of James, and her son Murray his legitimate issue, who had been supplanted by the queen."

The castle, situated in the county of Kinross, was built on an island in the middle of a small lake which bathed its walls and intercepted all flight. There she was treated by the Douglases with the respect due to her rank and misfortunes.

Queen Elizabeth saw with alarm the triumph of the revolt against the queen. She prevailed on Murray, who was respected by all parties, to undertake the government during Mary's captivity. Murray went to Lochleven to confer with his captive sister about the fate of the kingdom, and of James, the infant heir to the throne. Hopefully she saw him assume the supreme authority, believing with reason that he would be indulgent toward her.

She learned from him that Bothwell had fled to the Shetland Islands, where he had embarked for Denmark, there to resume, with his old companions, the sea-robbers, the life of a pirate and a brigand, the only refuge fortune had left him. We shall afterward find him closing in captivity and insanity a life passed alternately in disgrace and on a throne, in exploits and assassinations.

She made several attempts to escape from Lochleven to join Bothwell or to fly to England. The historian we quote, who has visited its ruins, thus describes the first prison of the queen:

"The sojourn at Lochleven, over which romance and poetry have shed their light, must be depicted by history only in its nakedness and horrors. The castle, or rather fortress, is a massive block of granite, flanked by heavy towers, peopled by owls and bats, eternally bathed in mists, and defended by the waters of the lake. There languished Mary Stuart, oppressed by the violence of the hostile lords, torn by remorse, troubled by the phantoms of the past and by the terrors of the future."

The English ambassador, Drury, thus relates to his sovereign the last unsuccessful attempt at escape:

"Toward the 25th of last month (April, 1568) she very nearly escaped, thanks to her habit of passing the mornings in bed. She acted in this way: The washerwoman came early in the morning, as she had often done, and the queen, as had been arranged, donned the woman's cap, took up a bundle of linen, and covering her face with her cloak, left the castle and entered the boat used in traversing the loch.

"After some minutes one of the rowers said laughingly, 'Let us see what kind of lady we have got,' at the same time attempting to uncover her face. To prevent him she raised her hands, and he remarked their beauty and whiteness, which made him immediately suspect who she was. She showed little fear, and ordered the boatmen, under pain of death, to conduct her to the coast. They refused, however, rowed back toward the island, promising secrecy toward the commander of the guard to whom she was confided."

It appears that she knew the place where, once landed, she could take refuge, for she saw, in Kinross (a little village near the banks of the loch), George Douglas and two of her former most devoted servants wandering about in expectation of her arrival.

George Douglas, the youngest son of that house, was passionately in love with the captive. His enthusiastic admiration for her beauty, rank, and misfortunes, determined him to brave all dangers in the attempt to restore her to liberty and her throne. He arranged signals with the Hamiltons and other chiefs, who, on the opposite side of the loch, awaited the hour for an enterprise in favor of the queen.

The signal agreed upon for the flight, which was to be a fire kindled on the highest tower of the castle, at length shone forth in the eyes of the Hamiltons. Soon an unperceived boat glides over the lake, and approaching its banks, delivers to them the fugitive queen. They throw themselves at her feet, carry her off

to the mountains, raise their vassals, form an army, revoke her abdication, fight for her cause under her eyes at Langside against the troops of Murray, and are a second time defeated. Mary, without refuge and without hope, fled to England, where the letters of Queen Elizabeth led her to expect the welcome due from one sovereign to another.

Elizabeth had the choice of two policies—the one magnanimous, to welcome and receive her unfortunate cousin; the other openly hostile, to profit by her reverses, or to dethrone her a second time by her freely expressed condemnation. She adopted a third policy, indefinite, dissembling, caressing in speech, odious in action, which delivered up her "sister" by turns to hope and to despair, wearing out the heart of her rival by endless longing, as if she had resolved that grief, anguish, and time should be her executioners.

This queen, so great in genius, so mean in heart, cruel by policy, and rendered more so by feminine jealousies, proved herself, in this instance, the worthy daughter of Henry the Eighth, all whose passions were slaked in blood.

She offered to Mary the castle of Carlisle as a royal refuge, and detained her there as in a prison. She wrote that she could not with propriety treat her as a queen and a sister till she should clear herself of the crimes imputed to her by her Scottish subjects. She thus evoked before her own tribunal, as a foreign queen, the great suit pending between Mary Stuart and her people.

By assuming this attitude, her influence in Scotland, whose queen she retained as a prisoner, and whose regent, Murray, had everything to hope or to fear from her, became all-powerful. She was about to rule over Scotland as arbiter, and even without an army. This policy—counseled, it is said, by her great minister, Cecil—was ignoble, but national.

These ideas were expedient in policy, but the avowal of them was humbling to a queen, and above all to a woman, the more so that Mary was her own kinswoman. The whole secret of this temporizing craft of Elizabeth lay in the impossibility of openly avowing a course which served her views, but which dishonored her in the eyes of Europe.

"No, madam," replied Mary from Carlisle Castle, "I have not come here to justify myself before my subjects, but to punish them, and to demand your succor against them. I neither can nor will reply to their false accusations; but knowing well your friendship and good pleasure, I am willing to justify myself to you, though not in the form of a suit with my subjects. They and I are in no wise equal; and should I even remain here forever, rather would I die than recognize such a thing!"

Already she was in reality a captive. The Spanish ambassador in London, Don Guzman da Silva, who had gone to Carlisle to offer to her the condolence of his court, thus describes her abode in the castle:

"The room occupied by the queen is dark, and has but one window, garnished with bars of iron. It is entered through three other rooms, guarded and occupied by armed men. In the last, which forms an antechamber to the queen's room, Lord Scrope is stationed, who is governor of the border district of Carlisle. The queen has only three of her women with her. Her attendants and domestics sleep outside of the castle. The gates are opened only at ten o'clock in the morning. The queen is allowed to go as far as the city church, but is always escorted by a hundred soldiers. On asking Lord Scrope to send her a priest to say mass, he replied that in England there were none."

Alarmed at the evidently evil intentions of Elizabeth, Mary implored the interference of France. Forgetting her secret hatred of Catherine de Medici, she wrote to her, and also to Charles IX. and the Duke of Anjou, asking them to aid her.

Mary's apprehensions were soon realized. Elizabeth determined to remove her from the Scottish Marches. On the 28th July, 1568, the august captive was conducted, in spite of her energetic protestations, to Bolton Abbey, in the county of York, which belonged to Lord Scrope, brother-in-law to the Earl of Norfolk.

It will be seen that, from the first days of her stay in England, while caressing Elizabeth with one hand she wove with the other, and with strangers as well as with her own subjects, that net in which she was herself caught at last. Captivity was her excuse, religion her pretext; oppression gave her a right to conspire; but if she could not urge her misfortunes as a reason for thus plotting, she could not, with truth, urge her innocence. She unceasingly demanded from Madrid and from Paris armed intervention against Scotland and against Elizabeth. Her whole life during her captivity was one long conspiracy; the inhuman and unprincipled duplicity of Elizabeth's policy justified all she did.

Murray, guardian of the infant king James and dictator of the kingdom, governed the unhappy country with vigor and address. But a proscribed gentleman of good family, James Hamilton of Bothwellhaugh, whose wife Murray had left to die in misery and madness on the threshold of her own dwelling, which had been bestowed by the regent on Bellenden, one of his partisans, swore to avenge at once his wife and his country. Gathering a handful of the earth which covered the bier of his wife, he wore it within his girdle as an eternal incentive to revenge; and, repairing in disguise to the small town of Linlithgow, through which Murray had to pass on his return to Edinburgh, he placed himself at a window, fired upon and killed the regent. He then mounted a horse ready for him behind the house, and by swift flight escaped the regent's guards. "I alone," cried the dying Murray, " could have saved the church, the kingdom, and the king; anarchy will now devour them all!"

The advisers of Elizabeth represented to her, for the first time, the necessity of the immediate trial and death of the Queen of Scots, to secure the peace of the kingdom, and perhaps even the safety of her own life. Her most eminent statesmen, Burleigh, Leicester, and Walsingham, were unanimous in recommending this sacrifice.

One of the Earl of Derby's gentlemen, named Babington, brought up in the household of the Earl of Shrewsbury, where he had become acquainted with the queen while she was a prisoner at Bolton Abbey, had resolved to serve and save her. Babington had gone over to the Continent, and was at Paris the agent of the correspondence in which the queen was engaged with France and Spain to bring about her deliverance and restoration.

Walsingham, the chief counselor and minister of Elizabeth, who had brought the spy-system to a state of what might be called infamous perfection, and had his tools and agents everywhere, who insinuated themselves into the confidence of the conspirators, urged them on to the execution of their designs, at the same time revealing all to him, and, with a malignant ingenuity, even adding to the reality by inventions of their own, in order, doubtless, to please their employer and lead the more certainly to the accomplishment of his aim.

One of these spies, named Gifford, whose earnestness seemed to place him above suspicion at the French embassy, in which was the repository of the correspondence, received letters, pretended he had forwarded them to their address, but conveyed them secretly to Walsingham.

These letters prove some hesitation at first on the part of the conspirators regarding the propriety of the assassination of Elizabeth, and afterward a more decided resolution in favor of the murder, after a consultation with Father Ballard, the Jesuit of Rheims. One of the letters, bearing the signature of Babington, thus addressed Mary:

"Very dear Sovereign: I myself, with six gentlemen, and a hundred others of our company and following, will undertake the deliverance of your royal person from the hands of your enemies. As for that which tends to rid us of the usurper, from the subjection of the . . . ."

At the subsequent trial the copy only of a letter from Mary in reply was produced, containing these words: "These things being prepared, and the forces, without as well as within the kingdom, being all ready, it is necessary that the six gentlemen should be set to work, and orders given that, their design being

effected, I may then be taken hence, and all the troops be at the same time in the field to receive me while awaiting the succurs from abroad, who must also hasten with all diligence. . . ."

Mary solemnly declared that she never wrote this letter; and although she insisted upon the original being shown, it never appeared, its only substitute being an alleged copy in the handwriting of Phellips, one of Walsingham's creatures, and an expert forger of autographs.

No trace of any such original letter has ever been found; and when we consider Elizabeth's evident anxiety to get rid of her troublesome captive, her subsequent remorse, the unscrupulous efforts of Walsingham to please his mistress, by fair means or foul, and the zeal of his spies and tools, we cannot but arrive at the conclusion that this letter, which was so fatal to Mary, but which no one ever saw, was a forgery executed by Phellips, who, besides, is proved to have added a postscript of his own to another of Mary's letters now extant.

The punishment of her friends impressed Mary with a presentiment of her own fate. Involved in their plots, and more feared than they were, she could not long remain in suspense as to her own destiny. She was carried, in fact, some days afterward, to Fotheringay Castle, her last prison. This feudal residence was solemn and gloomy, even as the hour of approaching death.

Elizabeth, after long and serious deliberation, at last named thirty-six judges to examine Mary and report to the council. The Queen of Scots protested against the right of trying a queen and of judging her in a foreign country, where she was forcibly detained as a prisoner.

"Is it thus," cried she, when she appeared before the commissioners, "that Queen Elizabeth makes kings be tried by their subjects? I only accept this place" (pointing to a seat lower than that of the judges) "because as a Christian I humble myself. My place is there," she added, pointing toward the dais. "I was a queen from the cradle, and the first day that saw me a woman saw me a queen!" Then turning toward Melvil, her esquire, and the chief of her household, on whose arm she leaned, she said: "Here are many judges, but not one friend!"

She denied energetically having consented to the plan for assassinating Elizabeth; she insinuated, but without formally asserting, that secretaries might easily have added to the meaning of the letters dictated to them, as none were produced in her own handwriting. "When I came to Scotland," she said to Lord Burleigh, the principal minister, who interrogated her, "I offered to your mistress, through Lethington, a ring shaped like a heart, in token of my friendship; and when, overcome by rebels, I entered England, I in my turn received from her this pledge of encouragement and protection." Saying these words, she drew from her finger the ring which had been sent by Elizabeth. " Look at this, my lords, and answer. During the eighteen years that I have passed under your bolts and bars, how often have your queen and the English people despised it in my person!"

The commissioners, on their return to London, assembled at Westminster, declared the Queen of Scots guilty of participation in the plot against the life of Elizabeth, and pronounced upon her sentence of death. The two houses of parliament ratified the sentence.

Mary asked, as a single favor, not to be executed in secret, but before her servants and the people, so that no one might attribute a cowardice to her unworthy of her rank, and that all might bear testimony to her constancy in suffering martyrdom. Thus she already spoke of her punishment, a consolatory idea most natural in a queen who desired that her death should be imputed to her faith rather than to her faults.

The scene at the execution of the unfortunate queen is touching, indeed.

She arrived in the hall of death. Pale, but unflinching, she contemplated the dismal preparations. There lay the block and the ax. There stood the executioner and his assistant. All were clothed in mourning. On the floor was scattered the sawdust which was to soak her blood, and in a dark corner lay the bier which was to be her last prison.

It was nine o'clock when the queen appeared in the funeral hall. Fletcher, Dean of Peterborough, and certain privileged persons, to the number of more than two hundred, were assembled. The hall was hung with black cloth; the scaffold, which was elevated about two feet and a half above the ground, was covered with black frieze of Lancaster; the armed chair in which Mary was to sit, the footstool on which she was to kneel, the block on which her head was to be laid, were covered with black velvet.

The queen was clothed in mourning like the hall, and as the ensigns of punishment. Her black velvet robe, with its high collar and hanging sleeves, was bordered with ermine. Her mantle, lined with marten sable, was of satin, with pearl buttons and a long train. A chain of sweet-smelling beads, to which was attached a scapulary, and beneath that a golden cross, fell upon her bosom. Two rosaries were suspended to her girdle, and a long veil of white lace, which, in some measure, softened this costume of a widow and of a condemned criminal, was thrown around her.

She was preceded by the sheriff, by Drury and Paulet, the earls and nobles of England, and followed by her two maidens and four officers, among whom was remarked Melvil, bearing the train of the royal robe. Mary's walk was firm and majestic. For a single moment she raised her veil, and her face, on which shone a hope no longer of this world, seemed beautiful as in the days of her youth. The whole assembly were deeply moved. In one hand she held a crucifix, and in the other one of her chaplets. The Earl of Kent rudely addressed her, "We should wear Christ in our hearts."

"And wherefore," she replied quickly, "should I have Christ in my hand if He were not in my heart?"

Paulet assisting her to mount the scaffold, she threw upon him a look full of sweetness.

"Sir Amyas," she said, "I thank you for your courtesy; it is the last trouble I will give you, and the most agreeable service you can render me."

Arrived on the scaffold, Mary seated herself in the chair provided for her, with her face towards the spectators. The Dean of Peterborough, in ecclesiastical costume, sat on the right of the queen, with a black velvet footstool before him. The Earls of Kent and Shrewsbury were seated, like him, on the right, but upon larger chairs.

On the other side of the queen stood the sheriff, Andrews, with white wand. In front of Mary were seen the executioner and his assistant, distinguishable by their vestments of black velvet, with red crape round the left arm. Behind the queen's chair, ranged by the wall, wept her attendants and maidens. In the body of the hall the nobles and citizens from the neighboring counties were guarded by the musketeers of Sir Amyas Paulet and Sir Drew Drury. Beyond the balustrade was the bar of the tribunal. The sentence was read; the queen protested against it in the name of royalty and innocence, but accepted death for the sake of the faith.

She then knelt down before the block, and the executioner proceeded to remove her veil. She repelled him by a gesture, and turning toward the earls with a blush on her forehead, "I am not accustomed," she said, "to be undressed before so numerous a company, and by the hands of such grooms of the chamber."

She then called Jane Kennedy and Elizabeth Curle, who took off her mantle, her veil, her chains, cross, and scapulary. On their touching her robe, the queen told them to unloose the corsage and fold down the ermine collar, so as to leave her neck bare for the ax. Her maidens weepingly yielded her these last services, Melvil and the three other attendants wept and lamented, and Mary placed her finger on her lips to signify that they should be silent.

"My friends," she cried, "I have answered for you, do not melt me; ought you not rather to praise God for having inspired your mistress with courage and resignation?" Yielding, however, in her turn to her own sensibility, she warmly embraced her maidens; then pressing them to descend from the scaffold, where they both clung to her dress, with hands bathed in tears, she addressed to them a tender blessing and a last farewell. Melvil and his companions remained, as if choked with grief, at a short distance from the queen. Overcome by her accents, the executioners themselves besought her on their knees to pardon them.

"I pardon you," she said, "after the example of my Redeemer."

She then arranged the handkerchief, embroidered with thistles of gold, with which her eyes had been covered by Jane Kennedy. Thrice she kissed the crucifix, each time repeating, "Lord, into thy hands I commend my spirit." She knelt anew, and leaned her head on that block which was already scored with the scored marks; and in this solemn attitude she again recited some verses from the Psalms. The executioner interrupted her at the third verse by a blow of the ax but its trembling stroke only grazed her neck; she groaned slightly, and the second blow separated the head from the body. The executioner held it up at the window, within sight of all, proclaiming aloud, according to usage, "So perish the enemies of our queen!"

The queen's maids of honor and attendants enshrouded the body, and claimed it, in order that it should be sent to France; but these relics of their tenderness and faith were pitilessly refused. Relics which might rekindle fanaticism were to be feared.

But that cruel prudence was deceived by the result. Mary's death resembled a martyrdom; her memory, which had been execrated alike by the Scottish Presbyterians and the English Protestants, was practically adopted by the Catholics as that of a saint. The passions were Mary's judges; therefore she was not fairly judged, nor will she ever be.

Elizabeth, having thus mercilessly sacrificed the life of her whom she had so long and so unjustly retained in hopeless captivity, now added the most flagrant duplicity to her cruelty. Denying, with many oaths, all intention of having her own warrant carried into execution, she attempted to throw the entire odium on those who in reality had acted as her blind and devoted agents.

This policy of the English queen was unsuccessful, however; posterity has with clear voice proclaimed her guilty of the blood of her royal sister, and the sanguinary stain will ever remain ineffaceable from the character of that otherwise great sovereign.

If we regard Mary Stuart in the light of her charms, her talents, her magical influence over all men who approached her, she may be called the Sappho of the sixteenth century. All that was not love in her soul was poetry; her verses, like those of Ronsard, her worshiper and teacher, possess a Greek softness combined with a quaint simplicity; they are written with tears, and even after the lapse of so many years retain something of the warmth of her sighs.

If we judge her by her life, she is the Scottish Semiramis; casting herself, before the eyes of all Europe, into the arms of the assassin of her husband, and thus giving to the people she had thrown into civil war a coronation of murder for a lesson of morality.

Her direct and personal participation in the death of her young husband has been denied, and nothing in effect, except those suspected letters, proves that she actually and personally accomplished or permitted the crime; but that she had attracted the victim into the snare; that she had given Bothwell the right and the hope of succeeding to the throne after his death; that she had been the end, the means, and the alleged prize of the crime; finally, that she absolved the murderer by bestowing upon him her hand—no doubt can be entertained regarding these points. To provoke to murder and then to absolve the perpetrator—is not this equivalent to guilt?

In fine, if she be judged by her death—comparable in its majesty, its piety, and its courage, to the most heroic and the holiest sacrifices of the primitive martyrs—the horror and aversion with which she had been regarded change at last to pity, esteem, and admiration.

THE FATAL LOVE INTRIGUES IN THE COURT OF PETER THE GREAT.

PETER THE GREAT AS AN EXECUTIONER—HIS FIRST WIFE AND HER LOVER—THE LOVER'S FEARFUL DEATH—IN LOVE AGAIN WITH A BREWER'S DAUGHTER—THE SECOND WIFE AND HER LOVER—THE EMPEROR'S VENGEANCE—HIS DEATH—CATHARINE FOLLOWS SUIT.

MANY popular histories of Russia represent Peter the Great of that country as a wise, humane, and energetic ruler, whose only ambition was the advancement of his empire, and the mental and moral improvement of his people.

On the other hand, some reliable historians assert that he was the most violent and the most cruel of monarchs; and that he not only bestowed personal chastisement on his courtiers, generals and ministers who committed the slightest offenses, but he was very frequently the executioner of the sentence of death which he had pronounced on his unfortunate victim.

The historians last alluded to relate many incidents tending to depict the cruel nature of this popular Russian hero, a few of which we will present, with the object of showing how savage Peter could be when aroused to anger by jealousy.

The first insurrection that occurred in Russia during the reign of Peter I. was occasioned by an order issued by him that all Russians "should leave off wearing beards."

This insurrection was crushed with great severity, and over eight thousand unfortunate persons were sentenced to be executed.

In order to dispatch so many victims with due formalities, the Czar selected a large spot of open ground convenient to one of his palaces near Moscow. This place was surrounded by palisades, through which might be easily seen what was passing within. Within the inclosure several blocks and logs had been placed, and the miserable wretches destined to lose their lives were conducted to them. Several executioners were employed in chopping off the heads of the unfortunates; and Peter himself, with a hatchet in his hand, set the example to the others.

On this occasion, as related by one historian, a boy, about twelve years old, went and placed his head upon the block of the Czar. The royal executioner stared at the child for a moment, and then, seizing him by the arm, pushed him back.

The little lad, without speaking a word, went and laid his head upon another block. The Czar perceived him, advanced towards the lad, lifted him in his arms, and again drove him away.

In an instant after the lad advanced again, and again placed his head on the block. The Czar then seized the child once more, lifted him up in his arms, and demanded, while his face was purple with passion:

"Boy, why do you insist on having your head cut off by me?"

The young lad looked at the tyrant with undaunted eyes, as he replied:

"Thou hast cut off that of my father, that of my brother, and those of all my relations, who were not more culpable than I am. Why, then, wilt thou not cut mine off, as I do not wish to live?"

The Czar made no reply, but ordered the child to be put out of the inclosure, flung down his hatchet, and went away. It is said that he was forcibly moved by the touching appeal.

About the same period the Czar invited M. Printz, the Prussian ambassador, to a magnificent repast. After the autocrat had partaken of a great deal of wine and brandy, according to his custom, he determined to amuse his guest in a very horrible manner.

Calling on one of his officers, he ordered that twenty of the unfortunate insurgent prisoners should be brought before him. And then, after each bumper, he amused himself by cutting off the head of one of the wretched creatures, laughing the while at the terror of the others.

The royal host then proposed that the Prussian ambassador should make a trial of his skill in the same manner, but that diplomat rejected the barbarous offer on the instant.

Peter was endowed with a fine figure, and he possessed a su-

perior mind. Although invested with supreme power, and passionately fond of the tender sex, it is not recorded that he ever won the sincere love of any woman.

Certain it is that he was deceived by all on whom he lavished his caresses.

Whilst he was yet very young he married a young woman known as Eudoxia Lapoukin, who was the mother of the unfortunate Alexis, a prince who suffered fearful persecutions at the hands of his own father.

A short time after his first marriage, the Czar became deeply infatuated with a certain Anne Moens, a very pretty Fleming, the daughter of a beer-brewer, who had settled in the Russian capital.

Eudoxia appeared at first to be greatly out of humor at the thought that her husband had deserted her for a damsel of humble birth; but she soon consoled herself and retaliated on the Czar by following his example.

The deserted empress fell in love with a young boyar named Kleboff; but, unfortunately for her young lover, as well as for herself, she did not employ sufficient mystery in carrying on her clandestine amours, and they were discovered.

Although the Czar felt that he could enjoy his love with perfect impunity, he could not tolerate the same conduct on the part of his wife.

The unfortunate woman was arrested, and sent to a cloister; and she was afterwards solemnly repudiated by the unforgiving Peter.

His revenge on Kleboff was far more cruel. The young man was seized and then impaled; and it is asserted as a fact that the unfortunate being remained in that horrible situation more than twenty-four hours before his sufferings were brought to a close by death.

Peter was eager to witness and enjoy the terrible punishment of his young rival. He did even more, for he ascended the pilaster of mason work upon which the stake was fixed, and exhorted the dying man to make a full confession of his crime.

"Approach me," said the victim, "that thou mayst hear me more distinctly."

The Czar advanced towards the stake, while the victim paused an instant or two in order to recover sufficient strength to speak out in a forcible manner.

"Now, tyrant," he cried, "the most execrable which hell ever sent forth, supposing that which thou imputest to me be true, dost thou believe that, not having confessed it before my punishment, and when I had still hope of obtaining pardon by that avowal, dost thou believe, I say, that I could be such an idiot, so weak, or such a coward, as to satisfy thee, now that it is out of thy power to give me my life? Go, horrible monster, and take my scorn with thee!"

And the dying man spat in the Czar's face.

Peter thought seriously of placing Anne Moens on the throne; but the young woman, who regarded the Czar's attentions as the greatest of misfortunes, found means to cunningly evade all his offers of marriage.

The royal lover continued to visit the young woman for some time, however, but at length, growing weary and disgusted at her coldness, he wandered elsewhere, and allowed her to marry an old lover, with whom she had carried on an intrigue for a long time. She became Madame Balk.

The next fair lady who inspired a passion in the breast of Peter was a winning young Livonian, who had been the wife of a Swedish dragoon, and successively the mistress of three prominent

Russian generals. This woman soon became Empress of Russia, under the name of Catharine I.

Although Catharine was indebted for every favor to the Czar, who had seated her on the throne, she was not as true to him as he had a right to expect.

Some years after obtaining her high honors, Catharine chose for her chamberlain a young man named Moens de la Croix, a brother to the mistress of the Czar who had rejected his hand.

Moens was a very handsome man; and it was not long before he made a powerful impression on the heart of the empress. The passion was quickly perceived by one of the Czar's favorites, who was base enough to inform his master of the proceedings of the lovers.

All the fierce jealousy of Peter was instantly aroused. He swore to avenge himself; but he resolved beforehand that he would be an eye-witness of the treachery of Catharine.

The jealous autocrat pretended to leave St. Petersburg with the design of passing some days in one of his country palaces, and then he returned in secret to the Winter Palace. He afterwards sent a page, on whom he could rely, to carry his compliments to Catharine, and to tell her that he was at Doupka, some leagues from the capital.

The page, who had received orders to take notice of all that passed, was not long in returning to confirm the worst suspicions of the jealous Czar, who immediately hastened to Catharine, and surprised her in the arms of her lover.

It so happened that Madame Balk, the sister of Catharine's lover, was a lady in waiting on the empress at the time of the discovery.

It was two hours after midnight, and Madame Balk was watching at some distance from the apartment of the empress. Peter rushed in in a great rage, overthrew a page whom he met on the way, and struck Catharine with his cane.

The enraged Czar did not say a word to Madame Balk or her guilty brother, as he had made up his mind to punish them in a more severe manner than by inflicting a few strokes of his cane.

Rushing from his wife's apartments in a transport of fury, Peter entered the sleeping chamber of Prince Repnin, who was his confidential minister and adviser, and the only man in Russia who could control the violent autocrat.

The prince, on seeing the agitated Czar, gave himself up for lost, as he was well aware that the passionate man conceived sudden hatreds.

"Get up," said Peter to the prince, "and listen to me. Thou hast no occasion to dress thyself."

The prince arose, pale and trembling.

Then Peter, in passionate tones, related what had just passed, and added:

"I am resolved to have the empress' head cut off as soon as it is day."

"You are offended, and you are absolute master," said Repnin; "but permit me, with the utmost deference, to make an observation to you. Why should you divulge the disgraceful adventure which irritates you? You have been obliged to destroy the rebels. Almost every year of your reign has been marked with bloody executions. You have conceived it your duty to condemn your own son to death. If you cut off the head of your wife, you will sully forever the glory of your name. Europe will regard you as a prince who thirsts for the blood of his people and all who approach him. Let Moens perish by the sword of justice; but, with regard to the empress, you must rid yourself of her in a manner at which your glory will have no reason to blush."

During the address Peter was violently agitated. He fixed his looks on the speaker for a long time, and left the chamber without uttering a syllable.

The destruction of the young lover was already determined on. He was arrested, and so was his sister.

They were both shut up in an apartment in the Winter Palace, into which no one was ever permitted to enter except the emperor himself, who carried them their provisions.

At the same time a report was spread that the brother and sister had permitted themselves to become corrupted by the enemies of the state, in the hope of gaining over the empress, in the face of the Czar, to oppose the interests of Russia.

On being interrogated by the emperor, in presence of one of his prominent generals, the young lover confessed everything required of him, and he was then condemned to be executed.

Madame Balk was also tried by the autocrat, and she was condemned to suffer the fearful punishment of the knout. It is asserted that the Czar struck the blows on the tender part of his former mistress with his own hand. The unfortunate woman was then banished to Siberia.

The young lover walked to the place of execution with the utmost fortitude. He always wore a bracelet of diamonds, in which was a miniature portrait of Catharine; but as it had not been discovered when he was arrested, he found means to conceal it under his garter. When he was on the scaffold he could not conceal the secret to the Lutheran priest who accompanied him, and under cover of his cloak slipped the bracelet in his hand, to be restored to the empress.

The Czar was a witness to the punishment of young Moens, which he beheld from one of the windows of the senate-house.

After the execution he ascended the scaffold, took the head of his dead rival by the hair, and expressed in a brutal and energetic manner how well satisfied he was with his vengeance.

On the same day he had the cruelty to convey Catharine, in an open carriage, to the stake on which the head of her unfortunate lover was nailed. Catharine was sufficient mistress of herself not to change countenance at the sight of the horrible spectacle, but it is asserted that, on returning to her apartment, she shed a torrent of tears.

From that period Peter never saw Catharine again except in public. The vengeful autocrat threw into the fire the will by which he had named his wife heiress to the throne; and he did not attempt to conceal the design which he had formed to revenge himself still farther upon the erring woman.

But Catharine was not a woman who could bear with patience all the indignities heaped upon her by her cruel husband, and she soon became attached to another lover.

This man was Menzikoff, one of the emperor's favorites, who was a secret intriguer against his master.

While they were in the height of their intrigues, Peter the Great was suddenly called away, and it was believed in Russia that his death had been hastened by his secret enemies.

On the death of her husband, and principally through the instrumentality of her lover, Catharine was proclaimed sovereign of all the Russians, and Menzikoff shared the supreme power with her.

The first days of Catharine's reign were very agreeable to the people, as she caused the taxes to be diminished, and she abolished some odious laws.

It may be interesting to know that the two persons thus placed at the head of one of the greatest nations of Europe were very ignorant in point of education. They could neither read nor write.

Catharine soon grew weary of the affairs of State, however, disdained all business details, and abandoned herself entirely to luxury and pleasure.

While retaining Menzikoff as her prime minister, she took up with two new favorites at the same time, and they were both young and handsome.

About the same time a brother of the empress arrived at St. Petersburgh, whom she called Count Skawronsky. This man brought with him a wife and three children. As it was always believed that the empress did not know one of her relations, it was rumored that the count had been one of her old lovers.

Catharine I. died in the year 1727, and while she was on her death-bed her ministers were wrangling about her successor to the throne.

THE INFAMOUS LOVE INTRIGUES OF CATHARINE II. OF RUSSIA.

THE EMPRESS ELIZABETH AND HER MASTER OF HOUNDS—THE FIRST FOLLY OF THE YOUNG PRINCESS—HER HUSBAND RETALIATES IN THE SAME MANNER—CATHARINE DISPOSES OF HER UGLY HUSBAND—LOVERS IN PLENTY—A VILE PLOT AGAINST A POOR GIRL—THE TRICK PLAYED ON THE GALLANT PAUL JONES—THE REWARDS GIVEN TO THE FAVORITES.

THE snow-storms of Russia had a terrible effect on the all-conquering armies of the great Napoleon, but they do not seem to have chilled the ardor of the sons and daughters of the country, and more especially of its rulers, if we are to judge them—as Judge them we must—according to the clear statements presented to us by the candid pen of the historian.

In the year 1742 Russia was ruled by Elizabeth, daughter of Peter the Great and his "fair and frail" wife, Catharine.

While Elizabeth resembled her beautiful mother, she was still more beautiful. She possessed a tall and admirably proportioned figure, and although her features were rather large, her physiognomy had a sweetness inexpressible. She was winning in her manners, and she could always command a lively flow of words in conversation.

But if Elizabeth rivaled her mother in those advantages which lend so great a charm to the society of women, if she surpassed her in the unbounded love of pleasure, she was far from possessing that greatness of soul which serves to gain an ascendancy over those by whom one is surrounded in public life.

Instead of possessing the art of ruling over others, Elizabeth allowed herself to be governed by her crafty and designing ministers.

In order the better to rise above the reach of dependence, Elizabeth—like her namesake, the "virgin" queen of England—constantly refused to take a husband, with whom she must have divided her empire; but she did not the less experience the delights of love in the meantime.

Elizabeth's master of hounds was a gay, handsome young man, of very humble origin. The amorous empress fixed her regards on this favored individual, and she married him in private. Two children—a boy and a girl—were the fruits of this clandestine marriage.

The vivacious empress was not always true to her master of hounds, however, for she had often occasion to change her favorite. Yet Elizabeth always loved the father of her children, humble though he was; and when she grew weary of her other favorites she would turn to her first love, clinging to him to the last.

As Elizabeth had no legitimate heirs to the throne of Russia, she nominated Peter Ulric, her nephew, as her successor. Peter was only fourteen years of age at the time.

Having selected an heir to the throne, Elizabeth cast around for a wife for the young prince, and she soon selected Anne, Princess of Zerbst, who was only in her thirteenth year.

This young girl, who was destined to become one of the most famous women that ever figured in the history of the world, was afterwards known as Catharine, having changed her name on being admitted into the fold of the Greek Church.

The young lovers met in St. Petersburgh, where they were received and entertained by Elizabeth in a cordial manner. Young Catharine was pretty and very winning, and the young prince was endowed with a fine person. An attachment soon sprang up between the young pair, and the marriage was hastened.

While fortune was thus smiling on the young heir, a terrible misfortune befell young Peter. He was seized with a violent fever, and in a short time it was discovered that he was seized with a malignant form of small-pox.

The young prince did not fall a victim to the cruel malady, but he retained frightful traces of it. The change was terrible indeed. He lost all the charms of his countenance, and he became deformed, and almost hideous to behold.

When Peter appeared in public again, his promised bride looked on him with secret horror. She contrived, however, to restrain her emotions, and, running to the prince, she embraced him with every appearance of joy. On returning to her apartment, Catharine became sensible of the whole extent of her misfortune, and she fell into a swoon, from which she did not recover for three hours.

The chagrin which Catharine had just suffered did not suggest any pretext for deferring her marriage with the ugly young prince. The aged empress looked forward to the alliance with pleasure, and the promptings of ambition, already influencing the heart of young Catharine, did not permit her to hesitate.

As the writer may be accused by some mock modest critics of presenting the scenes that followed this unhappy marriage in a manner too free and open, we state that we take the liberty of quoting from the work of F. Castra, an authentic French historian.

The work from which we quote is entitled: "The History of Catharine II., Empress of Russia." This work was translated into English by an English clergyman, Henry Hunter, D.D., and it can be found in the public libraries of our great cities.

M. Castra thus describes the life of the young couple after their unhappy marriage:

"The marriage was accordingly celebrated; but notwithstanding the attachment which had manifested itself between the grand duke and the princess from the first moment that they met, nature had not destined them to love each other long, and the alteration that had taken place in the features of the prince was not the only cause of the indifference of his youthful bride.

"Peter had a defect which, although easy to remove, seemed so much more cruel; the violence of his love, his ineffectual efforts, could not accomplish the consummation of his marriage.

"If the prince had confided his secret to some one who possessed a little experience, the obstacle which opposed itself to his desires might have been overcome. The lowest of the disciples of Moses, or the most insignificant surgeon, could have freed him from it. But such was the shame with which this misfortune overwhelmed him, that he had not the courage to reveal it; and the princess, who received his caresses with the utmost repugnance, and who was not at that time more experienced than himself, neither thought of consoling him, nor of making him employ the means to bring him back to her arms.

"Nevertheless, they lived for some time in apparent understanding, which Catharine prolonged as long as she thought it was necessary.

"This princess, educated not far from the court of the great Frederick, where everything breathed the love of the sciences and the fine arts, joined to beauty and to the superior understanding which she had received from nature extensive knowledge, and the facility of expressing herself with elegance in several languages.

"Peter likewise possessed sense, but his education had been dreadfully neglected. He had an excellent heart, but was delicient in politeness. He was of a very good stature, but ugly and deformed. He frequently blushed at the superiority of his wife, and his wife blushed to behold him so little worthy of her. In a word, he did not know how to make her happy. From thence arose that natural hatred which the courtiers were not slow in discovering, and which increased so rapidly."

The historian then tells of the intrigues of the court, in which the youthful Catharine mingled freely, while her husband was "playing soldier" at a castle in the country, and indulging in gambling and drunken debauchery.

M. Castra thus describes the first lover who attracted Catharine's attention:

"There was one in particular who rendered himself as much distinguished by his taste for the fine arts as by the graces of his person. This was Soltikoff Chamberlain to the prince, he was in all his parties, but was ashamed of them. He was tolerably well acquainted with French literature, he knew by heart the choicest morsels of Racine and Voltaire, to which his voice seemed to add new charms Although scarcely emerged from childhood, he had already obtained the favors of several of the court belles, and his success rendered him arrogant.

"Soltikoff, it is true, passed for being a little deficient in courage among men, but he was not the less presumptuous nor the less forward in the society of women. Perhaps he might have trembled at the sight of a naked sword, but to extend the number of his gallant conquests he had frequently appeared to brave the deserts of Siberia.

"In a word, the married men regarded him as the most agreeable and the most dangerous man in St. Petersburgh.

"It was not long before Soltikoff raised his eyes toward the wife of his master, and vanity, still more than love, inspired him with the bold design of captivating her heart. He began by carefully studying the inclinations of the princess. He perceived that, notwithstanding the constraint in which she lived, Catharine had a great fondness for pleasure, and that the solitude of Oranienbanm rendered dissipation necessary to her.

"He immediately procured for her some new amusement every day. He persuaded the grand duke to give festivals; he took upon himself the charge of inventing them, of directing them, and he did not allow the grand duchess to remain ignorant that she was their sole object, and that it was to him alone that she was indebted for them.

"Catharine was not insensible to attentions so gallant, so unremitting. The seducing figure and the wit of Soltikoff had made an impression upon her. His assiduities completely won her; but Soltikoff, well knowing that the heart of the grand duchess was not an ordinary conquest, dreaded explaining himself in an incautious manner. It is even possible that he only wished at that time to feign a passion which proved in the end altogether real. They at last had become attached to each other for a long time, without having declared their affection.

"A melancholy event accelerated the declaration. Soltikoff lost his father. His duty obliged him to take his departure for Moscow. He obtained permission to this effect from the grand duke, and on taking leave of Catharine he could not refrain from letting her see what pangs his departure cost him.

"The princess, who beheld his tears, was no less touched than himself with the motive which caused them to flow, and, fixing her eyes with a very expressive air upon Soltikoff, she conjured him to abridge the period of his absence as much as he could, and to return to forget his sorrows in the bosom of a court where without him it was impossible to enjoy pleasure.

"The character of Soltikoff may permit us easily to judge of what an impression these words were productive. He thought he perceived a return of affection on her part, and his pride redoubled. His journey lasted but a few days.

"What were domestic occupations when put in competition with the happiness which awaited him? What was Moscow to him in comparison of St. Petersburgh? He abandoned everything to hasten and to secure his triumph.

"However, on approaching the grand duchess, the presumptuous idea which had filled his mind at a distance from her began to vanish away. His audacity abandoned him. The most serious, the most melancholy reflections overwhelmed his spirit. He foresaw all the danger of his attachment. He durst not presume to flatter himself that Catharine would forget what she owed to her rank, to her husband, to receive the attentions of a simple chamberlain.

"But were he so happy as to find that she deigned to return to his passion, was it possible for him to believe he could exclude the penetrating observations of the jealous courtiers who surrounded her? How, in a word, risk an avowal of which perpetual banishment, or even the loss of life, might become the price.

"He trembled, he was struck with terror, he resolved to renounce those hopes, which he believed to have been too ambitiously conceived.

"In this state of inquietude and sorrow, Soltikoff could no longer display that brilliant gayety which had till then distinguished him. He tried in vain to assume an unembarrassed air. The deepest melancholy preyed upon his heart, and was depicted in his countenance, his health visibly declined.

"The grand duchess was alarmed at it, and one day, when she found herself alone with him, demanded the reason.

"Soltikoff being then unable to resist the passion which he felt made the confession. Catharine listened to it without anger; she even appeared to pity him; but advised him to renounce a propensity of which he could not but feel the impropriety and the danger.

"Although still very young, Soltikoff understood the female sex too well not to know that she who permits herself to listen to a lover already begins to approve him. He gained new confidence. He threw himself at the knees of the grand duchess, and had the presumption to embrace them.

"The princess was distressed; she let fall some tears, and flying precipitately from the transports of Soltikoff, to go and shut herself up in her closet, she repeated that line which Monimia addresses Xiphares in the tragedy of 'Mithridates':

"'And merit the tears you are going to cost me.'

"From this moment the chamberlain recovered his gayety with hope, and everything around him announced this alteration.

"Whilst the grand duke and the grand duchess passed the fine season at Oranienbaum, the Empress Elizabeth remained at Petershof, and from time to time invited the couple thither to partake of the pleasures of her court. It was on one of these occasions that Soltikoff became completely happy. In order to avoid spectacles and feasts, where too many indiscreet observations laid her under constraint, Catharine feigned indisposition.

"The grand duke was so blinded with respect to his chamberlain, that he himself entreated him to share the solitude of his wife, and to employ all the allurements of his wit in order to amuse her.

"This was precisely what the two lovers wished; accordingly they did not fail to take advantage of it. But scarcely had the grand duchess yielded than she abandoned herself to all the apprehension with which the idea of her weakness could inspire her. She foresaw the dangerous consequences of the pleasures which she tasted with Soltikoff, and imparted her fears to him.

"The chamberlain observed to her that if he could find a method to bring her husband to her arms, the consequences which she so much dreaded would become of advantage to her. He took upon himself at the same time to procure the success of his project.

"The grand duke had, as has already been said, begun to abandon himself to the excesses of the table, and when heated with wine, sometimes conversed with his friends respecting the obstacle which estranged him from his wife. The cause of his impotence was then known, and the method of removing it easy; but the grand duke feared to make use of this method.

"Soltikoff resolved to make him determine upon it. He wished, however, in the first place, to obtain the consent of the empress. An opportunity soon presented itself.

"Madame de Narischken, sister and confidante of Soltikoff, was pregnant. Soltikoff was chatting with her when Elizabeth approached Madame de Narischkin to congratulate her on the happiness she enjoyed in knowing how to create an heir.

"'I wish sincerely,' added she, 'you would communicate this virtue to the grand duchess.'

"Soltikoff saw that this was the favorable moment for letting the empress know what it was that opposed the happiness of the grand duke. He revealed it to her. He likewise informed her that he had formed the design of profiting by the ascendancy which he had over the prince to persuade him to rid himself of an obstacle so easy to be removed.

"Elizabeth approved it, and even recommended him to neglect nothing which could procure success in a project on which depended the tranquillity of her nephew, and that of the empire.

"Soltikoff, emboldened by this first step, proposed the very same day to the grand duke to submit to the operation prescribed by the legislator of the Hebrews. He represented to him that he would experience but very slight pain, and that he would only be obliged to keep his apartments for some days, to taste afterwards the most delicious pleasures.

"The prince, naturally timid, manifested an extreme repugnance. The wishes of his aunt, the enthusiasm of Soltikoff, the wish he himself felt of enjoying an unknown pleasure, the shame of not being like other men, nothing could make him come to a resolution.

"But Soltikoff was too much interested in this undertaking to be discouraged by these first difficulties. He gained over the other favorites of the grand duke by assuring them that what he had done was by the orders of the empress.

"One night this prince supped with him, and having, according to custom, drank to excess, they turned the conversation upon the pleasures of love. The prince permitted some expressions of regret to escape him on the impossibility of having the power of enjoying them.

"Upon this all the company threw themselves at his knees, and conjured him to yield to the advice of Soltikoff. The grand duke appeared irresolute. Some words which he stammered out were interpreted to consent. Everything was prepared. The famous physician, Boerhave, was introduced, with a skilful surgeon. He had no longer any power of defending himself, and the operation was very happily performed.

"The Empress Elizabeth was so well satisfied with the conduct of Soltikoff that she testified her gratitude by presenting him with a magnificent diamond.

"The young chamberlain had been till then too happy not to experience some disturbance of his happiness. The grand duchess did not always observe sufficient precaution to conceal the passion which she had for him. The courtiers, always malignant, always envious, began by remarking a preference which offended them, and they very soon discovered the real cause.

"Immediately the ruin of Soltikoff was resolved upon. Even those who testified the greatest friendship toward him, and, of course, had it most in their power to injure him, continued secretly to convey to the empress their suspicions respecting the attachment existing between the grand duchess and the chamberlain.

"Greatly addicted to gallantry herself, Elizabeth should not perhaps have been too deeply offended at this intrigue; but she was stately, and in the first moments of her indignation she declared that an exile to Siberia should be the price of the temerity of Soltikoff. She likewise declared that, as soon as the grand duke, perfectly cured of the consequences of the operation which he had undergone, would begin to enjoy the privileges of a husband, it was her will that the grand duchess should conform to the ancient custom of the Russians, and give the tokens of virginity, which she must have preserved till then.

"Soltikoff, informed of the danger which threatened him, immediately applied himself to devise the way of escaping it. He perceived that the best mode to prevent the storm from bursting on his head was to brave it. Assuming then an air of assurance, and with all the appearance of injured innocence, he flew to the grand duke to complain of the reports which had been so daringly spread. He reminded the prince that he had only presented himself before the grand duchess in conformity to the orders which he himself had given him, and he protested that he had never regarded that princess but with all the respect due to her rank. He observed, at the same time, that the calumniators who wished to ruin him sought by a roundabout but certain method to attack the heir of the empire, since by these infamous reports the honor of the throne would find itself much more deeply exposed than that of a simple chamberlain.

"He finally added, in order that he might no longer furnish a

pretext for the jealousy of his enemies, and to appease the empress, that he begged the good duke's permission to retire to Moscow.

"The discourse of Soltikoff not only deceived the credulous prince, but persuaded him that his own glory required he should retain the chamberlain in the service of his wife. He ordered him to remain; afterward he demanded an audience of the empress, in which he complained of the insolent language which was allowed; he defended Soltikoff with so much vehemence, and by such plausible reasons, that Elizabeth began herself to realize that the reports which had been made to her could be the offspring only of calumny.

"Whilst this scene was going forward in the apartment of Elizabeth, the grand duchess did not remain idle; she was more interested than any one in causing those injurious reports to be quashed, and in the preservation of her lover. And who could better than herself undertake her own defense?

"Informed by Madame de Narischkin of the pains which the grand duke had taken to justify Soltikoff, and of the success which he had just obtained, she presented herself immediately before the empress.

"Laying aside the mildness in which she had always, till then, appeared clothed in the presence of the sovereign, she broke out with reproaches for her having given credit to such odious suspicions. She represented how uncertain and deceitful the proof which the empress demanded of her virtue might be, and how such a request overwhelmed her with shame, since on occasions of the kind the smallest doubt left an indelible stain.

"Grief, revenge, passion, lent so great a force to her eloquence, that Elizabeth could not resist it; she appeared moved, softened, persuaded, and the victory of Catharine was still more complete than that of the grand duke.

"In the evening there was, according to custom, a grand party at the palace, and the empress hastened to take advantage of it, to testify in the eyes of her courtiers that Soltikoff had no longer anything to dread from her.

"The chamberlain was engaged at play. Elizabeth, advancing close to the back of his chair, asked him, with that grace which she knew how to infuse into everything she said, if he was happy.

"'Never, madame,' replied Soltikoff.

"'I am sorry for it,' rejoined she; 'but this is perhaps in some measure your own fault. It is said that you intended quitting the grand duke; I cannot believe it, and I invite you to remain with him. Depend upon it, that if your enemies make any further attempts to malign you, I will be the first to stand up in your defense.'

"Had it been true that Soltikoff was forming a serious design of withdrawing himself from court, these words would have been sufficient to retain him; and supposing the courtiers to have procured the most positive proof of his presumption, they would henceforth have imposed silence on them.

"However, the grand duke, feeling no longer any inconvenience from the operation which he had undergone, at last had the courage to enjoy his privilege as a husband. All was prepared; he passed the night with his consort, and believed himself perfectly happy.

"The next day he sent to the empress, at the instigation of Soltikoff, a sealed casket, which contained the tokens of the pretended virginity of the grand duchess. Elizabeth appeared to be persuaded of their authenticity.

"Some people, no doubt, laughed at this inwardly, but every one was eager loudly to felicitate the prince upon his happiness.

"From this period Soltikoff thought he had no danger to guard against. He enjoyed, without disturbance and without remorse, pleasures from which, the moment that the grand duke had passed into the arms of Catharine, did not permit him to apprehend any ill consequences.

"Catharine herself had no longer any occasion to employ extreme circumspection. Her first attempt had inspired her with greater courage.

"Besides, the example of the Empress Elizabeth, whose manners became more and more corrupted, and who abandoned herself every day to new propensities, seemed to excuse her own attachment. The empress entertained no suspicions of an intrigue, which she might easily have perceived, or, if she remarked it, she did not any longer discover at least either suspicion or anger.

"Time, which weakens, and frequently extinguishes the most ardent passions, did not in any degree diminish that of Catharine. That princess was on the point of becoming a mother ; Soltikoff gained every day a greater ascendancy over her heart ; but his good fortune had arrived at its summit; he became the artificer of his own destruction."

The historian then dwells on the intrigues of the courtiers against Catharine's favorite; about his implication in a plot; and of his banishment from the empire by the secret orders of the Empress Elizabeth.

The beautiful Catharine mourned for her handsome lover, but she did not mourn her heart away. She was scarcely "off with the old love before she was on with the new."

The next love affair of the amorous Catharine is thus described by the candid historian:

"The young Count Stanislaus Poniatowsky, to whom Catharine has since given, and afterwards taken away, the throne of Poland, was the happy successor of Soltikoff. Born a simple gentleman and unpossessed of fortune, but endowed with a fine figure and filled with ambition, Poniatowsky carried about through Germany, and in France for some time, his restlessness and vague expectations.

"He was at first tolerably successful at Paris, where the friendship of the Swedish ambassador procured him some distinguished connections; but his mother, who dreaded on his account the too seductive pleasures of that city, wrote to him, with orders to depart from it. She was in the right; for Poniatowsky had already been imprisoned for debt.

"He quitted France and went over to England, where he met again Sir Hanbury Williams, whom he had been acquainted at Warsaw, and who, nominated by the court of London as ambassador to St. Petersburgh, carried him in his suite.

"Without having any title which could attach him to the embassy, the young Polonese labored in the embassador's office, and served him in the quality of secretary. He at first intended to devote himself entirely to diplomatic pursuits; but the taste for dissipation which for a long time had led him away, his youth, the seducing opportunities which were every day presenting themselves to him, very soon hurried him back to pleasure. He was gay, genteel, brilliant, and formed to succeed in a court of which amusement seemed to be the principal concern. Accordingly, he was not slow in perceiving the impression he had made upon the heart of Catharine.

"Poniatowsky was bold even to presumption. However, the rank of the grand duchess intimidated him, and the numerous courtiers whose eyes were upon him restrained him still more.

"The two lovers for some time conversed only by their looks, but to these conversations in dumb-show some of another sort afterwards succeeded, in which they came to an explanation in regard to their attachment, and respecting the methods which they should adopt in order to give themselves up to it without restraint.

"Envy, which at that time studied the inclinations of the grand duchess only to censure and thwart them, hastened to inform the empress of the new intrigue of her adopted niece.

"Elizabeth did not esteem her nephew, and gave herself as little concern about the honor of the grand duchess; she did not in general observe greater severity with regard to the manners of others than to her own; in a word, she was always reluctant to punish; but her extreme facility in following councils of all who surrounded her, frequently caused her to act with a rigor entirely foreign to her character. She gave orders to Poniatowsky to quit Russia immediately. Poniatowsky obeyed."

But Catharine did not submit to the banishment of her second lover as easily as she did to that of the other. Through the connivance of the British embassador, Poniatowsky was recalled, high honors were conferred on him by the Polish government, and he was once more the recipient of Catharine's favors.

At length the jealous courtiers around the court aroused the jealousy of the husband.

The lovers had become so bold in their meetings that detection was not impossible; and the grand duke was informed of their proceedings.

The historian then presents us with some serio-comic scenes in the life of the unhappy couple:

"When the jealousy of the grand duke was once aroused, they were in haste to furnish him with positive proofs of the love of his wife for the Polonese, and of the criminal commerce which they carried on.

"The prince was overwhelmed, thunderstruck. He deplored his misfortune and his imprudence. He laid aside the deference, the respect which he had till then expressed for the grand duchess, and he forbade Poniatowsky her presence. He afterwards hastened to the empress, from whom he demanded vengeance for the insult he had received."

Catharine fell into disgrace after the *exposé*, and though she made every effort to conciliate the empress, she was not successful.

The wily young woman even played the part of the penitent sinner, in order to gain the pardon of the empress, well knowing that her august mistress had often sinned herself.

Yet the lovers still clung to each other, while the storm was gathering around them.

The historian then tells us of the situation after the discovery by the prince:

"Catharine remained there for some time in this painful situation. She had to support, at the same time, the hatred of the grand duke, the disdain of the empress, the insulting dereliction of a court which some days before had hastened to cringe at her feet, and—what afflicted her still more—the apprehension of losing Poniatowsky forever.

"Poniatowsky was not less tormented than her. The court of Warsaw had just recalled him, and he could not resolve on quitting Russia. Feigning indisposition, he kept himself, during the day, concealed in his hotel, and at night stole mysteriously to the grand duchess. But numerous spies observed the pair; their interviews were discovered, and care was taken to render an account of them to the empress.

"Upon the return of the summer season, the difficulties of meeting each other still increased.

"The grand duchess was under a necessity of following her husband to Oranienbaum, and Poniatowsky was obliged to employ every species of disguise in order to penetrate into the castle.

"One night that he had been at considerable pains to conceal his ribbon of the White Eagle, he was walking in an alley of the park where Catharine had given him a meeting; he was recognized by a servant, who ran to give the information to the grand duke.

"The prince, wishing to avenge himself on Poniatowsky, immediately ordered the stoutest of his Russian officers to be summoned, and, after having given one of them the signal by which to distinguish the Polonese, he ordered him to go and surprise him in the park, and to bring him, either by fair means or by force, to the corps-de-garde.

"The Russian immediately set out, joined the man who had been pointed out to him, and demanded who he was and what he wanted.

"Poniatowsky replied that he was a German tailor, and that he had come to Oranienbaum to take the measure of a Holstein-ese officer for a coat.

"'I have orders to conduct you to the corps-de-garde,' said the Russian to him.

"'I cannot consent to this; I have not sufficient time,' replied the Polonese.

"'Oh! whether thou hast time or not, thou must follow me,' replied the Russian.

"And, throwing a handkerchief over his neck, in which he made a slip-knot, he dragged him to the fort.

"As soon as the grand duke was sure of the arrest of Ponia towsky, he assembled a council of war, and insisted that the Polonese should be condemned to the gallows, for having intruded clandestinely within the limits of his fortifications.

"General Tottleben, whom the empress had placed about him in order to watch his conduct, pretended to applaud this resolution; but he observed that, as Poniatowsky was invested with the character of a foreign minister, the sentence could not be executed until after they had obtained the approbation of the empress.

"A courier was immediately dispatched to St. Petersburgh. Kratschinsky, attached to Poniatowsky by ties of friendship, and by the title of gentleman of the embassy, and lover of the Countess of Romanzoff, employed this lady with Elizabeth, whose confidante she was, to prevail on her to restore the Polish minister to liberty.

"During this time some courtiers of the grand duke had, at the instigation of Catharine, tempted the avarice of the prince's mistress; and through the medium of some money this young woman had persuaded her lover to release Poniatowsky.

"Poniatowsky was then conducted into the presence of the grand duke, as if the prince had been still ignorant who his prisoner was. He assumed even the air of being hurt that he had been treated with so much indignity on his account, and scolded the officers who had arrested him; but he afterwards amused himself greatly with this adventure, and took pleasure above all things to relate it in the presence of the grand duchess.

"It was a short time before this that, whether yielding to an involuntary inclination, or whether he wished to indemnify himself for the infidelities of his wife, the grand duke had chosen a mistress, one of the daughters of the Senator Woronzoff, brother of the new chancellor.

"These ladies were three sisters; the eldest of whom, Madame du Boulourlin, passed with reason for one of the most beautiful and most coquettish women in Russia.

"The youngest, who has since performed so courageous a part, under the name of the Princess d'Aschkoff, was not very handsome, but lively and very intelligent.

"As to the third, Elizabeth Woronzoff, to whom the grand duke gave the title of countess, and of whom he was so passionately enamored, she possessed neither wit, grace, nor beauty. Her complaisance seduced him, her caprices amused him, and the habit of living with her became very soon an imperious necessity.

"The Senator Woronzoff, a mean and ambitious courtier, prostituted his daughter to the prince in the basest manner.

"The grand duchess, who awaited with impatience the moment which was to reconcile the empress to her, thought it her duty, after a pretty long silence, to renew her attempts.

"She demanded pardon, but it would not be granted, except on conditions which shocked her. A proposal was made to her to acknowledge herself guilty, and to throw herself on the clemency of her husband and of the empress.

"Catharine, upon this, recovered all her haughtiness. She avoided making her appearance at court, kept herself shut up in her apartments, and asked permission of the empress to retire into Germany, a permission which she was certain would not be granted, since, knowing the extreme tenderness of Elizabeth for the young Paul Petrouitz, she had no reason to apprehend that this princess would remove the mother of a child whom she would by that expose to the hazard of being one day declared a bastard.

"This project of Catharine's procured the wished-for success. An accommodation followed it. At the very moment when she was thought to be completely ruined, and to the great astonishment of all the courtiers, she made her appearance at the play by the side of the empress, who lavished caresses on her.

"It is true that in the secret conversation which the grand

duchess had with Elizabeth, she promised not to see Poniatowsky any more, and from this moment in reality she infused a much greater portion of reserve into her conduct.

"Poniatowsky demanded almost immediately his audience of leave. But, as ambition still more than love attached him to Catharine, and as he was willing to neglect that which might kindle still further a flame, which since then procured him the throne of Poland, he found new pretexts to prolong still longer his stay in Russia."

The historian then goes on to tell of the various intrigues of the unhappy couple. The young prince was inspired by his mistress; and Catharine, who possessed the power of winning many friends, gained several of the powerful nobles over to her side.

The Empress Elizabeth died in the year 1762; and then Peter was elevated to the throne, while Catharine was made empress. And then a deadly conflict ensued between the emperor and his wife. Prompted by his mistress, Peter III. plotted to put aside his erring wife, to consign her to a dungeon or to death, and place his favorite beside him on the throne.

Count Poniatowsky was dismissed from St. Petersburgh before the death of the old empress; but Catharine soon found another lover, as well as a powerful ally, who is thus described by the historian:

"Gregory Orloff possessed the advantages neither of birth nor education, but he had received from nature some of the happiest endowments, beyond all doubt, courage and manly beauty.

"Grandson of a Strelitz who, in the grand execution at Moscow, was in the act of losing his head by the ax of Peter I., when his apathetic composure induced that prince to spare his life, Gregory served in the artillery, while two of his brothers were only common soldiers in the guards.

"Count Peter Schouwaloff, grandmaster of the ordnance, a man vain and stately, wished to have the handsomest of his officers for aide-de-camp, and made choice of Gregory Orloff. He had likewise for his mistress one of the most illustrious and most beautiful women at court, the Princess Kourakin, who speedily notified the aid-de-camp that she preferred him to the general.

"But unfortunately the general, who surprised them together, forbid Orloff his presence, and threatened to employ his influence to have him banished to Siberia.

"This adventure took place toward the close of Elizabeth's reign, and made some noise. It became the subject of conversation both at court and in the city, and the report of it reached the retreat to which Catharine had been obliged to condemn herself. Curiosity, perhaps compassion, inspired her to know the young officer whose misfortune she had heard of.

"Ivanowana, her confidential maid, procured her a sight of him, with all the accustomed precaution; and Orloff, without guessing at first who the beauty was that interested herself in his fate, found in her many more charms, and a much greater ardor of affection, than in the Princess Kourakin.

"This first and mysterious interview was followed by many others, in which Catharine discovered tenderness only; but when she believed herself fully assured of the intrepidity and discretion of her lover, she confided to him her ambitious designs.

"Orloff on this formed with her a conspiracy, in which he soon engaged his brothers and some intimate friends among the officers of the army.

"Catharine was as yet grand duchess only when her attachment to Orloff commenced, and her intrigue with him was not the only one which she conducted with equal address and good fortune. Several other officers, beside various persons of her court, had partaken of her favors; but as she did not find in them the devotedness and genius which were necessary to her, she was satisfied with securing their friendship, but did not impart to them her secret.

"Lieutenant-General Villebois was one of those whom that prince distinguished the most; and when he obtained the command of the artillery on the death of the general who discarded

Orloff, she prevailed with him to bestow the post of captain-pay-master to his corps on that favorite.

"Villebois did whatever she desired, without at once suspecting that he brought forward a preferred rival."

With the assistance of Orloff and the officers whom she had won over to her side, Catharine raised a successful revolution against her husband. That unfortunate man was taken prisoner, cast into a dungeon, and afterwards assassinated by the orders of his wife.

Then Catharine was declared empress of all the Russians, and she commenced her undivided reign by conferring high honors on her favorite, and in putting down with a severe hand several conspiracies organized against her by his jealous rivals.

The historian thus relates the new favorite's position after the death of the unfortunate Peter III.:

"In truth this favorite became every day more dear to the empress. His masculine beauty, which had given birth to the attachment of this princess, and which was still heightened by an air of confidence and self-sufficiency, which the high degree of favor he enjoyed could not fail to inspire, the important services he had rendered to Catharine, those which it was still in his power to contribute, the secret claims with which the certainty of beholding her again a mother furnished him; everything, in a word, secured the ascendant of Orloff.

"Catharine had endeavored from time to time to conceal her connection with him under the veil of decency; but, whether from excess of love, or from policy, she very soon laid aside all mystery, and even seemed to glory in openly avowing her attachment.

"Although Poniatowsky could not be ignorant that Orloff had been long the preferred lover of Catharine, he attempted still to rekindle, by his letters, the passion with which he had formerly inspired the princess. In hopes that, perhaps, his presence might insure him a triumph over his rival, he supplicated the empress to permit him to come to St. Petersburgh in the most private manner.

"But his solicitations were ineffectual. Catharine knew too well what she had to apprehend from the violence of Orloff to consent to a journey which could not fail of being discovered. She, therefore, ceased to dissemble with the Polonese; but in acknowledging that she no longer felt any love for him, she assured him of her constant friendship, and promised to give him proofs of it on every occasion which presented itself. She was not slow, as facts evinced, in realizing this promise."

Orloff reigned as mistress of Catharine's heart for some time, gaining in favor and power each day, until he earned the envy of Panim, who was prime minister to the empress, and a very able and cunning man.

The prime minister adopted a novel way of getting rid of the favorite, and he was successful for a time in weaning her from Orloff.

The historian gives us, in very clear words, the incidents of this movement of the minister:

"Orloff's credit was founded on claims of a nature more tender; but he employed it with little discretion, and incessantly shook it to the foundation. A lover satiated with his good fortune, the assiduity which Catharine exacted appeared to be a constraint on his liberty. He would go bear-hunting for weeks together, and dared to indulge himself on these occasions in infidelities which he was not sufficiently careful to conceal from his mistress, and the example of which she was naturally disposed to follow.

"Panim, who observed this conduct, imagined he could avail himself of it to ruin the arrogant favorite. He observed that the empress frequently cast a look of complacency on a young officer named Wissotzky. Henceforward he employed all his skill to strengthen this attachment. Wissotzky was soon made happy; and, directed by the crafty minister, inspired the empress with a passion sufficiently violent to create a belief that Orloff would be made a sacrifice.

'But this gentleman, who did not choose to surrender his right, showed himself by turns jealous and tender, dangerous and necessary. He resumed his ascendant over the heart of Catharine, and the new lover was dismissed with a handsome recompense, and an employment which fixed him in a distant province."

Orloff continued for some years to be the favorite of Catharine. She elevated him to the highest honors possible, and he was placed in command of one of her conquering armies. But the favorite wavered in his affections; and he was ambitious to become master of the empire as well as of her heart. The historian then writes of the actions of the lovers in 1772, after the genius of Catharine had placed Russia among the foremost nations of the earth:

"Catharine had been greatly attached to Orloff, and she loved him still. Orloff, on the contrary, had never been attached to Catharine but from complacence and ambition.

"For a long time, puffed up with the favors of his sovereign, he displayed a zeal to merit them; but when he thought he had acquired sufficient rights over her, his zeal cooled, and those favors even seemed to be frequently burdensome to him. The greater efforts Catharine made to allure him back to her, the more eager he appeared to avoid her, and to seek elsewhere charms which he no longer found in her.

"That princess was mortified at the coldness of an ingrate, and provoked at his infidelity; but she was still attached to him by such powerful ties that she durst not think of breaking them asunder.

"Their son Bobrinsky, above all, rendered the love of Orloff dear to her. She had him brought up in the house of the chamberlain Schkourin, and went frequently to see him, under a borrowed name, and disguised in such a manner as not to be recognized.

"One day, when she had just quitted his child, and was meditating how to cure Orloff of his inconstancy, she thought she had discovered a method by espousing him privately.

"She made him the proposition. Orloff rejected it in a haughty manner. He replied to the empress that he did not think himself worthy of bearing publicly the name of her husband, and of seating himself with her on a throne which he had preserved for her.

"Catharine, in astonishment, dissembled her displeasure, but discerned immediately that the pride of her favorite might be productive of fatal consequences to her, and did not delay overcoming an attachment which exposed her to too great humiliation.

"Panim, who carefully watched the inclinations of the empress, was not slow of perceiving that she frequently regarded with complacency a sub-lieutenant of the guards named Wassiltchikoff. He immediately conceived the idea of making this young man serve as an instrument for effecting the ruin of Orloff.

"Wassiltchikoff pleased her, because he was young and robust, but he was deficient in understanding, in talents, in experience, and even in personal courage. The empress was so well pleased with him that she nominated him her chamberlain, made him magnificent presents, and frequently treated him in public with a familiarity which rendered it very easy to perceive their good understanding.

"When Catharine had proposed to the haughty Orloff to espouse him in private, the favorite flattered himself that his refusal would only stimulate the desire of that princess, and that access to the throne would become by that means more easy. Accustomed to a love of which he had the most endearing proofs, he did not believe it possible that he could lose the heart of the empress.

"What must have been his thoughts when he learnt that she had availed herself of his absence to choose a new lover? He at first trembled with astonishment and rage. But pride soon came to his consolation. He imagined that his presence would be sufficient to rekindle a flame which he believed but ill extinguished.

"Full of this idea, he forgot negotiations, peace, all the interests of the empire, departed from Foskani without even demanding the permission of the empress, and arrived at the gates of St. Petersburgh.

"At the instant he presented himself, the officer of the guard advanced toward his carriage, and showed him the order which he had not to permit him to enter the capital. Orloff observed a perfect silence, and took the road to Galschina, one of his country residences."

The dismissal of the great favorite by Catharine served as a warning to other ambitious lovers. But while Orloff was never afterward fully reinstated in her favor, he was richly rewarded with presents, and he was made a prince of the empire.

This bold, handsome, unscrupulous man was a mere puppet in Catharine's hands, in everything where love was not concerned; and she engaged him in the most difficult and questionable enterprises, at home and in other countries.

The following account of a treacherous piece of work is presented by the historian, and it will serve to show the character of Alexis Orloff, brother of the favorite, as well as that of the renowned empress:

"Extravagances are not always crimes. But there is no crime so atrocious that the extravagant Alexis Orloff was incapable of perpetrating.

"At the time of his departure from St. Petersburgh he had received orders from Catharine to send her a young unfortunate female placed beyond the reach of her tyranny. Orloff knew but too well how to execute those barbarous orders.

"It has already been mentioned that the Empress Elizabeth had three children, the fruit of her clandestine marriage with the master of the hounds.

"The youngest of those children was a daughter, educated under the name of Princess Tarrakanoff. Prince Charles Radziwill, informed of this secret, and filled with indignation that Catharine should presume to trample under foot the rights of the Polonese, imagined that the daughter of Elizabeth furnished him with the means of executing final vengeance.

"He believed it was possible to raise a successful opposition to the sovereign whose armies were desolating his unhappy country, in the person of a rival, whom the name of her mother must endear to the Russians.

"Ambition, perhaps, presented to him still loftier pretensions. Perhaps he flattered himself with the hope of one day partaking the throne to which he wished to elevate the young Tarrakanoff. Be this as it may, he gained over the persons intrusted with the education of this young princess, carried her off, and conducted her to Rome.

"Catharine, apprised of this elopement, strained every nerve to render the designs of Radziwill abortive. Availing herself of his being the chief of the confederation of malcontents, she had all his property seized, and reduced him to the necessity of subsisting by the sale of his diamonds and other valuable effects which he had carried into Italy. These resources were speedily exhausted.

"Radziwill departed in quest of fresh supplies in Poland, and left the young Tarrakanoff at Rome, under the guardianship of a single governess, and in very narrow circumstances.

"Scarcely had he got back to his own country, when he was offered the restoration of his estates if he would bring the daughter of Elizabeth again into Russia. He refused to submit to that indignity, but had the weakness to promise that he would no longer take any interest in her.

"At that price he purchased his pardon from Catharine.

"Alexis Orloff, charged with the execution of her imperial majesty's sovereign will, on his arrival at Leghorn, lost no time in laying a snare for the Princess Tarrakanoff. One of those intriguers so common in Italy, repaired to Rome, and having discovered the residence of the Russian damsel, presented himself at her habitation under the name and in the garb of an officer of that nation. He pretended at first to be attracted thither simply by a wish to pay homage to a princess whose fate interested all his compatriots. He affected extreme concern at finding her in a destitute condition. He offered her relief,

while necessity obliged her to accept, and the traitor soon appeared to her, as well as to the woman who attended her, to be a savior graciously sent from heaven.

"When he thought that he had sufficiently insinuated himself into her confidence, he declared that he was empowered by Count Alexis Orloff to offer to the daughter of Elizabeth the throne which her mother had filled.

"He said that the Russian nation was dissatisfied with Catharine; Orloff in particular could never forgive her tyranny and ingratitude; and if the young princess would accept the services of that general, and reward him by the gift of her hand, she would soon behold the explosion of the revolution of which he had laid the train.

"Proposals so brilliant ought to have opened the eyes of Princess Tarrakanoff to discern the perfidy of the wretch who made them. But her inexperience and candor prevented all suspicion of foul play.

"Besides, the language of Orloff's emissary seemed analogous to the ideas which she had received from Prince Radziwill. She believed herself destined to the throne; and all the chimeras relative to that belief could not but be flattering to her. She abandoned herself, therefore, to the most delusive hope, and replied in terms of acknowledgment to the man who spoke only to betray.

"Some time after Orloff made his appearance at Rome.

"His agent had announced his arrival. He was received as a benefactor. Some persons, however, to whom the princess and her duenna had communicated the news of the good fortune which awaited them, cautioned them to be on their guard against the designs of a man whose abandoned character had long been notorious, and who, undoubtedly, had too many reasons to persevere in his fidelity to the empress to think of forming a conspiracy against her.

"So far from profiting by such counsels, the princess had the imprudent frankness to talk of them to Orloff, who found no difficulty in justifying himself, and learnt besides only to employ dissimulation and address.

"Not satisfied with feeding the ambition of the young Russian, he affected a violent passion for her, which quickly inspired her with a very serious one for him. As soon as he was sure of this, he conjured her to unite herself with him by the most sacred of bonds.

"In a most unfortunate moment she yielded consent; and it was even with transport that the unfortunate maiden promised to consummate a marriage which was to accomplish her destruction. She believed that the title of wife to Alexis Orloff would prove an impregnable security against the terrors with which she was haunted. She could not believe it possible for a man to abuse the sanctions of religion, and ties the most sacred, to pursue an innocent victim to perdition.

"But was there no obligation of religion, was there a sacredness of engagement that could bind the monster who deluded her? Could the man who strangled the unfortunate Peter III. feel remorse at dishonoring the daughter of Elizabeth?

"Affecting to wish the marriage ceremony might be celebrated conformably to the ritual of the Greek Church, he suborned villains of an inferior order to fill up the parts of priests and lawyers. Thus profanation allied itself to imposture to overwhelm the feeble and too confident Tarrakanoff.

"As soon as Orloff had become the husband, or rather the ravisher, of this unfortunate princess, he represented to her that a residence at Rome exposed her to too much observation, and that it would be better for her to retire to some other city of Italy, and wait for the moment when the match would be applied to the conspiracy which was to raise her to the throne.

"Believing the advice to be dictated by love and prudence, she replied to the perfidious Orloff that she would follow him wherever he pleased to carry her. He immediately conveyed her to Pisa, where he had some time before hired a magnificent palace.

"There he continued to treat her with every mark of respect and tenderness; but he never allowed her to be approached by any but persons in his own pay, and when she went to the theater or to the public walks he always accompanied her himself.

"The division of the Russian squadron under the command of Rear-Admiral Greig had just returned to the port of Leghorn. On communicating this intelligence to the princess, Orloff told her that it was necessary for him to repair thither to give orders to the fleet, and made her an offer to be of the party.

"She consented the more readily that she had frequently heard the beauty of Leghorn and the magnificence of the Russian ships of war highly extolled. Imprudent creature! The nearer she approached the point at which Orloff was to accomplish his horrible purpose, the greater the confidence she reposed in the tenderness and sincerity of that traitor.

"She left Pisa with her usual retinue. On arriving at Leghorn, she alighted at the house of the English consul, Dick, who had prepared apartments for her under his roof, and received her with every mark of the most profound respect.

"The ladies of the rear-admiral and of the consul hastened to present themselves to her, and never quitted her more. She beheld herself surrounded by a numerous court, every one vying with another to outrun her slightest wishes, and seeming to have no object but incessantly to procure for her new pleasures.

"When she went abroad the populace crowded into her way. At the theater all eyes were directed on her. Everything conspired to complete the delusion; everything kept out of sight the danger ready to burst upon her head.

"It is undoubtedly painful to think that a consul, an English admiral, and their wives could have been so vile, so lost to humanity, as to decoy into the snare, with perfidious homage and caresses, a victim whose youth, beauty, and innocence ought to have melted hearts the most insensible. Everything proves, nevertheless, that they were associates in the plot contrived to entrap her, and that they practiced every art to gain her confidence, only to betray her with more certain effect.*

"The young Tarrakanoff was so far from entertaining any apprehension of her misfortune that, after having passed some days in amusement and dissipation, she herself expressed a desire to visit the Russian squadron.

"This idea was highly applauded. The necessary orders were immediately issued; and next day, on rising from the table, all was prepared on the beach for the reception of the princess.

"Thither she went; she was put on board a barge, superbly decorated. The English consul, his wife, and the wife of Rear-Admiral Greig, took their seats beside her, and a second barge carried the rear-admiral and Orloff; and a third, filled with English and Russian officers, closed the procession.

"The barges left the shore in sight of an innumerable multitude of spectators, and were welcomed by the squadron with bands of music, salutes from the artillery, and repeated huzzas.

"When the princess approached the ship on board of which she was to be received, a magnificent accommodation chair was lowered, in which they made her sit down, and hoisted her gently on deck; observing to her that these were the particular honors paid to her rank.

"But scarcely is she on board when her hands are loaded with irons. To no purpose does she implore compassion from the unrelenting Orloff, whom she still addresses by the name of husband. To no purpose does she throw herself at his feet and bedew them with her tears. The barbarian does not as much as deign to reply.

"They carry her down to the bottom of the hold. The next day the vessel sails for Russia.

"Upon her arrival at St. Petersburgh the youthful victim was shut up in the fortress, and treated in the most barbarous manner. Six years afterwards the waters of the Neva put a period to her misery. She was drowned in her prison.

"The inhabitants of Leghorn, meanwhile, who had seen the

prisoner embark, soon learned with horror that, instead of a banquet, which she was taught to expect on board the squadron, she had found irons only.

"Leopold, Grand Duke of Tuscany, whose territorial rights had just been so shamefully violated, wrote immediately to Vienna and St. Petersburgh, complaining of the outrage. But Alexis Orloff insolently braved both the complaints of Leopold and the indignation of the public.

"Some of the English degraded themselves so far as to assist in the machinations of Orloff, but others were very far from approving his conduct. They even blushed to serve under him, and gave in their resignations. Of this number was Admiral Elphingston. Greig succeeded him."

In this connection it may be as well to give the author's account of the trick played on Paul Jones, the great naval hero of our Revolution, by the cunning Catharine.

It is well known that Paul Jones served in the Russian navy for a time, and that he was disgusted with his treatment therein; but the immediate cause of his retirement from Catharine's service is not so well understood.

The empress had given the command of a vessel to the pirate Paul Jones, who had distinguished himself by his intrepidity in the American war. The English officers employed in the Russian fleet had not been previously informed of this; and whether it was that some agent of their nation secretly irritated them, or that they were really offended at serving with a man whom they regarded as a traitor, they repaired to the President of the Board of Admiralty, and declared that they would no longer remain in a squadron to which Paul Jones belonged.

The empress, informed of this measure, and knowing that seven out of eight of her ships ran the risk of being totally deprived of officers, concealed her vexation, and withdrew Paul Jones from serving in the fleet.

"That she might not appear to yield to circumstances, she resolved to give him employment in the Black Sea, and ordered him to go and join Potemkin. Paul Jones departed immediately, and distinguished himself at the battle of Leinar, and was rewarded for it with the ribbon of St. Anne.

"But having accused the Prince of Nassau Siegen of not understanding how to profit by his advantages, he involved himself in a quarrel with that admiral, and returned to St. Petersburgh, where, in a very short time, means were found to get rid of him.

"A young girl was sent into the inn in which the sailor lodged, who, in offering him some trifles for sale, cast a few tender glances upon him. He thought himself in duty bound to reply to them. The young girl screamed out. The officers of the police, who were just at hand, entered, and Paul Jones was obliged to quit Russia."

What beautiful consistency the hireling Englishmen displayed in refusing to serve with Paul Jones, after they had assisted Orloff in one of the basest acts of treachery ever perpetrated on an innocent and defenseless woman!

But the brave Paul Jones had given them many a sound thrashing, and they could never forgive him for his noble work in defense of American liberty. They could serve under such wretches as Greig and Orloff, but they could not fight side by side with a man who had so often lowered the Union Jack in their own waters!

After Catharine had banished Gregory Orloff from Russia, the wretch spent ten years in traveling in other countries; but his eye was all the time fixed on the empress and the throne of Russia.

The historian cannot inform us whether he was recalled again by the empress, or whether he ventured before her of his own option, but certain it is that he appeared at St. Petersburgh again after two years of exile, and was received by his mistress in a kindly manner. Her last lover was dismissed, Orloff was appointed in his place as chamberlain; and Catharine, although she declared that she loved him no more, bestowed many marks of favor on the ambitious man whose audacity and power caused her much fear.

The historian then gives us a very lucid account of Catharine's next love adventure:

"The post of favorite had been restored to Gregory Orloff really from policy. Policy may assume the semblance of love, but does not command it. Catharine affected for her ancient lover a passion. She no longer felt she was lavish of her caresses, but she no longer opened her heart to him.

"Orloff deceived himself, then, in supposing he was the sole cause of Wassiltschikoff's dismission. This sacrifice had been made to another and not to him.

"A considerable period had elapsed since the empress had remarked the manly beauty and graceful demeanor of Potemkin. She recollected, with complacency, that on the day of the revolution in 1762, Potemkin, then a very young man, seized the instant of her mounting on horseback to present his sword-knot to her.

'She wished at length to know him more intimately; and the first interview she had with him secured to this new lover the advantage over all his rivals.

"Wassiltschikoff was dismissed. Orloff was resumed, and gave disgust. Potemkin alone administered consolation in secret for the solicitude occasioned by the war, the terrors which rebellion inspired, and the misunderstanding which prevailed between the ancient favorite and the prime minister Panin.

"Potemkin was presumptuous. His good fortune inebriated him. His pride soon met with its punishment.

"One day when he was playing billiards with Alexis Orloff he had the assurance to boast of the favor he enjoyed, and asserted that it depended entirely on himself to procure the banishment from court of all who fell under his displeasure. Alexis Orloff retorted in a haughty style. A scuffle ensued, and Potemkin received a blow which struck out one of his eyes.

"This was not the full extent of his misfortune. Gregory Orloff, informed of the whole affair by his brother, flew to the empress and insisted on Potemkin's dismission.

"Potemkin retired to Smolensko, the place of his birth, where he remained almost a year in solitude, suffering severely from his eye, and under the languor of banishment from court. He sometimes gave out that it was his intention to turn monk; at other times he predicted that he should become the most powerful man in Russia.

"At length he suddenly thought of writing to the empress, beseeching her to think of him. The empress instantly dispatches his recall, and completely restores him to power.

"Orloff had been out upon a hunting match for several days. Advantage was taken of his absence to install Potemkin in the palace; and when the ancient favorite returned, neither complaints nor reproaches could shake the credit of the new one.

"It may be necessary in this place to unfold what were the duties and the distinctions of Catharine's favorites. When that empress had made choice of a new favorite she conferred on him the rank of aide-de-camp, that he might accompany her wherever she went without furnishing any occasion for censure.

"From that time forward the favorite occupied apartments in the palace, under those of the empress, and which had a communication with them by a private staircase.

"The first day of his first installment he received a present of 100,-000 roubles, and every month found 12,000 on his toilet. The purveyor of the court had orders to keep up for him a table of twenty-four covers, and to defray the whole expense of his household.

"The favorite was obliged to attend the empress on all her excursions; he could not leave the palace without asking and obtaining permission. He scarcely durst venture to chat with other women; for if he meant to keep his place it was incumbent on him to take care how he awakened the sovereign's jealousy.

"As often as the empress fixed her eyes on a subject with the view of raising him to the post of favorite, she contrived to have him invited to dinner by some one of her confidants, to whom she paid a visit, as if by accident. There she conversed with the stranger, and endeavored to find out whether he was worthy of the favor to which she destined him.

"When her judgment proved favorable, a look conveyed the knowledge of it to the confidant, who in turn communicated the intelligence to him who had the honor to please. Next day he received a visit from the court physician, who came to inquire into the state of his health, and the same evening accompanied the empress to the hermitage, and took possession of the apartment prepared for him.

"It was when the choice fell upon Potemkin that these formalities were first settled. Since then they have been constantly observed.

"When a favorite ceased to please, there was likewise a particular mode of ousting him. He received orders to travel. From that moment he saw the empress no more. But he was sure of finding at the place to which he repaired rewards worthy of Catharine's pride."

The dismissal of Potemkin, and the taking up of another favorite by the volatile Catharine, is thus described by the French historian:

"Scarcely had she returned to St. Petersburgh when Potemkin ceased to be the object of her tender affections. She loaded him with benefits.

"It appeared as if she had not honors and dignities enough to lavish upon him. She professed to love him, and him only, and her heart was already decidedly bestowed on another.

"A young Ukranian, named Zawadoffsky, was secretly in possession of her favors. She began with making him her secretary. Almost immediately she openly avowed him to be her favorite.

"This change produced a scene very extraordinary at the court of Catharine. When she had once issued an order, there was an apparent impossibility of its remaining unexecuted. She insisted, in every case, on being obeyed.

"Now it is well known that the disgraced favorite always received orders to set out upon his travels, and that he was never more permitted to present himself to the empress till she vouchsafed to recall him.

"The lofty Orloff himself had submitted to the regulation. Potemkin had the boldness to neglect it.

"When he received the fatal order he feigned compliance, and the next day came and very calmly took his place opposite the empress, at the moment she was going to make up her party at whist.

"Without expressing displeasure at Potemkin's presumption and disobedience, Catharine held out a card to him, and told him he was a very fortunate player, without saying a word about him withdrawing from court. Potemkin retained his honors, his employments, his credit, and from being the lover, became the friend of the empress.

"Zawadoffsky possessed the art of pleasing; but Potemkin rendered himself useful; and his genius, more analogous to the genius of Catharine than that of any other of her lovers, ceased not to maintain its ascendancy.

"Orloff, however, who had been informed rather too hastily of Potemkin's disgrace, flew to St. Petersburgh. There he found his rival still enjoying, not the love, but the confidence of the empress.

"Orloff believed it possible for him to recover that confidence while a lover, young and unacquainted with politics, occupied the heart of Catharine. He was speedily undeceived.

"He made his appearance at the court, kissed the empress' hand, and observing Potemkin in habits of intimacy with her, instantly withdrew, and found his way back to Moscow.

"Courtiers the most habituated to study the empress could not divine which was the preferred lover. They did not believe that Potemkin would tamely surrender the claims which he had upon the heart of that princess. They forgot that in the presence of ambition love is mute.

"Gregory Orloff, who had returned to court without being recalled, seemed to have been insensibly reconciled to behold

Potemkin occupying the first place by the side of Catharine's throne. Potemkin, elated with the credit he possessed, and more solicitous to preserve unlimited power than the affections of the empress, permitted her to indulge her inclinations toward Zuwadoffsky.

"For eighteen months this last occupied the place of subaltern favorite, when all at once his ambition caught fire. He had the example of Potemkin before his eyes. He believed it possible, like him, to pass from the arms of the empress into the post of prime minister.

"But in order to do this it was necessary to drive Potemkin from it. To this arduous undertaking he vigorously applied himself. He endeavored to render the despotism of Potemkin hateful to the sovereign. He got himself seconded by discontented officers, by envious courtiers, by women of ability and intrigue.

"Potemkin, informed of these cabals, and more intelligent than his rival, resolved to supplant him. Chance almost instantly furnished him with an opportunity.

"A young Servian named Zoritz, an officer of hussars, had come to St. Petersburgh to solicit preferment. He was tall, very finely formed, and very well calculated to excite the inclinations of a voluptuous woman.

"Potemkin, who was well acquainted with Catharine's inconstancy and violence of appetite, gave Zoritz a captain's commission, and made him throw himself in the empress' way. She did not fail to distinguish him. The next day Zawadoffsky was dismissed. Zoritz replaced him.

"Zawadoffsky, who had already received so many substantial marks of Catharine's bounty, got, at the moment of his dismissal, a gratuity of 90,000 roubles, an addition of 40,000 to his annual pension, and a considerable landed estate.

"Zoritz at the same time received an estate in land worth 120,000 roubles, besides the usual presents, a great part of which the greedy Potemkin took care to squeeze out of him.

"This new lover, without education, without experience, could not possibly give umbrage to the lofty Potemkin. Content with ministering in obscurity to the pleasures of the empress, the only advantage he derived from the favor he possessed was to strengthen the credit of the man to whom he was indebted for it.

"It was with Potemkin alone that Catharine weighed the destinies of Europe.

"But though Catharine frequently changed her lover, her inclination to love was always the same. The Servian Zoritz had fixed her during a year, and had received considerable presents and the rank of major general.

"Potemkin was neither jealous of the fortune nor the favors which Zoritz enjoyed. He supported him, on the contrary, in the apprehension of seeing him succeeded by some more dangerous rival.

"Catharine herself appeared every day more satisfied with her favorite. But all at once she sent him an order to quit the court.

"Zoritz immediately hastened to complain to Potemkin, who took upon him to demand of the empress what could be the cause of the disgrace of his protégé.

"'Last night I loved him; to-day I love him no longer,' replied the empress. 'Perhaps had he been better educated I should love him still; but his ignorance makes me blush. He can speak nothing but Russian. He must travel through France and England in order to learn foreign languages.'

"Potemkin respected the caprice of his sovereign. Zoritz took his departure for France.

"The same day Potemkin, employing himself in looking out for a successor to Zoritz, and going to pass the evening at the hermitage, perceived with astonishment, behind the arm-chair of Catharine, a chamberlain whom he did not know.

"This was Rinsky Korzakoff. From the obscure rank of sergeant of the guards, Korzakoff had been suddenly elevated to that of aid-de-camp to the empress, and honored with all the

benefits which the generosity of that empress usually lavished upon her favorites.

"Korzakoff was endowed with a fine figure and a very elegant air; but having neither wit nor understanding, it was not in his power, any more than Zoritz, to undermine the credit of Potemkin. Besides, he disarmed his jealousy by sacrificing to his avarice.

"A single fact will suffice to unfold the character of Korzakoff. As soon as he had obtained the place of favorite, he thought a man like him should of necessity purchase a library. He immediately summoned the most famous bookseller in St. Petersburgh, and told him he wished to have some books, that he might place them in the palace of Wassiltschikoff, of which the empress had just made him a present.

"The bookseller ask ed him what kind of books he preferred.

"'You know better than I do,' replied the favorite; 'that is your concern. Large books at the bottom, small ones atop. This is the way they are placed in the library of the empress.'"

The fall of this favorite was brought about by his own caprice and vanity. The historian disposes of him as readily as Catharine could take up with a new lover.

"Korzakoff was at that time beloved of the empress. The benefits, the honors with which she overwhelmed him, ought to have inspired him if not with love, at least with gratitude; but he possessed only thoughtlessness and vanity.

"The Countess de Brisac, who saw him every day about the empress, conceived an inclination for him. She could not, however, give herself up at first to this propensity. The constraint in which the lovers of Catharine lived allowed them but little opportunity for infidelities.

"Potemkin assisted the Countess de Brisac to overcome every obstacle. He took upon himself the charge of being her confidant; he furnished her with the means of having secret interviews with Korzakoff; and although he had some esteem for the favorite, he resolved to sacrifice him, in the hope of involving in his ruin the sister of Romanzoff.

"The project of Potemkin succeeded. The empress was not slow of discovering that she was deceived by her favorite and by her friend. She immediately ordered the one to travel out of her empire, and the other to repair to Moscow.

"She resolved henceforth that she would not again have a female friend, but she could not so easily form the resolution to dispense with a favorite.

"The same day Lanskoi, a chevalier-garde of the most beautiful and most interesting figure, was upon duty at the door of the empress, when General Tolstoi was struck with his graceful mien, and caused his sovereign to remark it.

"From this moment the choice of Catharine was decided; and it will be seen in the sequel of this work that of all her lovers, Lanskoi was the one whom she most loved, and who was the most worthy of being loved."

The miserable death of Gregory Orloff is thus described by the historian:

"A destiny still more tremendous was reserved for Gregory Orloff. Though he continued to be under an accumulation of benefits from the empress, and was the husband of a young and beautiful woman, the sight of new favorites was insupportable to him.

"He passed by far the greater part of the last years of his life in travelling. In 1782 he stopped at Lausanne, where he saw his wife breathe her last. This loss plunged him into a deep melancholy.

"He immediately returned to court, but only to exhibit the mournful spectacle of mental derangement. Sometimes he gave vent to excessive gayety, which exposed him to the derision of the courtiers. Sometimes the reproaches he thundered out against the empress made all who heard him to shudder and sink herself in sorrow and disquietude.

"At last it was found necessary to oblige him to retire to Moscow. There his remorse awoke with redoubled fury. The bloody shade of Peter III. pursued him wherever he went; he saw it incessantly calling for vengeance, and perished in despair."

Then we have an account of the death of the Catharine's favorite lover, her anguish on the occasion, and the intrigues set on foot as to the selecting of his successor.

"Lanskoi lived on good terms with Potemkin, and became every day dearer to the empress. The education of this favorite had been neglected. Catharine exerted herself to remedy the defect. She enriched his mind with knowledge the most useful, and admired in him the fruits of her own labor. But this satisfaction came to a period.

"Lanskoi excited Potemkin's jealousy. Perhaps he failed in paying proper respect to that despot. He was seized with a violent distemper, and expired, in the flower of life, in the empress' arms, who lavished on him, to the very last moment, every expression of the most passionate love.

"When he ceased to breathe, she abandoned herself to all the bitterness of grief. For several days she refused nourishment of every kind, and remained three months at one of her private palaces without stirring abroad.

"She afterwards reared a very beautiful mausoleum to Lanskoi; and more than ten years after, her attendants having accidentally conducted her within sight of that monument, she was seen suddenly to dissolve into a flood of tears.

"Potemkin undertook to cure Catharine of this excess of sorrow. He was almost the only person who could penetrate into the solitude in which she had buried herself. He acquired still more of the ascendancy he had over her, and whether from gratitude, whether from weakness, she wished, it is said, to unite herself to him by indissoluble bonds, and gave him her hand in secret.

"Marriage could no more fix the inclinations of Potemkin than those of Catharine. He soon thought of liberating himself from the duties which that tie imposed, and of delegating them to a favorite younger and more complaisant than himself.

"Every courtier who looked for preferment wished to see the place left open by the death of Lanskoi filled up by a personage who would share with them the favors annexed to it.

"The Princess d'Aschkoff employed all her arts to procure it for her son. Her intrigues appeared for a moment to be crowned with success.

"The young Prince d'Aschkoff was tall, well made, and of a figure well adapted to make some impression on the heart of the empress.

"Potemkin, who perceived the engines put in motion to bring it about, took care not to give it an avowed opposition, lest contradiction should whet Catharine's appetite and determine her choice.

"Affecting, on the contrary, an inclination to favor young D'Aschkoff, he tendered civilities to his family, with whom he had hitherto lived on very indifferent terms.

"He had the skill of catching and mimicking with facility the ridiculous traits of the persons with whom he was intimate, and did not neglect to point out to Catharine those of the Princess d'Aschkoff and her son. The empress was highly diverted at it.

"Potemkin next day sent for, one after another, two officers of the guard, Yermoloff and Momonoff, on some trifling commission, to give her an opportunity of seeing them. Catharine decided in favor of the former.

"There happened to be a ball at court, and young D'Aschkoff displayed uncommon magnificence on the occasion. The courtiers imagined his triumph was at hand, and already treated him with the deference which attached to the person of the favorite.

"Potemkin redoubled his attentions to the Princess d'Aschkoff. She was so well pleased with them that, the day after, she wrote him a billet, requesting he would admit into the number of his aides-de-camp the young Count de Bouthourlin, her nephew.

"Potemkin maliciously replied that every place of aide-de-camp was filled, and that the last had just been given away to Lieutenant Yermoloff.

"Both the name and the person who bore it were strange to

Princess d'Aschkoff. That very day she learned to know them, by seeing Yermoloff at the hermitage with the empress."

The fall of Yermoloff was due to his own imprudence and ingratitude. Like very many others in this vain world, he could not stand prosperity.

The historian thus describes his fall:

"Yermoloff had risen to the highest degree of favor. His imprudence tumbled him from it. This favorite, tall, fair, and of a figure which announced total want of feeling, was replete with jealousy.

"He soon showed himself ungrateful to Potemkin, to whom he owed his fortune. He eagerly seized every opportunity of injuring him; and, merely in the view of thwarting him, defended the unfortunate Khan Sahim-Gherai, the payment of whose pension was most scandalously neglected.

"The empress, who became weaker every day, where her lovers were concerned, discovered a degree of coldness towards Potemkin, and also to the French Ambassador, whose credit gave umbrage to Yermoloff.

"Some of the courtiers contributed, by underhand instigations, to sour the temper of Potemkin.

"Yermoloff had an uncle whom Potemkin dismissed with ignominy from the service, in consequence of a quarrel at play, in which the uncle had been on the wrong side. Yermoloff complained to the empress.

"Potemkin had to stand the brunt of the empress' reproaches, and he felt himself so keenly hurt that he haughtily said to her:

"'Madame, make your choice, and dismiss Yermoloff or me; for so long as you keep that white negro my foot shall not enter your doors.'

"That very day Yermoloff received orders to set out on his travels. Momonoff replaced him.

"These intrigues were known only at court. Elsewhere the glory of Catharine was blazoned.

"Momonoff was very much beloved of the empress, and did not requite her tenderness.

"After the example of Potemkin, not content with the magnificent presents which the empress lavished on him, he fraudulently extorted from her immense sums. But he lived with her as a slave, the gold of whose chains did not prevent him from feeling their weight, and not as a lover delighted to please. His heart was not, however, insensible.

"Catharine had in the number of her maids of honor the daughter of Prince Scherbatoff, a pretty young girl, very witty, and with a considerable propensity to gallantry.

"Momonoff was soon captivated with her charms, and made successful love to her. His passion had not yet passed the bounds of respect, when one day he heard Potemkin vaunting of the favor of the Princess Scherbatoff. Momonoff shuddered at it. He knew the unlimited power of Potemkin; he knew that it was sufficient for him to form desires to assure their accomplishment.

"He flew to throw himself at the feet of Princess Scherbatoff, and imparted to her his inquietude. To set his heart at rest, she granted him that which he dreaded being carried off by his rival. But in a short time he had fresh reason to be easy. Potemkin departed for the army.

"This intrigue lasted a considerable time. It was known to all the court. Catharine alone had not perceived it.

"However, the jealousy of the courtiers opened her eyes. She was apprised that Momonoff deceived her, and she had very shortly clear proof of it. However offended she might be at this discovery, she dissembled her resentment. This was during the summer of 1789.

"The court was held at Tzarsko-Zebo, and the daughter of Count de Bruce, one of the richest heiresses of the empire, came to be presented there.

"Catharine, seizing this opportunity, said to Momonoff that she wished him to marry Countess de Bruce. Momonoff supplicated not to exact it of him.

"The empress demanded the reason of his refusal. He was

embarrassed. She insisted; and he fell at at her feet, acknowledging to her that he had pledged his faith to the Princess Scherbatoff.

"She wished for no other explanation. The two lovers were affianced immediately, and a few days after they were married in the chapel of the palace.

"Momonoff ought to have been grateful for the benefits of Catharine, and for the extreme moderation which she exercised towards him. But it is asserted that he had the imprudence to disclose to his wife the details of his secret interviews with the empress, and that the wife revealed them with a levity injurious to the sovereign.

"It is added that the empress avenged herself in a terrible manner.

"At a time when Momonoff and his wife were in bed, the chief of the police at Moscow entered their apartment, and after having shown them an order from the empress, left them in the hands of six women, and withdrew himself into a neighboring room.

"Upon this the six women, or rather the six men dressed in women's clothes, seized the babbling offender, and having stripped her entirely naked, whipped her with rods in presence of Momonoff, whom they had obliged to remain on his knees.

"When the chastisement had been inflicted, the chief of police re-entered and said:

"'This is the mode in which the empress punishes a first indiscretion. For the second, the delinquent is banished to Siberia.'

"The very day of Momonoff's marriage, the place of favorite was bestowed on Plato Zouboff, an officer of the horse-guards.

"Potemkin heard with no little vexation that the choice of Catharine had fallen upon Zouboff. He wrote to her on the subject, and made use of all his efforts to prevail on her to change 'r lover. But from the first day of his elevation, Zouboff had , well understood how to please, that he no longer feared a rival.

"The empress sent word to Potemkin that, as he had no just reason to complain of Zouboff, she could not resolve to give him his dismissal.

"Notwithstanding this, Potemkin still insisted for some time longer.

"'When thou seest the empress,' he said, to one of the courtiers who carried his dispatches to court, 'remark to her that I have teeth from which I suffer considerable uneasiness, and that I shall not be quiet until I have got rid of them.'

"This was a silly play on words. The name of Zouboff signifies teeth in the Russian language."

The death of this ambitious and voluptuous woman, who had had extended the power of Russia by conquest and policy, is thus described by the historian:

"But death blasted her hopes. On the morning of November 6th, 1796, she was tolerably gay, and drank coffee as usual. Some time after she retired to her closet as usual.

"After an interval of half an hour, her female attendants, finding that she did not reappear, began to be uneasy. They went in, and found the empress stretched on the floor, with her feet against the door.

"Dr. Rogerson, her first physician, was called in, who, supposing it to be a fit of apoplexy, ordered her to be bled twice.

"The empress appeared at first to be somewhat relieved, but it was impossible for him to give a decided opinion, and at ten in the evening she expired."

The French author concludes his history of this very remarkable woman by giving a statement of the amounts received by her numerous favorites during her lifetime. As this is a very interesting document, we present it to our readers as we find it in the history:

	Roubles
The five brothers ORLOFF received 45,000 peasants, and in lands, palaces, jewels, plate, and ready money	17,000,000
WISOTSKY, an officer of the guards, in favor about two months	300,000
WASSILTSCHIKOFF, a simple lieutenant of the guards, received the twenty months he was in favor, an estate of land, with 7,000 peasants valued at	600,000
In ready money	100,000
In jewels	60,000
In plate	60,000
A palace furnished	100,000
A pension of 20,000 roubles, worth about . .	200,000
	1,110,000
POTEMKIN received the two first years about nine millions. He afterwards accumulated vast wealth. He had great estates in Poland, and in all the provinces of Russia. One of his chests was filled with gold, diamonds, and bank-bills on London, Amsterdam and Venice. His fortune was valued at.	50,000,000
ZAWADOFFSKY received, in eighteen months, lands in Poland, with 2000 peasants, in the Ukraine with 5000, and in Russia with 1800. The whole valued at . . .	1,000,000
He received in money, ...	150,000
In plate	60,000
In jewels.	80,000
And a pension from the privy purse of 10,000 roubles, worth	100,000
	1,390,000
ZORITZ received, in one year, the Ribbon of the Swedish order of the Sword, and that of the White Eagle of Poland. An estate in Poland of	500,000
One in Lithuania of fifty hacks, worth . .	100,000
In money	600,000
In jewels	200,000
	1,420,000
KORSAKOFF received, in sixteen months, the Ribbon of the White Eagle of Poland, and the palace of Wassiltschikoff, which had been repurchased	100,000
An estate with 4,000 peasants	400,000
In money and jewels	150,000
To pay his debts	100,000
To equip him for traveling	100,000
Gratuity on his travels	70,000
	820,000
LANSKOI received in money or lands . . .	7,000,000
In diamonds	80,000
To pay his debts	80,000
A palace valued at	100,000
	7,260,000
Besides, his sister and cousin were admitted into the number of the maids of honor of the empress, and received many presents, of which no valuation can be made.	
YERMOLOFF received, in sixteen months, the Ribbon of the White Eagle of Poland, and an estate valued at . .	100,000
Another, with 3,000 peasants	300,000
In money	150,000
	550,000
MOMONOFF received, in twenty-six months, in land . .	900,000
In money	200,000
In jewels	80,000
	880,000
PLATO ZOUBOFF was decorated with the title of prince and with several ribbons, and appointed grand-master of artillery. He received immense estates in Russia, in Poland, and in Courland. His fortune, exclusive of movables and jewels, amounted to an annual revenue of about 100,000 roubles, and is consequently estimated at . 2,500,000	
Furniture and jewels	200,000
	2,700,000
VALERIAN ZOUBOFF received a great deal of money, lands in Poland and Courland,and a pension of 12,000 roubles, payable in gold. The whole may be estimated at	800,000
	84,000,000
To these presents must be added the expense of the favorite, calculated at 250,000 roubles a year, which amounts, during the 34 years that Catharine's reign lasted, to . .	8,500,000
Total	92,820,000

This sum is about equal to $96,650,000.

Hence it appears how magnificently Catharine rewarded the attachment of her lovers.

She was equally generous to her ministers, her generals, and to any one about her person.

In excuse for a profusion which sometimes had the appearance of bearing an extravagant proportion to the state of other finances, she used to say:

"My pretended prodigality is real economy. All this remains in the country, and returns to me one day."

THE FATAL LOVE INTRIGUES OF ANNE BOLEYN, SECOND WIFE OF HENRY VIII., OF ENGLAND.

ANNE BOLEYN'S FRAIL SISTER—THE KING DISCOVERS AN ANGEL—JEALOUSY AND RAGE—THE INJURED QUEEN'S PREDICTION—QUEEN ANNE'S LOVERS—THE SAUCY RIVAL—THE SCENE AT THE MASKED BALL—RETRIBUTION IN DEATH.

"BLUFF King Harry," he was called by the stout English yeomen of the time; for he was brave and strong and handsome, and he delighted in all the sports of the field, in rough tournaments, and in stirring warfare.

He is famed in history as the "King of Many Wives," some of whom he disposed of in a summary manner, while it would be impossible to give a correct account of his numerous mistresses.

When he was in his nineteenth year, King Henry married Catherine of Arragon, who was his brother's widow. Catherine was some years older than her royal husband, but she was a very beautiful and highly accomplished woman, tender and loving, and she was devotedly attached to her handsome young husband.

After he had lived with Catherine for some eighteen years, during which time several children were born to them, it suddenly dawned on the conscience-stricken Henry that he was committing a great crime while sharing his couch with the widow of his brother. The mere fact that Catherine's charms were on the decline had no influence with the good king whatever. He only thought of the salvation of his soul; and to save that immortal soul, it was very necessary to put his wife aside, and take up with one who was not connected with him by any former ties of kindred.

About the time that King Harry became inspired with the idea that he was committing mortal sin while living with his brother's widow, it happened that his queen had a very charming young maid of honor whose name was Mary Boleyn. Queen Catherine soon noticed that her conscience-stricken husband was often found paying homage to this young damsel, and that Mary was not averse to receiving the smiles and the favors of her royal master.

Perhaps the young girl pitied the penitent Harry, who was a very handsome fellow, and that she endeavored to offer him consolation in pure sympathy only; but it does seem strange that the unreasonable queen should grow jealous of the young favorite, and that she should offer to chide her for her charitable and innocent conduct. Kings will repent in company, and queens should not be jealous of their maids of honor.

This very unreasonable queen carried her jealousy so far, on a certain evening, as to invite Mary Boleyn into her private chamber, and to then and there question her as to the nature of the consolation offered to King Harry. Poor Mary, with tears in her eyes, was obliged to confess her fault. She had loved the handsome Harry "not wisely but too well."

Poor Mary Boleyn, in order to hide the consequences of her fault, soon married a poor young gentleman named William Carey, and then the penitent King Harry had to seek consolation in another quarter.

Now it so happened that Mary Boleyn had a younger sister, who was called Anne. This Anne was still more charming than her older sister; she was very witty and highly accomplished; and as she had passed some years of her young life in the gay court of France, she was well skilled in all the arts of coquetry.

Moreover, while Anne was a great lover of pleasure, and while it was asserted that she had lavished her smiles and caresses on other lovers of her youth, she was possessed of an ambitious spirit.

The penitent King Harry was still seeking consolation in the country when he first encountered the fair Anne Boleyn in her father's garden at Hever. The meeting was accidental, but it was not the less pleasant for all that. The king was so delighted with Anne that on his return to Westminster he told Cardinal Wolsey "that he had been conversing with a young lady who had the wit of an angel, and who was worthy of a crown."

Very soon after that chance meeting Anne was appointed maid of honor to the queen.

The first thing the winning Anne did on entering her new career was to engage in a love affair with Henry, Lord Percy, the eldest son of the Earl of Northumberland, and at the very time when she was engaged in marriage to another gentleman.

In the meantime King Harry had his eye on the two lovers, and more especially on Anne, to whom he had become very much attracted.

Young Percy was compelled to wed a young lady to whom he had been engaged, and Anne was sent back to her father's house.

Anne was not fully aware of the king's jealousy, and she could not understand why her intrigue with the noble Percy was crushed in such a summary manner. On due reflection, she blamed Cardinal Wolsey for her great love disappointment, and she became the enemy of that powerful prelate during her lifetime.

When Anne was in retirement for some time, the penitent king paid her a visit at her father's house, but Anne would not receive him. On his arrival, she withdrew to her chamber, and pleaded indisposition as the cause of her not appearing in the reception-room.

The young beauty soon learned that she had made an impression on Harry; but she was determined that she would not offer consolation to the penitent after the manner of her erring sister.

Then Harry commenced the siege by conferring great honors on Anne's father, who was base enough to countenance the disgrace of his daughter in order to advance his own fortunes. The coy maiden was also invited to return to court.

There is no doubt that Anne was deeply in love with Percy at that time, and that this love inspired her to reject the dishonorable proposals made to her by the amorous king.

The blunt king was not long in finding an opportunity of declaring his love for Anne. Finding her alone in one of the private chambers of the court he presented her with some costly jewels, and declared that he loved her only too well. Anne recoiled from the king with real apparent abhorrence, and falling on her knees before him she replied:

"I think, most noble and worthy king, your majesty speaks those words in mirth to prove me, without the intent of degrading your princely self. Therefore, to ease you of the labor of asking me any such question hereafter, I beseech your highness most earnestly to desist, and take this my answer (which I speak from the depth of my soul) in good part. Most noble king, I would rather lose my life than my virtue, which will be the greatest and best part of the dowry I shall bring to my husband."

Henry was a little nonplussed at this decided refusal, as he was not accustomed to rebuffs from the fair maids of his court.

After pressing his suit with all the ardor of a royal lover, and still feeling that Anne was not to be conquered, he inquired:

"May I not hope, at least?"

"I understand not, most mighty king," replied Anne in proud tones, "how you shall retain such hope. Your wife I cannot be, both in respect of mine own unworthiness and also because you have a queen already. Your mistress I will not be."

Very soon after this interview, Anne Boleyn returned to the Court of France; and it was four years afterwards ere her royal lover had another opportunity of paying his addresses.

Through the instigations of her base and ambitious father, the young charmer was again induced to resume her place as maid of honor to Catherine of Arragon, who was then in great distress

"No," replied Anne. "Let this dame be dismissed."

"I shall not go at your bidding, minion!" cried Catherine, fiercely.

"Ah!" cried Anne, starting, "whom have we here!"

"One you had better have avoided," whispered Henry.

"The queen!" exclaimed Anne, with a look of dismay.

"Ay, the queen!" echoed Catherine, unmasking, "Henry, if you have any respect left for me, I pray you, order this woman from my presence. Let me depart in peace."

"Lady Anne, I pray you retire," said Henry.

But Anne stood her ground resolutely.

"Nay, let her stay, then," said the queen; "and I promise you she shall repent her rashness. And do you stay too, Henry, and regard well her whom you are about to make your spouse. Question your sister Mary, somewhile consort to Louis the Twelfth, and now Duchess of Suffolk—question her as to the character and conduct of Anne Boleyn, when she was her attendant at the court of France—ask whether she had never to reprove her for levity—question the Lord Percy as to her love for him—question Sir Thomas Wyatt, and a host of others."

"All these charges are false and calumnious," cried Anne Boleyn.

"Let the king inquire and judge for himself," rejoined Catherine, "and if he weds you, let him look well to you, or you will make him a scoff to all honorable men. And now, as you have come between him and me—as you have divided husband and wife—for the intent, whether successful or not, I denounce you before Heaven, and invoke the wrath upon your head. Night and day, I will pray that you may be brought to shame; and when I shall be called hence, as I may be soon, I will appear before the throne of the Most High, and summon you to judgment."

"Take me from her, Henry," cried Anne, faintly; "her violence affrights me."

"No, you shall stay," said Catherine, grasping her arm, and detaining her, "you shall hear your doom. You imagine your career will be a brilliant one, and that you will be able to wield the scepter you wrongfully wrest from me, but it will molder into dust in your hand—the crown unjustly placed upon your brow will fall to the ground, and it will bring the head with it."

"Take me away, Henry, I implore you!" cried Anne.

"You *shall* hear me out," pursued Catherine, exerting all her strength, and maintaining her grasp—"or I will follow you down you aisles, and pour forth my malediction against you in the hearing of all your attendants. You have braved me, and shall feel my power. Look at her, Henry—see how she shrinks before the gaze of an injured woman. Look me in the face, minion—you cannot!—you dare not!"

"Oh, Henry!" sobbed Anne.

"You have brought it upon yourself," said the king.

"She has," replied Catherine; "and unless she pauses and repents, she will bring yet more upon her head. You suffer now. minion, but how will you feel when, in your turn, you are despised, neglected, and supplanted by a rival—when the false glitter of your charms having passed away, Henry will see only your faults—and will open his eyes to all I now tell him?"

A sob was all the answer Anne could return.

"You will feel as I feel towards you," pursued the queen—"hatred towards her; but you will not have the consolations I enjoy. You will have merited your fate; and you will then think upon me and my woes, and will bitterly, but unavailingly, repent your conduct. And now, Henry," she exclaimed, turning solemnly to him, "you have pledged your royal word to me, and given me your hand upon it, that if you find this woman false to you, she shall expiate her offense on the block. I call upon you to ratify the pledge in her presence."

"I do so, Catherine," replied the king. "The mere suspicion of her guilt shall be enough."

"Henry!" exclaimed Anne.

"I have said it," replied the king.

"Tremble, then, Anne Boleyn!" cried Catherine, "tremble! and when you are adjudged to die the death of an adulteress,

bethink you of the prediction of the queen you have injured. I may not live to witness your fate, but we shall meet before the throne of an eternal judge."

"Oh, Henry, this is too much!" gasped Anne. And she sank fainting into his arms.

"Begone!" cried the king, furiously. "You have killed her!'

"It were well for us both if I had done so," replied Catherine. "But she will recover to work my misery and her own. To your hands I commit her punishment. May God bless you, Henry!" With this she replaced her mask, and quitted the chapel.

Henry, meanwhile, anxious to avoid the comments of his attendants, exerted himself to restore Anne Boleyn to sensibility, and his efforts were speedily successful.

"Is it, then, reality?" gasped Anne, as she gazed around. "I hoped it was a hideous dream. Oh, Henry, this has been frightful! But you will not kill me, as she predicted! Swear to me you will not!"

"Why should you be alarmed?" rejoined the king. "If you are faithful, you have nothing to fear."

"But you said suspicion, Henry—you said suspicion!" cried Anne.

"You must put the greater guard upon your conduct," replied the king, moodily. "I begin to think there is some truth in Catherine's insinuations."

"Oh! no; I swear to you there is not," said Anne—"I have trifled with the gallants of Francis's court, and have listened, perhaps too complacently, to the love-vows of Percy and Wyatt, but when your majesty deigned to cast eyes upon me, all others vanished as the stars of night before the rising of the god of day. Henry, I love you deeply, devotedly—but Catherine's terrible imprecations make me feel more keenly than I have ever done before the extent of the wrong I am about to inflict upon her—and I fear that retributive punishment will follow it."

"You will do her no wrong," replied Henry. "I am satisfied of the justice of the divorce, and of its necessity; and if my purposed union with you were out of the question, I should demand it. Be the fault on my head."

"Your words restore me, in some measure, my liege," said Anne. "I love you too well to risk body and soul for you. I am yours forever—ha!" she exclaimed, with a fearful look.

"What ails you, sweetheart?" exclaimed the king.

"I thought I saw a face at the window," she replied—"a black and hideous face like that of a fiend!"

"It was mere fancy," replied the king. "Your mind is disturbed by what has occurred. You had better join your attendants, and retire to your own apartments."

"Oh, Henry!" cried Anne—"do not judge me unheard—do not believe what any false tongue may utter against me. I love only you—and can love only you. I would not wrong you, even in thought, for worlds."

"I believe you, sweetheart," replied the king, tenderly.

So saying, he led her down the aisle to her attendants. They then proceeded together to the royal lodgings, where Anne retired to her own apartments, and Henry withdrew to his private chamber.

Notwithstanding the ravings of his lawful wife, or her own suspicions, Henry procured a divorce, married Anne, and made her queen.

After some years of wedded life, Anne was doomed to feel all the pangs which she had inflicted on poor Catharine of Arragon. Her enemies began to whisper that she was playing false to the king, and latterly had become evident that his passion for her was fast subsiding, if indeed it had not altogether expired.

Though Anne had never truly loved her royal consort, and though at that very time she was secretly encouraging the regards of another, she felt troubled by this change, and watched all the king's movements with jealous anxiety, to ascertain if any one had supplanted her in his affections.

At length her vigilance was rewarded by discovering a rival in one of the loveliest of her dames, Jane Seymour. This fair creature, the daughter of Sir John Seymour, of Wolff Hall, in Wiltshire, and who was afterwards, it is almost needless to say, raised to as high a dignity as Anne Boleyn herself, was now in the very pride of her beauty. Tall, exquisitely proportioned, with a complexion of the utmost brilliancy and delicacy, large, liquid blue eyes, bright chestnut tresses, and lovely features, she possessed charms that could not fail to captivate the amorous monarch. It seems marvelous that Anne Boleyn should have such an attendant; but perhaps she felt confident in her own attractions.

Skilled in intrigue herself, Anne, now that her eyes were opened, perceived all the allurements thrown out by Jane to ensnare the king, and she intercepted many a furtive glance between them. Still she did not dare to interfere. The fierceness of Henry's temper kept her in awe, and she well knew that the slightest opposition would only make him the more determined to run counter to her will. Trusting, therefore, to get rid of Jane Seymour by some stratagem, she resolved not to attempt to dismiss her except as a last resource.

A slight incident occurred, which occasioned a departure from the prudent course she had laid down to herself.

Accompanied by her dames, she was traversing the great gallery of the palace at Greenwich, when she caught the reflection of Jane Seymour, who was following her, in a mirror, regarding a jeweled miniature. She instantly turned round at the sight, and Jane, in great confusion, thrust the picture into her bosom.

"Ah! what have you there?" cried Anne.

"A picture of my father, Sir John Seymour," replied Jane, blushing deeply.

"Let me look at it!" cried Anne, snatching the picture from her. "Ah! call you this your father? To my thinking, it is more like my royal husband. Answer me frankly, minion—answer me, as you value your life! Did the king give you this?"

"I must decline answering the question," replied Jane, who by this time had recovered her composure.

"Ah! am I to be insolently treated by one of my own dames?" cried Anne.

"I intend no disrespect to your majesty," replied Jane; "and I will, since you insist upon it, freely confess that I received the portrait from the king. I did not conceive there could be any harm in doing so, because I saw your majesty present your own portrait, the other day, to Sir Henry Norris."

Anne Boleyn turned as pale as death, and Jane Seymour perceived that she had her in her power.

"I gave the portrait to Sir Henry as a recompense for an important service he rendered me," said Anne, after a slight pause.

"No doubt," replied Jane; "and I marvel not that he should press it so fervently to his lips, seeing he must value the gift highly. The king likewise bestowed his portrait on me for rendering him a service."

"And what was that?" asked Anne.

"Nay, there your majesty must hold me excused," replied the other. "It were to betray his highness's confidence to declare it. I must refer you to him for an explanation."

"Well, you are in the right to keep the secret," said Anne, forcing a laugh: "I dare say there is no harm in the portrait—indeed, I am sure there is not, if it was given with the same intent that mine was bestowed upon Norris. And so we will say no more upon the matter—except that I must beg you to be discreet with the king. If others should comment upon your conduct I may be compelled to dismiss you."

"Your majesty shall be obeyed," said Jane, with a look that intimated that the request had but slight weight with her.

"Catherine will be avenged by means of this woman," muttered Anne, as she turned away. "I already feel some of the torments with which she threatened me. And she suspects

Norris. I must impress more caution on him. Ah! when a man loves deeply, as he loves me, due restraint is seldom maintained."

But though alarmed, Anne was by no means aware of the critical position in which she stood. She could not persuade herself that she had entirely lost her influence with the king; and she thought that when his momentary passion had subsided, it would return to its old channels.

She was mistaken. Jane Seymour was absolute mistress of his heart; and Anne was now as great a bar to him as she had before been an attraction. Had her conduct been irreproachable, it might have been difficult to remove her; but unfortunately, she had placed herself at his mercy, by yielding to the impulses of vanity, and secretly encouraging the passion of Sir Henry Norris, groom of the stole.

This favored personage was somewhat above the middle size, squarely and strongly built. His features were regularly and finely formed, and he had a ruddy complexion, brown curling hair, good teeth and fine eyes of a clear blue. He possessed great personal strength; was expert in all manly exercises, and shone especially at the jousts and the manege. He was of an ardent temperament, and Anne Boleyn had inspired him with so desperate a passion that he set at naught the fearful risk he ran to obtain her favor.

In all this seemed traceable the hand of fate—in Henry's passion for Jane Seymour, and Anne's insane regard for Norris—as if in this way, and by the same means in which she herself had been wronged, the injured Catherine of Arragon was to be avenged.

How far Henry's suspicions of his consort's regard for Norris had been roused did not at the time appear. Whatever he felt in secret, he took care that no outward manifestation should betray him. On the contrary, he loaded Norris, who had always been a favorite with him, with new marks of regard, and encouraged rather than interdicted his approach to the queen.

On the day, after the solemnization of the Grand Feast of the Order of the Garter, a masked fête of great splendor and magnificence was held within the castle. The whole of the state apartments were thrown open to the distinguished guests, and universal gayety prevailed. No restraint was offered to the festivity by the king, for though he was known to be present, he did not choose to declare himself.

The queen sat apart, on a fauteuil in the deep embrasure of a window—and as various companies of fantastic characters advanced towards her, she more than once fancied she detected amongst them the king, but the voices convinced her of her mistake. As the evening was wearing, a mask in a blue domino drew near her, and whispered, in a devoted and familiar tone, "My queen!"

"Is it you, Norris?" demanded Anne, under her breath.

"It is," he replied. "Oh, madam! I have been gazing at you the whole evening, but have not dared to approach you till now."

"I am sorry you have addressed me at all, Norris," she rejoined. "Your regard for me has been noticed by others, and may reach the king's ears. You must promise never to address me in the language of passion again."

"If I may not utter my love, I shall go mad," replied Norris. "After raising me to the verge of Paradise, do not thrust me to the depths of Tartarus."

"I have neither raised you, nor do I cast you down," rejoined Anne. "That I am sensible of your devotion, and grateful for it, I admit, but nothing more. My love and allegiance are due to the king."

"True," replied Norris, bitterly; "they are so, but he is wholly insensible to your merits. At this very moment he is pouring his love-vows in the ear of Jane Seymour."

"Ah! is he so?" cried Anne. "Let me have proof of his perfidy, and I may incline a more favorable ear to you."

"I will instantly obtain you the proof, madam," replied Norris, bowing and departing.

Returning soon after, Norris led the queen away from the

apartment. Passing from the great hall in which the crowd of dancers was assembled, they descended a short flight of steps, when Norris pointed with his right hand to a chamber partly screened by the folds of a curtain.

At this intimation, the queen and her companion stepped quickly on, and as she advanced, Anne Boleyn perceived Jane Seymour and the king seated on a couch within the apartment. Henry was habited like a pilgrim, but he had thrown down his hat, ornamented with the scallop-shell, his vizard, and his staff, and had just forced his fair companion to unmask.

At the sight, Anne was transfixed with jealous rage, and was for the moment almost unconscious of the presence of Norris, who remained behind the curtain, pointing to what was taking place.

"Your majesty is determined to expose my blushes," said Jane Seymour, slightly struggling with her royal lover.

"Nay, I only want to be satisfied that it is really yourself, sweetheart," cried Henry, passionately. "It was in mercy to me, I suppose, that you insisted upon shrouding those beauteous features from my view."

"Hear you that, madam?" whispered Norris to Anne.

The queen answered by a convulsive clasp of the hand.

"Your majesty but jests with me," said Jane Seymour.

"Jests!" cried Henry, passionately. "By my faith, I never understood the power of beauty till now. No charms ever moved my heart like yours; nor shall I know a moment's peace till you become mine."

"I am grieved to hear it, my liege," replied Jane Seymour, "for I never can be yours, unless as your queen."

Again Norris hazarded a whisper to Anne Boleyn, which was answered by another nervous grasp of the hand.

"That is as much as to say," pursued Jane, seeing the gloomy reverie into which her royal lover was thrown, "I can give your majesty no hopes at all."

"You have been schooled by Anne Boleyn, sweetheart," said Henry.

"How so, my liege?" demanded Jane Seymour.

"Those are the very words she used to me when I wooed her, and which induced me to divorce Catherine of Arragon," replied Henry. "Now they may bring about her own removal."

"Just Heaven!" murmured Anne.

"I dare not listen to your majesty," said Jane Seymour, in a tremulous tone; "and yet, if I dared speak——"

"Speak on, fearlessly, sweetheart," said Henry.

"Then I am well assured," said Jane, "that the queen no longer loves you; nay, that she loves another."

"It is false, minion," cried Anne Boleyn, rushing forward, while Norris hastily retreated—"it is false! It is you who would deceive the king for your own purposes. But I have fortunately been brought hither to prevent the injury you would do me. Oh! Henry, have you overheard this of you?"

"You have chanced to overhear part of a scene in a masquerade, madam—that is all," said the king.

"I have chanced to arrive most opportunely for myself," said Anne. "As for this slanderous and deceitful minion, I shall dismiss her from my service. If your majesty is determined to prove faithless to me, it shall not be with one of my own dames."

"Catherine of Arragon should have made that speech," retorted Jane Seymour, bitterly; "she had reason to complain that she was supplanted by one much beneath her. And she never played the king falsely."

"Nor have I," cried Anne, fiercely. "If I had my will I should strike thee dead for the insinuation. Henry—my lord—my love—if you have any regard for me, instantly dismiss Jane Seymour."

"It may not be, madam," replied Henry, in a freezing tone. "She has done nothing to deserve dismissal. If any one is to blame in the matter it is myself."

"And will you allow her to make these accusations against me without punishment?" cried Anne.

"Peace, madam!" cried the king, sternly; "and thank my

good nature that I go no further into the matter. If you are weary of the masque, I pray you to retire to your own apartments. For myself, I shall lead Jane Seymour to the bransle."

"And if your majesty should need a partner," said Jane, walking up to Anne, and speaking in a low tone, "you will doubtless find Sir Henry Norris disengaged."

The queen looked as if stricken by a thunderbolt. She heard the triumphant laugh of her rival; she saw her led forth, all smiles and beauty and triumph, by the king to the dance; and she covered her face in agony. While she was in this state, a deep voice breathed in her ears: "The vengeance of Catherine of Arragon begins to work!"

Tottering to the seat which Henry and Jane had just quitted, Anne sank into it. After a little time, having in some degree recovered her composure, she was about to return to the great hall, when Norris appeared.

"I did not deceive you, madam," he said, "when I told you the king was insensible to your charms. He only lives for Jane Seymour."

"Would I could dismiss her!" cried Anne, furiously.

"If you were to do so, she would soon be replaced by another," rejoined Norris. "The king delights only in change. With him the last face is ever the most beautiful."

"You speak fearful treason, sir!" replied Anne—"but I believe it to be the truth."

"Oh, then, madam!" pursued Norris, "since the king is so regardless of you, why trouble yourself about him?—there are those who would sacrifice a thousand lives, if they possessed them, for your love."

"I fear it is the same with all men," rejoined Anne. "A woman's heart is a bauble which, when obtained, is speedily tossed aside."

"Your majesty judges our sex too harshly," said Norris. "If I had the same fortune as the king, I should never change."

"The king himself once thought so—once swore so," replied Anne, petulantly. "It is the common parlance of lovers. But I may not listen to such discourse longer."

"Oh, madam!" cried Norris, "you misjudge me greatly. My heart is not made of the same stuff as that of the royal Henry. I can love deeply—devotedly—lastingly."

"Know you not that by these rash speeches, you place your head in jeopardy?" said Anne.

"I would rather lose it than not be permitted to love you," he replied.

"But your rashness endangers me," said the queen, "your passion has already been noticed by Jane Seymour, and the slightest further indiscretion will be fatal."

"Nay, if that be so," cried Norris, "and your majesty should be placed in peril on my account, I will banish myself from the court, and from your presence, whatever the effort may cost me!"

"No," replied Anne, "I will not tax you so hardly. I do not think," she added, tenderly—"deserted as I am by the king, that I could spare you."

"You confess, then, that I have inspired you with some regard?" he cried rapturously.

"Do not indulge in these transports, Norris," said Anne, mournfully. "Your passion will only lead to your destruction—perchance to mine! Let the certainty that I do love, content you, and seek not to tempt your fate further."

"Oh! madam, you make me the happiest of men by the avowal," he cried. "I envy not now the king, for I feel raised above him by your love."

"You must join the revel, Norris," said Anne; "your absence from it will be observed."

And extending her hand to him, he knelt down, and pressed it passionately to his lips.

The first outbreak between King Henry and Anne occurred at a grand tournament which took place soon after the night of the masked ball. The king had challenged Sir Henry Norris to a tilt at arms, and the knight accepted the challenge.

By the time Norris had placed his lance in the rest the trumpet sounded. The next moment the word was given, and the champions started. Henry rode with great impetuosity, and struck Norris in the gorget with such good-will that both he and his steed were shaken.

But Norris was more fortunate. He made the upper part of the king's helmet his mark, and the blow was so well dealt that, though it did not dislodge the royal horseman, it drove back his steed on its haunches.

The success was so unequivocal that Norris was at once declared the victor by the judge. No applause, however, followed the decision, from a fear of giving offense to the king.

Norris dismounted, and committing his steed to the care of an esquire, and his lance to a page, took off his helmet, and advanced toward the royal gallery, near which the Earl of Surrey and Sir Thomas Wyatt were standing talking with the other dames. As Norris drew near, Anne leaned over the edge of the gallery and let fall her embroidered handkerchief.

Norris stooped to pick it up, regarding her, as he did so, with a glance of the most passionate devotion. A terrible gaze, however, was fixed on the unfortunate pair at that moment. It was that of the king. While Henry was careering in front of the gallery to display himself before Jane Seymour, some one said, "Look at Sir Henry Norris!"

Thus addressed, Henry raised his beaver, that he might see more distinctly, and beheld Norris take up the embroidered handkerchief, which he recognized as one that he had given in the early days of his affection to the queen.

The sight stung him almost to madness, and he had great difficulty in repressing his choler. But if this slight action, heightened to importance, as it was, by the looks of the parties, roused his ire, it was nothing to what followed. Instead of restoring it to the queen, Norris, unconscious of the danger in which he stood, pressed the handkerchief fervently to his lips.

"I am hitherto the victor of the jousts," he said; "may I keep this as the prize!"

Anne smiled assent.

"It is the proudest I ever obtained," pursued Norris. And he placed it within his helmet.

"Death of my life!" exclaimed Henry, "it is the very handkerchief I gave her before our union! I can contain myself no longer, and must perforce precipitate matters. What, ho!" he cried, riding up to that part of the gallery where the Duke of Suffolk was seated—"let the jousts be stopped!"

"Wherefore, my dear liege!" said Suffolk. "The Earl of Surrey and Sir Thomas Wyatt are about to run a course."

"Let them be stopped, I say!" roared Henry, in a tone that admitted of no dispute. And wheeling round his charger, he dashed into the middle of the barriers, shouting in loud, authoritative accents,—"The jousts are at an end. Disperse!"

The utmost consternation was occasioned by the announcement. The Duke of Suffolk instantly quitted his seat, and pressed through the crowd to the king, who whispered a few hasty words in his ears. Henry then called to the Earl of Surrey, the Marquis of Dorset, the Lord Clifford, Wyatt, and some others, and bidding them attend him, prepared to quit the court. As he passed the royal gallery, Anne called to him, in an agonized voice:

"Oh, Henry, what is the matter? what have I done?"

But without paying the slightest attention to her, he dashed through the Norman Gate, galloped down the lower quadrangle, and quitted the castle.

The confusion that ensued may be imagined. All saw that something extraordinary and terrible had taken place, though few knew precisely what it was. Dismay sat in every countenance, and the general anxiety was heightened by the agitation of the queen, who, uttering a piercing scream, fell back, and was borne off in a state of insensibility by her attendants.

Unable to control himself at the sight, Norris burst through the guard, and rushing up the great staircase, soon gained the apartment to which the queen had been conveyed. Owing to the timely aid afforded her, she was speedily restored; and the first

person her eyes fell upon was her lover. At the sight of him a glance of affection illumined her features, but it was instantly changed into an expression of alarm.

At this juncture the Duke of Suffolk, who, with Bouchier and a party of halberdiers, had entered the room, stepped up to the queen and said:

"Will it please you, madam, to retire to an inner apartment? I grieve to say you are under arrest."

"Arrest!" exclaimed Anne; "for what crime, your grace?"

"You are charged with incontinency towards the king's highness," replied Suffolk, sternly.

"But I am innocent!" cried Anne—"as Heaven shall judge me, I am innocent!"

"I trust you will be able to prove yourself so, madam," said Suffolk. "Sir Henry Norris, your person is likewise attached."

"Then I am lost, indeed!" exclaimed Anne, distractedly.

"Do not let these false and malignant accusations alarm you, madam," said Norris. "You have nothing to fear. I will die protesting your innocence."

"Sir Henry Norris," said the duke, coldly, "your own imprudence has brought about this sad result."

"I feel it," replied Norris; "and I deserve the worst punishment that can be inflicted upon me for it. But I declare to you—as I will declare upon the rack, if I am placed upon it—that the queen is wholly innocent. Let her not suffer for my fault."

"You hear what Sir Henry says," cried Anne; "and I call upon you to recollect the testimony he has borne."

"I shall not fail to do so, madam," replied Suffolk. "Your majesty shall have strict justice."

"Justice!" echoed Anne, with a laugh of bitter incredulity. "Justice from Henry the Eighth!"

"I beseech you, madam, do not destroy yourself!" said Norris, prostrating himself before her. "Recollect by whom you are surrounded. My folly and madness have brought you into this strait, and I sincerely implore your pardon for it."

"You are not to blame, Norris," said Anne; "it is fate, not you, that has destroyed me. The hand that has dealt this blow is that of a queen within the tomb."

"Captain Bouchier," said the Duke of Suffolk, addressing that officer, who stood near him, "you will convey Sir Henry Norris to the strong-room in the lower gateway, whence he will be removed to the Tower."

"Farewell, forever, Norris!" cried Anne. "We shall meet no more on earth. In what has fallen on me, I recognize the hand of retribution. But the same measure which has been meted to me shall be dealt to others. I denounce Jane Seymour before Heaven! She shall not long retain the crown she is about to snatch from me!"

"That imprecation had better have been spared, madam," said the duke.

"Be advised, my gracious mistress," cried Norris, "and do not let your grief and distraction place you in the power of your enemies. All may yet go well."

"I denounce her!" persisted Anne, wholly disregarding the caution; "and I also denounce the king. No union of his shall be happy, and other blood than mine shall flow!"

At a sign from the duke she was here borne, half-suffocated with emotion, to an inner apartment, while Norris was conveyed by Bouchier and a company of halberdiers to the lower gateway, and placed within the prison chamber.

Anne Boleyn's arraignment took place very soon after.

Notwithstanding an eloquent and impassioned defense, Anne was found guilty; and, having been required to lay aside her crown and the other insignia of royalty, was condemned to be burned or beheaded at the king's pleasure.

On the following day, she was summoned to the archiepiscopal palace at Lambeth, whither she was privately conveyed; and her marriage with the king was declared by Cranmer to be null and void, and to have always been so. Death by the ax was the doom awarded to her by the king, and the day appointed for the execution was Friday, the 19th of May, at the hour of noon.

Leaving the conduct of the fatal ceremony to the Duke of Suffolk—who had orders to have a signal gun fired from the summit of the White Tower, which was to be answered from various points, when all was over—Henry repaired to Windsor Castle on the evening of Thursday. Before this, he had formally offered his hand to Jane Seymour; and, while the unfortunate queen was languishing within the Tower, he was basking in the smiles of his new mistress, and counting the hours till he could make her his own. On the Tuesday before the execution, Jane Seymour retired

to her father's mansion, Wolf Hall, in Wiltshire, where preparations were made for the marriage, which it was arranged should take place there in private on the Saturday!

Anne met her death with great courage and fortitude; but it is said that, in her last moments, she was haunted by the thought that she would soon have to encounter the spirit of the injured Catherine of Arragon.

Sir Henry Norris was also executed by the orders of the jealous king.

THE EARLY LOVE INTRIGUES OF KATHARINE HOWARD, FIFTH WIFE OF HENRY VIII. OF ENGLAND.

HUNTING THE RABBIT TO A TRYSTING-PLACE—KATE RECEIVES A LAST EMBRACE FROM ONE BOLD LOVER—A BOLDER ADVENTURER APPEARS ON THE SCENE—A NIGHT'S CAROUSE IN SECRET—EXPOSED AGAIN—KATE BECOMES A MISTRESS AND A QUEEN—HUNTED BY HER OLD LOVER—SHARING ANNE BOLEYN'S FATE.

A FINE old English mansion, with a spreading lawn in front, gardens and orchards at each side, and a dark wood in the rear, was the scene presented to a young girl of fourteen, as she stood on a hill overlooking the Norfolk mansion, over three hundred years ago.

The young maiden was plump and fair to look at, with a form that was fast developing into womanhood, and with an eye that was at once sprightly, passionate, and full of fire.

A large dog frisked around near the girl, every now and again running to receive a pat on the head from the hand of his mistress, who was gazing wistfully towards the wood at the back of the great mansion.

"I wish we had never come here, Nero," sighed the young girl, addressing the dog. "I am not at all happy, and I know you are not."

The great dog barked, as if giving his assent to the assertion, and then scampered off again.

"I won't go to the wood to meet him," continued the maid in petulant tones. "He's a nasty fellow, and I begin to hate him. Oh, what would grandmother say if she knew that he kissed me!"

The great dog started a rabbit from the bushes at the moment; the little animal darted off towards the wood with Nero bouncing after him; and then young Katharine Howard, clapping her hands in half-childish glee, ran after the dog, as she said:

"Chase him, Nero! Catch him before he gains the wood, or he will escape you altogether!"

Across the lawn, into the kitchen garden, and then out into the dark wood, the little rabbit kept on its flight for life, and after it ran the eager Nero, yelling the while in full cry.

On after the flying animals, and forgetting all else beside in the excitement, flew little Katharine, her flaxen ringlets streaming behind her, as she kept crying to the dog:

"Catch him, Nero, before he gets to the wood, or he will escape you! Ha, ha! he's got him!"

The great dog had caught the rabbit on the edge of the wood, and he was holding up his prize when the flushed maiden reached the spot.

"Good dog," she said, as she patted the animal on the head. "You have not forgotten your early lessons. Now we'll return to the house, and—"

"Katharine—Lady Kate!" cried a voice from the wood, "have you forgotten your tryst with me?"

The young girl started, and a deep blush overspread her young face, as she said:

"I don't want to meet you any more, sir. You are too rude. You forget your place."

"Come in here, my dear young mistress, and I will crave your pardon on my bended knees," cried the voice from the wood. "Do not speak so loud, or you may be overheard. Come in, I pray you."

"I will not, sir."

"Why, what has come over you, my sweet little lady? Yesterday you were all smiles, and——"

"I hate you to-day, Henry Manox. You are rude and low-born. My father would kill you if he knew that you had dared to kiss me."

"But you kissed me also, little lady. I am not rude or low-born, if I wear the guise of a player on the virginals at present. Draw near, I pray you, and I will not be rude again."

"You will not offer to kiss me?"

"On my oath, I will not."

"You will not press your arms around my waist?"

"I will not touch you, dear little lady."

The young girl advanced into the wood, as she said in pouting tones:

"If you do, Henry Manox, I will set Nero on you. You are a very rude man."

Henry Manox had all the appearance of being a very rude man at that moment.

He was a young man of twenty-two, with a face that was pleasing enough were it not for the thick lips and the gross expression of the dark eyes.

"What do you want with me?" demanded Katharine, as she gained the shelter of the wood.

"I wanted to tell you, my dear little lady, that I am going away to the wars."

"Going away to the wars, indeed, Henry Manox! Well, all brave young men shall go to the wars."

"Yes, dear lady Kate, I hope to win a fortune and fame. I hope to reclaim my birthright."

"You are really nobly born, then?"

"Can you doubt my word, my little lady? Will you not give me one farewell kiss?"

"You said you would not touch me, sir."

"Only one kiss, then, little angel. How can you refuse me after all our sweet endearments?"

"I don't like you any more, sir. You are a very naughty, wicked man, and——"

The rest of the sentence was stopped by the meeting of two lips, while the man stole his arm around the young maiden's plump waist.

"Oh, you wretch!" she cried, while she struggled, in a very feeble manner, to break away. "You said you would not touch me again."

"How could I leave you, perhaps forever, dear Kate, without taking a farewell embrace? Come with me into the bower, my dear one."

"I will not, sir. Oh, if Lady Norfolk should know of this, I would be disgraced."

"Pshaw, little Kate, your noble grandmother, old as she is,

has lovers of her own. I will bear you into the bower. Why, how heavy you are."

The young man had lifted the young maiden in his arms, and he was bearing her through the wood, when a noble-looking old lady strode out from behind a tree, and confronted the lovers.

"Hold, wretch," she cried, as she held up a heavy riding-whip, "and release that silly maiden."

Katharine was on the ground even before her grandmother had ceased speaking, and she was crouching behind her crest-fallen lover as the old lady advanced on him with the uplifted whip, crying:

"And so I have lovers—have I—as old as I am?" she said, as her eyes attempt to stir, villain, or I will have you torn limb from limb by the dogs."

The bold lover was dumbfounded for a moment, but he soon recovered his composure, and, staring at the old lady in an impudent manner, he replied:

"What crime have I committed, my Lady Norfolk? I have said you had lovers, and I spoke but the truth. Do you wish me to——"

"Silence, wretch! Get thee to the house, Katharine, and retire to my apartments. I will punish you for your gross conduct, you wicked wench."

"Do not stir, Lady Kate," cried her saucy lover. "Lady Norfolk, I have eyes, and ears, and a tongue. If you dare to strike me, or punish the young lady, I will denounce you to your noble husband. I will tell him of the doings with——"

"Silence, wretch! Kate, hie thee away to the mansion, and never mention what you have heard."

"You promise not to punish her, Lady Norfolk?"

"I will be silent, for the honor of our house, sir. I tell thee go hence, wicked girl."

"Get thee away, Kate," said the young man, as he bent down to kiss the trembling maiden. "Nay, Lady Norfolk, hold thy hand. That is the last kiss, perchance, I may ever offer the child."

"You deserve death, wretch," cried Lady Norfolk, as Katharine darted away through the wood.

"On my oath, Lady Norfolk," returned the brazen rascal, "but that would be your sentence, did your noble lord know that you stooped to receive the embraces of your head groom."

"Silence, you lying wretch, or I will strike you dead on the instant. How dare you?"

"That you may not do, my lady, while I wear this good sword. What crime have I committed, as compared to yours? The pretty little maiden, who is treated as a servant in your house, fell in love with her music-master, and she received his caresses with open arms. You——"

"No more of that, wretch. Get thee away from here, or I will have you murdered."

"Not before I will send this letter to your valiant husband, Lady Norfolk," said the desperate wretch, as he drew a sealed packet from his breast.

"Oh, you infamous wretch! What does that packet contain? Let me have it."

"This packet contains two of your letters to your late headgroom, who is now residing in London, Lady Norfolk. They speak of the boy born to you, while your husband was away in the wars in France for two years. I had the good fortune to intercept the precious documents on a certain night that I relieved the messenger of his purse on the high-road."

"Then you are a robber, as well as a vile seducer, wretch? I will have thee hung."

"Not until I have spent the two hundred golden pieces which you will present me with, for restoring these very interesting letters, my dear Lady Norfolk. I am certain that your noble husband would give even three hundred for them; but the road to Scotland is very dangerous at present, and I have found this Norfolk a very pleasant abiding-place."

"You demand two hundred pieces for these letters, wretch? I will give thee two hundred lashes on your rascally back!"

"Nay, my lady; you would not be so cruel as to scourge the back of your old lover's son. My real name is John Pollock, son of James Pollock, your late head groom."

"You are a son of James Pollock—you!"

"In truth I am, my good lady. You may be my mother, for all I know. I never heard that my worthy father had a wedded wife."

"Oh, I'm a miserable woman!" exclaimed the distracted old lady. "I will give three hundred golden pieces, and the best horse in the stable, and you but swear to ride hence, and never approach young Katharine Howard again. Will you swear?"

"A hundred oaths, if necessary, my lady. On my oath, but the damsel was growing cold. She is over young for a lasting affection. Heed my advice, and watch her well in the future, or she will be straying into pleasant paths again. When can I receive the heavy purse and the good horse, lady?"

"This very day—this very hour. Follow me to the house, and beware how you dally with the maid again."

"On my oath, but my ardor is cooled, bounteous old lady. I can now away to London and find sweethearts in plenty while I rattle the gold pieces in my purse. Adieu, sweet Katharine Howard. I may never look on your comely face again."

"And I pray that I may never look on yours, wretch," muttered the old lady, as she withdrew from the wood.

Young Katharine Howard was peeping out of a window in the castle half an hour after, when she beheld her lover riding away on a gallant steed.

"Dear me," she muttered, with a sigh, "I will never see him again. Well, well, if grandmother offers to chide me, I will soon close her mouth."

The grandmother did not offer to chide the young maiden, but she endeavored to keep a strict watch on her actions; and she did not offer to employ another young musician for her instruction.

Katharine was the daughter of Lord Edmund Howard, a gallant soldier-sailor, who had distinguished himself in many engagements, and more especially at the great battle of Flodden Field, where the Scotch met with the greatest disaster ever endured by that brave nation at the hands of their English invaders.

Lord Edmund was very poor, notwithstanding his great services to the crown, and he was often compelled to seek a hiding-place when his numerous creditors pressed him for payment. Lady Howard, his good wife, died under her sorrows, leaving several children to the tender charities of her numerous wealthy relatives.

Katharine was brought up in the house of her uncle, Sir John Culpepper, of Hollingbourne, where she had for a playfellow her young cousin, Thomas Culpepper, who was afterwards accused of being her paramour.

In an evil hour the young girl was received into the house of her father's step-mother, the Duchess-Dowager of Norfolk. There young Katharine was obliged to herd with the female servants, an unprincipled, degraded, licentious lot, who gave vent to the worst expressions in presence of the neglected child.

One of these criminal creatures, a nurse, named Mary Lassells, encouraged Katharine in her amour with Henry Manox, as she seemed to take a pride in the downfall of the unprotected little lady.

Some months after the departure of the unprincipled lover, Lady Norfolk's husband was killed in battle, and very soon after that event occurred, Katharine's uncle, the Duke of Norfolk, returned from the war, bringing with him a goodly train of gentlemen retainers.

One of these bold spirits was a certain Francis Derham, a cousin of young Katharine.

Derham was a handsome, dashing, fearless young fellow, and he was as unprincipled in his love affairs as he was bold and reckless in war.

He was not long installed in the mansion before he became attracted to his young cousin, who was then blooming fairer every day.

The young adventurer commenced his love-making by making Katharine trifling presents of handkerchiefs and lace; and as the neglected creature was not supplied with pocket-money, she readily accepted the gifts bestowed by her kinsman.

And it appears that she did not reject the more tender advances made to her at the same time.

Tender love scenes soon followed, vows of eternal faith were interchanged, and young Derham addressed Katharine in secret as "his dear wife," while she called him her "sweet husband."

While this dallying was going on the only care the old duchess seems to have taken of the young girl's honor was to lock the chamber door where Katharine and the women servants slept, and to place the keys in her own sleeping-room, and in the charge of her waiting-woman.

One night young Derham met Katharine in the hall as she was about to retire to her sleeping-room, and he inquired:

"Where away so early, my sweet little wife?"

"I am about to retire for the night, Francis. But you must not call me wife, as you may be overheard. The old lady is very watchful."

"The fiend take the old lady. Stay thee here with me awhile, dear one."

"I may not, Francis. The hour approaches for locking the chamber-door."

"Locking the chamber-door! And does she lock you in every night, the old prude?"

"Ah, that she does, Francis. She fears, I presume, that some of you gay gallants would be seeking stolen interviews with the maids."

"A fig for the maids, little wife. The drowsy damsels are weary and soon fall asleep, I presume."

"Indeed, and they do not, Francis. They sit and talk of their lovers for hours."

"And wish that their door was not locked, I'll wager then, Kate. I will even pay them a visit this very night and take some good strong wine to cheer them in their solitude. You will share, Kate?"

"You are in jest, Francis. How could you enter and the door locked? The casements cannot be reached from the ground, as we sleep in the dormitory."

"Fear thee not, sweet Kate. I will visit thee this very night, even had I to steal the keys from the old lady's chamber."

"You do but jest, Francis."

"Faith, and I do not, sweetheart; one more kiss now, and I will return it hereafter."

"There calls the old lady's waiting-woman; Francis, I must hasten to the chamber."

"But not to sleep, Kate. I will return that kiss to-night, on the word of your true lover."

Kate hastened away to her chamber, where she told her sleeping companions in a laughing manner what her cousin had promised to entertain them with that very night.

"I pray that he may come" responded one lively damsel; "but 'tis news that will not come to pass. The old duchess will not part with her keys unless she is strangled to death."

"He is a bold youth, Kate," remarked another, "and he loves you dearly. Alack-a-day, I would that my Jock had half his spirit."

"And he but comes and brings the good wine, we will all sleep without dreams," suggested a third, as she winked at the others.

"Do not partake of much of the wine, my sweet young lady," said another. "I am but a light sleeper, and I will drink thy portion."

"Marry! and we will all drink merrily," said Mary Lassells "The young lady will not fall asleep while her young lover is present."

While they were chatting away in a lively strain, an hour passed away.

Kate did not expect her lover, as she did not dream, wild and reckless as he was, that he would dare to venture into the old lady's chamber to steal the coveted keys.

"He will not come to-night," remarked Mary Lassells, with a yawn. "We must even retire without the good wine."

"Hist!" said another. "There is something in the keyhole. As I live in sin, but there comes the gallant!"

As the woman spoke, the door was gently opened, and Francis Derham, in his vamps, slipped into the chamber, closing the door cautiously after him.

"I greet thee, merry women," he said, as he drew two large bottles from under his coat.

"Oh, cousin, why did you come here?" asked Kate, as she retreated behind a bed. "Get thee away, or we will be undone."

"Not until the ladies partake of this good wine, Kate. Sit thee down here with me."

"Sit thee down, Lady Kate," said Mary Lassells. "On my faith, but you are a brave gallant, sir. And did you steal into the old lady's chamber?"

"Nay, nay, Mary, I but looked under the waiting-woman's pillow, while I slipped a bread gold piece into her hand. Come here, Kate, and drink to my success on other nights."

Kate Howard did sit down, and she drank of the wine, while her lover's arm was around her waist.

Francis Derham did not leave that chamber until the day was breaking.

Night after night the bold lover entered to pay his stolen visits to the chamber, and as he always went supplied with wine and other sleep-inviting refreshments, he was welcomed by the women with great glee.

At length the suspicions of the lady were aroused by one of the faithless women, who had been discharged from the house for an open amour with one of the retainers.

The old lady watched herself; she saw Derham getting the keys from her faithless waiting-woman; and she followed him to the room where Katharine was wont to receive him nightly.

A fearful uproar followed the discovery, and during the excitement our adventurer escaped from the house and hastened away to Ireland, in order to escape the vengeance of Katharine's enraged relatives.

The erring girl was immediately placed in strict confinement; but she managed, through the instrumentality of another corrupt female, to carry on a correspondence with him, while he lived an outlawed life in Ireland.

Some years passed away, and erring Katharine Howard became a refined, beautiful woman. She even became remarkable for her modest and maidenly deportment.

When Derham returned from Ireland in a secret manner, with his early love still strong in his breast, she positively refused to hold any communication with him. He was still devotedly attached to her, however, and he found means to gain an interview with the proud damsel.

It was reported at the time that Katharine was engaged in marriage to her cousin, Thomas Culpepper; and Derham was in a high state of jealous excitement when he broke in on Katharine.

"Will you be my wife, Kate?" he demanded.

"I will not wed you, sir," she replied. "I do not wish to ever look on you again."

"You are going to marry Thomas Culpepper, Kate, and that is why you forget me."

"If there was not another man in the world, sir, I would not be your wife," was the reply, as Kate turned to leave the apartment.

"Stay a moment, Kate," said the jealous lover. "I hear that you are going to court soon."

"That may be, sir."

"Then beware how you trifle with me. I will seek you and

claim you, even though you were the wife of the king. I love you still; and I will hold you, or perish in the striving."

King Henry had just married his fourth wife, Anne of Cleves, when he first met Katharine Howard at a banquet given by the Bishop of Winchester, and he became enamored of the young girl at their introduction.

The king had buried his third wife, Jane Seymour, who had died in childbirth; he had chosen the ugly and unprepossessing Anne of Cleves on the strength of a flattering portrait, which his favorite painter had taken; and he was already taking measures to set her aside by a divorce.

It was only natural, then, for the beauty-loving king to pay his attentions to the fair Katharine Howard, who was then in the full bloom of womanhood. Katharine was immediately appointed maid of honor to the queen; her royal lover pressed his attentions on her in his own ardent fashion, and she was soon looked upon as the future queen.

Francis Derham vanished from England at this time, and it was reported that he had been killed at sea, while cruising on a pirate ship.

The divorce was at length procured; the favorite mistress became the best-beloved wife of the powerful king, and peace and happiness appeared to dawn on the pathway of the once erring woman.

But the shadow of her past life was following her in her brightest moments.

The king undertook a northern journey, and his fair wife accompanied him. She met Derham at a castle on the coast, and he compelled her to introduce him into the royal household as her private secretary, while the king had never heard of the young adventurer before.

While at Lincoln Katharine admitted her cousin, Thomas Culpepper, with her at night in her private chamber; and that interview lasted many hours.

At length the king, who adored Katharine even more than all his former wives, heard some stories concerning her early life; and these stories were circulated by her former base companions.

An investigation was ordered; Katharine's old confidante, Mary Lassells, was arrested and questioned by the king's agents; and the faithless woman confessed all about the frail girl's connection with Henry Manox and Francis Derham.

Then Katharine's days were numbered. She was doomed to share the fate of Anne Boleyn, who was her cousin; and her lover, Francis Derham, was also seized and put to death.

THE LOVE INTRIGUES OF ELIZABETH, THE VIRGIN QUEEN OF ENGLAND.

THE FIRST LOVE OF A PRINCESS—HER JEALOUS SISTER IMPRISONED—THE QUEEN IN LOVE WITH ANOTHER WOMAN'S HUSBAND—ROYAL FAVORITES VYING FOR HER—SIR WALTER RALEIGH AND HIS ROYAL MISTRESS—ESSEX AS A YOUNG LOVER TO AN OLD QUEEN—HIS PRESUMPTION AND HIS DEATH.

It must not be imagined, because Elizabeth of England never shared her throne with a husband, that she was a confirmed man-hater.

On the contrary, even in her old age she was a great admirer of manly beauty, and her favorite courtiers were always noted for their graces of person as much as for their mental endowments.

This famous queen was the child of two personages in history who were noted for their warm and guilty attachments. She was the daughter of Henry VIII. and the unfortunate Anne Boleyn.

When her sister Mary was Queen of England, the Princess Elizabeth became attached to Edward Courtney, Earl of Devonshire, a very handsome and highly accomplished young nobleman, who returned her affection in a sincere and ardent manner. Queen Mary, who was in a state of single blessedness at the time, had also conceived a violent passion for young Courtney, and it is said that she would have placed him on the throne with herself were it not that his attachment for Elizabeth caused him to look on the queen with feelings of abhorrence.

Although Mary was regarded as a very beautiful woman in her youthful prime, she was anything but attractive at the time when she became enamored of Elizabeth's young lover. Besides, Mary was some eighteen years older than her young sister, who was then in the pride of youth and beauty, as well as being noted for her brilliant wit and high accomplishments.

While Elizabeth was fully assured of Edward Courtney's love, she was terribly afraid that her royal sister, who was the daughter of Catherine of Arragon, would bear away the prize.

One evening, as the two young lovers were strolling in the royal gardens, Elizabeth seated herself on a rustic seat, saying:

"I am weary, Edward. I have been dancing attendance on the queen all the live-long day."

The young nobleman took a seat by her side and seized her hand, as he responded, in warm tones:

"Would to Heaven, my beloved lady, that we could be wedded and retire to my castle."

"To be dragged from thence to the scaffold, Edward? You know that the queen would have our heads if we were guilty of such folly."

"I fear you are right, sweet princess. And yet it is almost death to me—this life of anxiety and hopeless waiting. Why shall we not be married in secret, my adored one?"

"I cannot consent to that, dear Courtney. If the queen were to know of it, we should be sent to the Tower on the instant. You know that she loves you, and that she seeks your hand."

"And may that hand be withered on my arm ere I give it to her in marriage, dear princess. I respect her as my queen, but I could never love her. My heart is yours, and yours only."

"I feel it, Edward. If I cannot wed you, I will never wed another. If I were queen of England to-morrow, you would be my husband. If we are separated for life, no other—not even the mightiest prince in Christendom—will share the throne."

While the lovers were thus conversing a pale face was peering out at them from some shrubbery at the side of the path above them, while a low, threatening voice could be heard muttering:

"I will soon put an end to this dallying. The guilty pair will soon find other quarters. I will cool their guilty love—the deceitful wretches!"

On the following morning, the young Earl of Devonshire was banished from the court, and the Princess Elizabeth was sent to the Castle of Alfreidge as a prisoner, and commanded, under severe penalties, not to hold any conversation with her lover.

But the devoted lovers were not to be baffled in their desires. Young Courtney managed to find the opportunities of holding secret interviews with the young princess, and several tender letters were also interchanged. Two of these letters were intercepted by the queen's emissaries, who conveyed them to the jealous creature.

The first letter opened by Mary was from her young sister to her lover, and it contained the following declarations of a violent passion:

"My Lord,—I do not doubt your love, but I fear this passion will be to your prejudice. It is this which obliges me to conceal my preference for you, having so little hope; but I am sensible

SOME OF THE LOVE INTRIGUES OF THE FAMOUS CARDINAL RICHELIEU.

THE GREAT SOLDIER-STATESMAN AS A LOVER—HIS INTRIGUE WITH FAIR MARION—THE FAVORED LOVER AND HIS FATE—LOOKING UP TO THE QUEEN—HIS GREAT ENGLISH RIVAL IN LOVE AS WELL AS IN WAR.

Lovers of the drama, who have witnessed our leading actors in Bulwer's popular play, are apt to regard the tottering old cardinal as a great statesman who had not yet lost his tact for state intrigues, and as one who, after years of warfare and state craft, declared that "the pen was mightier than the sword."

Students of history, reading of his great conquests, whereby he raised France to a proud and powerful position as a nation, are wont to look upon him as the greatest soldier of his age.

And many historians, who regarded the great cardinal only as a stern and unflinching prelate, have declared that his whole life was engrossed in the advancement of his religious views, and that he had neither the time nor the inclination to indulge in the weaker passions so common to the rulers of the age in which he lived—and in all ages, for that matter.

Yet the great statesman did have a soft spot in his stern heart, and he had an eye for female beauty as well as for ambition.

When Richelieu was in the prime of manhood and power, he heard of the charms of a certain young lady who was attached to the court of Louis XIII. of France, and who was known as Marion de Lormes.

Being excited by curiosity, he managed to get a fair view of the maiden without being seen himself, and he then found that she was even ten times more beautiful and fascinating than he had ever imagined she could be from the reports he had heard.

Anne of Austria was the neglected wife of the French king at the time, as the fickle monarch basked in the open smiles of more than one fair dame; and he even rode with two of his favorites in the same open carriage while attending the chase in the royal forests.

When Richelieu became attracted to Marion, that bewitching creature was carrying on an intrigue with Saint Mars, one of the king's male favorites. The bold prelate immediately set himself up as a rival to Saint Mars, and he made love to the fickle lady in secret.

The lady received the addresses of the great statesman with apparent satisfaction, knowing full well that it would be dangerous to incur the enmity of such a powerful lover.

But Richelieu, who was watchful and jealous in love as well as in war, had grave doubts of the damsel's faith, and he set himself as a spy on her actions.

One evening, while looking out from a window of the palace, he observed Marion walking along a pathway in the garden, as if hastening to meet some favored lover.

Hastily donning a suitable disguise, Richelieu hastened out into the garden, and stole along the path which his fair mistress had taken. He moved along in a silent manner until he reached a small grove, in the center of which was a small hunting-lodge, which afforded shelter to the gamekeepers of the forest during the severe storms of winter, and which was usually deserted in the summer season, save when occupied by some devoted lovers of the gay court during their tender and clandestine meetings.

Stealing along to the side of the lodge, with his ears wide open and his eyes glaring with jealous rage, Richelieu heard soft voices within, as well as other sounds that did not serve to allay his angry emotions.

"And so you have a new lover, Marion?" said a male voice, which Richelieu did not recognize.

"I have, my dear friend. I did but try with Saint Mars to flatter his vanity, while I was advancing your interests. And now the great cardinal is at my feet."

"Beware that he does not enter your heart, my Marion. He is not one to be trifled with, I assure you. I fear him as a rival, and I dread him as an enemy, should he learn that you are attached to me."

"But if I can advance your interests through him, dear Desbarreau. If I could——"

"He would never be content to have you share your favors with another, dear Marion. You must keep our love a secret. If we are discovered, my doom is sealed."

"That is folly, my dear friend. If Richelieu should discover our intrigue—or pretend to discover it you should make the report a matter of jest. Laugh at the idea of the great cardinal being your rival, and leave the rest to me. I assure you that I will cajole the great man, for he loves me too much to give me any great pain or displeasure."

The cardinal was sorely tempted to break in on the happy pair, more especially as every sentence uttered by them was accompanied with fond kisses and caresses, but he controlled his rage, and listened from the spot, in order to lay his plans for securing Marion's undivided embraces.

On the following day Monsieur Desbarreau, who was a counselor of the Parliament, and a young man of good figure and lively wit, received a visit from one of the cardinal's confidential agents.

The agent, in a very diplomatic manner, informed the young man that if he would give up Marion in favor of the cardinal, the sacrifice would be acknowledged in a form that would lead to the advancement of his fortune.

The young lawyer made light of the proposal, and rejoined, in a pleasant manner:

"The great cardinal does but jest with me, monsieur. I cannot imagine our eminent statesmen being capable of such a weakness."

Richelieu became so angry at this reply that he commenced to persecute the favored lover; he drove him from his position, and he compelled him to leave the kingdom, and the charming Marion.

Richelieu has been accused of making love to other fair dames, but his admiration for this neglected queen, Anne of Austria, is a matter of historical record.

The queen was at first inclined to receive the attentions of the powerful minister; but when she found that he was too ardent in his manner, and that he desired to overstep the bounds of decorum, she met his fervent advances with great contempt and disdain.

A historian of a later time, in speaking of the persecutions to which the queen was subjected by her cruel and adulterous king, speaks of Richelieu and a favored rival in the following strain:

"If we are to believe the annals of the times, those persecutions against a queen, the beauty, graces and sweetness of whose temper were worthy a happier fate, were instigated by love. The Cardinal Richelieu, that great minister, had been audacious enough to cast a wishful eye on the queen, from whom his passion met no return but contempt. It was therefore to avenge himself of that rebuke that he thus persecuted her. To such a cause are we to attribute the divisions which arose at that period between France and England, and which occasioned so much bloodshed.

"The Duke of Buckingham, who ruled over Great Britain, while Richelieu did the same in France, came into the latter kingdom on the occasion of his master's marriage. He was no less daring than the cardinal, and he fell in love with the queen, and had the boldness to tell her so in a long interview which he had with her. The Marchioness de Leucey, lady of honor, tired of the long conversation, said to him, in a severe tone:

"'Hold your tongue, sir; the Queen of France is not to be spoken to in that strain.'

"It is said that when taking leave of the queen he kissed her gown and shed some tears. It is further said that the king was informed of all that had transpired during his absence, and discharged some of the queen's attendants from her service. The cardinal, who was also informed of this, conceived the greatest jealousy, and soon made his rival feel the effects of it.

"The duke, having caused himself to be sent on a second embassy to France, merely to see the queen, was forbidden to set his foot into the kingdom. Such is the version given us by an Italian author.

"Richelieu and Buckingham were pitted one against another for reasons which were kept a secret because they were disgraceful in themselves, and afterwards the people had to pay out of their pockets for the follies and quarrels of these two rivals. Mr. Hume ascribes the rupture between England and France to the rivalship of those two ministers. The cardinal's jealousy was all the stronger as he knew the duke had been received with some favor, for that historian maintains that the apparent merit of the

duke had made some impression on the queen, and that she permitted herself at least 'that attachment of the soul, which conceals so many dangers under a delicious surface.'

"However, the duke having sworn he would see the queen in spite of all the power of France, he excited a war, the consequences of which were not of much credit, and he returned to England dishonored and more hated than ever.

"Another author asserts that while the Cardinal Richelieu was besieging La Rochelle, the Rochellese sent to England for new assistance, and that the Duke of Buckingham, animated with all the stimulus of love and jealousy, armed quickly a considerable fleet, which might have occasioned the ruin of the cardinal. They say that in this crisis they compelled the queen to write to the duke and beg him to suspend his armament, and to this letter was owed the taking of La Rochelle."

THE "MERRY MONARCH" OF ENGLAND AND HIS WITTY FAVORITE, NELL GWYNNE.

CHARLES II. AS A HUSBAND AND A LOVER—NELL GWYNNE'S EARLY LIFE—HER FIRST APPEARANCE ON THE STAGE—MEETING WITH CHARLES—FIGHTING HIS FORMER FAVORITES—THE REIGN OF AN AMOROUS FAMILY.

CHARLES II. of England was one of the greatest libertines that ever disgraced a throne, and he never pretended to hide his amorous intrigues.

After the death of his unfortunate father, Charles I., who was defeated and beheaded by Oliver Cromwell, the young king had to fly to France, where his morals were not at all improved by associating with the titled ladies of a gay court.

On the death of Cromwell, Charles was restored to his kingdom; and his ministers began negotiations for his marriage with Catharine of Braganza, who was one of the richest princesses in Europe.

While the marriage negotiations were going on, Charles carried on an open intrigue with a certain Mrs. Palmer; while his court was so riotous and unruly as to attract the censures of the more sober-minded people of England.

When Catharine was wedded to Charles she was well aware of his connection with Mrs. Palmer, but she was not prepared for the insult offered to her on her arrival in England. The king then presented her with a list of the ladies of honor which he had chosen for her, and at the head of the list was the name of his infamous paramour, Mrs. Palmer.

The indignant queen seized a pen on the instant and erased the odious name. Charles was then in some perplexity as to the course he would pursue in attempting to force his favorite into a position at court; but the witty lover was not to be baffled at a first repulse.

Nearly six weeks of married serenity had passed away, when a lady of majestic figure, and with a very beautiful face, was presented to the queen at one of her receptions, under the title of Lady Castlemaine. As the title was new to the queen, she was about to address the person in kindly tones, when one of her ladies whispered into her ear:

"That is the notorious Mrs. Palmer."

The queen was so indignant at this fresh outrage that she could scarcely subdue her feelings; and in the struggle the blood rushed from her nostrils and she fell in a fit.

Charles soon grew tired of Mrs. Palmer, and turned his attentions to his cousin, Lady Frances Stuart, one of the queen's maids of honor. She repelled his dishonorable advances, and she soon afterwards married the Duke of Richmond.

While the queen was residing at Tunbridge Wells, which was then a favorite watering-place, she sent for a company of actors, in order to amuse her and her friends. At that time the Merry Monarch was leading a life of the wildest dissipation, extending

his adventures and his amours over the country for miles around London.

When the players arrived at the watering-place, Charles became attracted by one of the actresses, who proved to be the famous Nell Gwynne.

Although Nell led a wild life from childhood, it is asserted that she maintained her virtue until she fell a victim to the wiles of the Merry Monarch. As an account of her early career will prove very interesting, we will draw on the historian for the facts recorded thereof, as well as for an account of her introduction to the stage:

The district of Alsatia, denominated Whitefriars, in London, had formerly been under the government of a republic, which, though often visited with revolutionary movements, had existed through the whole of the commonwealth. But about the same time that Cromwell, with the aid of the army, usurped the government of the nation, that of Alsatia also underwent a change, and the chief authority was seized by an adventurous washerwoman. This lady, being of an unscrupulous disposition, not soon or easily intimidated, maintained her position till the Restoration, when, like the mother realm, Alsatia became the seat of a monarchy. Its post of honor had since been successfully filled by several eminent criminals; but, among other things, the visitation of the Plague, in the year 1664, had brought about an interregnum, which lasted nearly a year.

The realm was still in a state of anarchy, when it was invaded, with every other part of the metropolis, by the Great Fire. The deeds of violence, rapine, and bloodshed, unrestrained by any law, fear, or scruple, which then took place, amidst the general confusion and helplessness, made an impression even on the Alsatians. When a knot of ruffians, herded for the nonce, were reveling among them in every kind of outrage, they were suddenly called upon by a stranger, whom none of them seemed to be acquainted with, to put them down.

That done, the stranger subsequently engaged them in other arrangements—formed them, with the general concurrence, into several distinct companies—directed some to transport the maimed and helpless over the river—some to guard and remove whatever could be saved from the fire; and finally, when flight could no longer be deferred, brought the majority of them safe to an encampment on St. George's Fields.

On the return of the Alsatians to the sanctuary, the stranger, who was now known by the name of Barker, bore them company, and was unanimously elected their chief. He had filled this

station for about a year, when he was joined, one day, without any previous intimation, by a woman and child; but, however the former might be allied to him, he claimed no consanguinity with the latter. Indeed, the little girl—for such she was—did not even possess his name; and it was soon generally known that she bore the appellation of Nell Gwynne.

He was well adapted for the post he had attained—possessing, among other qualifications, a strong and ready hand, and a dauntless spirit, with all the worst characteristics of the old royalist soldiers, softened by a dash of their chivalry. Thus qualified, and supported, whenever occasion arose, by many of his former companions in arms and quondam adversaries, he held his ground again, and met every attempt to depose him with the most severe retribution.

After a lapse of years, the woman died, and the girl, now verging on womanhood, removed from the lodgings of the Rum-dumber and began to reside alone. But, protected by the influence of her guardian, she still lived securely, and though her calling of a fruit-vender, which she pursued at the theater of the Duke of York, at Dorset Gardens, frequently kept her abroad at night, her connection with the Rum-dumber surrounded her with a constant safeguard, which the vilest bravo in Alsatia durst not infringe.

Nell's business as fruit-vender brought her into contact with the actors and actresses at the theater, and she soon acquired a passion for the profession. After struggling for some time, under the tuition of an able master, who had taken a great fancy to the beautiful fruit-girl, she was privately engaged to appear in a play written by the celebrated Otway.

On a certain morning a number of distinguished persons had assembled on the stage of the new theater in Lincoln's Inn Square, to witness the first rehearsal of the new play.

The foremost of the party—a tall, intellectual-looking man, dressed in grave habits, laced with black—was Betterton himself, in speaking of whom it was said, by a celebrated critic, that "Shakespeare conceived, and Betterton realized. There had never been two Shakespeares, and there could only be one Betterton."

A cavalier of middle age, dressed in a frock of tissue, whose noble features and engaging manner, free from the least affectation, at once denoted him a gentleman and courtier, stood next to him. It was Lord Buckhurst.

He smiled at Betterton's observation, and, wheeling round, turned the conversation to a person in his rear—a man of middle age, dressed, like Betterton, in grave habits, and having a slight inclination to stoop, but whose countenance, notwithstanding a look of gloom about the eyes, fairly beamed with expression. "Thinkst thou this is true, Master Dryden?" he said. "Is this some hoax of our playful Otway?"

"Nay, nay, my lord," smiled the illustrious Dryden. "He would not mar his play, methinks, with a jest."

Before the nobleman could utter a rejoinder, a fourth person interposed, a dashing, martial-looking cavalier, who was, indeed, no other than Sir George Etherege. As he stepped forward to speak, he involuntarily displayed, in his handsome and winning countenance, that look of innate kindness and immovable good temper, which had procured him universal esteem, and, in an age which dwelt more in scandal than eulogy, earned him the name of "easy George and gentle Etherege."

"'Tis most honestly said, brother John," he remarked; "I will wager my Hanover mare, which is the best blood in town, on Otway's earnestness."

"That mare of thine will certainly fall thee one day," cried Lord Buckhurst. "It hath, to my knowledge, been thy constant stake and wager for two whole months. But here is our fair cousin Davenant, who only lives in vivacity, as silent as a ghost. What mystery art thou fraught withal, good Charley? An' thou love us, unfold!—unfold, man, and shame the devil!"

The person addressed was a slight young man, attired in habiliments of some pretensions. But his chief attraction, as far as appearances were concerned, lay in his face, which presented so

marked a resemblance to that of Shakespeare, that, had they lived in the same age, he might have passed for the poet himself. "Nay, nay, I seek not to shame the devil," answered Davenant, "but to amaze your lordship! 'Tis a piece of woman's wit."

"How wondrous deep!" cried Betterton. "Of a verity I may say to thee, Charley, as Sir John Suckling said to thy father:

> "'Thou hast redeemed us, Will, and future times
> Shall not account unto the age's crimes
> Dearth of pure wit.'"

"Or, to go further," observed the nobleman, "as dear Will Shakespeare *may* have said to my grandmother,[*] 'Make the doors upon a woman's wit, and 'twill out at the keyhole; stop that, 'twill fly with the smoke out of the chimney.'"

"Truly, 'tis marvelous dark!" remarked Dryden.

"Nay, nay, not if it be *woman's* wit," suggested Sir George Etherege.

"Gentle George, methinks, is driving after Barry,"[†] said the nobleman.

There was a general laugh.

"*Parbleu,* my lord!" said Etherege, with a slight smile, "this is unfair of thee. But *vive la bagatelle!* Did not I see thee last night, at Dorset Gardens, coqueting with the pretty orange-girl?"

"Oh! oh!" cried Betterton and Davenant.

"My lord, nay, this is not well," smiled Dryden. "Fair Nelly will beat thee off!"

"And so will Master Hart," observed Davenant.

"Aud Lacy!" said Betterton. "But talk of the devil——"

"And he appears!" cried a new-comer.

It was the dramatic Adonis—Lacy, who, like Sir George Etherege, had won a good name in an evil age, and, both in person and conversation, was considered "the prettiest fellow about town." He was followed by a military-looking man, apparently about thirty, whose fine person, though set off with every advantage of taste and dress (approaching almost to dandyism), revealed marked traces of dissipated habits: it was Otway, the poet. By his side walked his double, Duke, whose poetry, as far as respects the world at large, has long since been sunk in Lethe, but whose friendship for Otway has rendered him immortal. He was leaning on the arm of a player named Hart, who, like Davenant, bore a remarkable resemblance to Shakespeare, and was, indeed, the grandson of the poet's sister. Finally, two ladies, if one may so call them, brought up the rear, and immediately secured universal attention.

One of the ladies, who was the taller of the two, wore a mask; the other was a pleasing-looking creature, though drawing fast on thirty, and might, if she had been less affected, have been considered pretty. She was instantly recognized as Mrs. Barry; and Sir George Etherege, whose passion for her was as earnest as it was unlawful, sprang forward to meet her.

"Fair Mistress Barry! how goes the day with you?" he whispered. "'Tis now high noon with *me.*"

"Now, Sir George, I protest, by my troth, and by every pretty oath I can swear," answered Mrs. Barry, "you frighten me out of my wits. Oh! Sir George! 'tis vastly cruel of you."

While Sir George, in an undertone, sought to reassure the alarmed lady, Lord Buckhurst addressed himself to the company generally.

"Fair Mistress Barry, accept my entire devotion," he said. "Master Lacy, you are fresh from the opera; how fares it, sir, with your cousin Purcell and the dames of Charter-house Square? Master Duke, I give you good-morrow; I owe you a rundlet of canary. Fair Master Hart, I hope all is well at the cockpit. Killegrew, methinks, is not doing amiss. Master Otway, I avow myself, as ever, your most true admirer. And beauteous un-

---

* Sir William, father of Charles Davenant, was reported to be the natural son of Shakespeare, by the beautiful hostess of the Crown, at Oxford.

† Alluding, perhaps, to Sir George's *liaison* for Mrs. Barry, the actress.

known," he concluded, as he presented himself before the mask, "who has taken me captive with thy half-hidden glance, let me remove thy cruel vizard, and look on all thy charms."

He raised his hand, but, while it was yet only half lifted, he was drawn back by Otway.

"Gramercy, my lord, the mask will scratch you!" cried the poet. "But let her have her will. The play is mine, and, if it fail, 'twill be my loss."

" 'Tis well spoken," observed Master Duke.

"Then suffer it to stand so," interposed Betterton; "but, for the sake of order, let us waste no more time. Ho, prompter, ring thy bell! Now, lords and gallants, leave us a fair stage. Dames and gentlemen, think of your parts, and let us, for Master Otway's sake, do our best for 'Friendship's in Favor.' "

Such was the title of the play which, after a long interval of preparation, was now to be rehearsed, and, as the manager ceased speaking, the necessary arrangements for the exhibition were speedily effected. But, interesting as the piece was, it was by the character of Lady Squeamish, which was sustained by the fair mask, that admiration was especially excited; and the conception of the part seemed to be strengthened and enlarged by the performance of the actress. Plaudit after plaudit burst from the admiring spectators; and Lord Buckhurst, in particular, seemed unable to give expression to his feelings. At the conclusion of the play, he broke away from his friends, and, pushing through the leading players, who were breaking off into groups, and past his favorite Betterton, made his way directly to the fair *debutante*.

"Mysterious divinity, whose very lisping is wit," he said, "wilt thou still repel thy poor admirer?"

The mask, who was pushing past him, drew up—perhaps gratified that so noble a gentleman, the mirror and Mæcenas of his age, who was less distinguished by his rank than his wealth —less by his wealth than his generosity—should offer her a tribute of applause. But, if such were her feeling, it soon subsided, and she answered his salutation with a little laugh.

"Laugh on, cruel scorner!" said the nobleman; "I would that, for the future, I might provoke thy scorn forever, so that I could hear that sweet laugh!"

"Hold! hold! an' thou wouldst not have me die!" answered the mask. "Bethink thee! how many times, and how vainly, hast thou uttered and repeated those false words!"

"*False* words!" echoed the nobleman. "By my hand, they are most veritably true!"

"Thou art an absolute Lothario!" returned the mask. "Didst thou not now, no longer since than yester-even, urge a lady with this same protest!"

"On my faith, no!" replied the peer, musingly. "And yet, I cry you mercy! I did, out of pure jest, say some sort of words to an orange-wench. No more, I promise you."

"An orange-wench!" laughed the mask. "Ho! ho!"

"A good jest, I promise you!" said the peer, also laughing; "and it pleased her mightily. To speak the truth, she is a marvelous fair wench!"

"Still a wench!" answered the mask.

"No more of her, I prithee!" returned the nobleman. "She is, I doubt not, a mere drab. But thou, sweet goddess——"

"Nay, nay, nay!" laughed the mask.

"Those eyes!——"

"But the orange wench!" cried the mask.

"That fair face!——"

"Tell me of the drab!" said the mask.

"Hang her!" cried the peer.

"Nay, false lord!" returned the lady, "thou wouldst not surely hang me!"

With these words she threw off her vizard, and the nobleman, looking up, recognized the fair orange-girl, Nell Gwynne.

He dropped his glance directly; and with one hand raised to his face, and the other, which was ungloved, pressed on his heart, fell on one knee at her feet. The part of the stage they occupied, owing to the interposition of a side scene, was screened from observation; and, in the bustle attending the general dispersion, they had hitherto escaped remark. At this moment, however, two persons came in sight of them, who evidently beheld their situation with anything but indifference. They were the two players, Hart and Lacy.

"False lord," said Nell, "what should be thy punishment?"

"Eternal disdain!" answered the peer. "Death."

"What if I forgive thee?" asked Nell.

The nobleman, seemingly electrified by the mere thought, sprung to his feet, and pressed her hand to his lips. As he did so, Nell, looking around, discovered her two former admirers, and, prompt in her perceptions, quickly perceived their discomposure.

"Soh, gallants!" she cried, laughing, "who is dead? Fair Master Hart, give me thy hand! Master Lacy, pull forth thy kerchief, and wipe that cloud from thy brow. For thee, my lord, thou must bear my vizard for me."

And seeing that all were pleased, Nell checked her laugh, and smiled on each alike.

Master Otway's play, so carefully and effectively put forward, with every advantage of scene, decoration, and cast, was received by the public with unmingled approbation. Yet it was by the representative of the baffled *intriguante*, Lady Squeamish, that the applause of the spectators was most frequently elicited. Her singular beauty, her winning manner, and her admirable art, which was continually throwing forward some new and unexpected attraction, were the theme of universal applause; and as the play was again and again repeated, her personal loveliness and professional merit became one of the topics of the day.

It will readily be imagined that in so vicious and licentious an age this necessarily laid her open, in the course of time, to many temptations—to the snares of the envious and the solicitations of the corrupt. Apparently unfriended and defenseless, she received more than one offer of distinguished protection; but, cautiously threading the quicksands around her, she held straight to her course, and was deaf alike to the jeers of her rivals and the seductions of her admirers.

But, though undaunted, the poor girl, thus mocked and harassed, was not indifferent to the peril of her situation. In her solitary moments she felt it severely, and the epithets she had won in public, and which are still applied to her, of "merryhearted Nell," "gay, laughing Nell," and "jocund Nelly," fell on her ears like bitter mockery, as false and hollow as the world itself.

Often, in the depth of night, when no eye could observe her, did she bend thought after thought on her melancholy condition; often did it recall the tears to her sleepless eyes; and think as she might, she could still start only the one reflection, "I MUST FALL!"

Thus, sad and anxious, but, over all, wearing an air of uniform gayety, she passed nearly a month; and, as each day increased her popularity, so every hour, in her progress onward, aggravated her embarrassment. At last she began to falter.

One evening, after an unusually brilliant performance, which drew from every part of the theater the most rapturous applause, she hurried from the stage alone. Anxious to avoid observation, she stole away from the company, and proceeded, with a quick step and a heavy and drooping heart, to what, according to Pepys, was called "The Woman's Shift." Here, as the room was devoted exclusively to the female portion of the company (and, indeed, was appropriated by them to the purposes of the toilet), she hoped to enjoy a short period of seclusion; but she had been its occupant only a few minutes, when she was startled by the approach of a footstep.

Indignant at this invasion of her privacy, she hastily arose, determined that the intruder, however elevated his rank, should not triumph in his effrontery. Hardly had the resolution occurred to her, when the chamber door, which she had neglected to fasten, was thrown open, and, to her great surprise, she found herself confronted by a stranger.

He was a man of good stature and commanding figure, al-

returned from a great naval battle, in which he had particularly distinguished himself; and he was looked upon as one of the great lions of the day, besides being young, attractive, and possessed of a very fascinating appearance.

Marie Antoinette's third lover was the celebrated Cardinal de Rohan, who loved the beautiful woman long and only too well, and who became involved in a disgraceful intrigue through that misguided and daring infatuation

The Cardinal Louis de Rohan was a man in the prime of life, and of an imposing figure and noble bearing; his eyes shone with intelligence, his mouth was well cut and handsome, and his hands were beautiful. A premature baldness indicated either a man of pleasure or a studious one—and he was both. He was a man no little sought after by the ladies, and was noted for his magnificent style of living; indeed, he had found the way to feel himself poor with an income of 1,500,000 francs.

The king liked him for his learning, but the queen hated him. The reasons for this hate were twofold; first, when ambassador to Vienna he had written to Louis XV, letters so full of sarcasm on Maria Theresa, that her daughter had never forgiven him; and he had also written letters opposing her marriage, which had been read aloud by Louis XV at a supper at Madame Dubarry's, one of his mistresses. The embassy at Vienna had been taken from M. de Breteuil and given to M. de Rohan; the former gentleman, not strong enough to revenge himself alone, had procured copies of these letters, which he had laid before the dauphine, thus making her the eternal enemy of M. de Rohan.

This hatred rendered the cardinal's position at court not a little uncomfortable. Every time he presented himself before the queen he met with the same discouraging reception. In spite of this he neglected no occasion of being near her, for which he had frequent opportunities, as he was chaplain to the court: and he never complained of the treatment he received. A circle of friends, among whom the Baron de Planta was the most intimate, helped to console him for these royal rebuffs, not to speak of the ladies of the court, who by no means imitated the severity of the queen towards him.

Certain friends of the cardinal, among whom was Madame de la Motte, encouraged the enamored prelate in his love intrigue, and even hinted that the queen's apparent dislike was all assumed. It was this intriguing creature who afterwards embroiled the cardinal in the celebrated necklace affair, which caused a great commotion as well as scandal at the time, and in which he was made a dupe of the cunning and charming woman. As this artful woman will figure in the adventures of the three lovers, it will be well to give a brief account of her history.

One day Madame de Boulainvilliers, wife of the Provost of Paris, met in a village in Burgundy a little girl, who held out her hand, saying: "My beautiful lady, for the love of God, give something to the descendant of the former Kings of France."

The words surprised Mdme. de Boulainvilliers; she asked the child to explain her singular way of begging. The curate of the village, who was passing by, told Madame that the child said the truth, and that she was the lineal descendant of Henri de Saint-Rémy, bastard of Henry II. and of Nicole de Savigny.

Madame de Boulainvilliers also heard that the child was an orphan, and that she lived on public charity. She took her to Paris; her genealogy was examined, and it was discovered that the little Jeanne de Valois, her brother, and her sister, were really scions of the old royal stock. A petition was presented to the Queen and to M. de Maurepas by the Duke de Brancas-Céreste. Pensions were granted to the three children. The boy entered the navy; he became a lieutenant, and died under the name of Baron de Saint-Rémy de Valois.

In 1780 Jeanne de Valois married a member of Monsieur's private guard, Comte de la Motte. This officer was poor; his wife's portion consisted of a small pension, and this was insufficient for the ambition of La Motte and his wife. Madame de la Motte was considered to be a very beautiful woman; she was witty and attractive, and expressed herself with elegance and facility. She

became acquainted with the Cardinal de Rohan, who lent her money and protected her.

It is difficult to say whether the prelate's generosity was quite disinterested; but there is reason to believe that it was not, especially as he lent Madame de la Motte, without any plausible reason, a sum amounting to one hundred and twenty thousand livres, previous to the necklace affair. Howbeit Mdme. de la Motte enjoyed the intimacy of the fastidious prelate, and discovered his secret aspirations. She found out that his desire was to have over the Queen, who, it is said, exercised a sovereign domination over her husband, the same influence as Cardinal Mazarin had had with Anne d'Autriche. She flattered his hobby, and used it as the basis of her future fortunes.

The almost stupid simplicity through which M. de Rohan fell a victim to the snare of this wily woman will afford an idea of the prelate's intellectual caliber. Mdme. de la Motte persuaded the Cardinal that she was on terms of intimacy with the Queen; that, conscious as she was of the Cardinal's eminent qualities, she had so often spoken of him to her Majesty that the Cardinal was on his way to favor; that Marie Antoinette authorized him to send her the justification of his supposed blunders during his embassy in Austria; that she further wished to have with M. de Rohan a correspondence which was to remain secret until she could openly manifest her preference for him; that Mdme. de la Motte was to be the bearer of this correspondence, the result of which must infallibly lead the Cardinal to the highest favor and influence.

The charming queen received the young soldier from America in the most gracious manner, and invited him to accompany her on a skating excursion on the French lake, on the following day.

It so happened that, while young Tavernay was the soul of honor and manhood, he had a corrupt and unscrupulous father, who was ever involved in the scandals and intrigues of the court.

This old reprobate was standing on the shore as his son was sending Marie Antoinette along the ice in a manner that raised the envy of the most expert skaters on the frozen lake. The young soldier had practiced skating on the great American lakes, and so pleased the queen in the highest degree by the swiftness and grace of his movements, as he pushed her along on the little sleigh; but he was not accustomed to the manners and customs of a corrupt court.

When the young man reached the shore, his father drew him aside in an energetic manner, saying:

"Listen, M. Philippe. America is, I know, a country a long way from this, and where there is neither king nor queen."

"Nor subjects."

"Nor subjects, M. Philosopher; I do not deny it; that point does not interest me; but what does so is, that I fear also to have to come to a conclusion——"

"What, father?"

"That you are a simpleton, my son; just trouble yourself to look over there."

"Well, sir."

"Well, the queen looks back, and it is the third time she has done so: there! she turns again, and who do you think she is looking for, but for you, M. Puritan?"

"Well, sir," said the young man, "if it were true, which it probably is not, that the queen was looking for——"

"Oh!" interrupted the old man, angrily, "this fellow is not of my blood; he cannot be a Tavernay. Sir, I repeat to you, that the queen is looking for you."

"You have good sight, sir," said his son, dryly.

"Come," said the old man, more gently, and trying to moderate his impatience, "trust my experience; are you, or are you not, a man?"

Philippe made no reply.

His father ground his teeth with anger, to see himself opposed by this steadfast will; but making one more effort, "Philippe, my son," said he, still more gently, "listen to me."

"It seems to me, sir, that I have been doing nothing else for the last quarter of an hour."

"Oh," thought the old man, "I will draw you down from your stilts. I will find out your weak side." Then aloud, "You have overlooked one thing, Philippe."

"What, sir!"

"When you left for America, there was a king, but no queen, if it were not the Dubarry; hardly a respectable sovereign. You came back and see a queen, and you think you must be very respectful."

"Doubtless."

"Poor child,' said his father, laughing.

"How, sir! You blame me for respecting the monarchy—you, a Tavernay Maison Rouge, one of the best names in France."

"I do not speak of the monarchy, but only of the queen."

"And you make a difference?"

"Pardieu, I should think so. What is royalty? a crown, that is unapproachable. But what is a queen? a woman, and she, on the contrary, is very approachable."

Philippe made a gesture of disgust.

"You do not believe me," continued the old man, almost fiercely; "well, ask M. de Coigny, ask M. de Lauzun, or M. de Vaudreuil."

"Silence, father!" cried Philippe; "or for these three blasphemies, not being able to strike you three blows with my sword, I shall strike them on myself."

The old man stepped back, murmuring, "Mon Dieu, what a stupid animal. Good-evening, son, you rejoice me; I thought I was the father, the old man, but now I think it is I who must be the young Apollo and you an old man;" and he turned away.

Philippe stopped him: "You did not speak seriously, did you, father? It is impossible that a gentleman of good blood like you should give ear to these calumnies, spread by the enemies, not only of the queen, but of the throne."

"He will not believe, the double mule," said the old man.

"You speak to me as you would before God!"

"Yes, truly."

"Before God, whom you approach every day?"

"It seems to me, my son," replied he, "that I am a gentleman, and that you may believe my word."

"It is, then, your opinion that the queen has had lovers?"

"Certainly."

"Those whom you have named?"

"And others, for what I know. Ask all the town and the court. One must be just returned from America, to be ignorant of all they say."

"And who says this, sir? some vile pamphleteers."

"Oh! do you, then, take me for an editor?"

"No; and there is the mischief, when men like you repeat such calumnies, which, without that, would melt away like the unwholesome vapors which sometimes obscure the most brilliant sunshine; but people like you repeating them, give them a terrible stability. Oh, monsieur, for mercy's sake, do not repeat such things."

"I do repeat them, however."

"And why do you repeat them?" cried Philippe, fiercely.

"Oh!" said the old man, with his satanic laugh, "to prove to you that I was not wrong when I said 'Philippe, the queen looks back; she is looking for you. Philippe, the queen wishes for you; run to her."

"Oh! father, hold your tongue, or you will drive me mad."

"Really, Philippe, I do not understand you. Is it a crime to love? It shows that one has a heart: and in the eyes of this woman, in her voice, in everything, can you not read her heart? She loves; is it you? or is it another? I know not, but believe in my own experience, at this moment she loves, or is beginning to love, some one. But you are a philosopher, a Puritan, a Quaker, an American; you do not love; well, then, let her look; let her turn again and again; despise her, Philippe, I should say Joseph de Tavernay."

The old man hurried away, satisfied with the effect he had produced, and fled like the serpent who was the first tempter into crime.

Philippe remained alone, his heart swelling and his blood boiling. He remained fixed in his place for about half an hour, when the queen having finished her tour, returned to where he stood, and called out to him:

"You must be rested now, M. de Tavernay; come, then, for there is no one like you to guide a queen royally."

Philippe ran to her, giddy, and hardly knowing what he did. He placed his hand on the back of the sledge, but started as though he had burned his fingers; the queen had thrown herself negligently back into the sledge, and the fingers of the young man touched the locks of Marie Antoinette.

From that moment until the day of his death, the young soldier was the slave of the bewitching queen.

De Charny was also received by Marie Antoinette in a very gracious manner; and then the gallant sailor, who was not quite so high-souled as the soldier in his gallantries, soon conceived a guilty passion for his mistress.

The two young lovers became exceedingly jealous of each other; a quarrel and a duel ensued, and De Charny received a severe wound, which was the forerunner of a violent fever.

While he was in a state of delirium, raving wildly about the queen, she who was the cause of all his trouble paid him a secret visit, in company with the doctor who was in attendance on him.

The queen stood in an anteroom, listening to the wild expressions, when the doctor said:

"Do you hear, madame?"

"It is frightful," continued Charny, "to love an angel, a woman—to love her madly—to be willing to give your life for her; and when you come near her to find her only a queen—of velvet and of gold, of metal and of silk, and no heart."

"Oh! oh!" cried the doctor again.

"I love a married woman!" Charny went on, "and with that wild love which makes me forget everything else. Well, I will say to her, there remains for us still some happy days on this earth. Come, my beloved, and we will live the life of the blessed, if we love each other. Afterwards there will be death—better than a life like this. Let us love at least."

"Not badly reasoned for a man in a fever," said the doctor.

"But her children!" cried Charny, suddenly, with fury; "she will not leave her children. Oh! we will carry them away also. Surely I can carry her, she is so light, and her children, too." Then he gave a terrible cry—"But they are the children of a king!"

The doctor left his patient and approached the queen.

"You are right, doctor," she said; "this young man would incur a terrible danger if he were overheard."

"Listen again," said the doctor.

"Oh, no more."

But just then Charny said, in a gentler voice:

"Marie, I feel that you love me, but I will say nothing about it. Marie, I felt the touch of your foot in the coach; your hand touched mine, but I will never tell; I will keep this secret with my life. My blood may all flow away, Marie, but my secret shall not escape with it. My enemy steeped his sword in my blood, but if he guessed my secret, yours is safe. Fear nothing, Marie, I do not even ask you if you love me; you blushed, that is enough."

"Oh!" thought the doctor; "this sounds less like delirium than like memory."

"I have heard enough," cried the queen, rising and trembling violently; and she tried to go.

The doctor stopped her; "Madame," said he, "what do you wish?"

"Nothing doctor, nothing."

"But if the king ask to see my patient?"

"Oh! that would be dreadful!"

"What shall I say?"

"Doctor, I cannot think; this dreadful spectacle has confused me."

"I think you have caught his fever," said the doctor, feeling her pulse."

She drew away her hand, and escaped.

The young man recovered soon after and went to reside on his estate in the country; but he was so impatient to be near his adored mistress that he set off at midnight and returned to Versailles in secret. Having hired a little cottage outside the park, De Charny spent his days and nights in watching the queen during her rambles with her ladies, and in gazing at her windows at night.

One night the ardent lover uttered a cry of joy, for he perceived the queen in the park attended by a single female. Springing over the walls, with the purpose of throwing himself at the feet of the woman he adored so much, he had just gained a position behind a tree, when he saw a tall man, enveloped in a great coat, and wearing a slouched hat, approaching Marie Antoinette, who hastened to meet him in a secluded spot, while the female attendant remained behind.

In approaching the queen, the man raised her hand to his lips, and then he embraced her in a more affectionate manner.

Mad with rage, the jealous lover flew from the spot, moaning: "She loves another. Oh! this is more than I can bear. My hated rival is successful."

There were many strange rumors afloat at this time about the adventures of the queen in places and in company that did not redound to the credit of her fair name, and the name of Cardinal de Rohan was mixed up with these rumors.

It was also asserted that the amorous cardinal had presented the queen with a very valuable necklace, which had been made for one of the mistresses of the late king.

On the next night, Charny was again in the park at the same hour, and the two ladies appeared at the rendezvous.

Charny had taken his resolution, he would find out who this lover was; but when he entered the avenue he could see no one, they had entered the baths of Apollo. He walked toward the door and saw the confidante who waited outside.

The queen then was in there alone with her lover; it was too much. Charny was about to seize this woman, and force her to tell him everything, but the rage and emotion he had endured was too much for him; a mist passed over his eyes, internal bleeding commenced, and he fainted; when he came to himself again the clock was striking two, the place was deserted, and there was no trace of what had passed there. He went home, and passed a night almost of delirium.

The next morning he arose pale as death, and went toward the castle of Trianon, just as the queen was leaving the chapel. All heads were respectfully lowered as she passed. She was looking beautiful, and when she saw Charny she colored and uttered an exclamation of surprise:

"I thought you were in the country, M. de Charny," she said.

"I have returned, madame," said he, in a brusque, and almost rude tone.

She looked at him in surprise; then turning towards the ladies, "Good-morning, countess," she said to Madame Jeanne de la Motte, who stood near.

Charny started as he caught sight of her, and looked at her almost wildly. "He has not quite recovered his reason," thought the queen, observing his strange manner; then turning to him again, "How are you now, M. de Charny?" she said, in a kind voice.

"Very well, madame."

She looked surprised again, then said, "Where are you living?"

"At Versailles, madame."

"Since when?"

"For three nights," replied he, in a marked manner.

The queen manifested no emotion, but Jeanne trembled.

"Have you got something to say to me?" asked the queen again with kindness.

"Oh, madame, I should have too much to say to your majesty."

"Come," said she, and she walked towards her apartments, but to avoid the appearance of a tete-a-tete she invited several ladies to follow her. Jeanne, unquiet, placed herself among them, but when they arrived she dismissed Madame de Misery, and the other ladies, understanding that she wished to be alone, left her. Charny stood before her—"Speak," said the queen, "you appear troubled, sir."

"How can I begin?" said Charny, thinking aloud, "how can I dare to accuse honor and majesty?"

"Sir!" cried Marie Antoinette, with a flaming look.

"And yet I should only say what I have seen."

The queen rose. "Sir," said she, "it is very early in the morning for me to think you are intoxicated, but I can find no other solution for this conduct."

Charny, unmoved, continued, "After all what is a queen? a woman; and am I not a man as well as a subject?"

"Monsieur!"

"Madame, anger is out of place now. I believe I have formerly proved that I had respect for your royal dignity. I fear I proved that I had an insane love for yourself. Choose, therefore, to whom I shall speak. Is it to the queen, or the woman, that I shall address my accusation, of dishonor and shame?"

"Monsieur de Charny," cried the queen, growing pale; "if you do not leave this room, I must have you turned out by my guards."

"But I will tell you first," cried he, passionately, "why I call you an unworthy queen and woman. I have been in the park these three nights."

Instead of seeing her tremble, as he believed she would on hearing these words, the queen rose, and approaching him, said:

"M. de Charny, your state excites my pity, your hands tremble, you grow pale, you are suffering; shall I call for help?"

"I saw you," cried he, again; "saw you with that man to whom you gave the rose—saw you when he kissed your hands—saw you when you entered the baths of Apollo with him."

The queen passed her hands over her eyes, as if to make sure that she was not dreaming.

"Sit down," said she, "or you will fall."

Charny, indeed unable to keep up, fell upon the sofa. She sat down by him.

"Be calm," said she, "and repeat what you have just said."

"Do you want to kill me?" he murmured.

"Then let me question," she said. "How long have you returned from the country?"

"A fortnight."

"Where do you live?"

"In the huntsman's house, which I have hired."

"At the end of the park?"

"Yes."

"You speak of some one whom you saw with me."

"Yes."

"Where?"

"In the park."

"When?"

"At midnight; Tuesday, for the first time, I saw you and your companion."

"Oh! I had a companion. Do you know her, also?"

"I thought just now I recognized her, but I could not be positive, because it was only the figure. She always hid her face, like all who commit crimes."

"And this person, to whom you say I gave a rose?"

"I have never been able to meet him."

"You do not know him, then?"

"Only that he is called monseigneur."

The queen stamped her foot—"Go on," said she; "Tuesday, I gave him a rose——"

"Wednesday you gave your hands to kiss, and yesterday you went alone with him into the baths of Apollo, while your companion waited outside."

"And you saw me?" said she, rising.

He lifted his hands to heaven, and cried, "I swear it."

"Oh, he swears."

"Yes, on Tuesday you wore your green dress, moirée, with gold; Wednesday, the dress with great blue and brown leaves; and yesterday the same dress that you wore when I last kissed your hand. Oh, madame, I am ready to die with grief and shame, while I repeat, that on my life, my honor, it was really you."

"What can I say?" cried the queen, dreadfully agitated. "If I swore he would not believe me."

Charny shook his head.

"Madman," cried she, "thus to accuse your queen; to dishonor thus an innocent woman. Do you believe me, when I swear by all I hold sacred, that I was not in the park on either of those days after four o'clock? Do you wish it to be proved by my women—by the king. No, he does not believe me."

"I saw you," replied he.

"Oh, I know," she cried; "did they not see me at the ball at the opera—at Mesmer's, scandalizing the crowd? You know it; you who fought for me."

"Madame, then I fought because I did not believe it; now I might fight, but I believe."

The queen raised her arms to heaven, while burning tears rolled down her cheeks—"My God," she cried, "send me some thought which will save me. I do not wish this man to despise me."

Charny, moved to the heart, hid his face in his hands.

Then, after a moment's silence, the queen continued—"Sir, you owe me reparation. I exact this from you; you say you have seen me three nights with a man; I have been already injured through the resemblance to me of some woman, I know not whom, but who is like her unhappy queen. But you are pleased to think it was me. Well, I will go with you into the park, and if she appears again, you will be satisfied. Perhaps we shall see her together; then, sir, you will regret the suffering you have caused me."

Charny pressed his hands to his heart—"Oh, madame, you overwhelm me with your kindness."

"I wish to overwhelm you with proof; not a word to any one, but this evening, at ten o'clock, wait alone at the door of the park. Now, go, sir."

Charny kneeled, and went away without a word.

Jeanne, who was waiting in the ante-chamber, examined him attentively as he came out. She was soon after summoned to the queen.

The intriguing Jeanne de la Motte was playing a very deep game; and when she saw the queen and Charny together she was in agony lest an exposure should ensue. When she was summoned to the presence of the queen she hoped to gain some important information; but Marie Antoinette was beginning to learn caution, and she guarded herself carefully.

Jeanne was, therefore, reduced to conjectures; she had already ordered one of her footmen to follow M. de Charny. The man reported that he had gone into a house at the end of the park.

"Then there is no more doubt," thought Jeanne; "it is a lover who has seen everything, it is clear. I should be a fool not to understand. I must undo what I have done."

On leaving Versailles she drove to the Rue St. Claude; there she found a superb present of plate, sent to her by the cardinal. She then drove to his house, and found him radiant with joy and pride. On her entrance he ran to meet her, calling her "Dear countess," and full of protestations and gratitude.

"Thank you, also, for your charming present. You are more than a happy man; you are a triumphant victor."

"Countess, it frightens me; it is too much."

Jeanne smiled.

"You came from Versailles?" continued he.

"Yes."

"You have seen her?"

"I have just left her."

"And she said nothing?"

"What do you expect that she said?"

"Oh! I am insatiable."

"Well, you had better not ask."

"You frighten me. Is anything wrong? Have I come to the height of my happiness, and is the descent to begin?"

"You are very fortunate not to have been discovered."

"Oh, with precautions, and the intelligence of two hearts and one mind——"

"That will not prevent eyes seeing through the trees."

"We have been seen!"

"I fear so."

"And recognized!"

"Oh, monseigneur, if you had been—if this secret had been known to any one, Jeanne de Valois would be out of the kingdom, and you would be dead."

"True; but tell me quickly. They have seen people walking in the park; is there any harm in that?"

"Ask the king."

"The king knows?"

"I repeat to you, if the king knew, you would be in the Bastile. But I advise you not to tempt Providence again."

"What do you mean, dear countess?"

"Do you not understand?"

"I fear to understand," he replied.

"I shall fear, if you do not promise to go no more to Versailles."

"By day?"

"Or by night."

"Impossible."

"Why so, monseigneur?"

"Because I have in my heart a love which will end only with my life."

"So I perceive," replied she, ironically; "and it is to arrive more quickly at this result that you persist in returning to the park, for most assuredly if you do, your love and your life will end together."

"Oh, countess, how fearful you are; you who were so brave yesterday!"

"I am always brave when there is no danger."

"But I have the bravery of my race, and am happier in the presence of danger."

"But permit me to tell you——"

"No, countess, the die is cast. Death, if it comes; but first, love. I shall return to Versailles."

"Alone, then."

"Is that what you were sent to tell me?"

"It is what I have been preparing you for."

"She will see me no more?"

"Never. And it is I who have counseled it."

"Madame, do not plunge the knife into my heart," cried he, in a doleful voice.

"It would be much more cruel, monseigneur, to let two foolish people destroy themselves for want of a little good advice."

"Countess, I would rather die."

"As regards yourself, that is easy; but subject, you dare not dethrone your queen; man, you will not destroy a woman."

"But confess that you do not come in her name, that she does not throw me off."

"I speak in her name."

"It is only a delay she asks."

"Take it as you wish; but obey her orders."

"The park is not the only place of meeting. There are a hundred safer spots—the queen can come to you, for instance."

"Monseigneur, not a word more. The weight of your secret is too much for me, and I believe her capable, in a fit of remorse, of confessing all to the king."

"Good God! impossible."

"If you saw her you would pity her."

"What can I do, then?"

"Insure her safety by your silence."

"But she will think I have forgotten her, and accuse me of being a coward."

"To save her."

"Can a woman forgive him who abandons her ?"

"Do not judge her like others."

"I believe her great and strong. I love her for her courage and her noble heart. She may count on me, as I do on her. Once more I will see her; lay bare my heart to her; and whatever she then commands, I will sacredly obey."

Jeanne rose. "Go, then," said she, "but go alone. I have thrown the key of the park into the river. You can go to Versailles—I shall go to Switzerland or Holland. The further off I am when the shell bursts the better."

"Countess, you abandon me. With whom shall I talk of her?"

"Oh ! you have the park and the echoes. You can teach them her name !"

"Countess, pity me; I am in despair."

"Well, but do not act in so childish and dangerous a manner. If you love her so much, guard her name, and if you are not totally without gratitude, do not involve in your own ruin those who have served you through friendship. Swear to me not to attempt to see or speak to her for a fortnight, and I will remain, and may yet be of service to you. But if you decide to brave all, I shall leave at once, and you must extricate yourself as you can."

"It is dreadful," murmured the cardinal; "the fall from so much happiness is overwhelming. I shall die of it."

"Suffering is always the consequence of love. Come, mon seigneur, decide. Am I to remain here, or start for Lausanne?"

"Remain, countess."

"You swear to obey me ?"

"On the faith of a Rohan."

"Good. Well, then, I forbid interviews, but not letters."

"Really! I may write ?"

"Yes."

"And she will answer ?"

"Try."

The cardinal kissed Jeanne's hand again, and called her his guardian angel. The demon within her must have laughed.

That day, at four o'clock, a man on horseback stopped in the outskirts of the park, just behind the baths of Apollo, where M. de Rohan used to wait. He got off, and looked at the places where the grass had been trodden down.

"Here are the traces," thought he; "it is as I supposed, M. de Charny has returned for a fortnight, and this is where he enters the park." And he sighed "Leave him to his happiness. God gives to one, and denies to another. But I will have proof to-night. I will hide in the bushes, and see what happens."

As for Charny, obedient to the queen's commands, he waited for orders; but it was half-past ten, and no one appeared. He waited with impatient anxiety. Then he began to think she had deceived him, and had promised what she did not mean to perform. "How could I be so foolish—I, who saw her—to be taken in by her words and promises!" At last he saw a figure approaching, wrapped in a large black mantle, and he uttered a cry of joy, for he recognized the queen. He ran to her, and fell at her feet.

"Ah, here you are, sir! it is well."

"Ah, madame! I scarcely hoped you were coming."

"Have you your sword?"

"Yes, madame."

"Where do you say those people came in?"

"By this door."

"At what time?"

"At midnight each time."

"There is no reason why they should not come again to-night. You have not spoken to any one?"

"To no one."

"Come into the thick wood and let us watch. I have not spoken of this to M. de Crosne. I have already mentioned this creature to him, and if she be not arrested, he is either incapable, or in league with my enemies. It seems incredible that any one

should dare to play such tricks under my eyes, unless they were sure of impunity. Therefore, I think it is time to take the care of my reputation on myself. What do you think?"

"Oh, madame, allow me to be silent! I am ashamed of all I have said."

"At least you are an honest man," replied the queen, "and speak to the accused face to face. You do not stab in the dark."

"Oh, madame, it is eleven o'clock! I tremble."

"Look about, that no one is here."

Charny obeyed. "No one," said he.

"Where did the scenes pass that you have described!"

"Oh, madame, I had a shock when I returned to you; for she stood just where you are at this moment."

"Here!" cried the queen, leaving the place with disgust.

"Yes, madame; under the chestnut tree."

"Then, sir, let us move, for they will most likely come here again."

He followed the queen to a different place. She, silent and proud, waited for the proof of her innocence to appear. Midnight struck. The door did not open. Half an hour passed, during which the queen asked ten times if they had always been punctual.

Three-quarters struck—the queen stamped with impatience.

"They will not come," she cried; "these misfortunes only happen to me;" and she looked at Charny, ready to quarrel with him, if she saw any expression of triumph and irony; but he, as his suspicions began to return, grew so pale, and looked so melancholy, that he was like the figure of a martyr.

At last she took his arm, and led him under the chestnut tree.

"You say," she murmured, "that it was here you saw her!"

"Yes, madame."

"Here, that she gave the rose!"

And the queen, fatigued, and wearied with waiting and disappointment, leaned against a tree, and covered her face with her hands, but Charny could see the tears stealing through. At last she raised her head.

"Sir," said she, "I am condemned. I promised to prove to you to-day that I was calumniated; God does not permit it, and I submit. I have done what no other woman, not to say queen, would have done. What a queen! who cannot reign over one heart, who cannot obtain the esteem of one honest man. Come, sir, give me your arm if you do not despise me too much."

"Oh, madame!" cried he, falling at her feet, "if I were only an unhappy man who loves you, could you not pardon me!"

"You!" cried she, with a bitter laugh, "you love me! and believe me infamous!"

"Oh, madame!"

"You accuse me of giving roses, kisses, and love. No, sir, no falsehoods; you do not love me."

"Madame, I saw these phantoms. Pity me, for I am on the rack."

She took his hands.

"Yes, you saw, and you think it was I. Well, if here under this same tree, you at my feet, I press your hands, and say to you, M. de Charny, I love you, I have loved, and shall love no one else in this world, may God pardon me—will that convince you? Will you believe me then?"

As she spoke she came so close to him that he felt her breath on his lips.

"Oh!" cried Charny, "now I am ready to die."

"Give me your arm," said she, "and teach me where they went, and where she gave the rose—and she took from her bosom a rose and held it to him. He took it, and pressed it to his heart.

"Then," continued she, "the other gave him her hand to kiss?"

"Both her hands," cried Charny, pressing his burning lips passionately on hers.

"Now they visited the baths—so will we; follow me to the place."

He followed her, like a man in a strange, happy dream. They

looked all round, then opened the door, and walked through.
When they came out again two o'clock struck.

"Adieu," said she; "now go home until to-morrow."
And she walked away quickly towards the chateau.

When they had gone a man rose from among the bushes.
He had heard and seen all.

That man was young Philippe Tavernay.

The queen went out riding on the following day. She seemed
full of joy, and was generous and gracious to every one. The road
was lined as usual on her return with ladies and gentlemen.
Among them was Madame de la Motte and M. de Charny, who
was complimented by many friends on his return, and on his
radiant looks. Glancing round he saw Philippe standing near
him, whom he had not seen since the day of the duel.

"Gentlemen," said Charny, passing through the crowd, "allow me to fulfill an act of politeness;" and advancing towards
Philippe he said, "Allow me, M. de Tavernay, to thank you for
the interest you have taken in my health. I shall have the honor
to pay you a visit to-morrow. I trust you preserve no enmity
towards me."

"None, sir," replied Philippe.

Charny held out his hand, but Philippe, without seeming to
notice it, said:

"Here comes the queen, sir,"

As she approached she fixed her looks on Charny with that
rash openness which she always showed in her affections, while
she said to several gentlemen, who were pressing round her:

"Ask me what you please, gentlemen, for to-day I can refuse
nothing."

A voice said, "Madame."

She turned, and saw Philippe, and thus found herself between
two men, of whom she almost reproached herself with loving one
too much and the other too little.

"M. de Tavernay, you have something to ask me; pray
speak——"

"Only ten minutes' audience at your majesty's leisure," replied
he, with grave solemnity.

"Immediately, sir—follow me."

A quarter of an hour after, Philippe was introduced into the
library, where the queen waited for him.

"Ah! M. de Tavernay, enter," said she, in a gay tone, "and
do not look so sorrowful. Do you know I feel rather frightened
whenever a Tavernay asks for an audience. Reassure me quickly, and tell me that you are not come to announce a misfortune."

"Madame, this time I only bring you good news."

"Oh! some news?"

"Alas! yes, your majesty."

"There! an 'alas' again."

"Madame, I am about to assure your majesty that you need
never again fear to be saddened by the sight of a Tavernay; for,
madame, the last of this family, to whom you once deigned to
show some kindness, is about to leave the Court of France forever."

The queen, dropping her gay tone, said, "You leave us?"

"Yes, your majesty."

"You also?"

Philippe bowed. "My sister, madame, has already had that
grief; I am much more useless to your majesty."

The queen started as she remembered that Andree or his
sister had asked for her congé on the day following her first visit
to Charny in the doctor's apartments. "It is strange," she murmured, as Philippe remained motionless as a statue, waiting his
dismissal. At last she said, abruptly:

"Where are you going?"

"To join M. de la Perouse, madame."

"He is at Newfoundland."

"I have prepared to join him there."

"Do you know that a frightful death has been predicted for
him?"

"A speedy one," replied Philippe; "that is not necessarily a
frightful one."

"And you are really going?"

"Yes, madame, to share his fate."

The queen was silent for a time, and then said: "Why do you
go?"

"Because I am anxious to travel."

"But you have already made the tour of the world?"

"Of the New World, madame, but not of the Old."

"A race of iron, with hearts of steel, are you Tavernays. You
and your sister are terrible people—you go not for the sake of
traveling, but to leave me. Your sister said she was called by
religious duty; it was a pretext. However, she wished to go,
and she went. May she be happy. You might be happy here,
but you also wish to go away."

"Spare us, I pray you, madame. If you could read our
hearts you would find them full of unlimited devotion towards
you."

"Oh," cried the queen, "you are too exacting; she takes the
world for a heaven, where one should only live as a saint; you
look upon it as a hell—and both fly from it; she, because she
finds what she does not seek, and you, because you do not find
what you do seek. Am I not right? Ah, M. de Tavernay,
allow human beings to be imperfect, and do not expect royalty
to be superhuman. Be more tolerant, or rather less egotistical."

She spoke earnestly, and continued:

"All I know is, that I loved Andree, and that she left me;
that I valued you, and you are about to do the same. It is humiliating to see two such people abandon my court."

"Nothing can humiliate persons like your majesty. Shame
does not reach those placed so high."

"What has wounded you?" asked the queen.

"Nothing, madame."

"Your rank has been raised, your fortune was progressing."

"I can but repeat to your majesty that the court does not
please me."

"And if I ordered you to stay here!"

"I should have the grief of disobeying your majesty."

"Oh! I know," cried she, impatiently, "you bear malice, you
quarreled with a gentleman here, M. de Charny, and wounded
him; and because you see him returned to-day, you are jealous,
and wish to leave."

Philippe turned pale, but replied:

"Madame, I saw him sooner than you imagine, for I met him
at two o'clock this morning by the baths of Apollo."

It was now the queen's time to grow pale, but she felt a kind
of admiration for one who had retained so much courtesy and
self-command in the midst of his anger and grief.

"Go," murmured she at length, in a faint voice. "I will keep
you no longer."

Philippe bowed, and left the room, while the queen sank, terrified and overwhelmed, on the sofa.

And now the strangest portion of this strange historical affair
remains to be told, which explains the mystery of the queen's
appearance in the park, and her apparent amours with the man
wearing the slouched hat.

A magnificent necklace had been ordered by Louis XV.
of MM. Boemer and Bossange, the crown jewelers. It was made
for Madame du Barry. The king died before it was finished; his
favorite mistress was exiled by the new monarch, and the beautiful jewel remained in the hands of the makers. They offered it
to the queen; but the price, which amounted to 1,800,000 livres,
was thought too high. Madame de la Motte saw the necklace.

The jewelers told her they were much embarrassed by the
Queen's refusal to purchase it; they were impeded in their trade
by such a considerable outlay of money, and they offered to make
a rich present to whoever could find a buyer.

The Countess thought that the Queen would be only too glad
to get the necklace if she had not to pay for it; and she inferred
that Marie Antoinette could not but feel very grateful to the
person who would get it for her. Her husband, M. de la Motte,
entered into the plot.

They obtained the support of the Comte de Cagliostro, who exercised a powerful influence over M. de Rohan, and at length Madame de la Motte persuaded the Cardinal that the Queen wished to purchase the necklace with her own money; that, as a token of good feeling toward the Cardinal, she requested him to buy the jewel in her name; and that she would send him a receipt written and signed with her own hand.

This document was handed to M. de Rohan by Madame de la Motte; it was dated from Trianon, and signed "Marie Antoinette de France."

How the Cardinal could fail to discover the forgery when he saw this signature, it is difficult to say. The Queen, like all the princesses who had preceded her on the throne, signed her Christian name only, and the words "de France," due to the imagination of the forger (Retaux de Villette) were a sufficient indication of the origin of the document.

But he had no suspicion; and really believing that he was acting in accordance with the wishes of his sovereign, and thinking that the highest favor would be accorded to him for his intervention, he sent for the jewelers, and showed them the Queen's receipt.

They accepted the arrangements he proposed, and on the 1st of February the casket was handed to Mdme. de la Motte at Versailles; and it was remitted by her, in the Cardinal's presence, to a so-called valet de chambre of the royal household, who was no other than the forger, Retaux de Villette. This bold fraud was brought to a conclusion by the departure for England of M. de la Motte with the rich booty.

After thus gaining possession of the necklace, Mdme. de la Motte was not satisfied; she hoped to compromise the Queen and the Cardinal still more. She therefore set to work again. Retaux de Villette wrote other letters, by which the Queen informed M. de Rohan that, being unable to give him public marks of her esteem, she wished to see him between eleven and midnight in the suburbs of Versailles. Mdme. de la Motte had met an abandoned girl of the name of Oliva whose resemblance to Marie Antoinette had struck her, and who acted the part of the Queen. The meeting took place in the park and in the Baths of Apollo. Mdlle. Oliva's performance was admirable; she gave a rose to the Cardinal, who was choking with emotion, and then sent him away in a state of high exultation.

De Rohan felt assured that he had received the embraces of the Queen whom he had loved so long, and he was in raptures.

But the date fixed for the payment of the first installment of the price of the necklace was drawing near, and the jewelers were somewhat uneasy. They tried to ascertain whether the necklace was in the Queen's possession; but they could not obtain an audience, and they soon discovered they were the victims of a robbery. In their indignation they made known the whole affair; and it was reported to M. de Breteuil, minister of the King's household.

M. de Breteuil was the Cardinal's personal enemy, and he eagerly seized the opportunity of manifesting his dislike. He had a secret conversation with the Queen; informed her of the rumors that were being circulated concerning herself, the Cardinal, and Mdme. de la Motte; and besought her to tell him if she had any reason to fear a public investigation.

The Queen answered that she had no apprehension whatever, and that the sooner the mystery was explained the better. On August 15th, the Cardinal, as great almoner, was to officiate in the chapel. He was about to assume his religious robes when an usher came to inform him that the King wished to speak to him. Louis XVI., Marie Antoinette, and M. de Breteuil were together when the Cardinal appeared in the royal presence. The King spoke to him in a strongly irritated tone:

"Sir, you have, I believe, bought diamonds at Boemer's?"

"I have, your Majesty," answered De Rohan.

"Where are they?"

M. de Rohan hesitated. "I thought, Sire," said he, at length, "that these diamonds were in the possession of the Queen."

"Who directed you to send them to the Queen?"

"A lady named Madame la Comtesse de la Motte Valois. She

gave me a letter from the Queen, whose orders I thought I obeyed by purchasing the diamonds."

The Queen here interrupted him. "How could you believe, sir," she exclaimed, "that after looking upon you with disfavor for more than eight years I could select you for such a piece of business, and through the intervention of such a woman?"

"I now perceive," answered the Cardinal, "that I have been cruelly deceived. My wish to please your Majesty led me astray. I will pay for the necklace. . . . . I am the victim of a fraud of which before this I had no suspicion. I am extremely sorry."

He produced his pocket-book, and selected the Queen's receipt. The King looked at it: "Why," he said, "this is neither the Queen's handwriting nor her signature. How could you, a prince of the house of Rohan, and the great almoner of France, believe that the Queen signed 'Marie Antoinette de France?' Everybody knows that queens only sign their Christian names."

The Cardinal was getting more and more disconcerted. He was obliged to lean against a table. The King saw this, and told him to go to an adjoining room, where he could write his justification. M. de Rohan obeyed, and reappeared a quarter of an hour after, with a paper which he handed to Louis. At the door he found M. de Jouffroy, lieutenant of the guards, who arrested him, and handed him over to M. d'Agoult, who took him to the Bastile.

Mdme. de la Motte was arrested on the following day. She denied having in any way participated in the theft of the necklace, and she charged M. de Cagliostro with the crime, alleging that he persuaded the Cardinal to buy the necklace. Cagliostro and his wife were arrested.

Mdme. de la Motte hoped, no doubt, to escape by insinuating that the Cardinal as well as Cagliostro was responsible for the necklace; but, unfortunately for her, Mdlle. Oliva was arrested in Brussels, and her revelations threw some light on the mystery. Some time after, Retaux de Villette was taken, and he was confronted with M. de la Motte. In the night of the 29th all the accused were transferred from the Bastile to the Conciergerie; and on September 5 letters patent of the King sent the case before the Parliament.

The letters were couched in strong and bitter terms, and brought against the Cardinal a terrible charge. The affair, which was now publicly known, produced deep sensation. The nobility and the clergy were equally interested in the issue of the trial, the two principal parties being the Queen and a prince of the Church.

The trial was commenced on December 22. Madame la Motte, who was dressed with great care and elegance, was brought in; her face was undisturbed, and she answered all the questions put to her by the president with the utmost coolness and presence of mind. The Cardinal appeared after her. The members of the bench showed him much regard, and it was easy to perceive that, perhaps, through a spirit of opposition to the Court of Versailles, they were favorable to him.

On December 29 the procureur-général read out his conclusions; they were extremely hostile to the Cardinal. The procureur demanded such humiliating admissions as M. de Rohan could not have made, and which must have left him in prison for the remainder of his life. These conclusions met with strong disapprobation on the part of the bench. Sentence was pronounced on the 31st. The court condemned La Motte, in contumaciam, to hard labor for life; Jeanne de Saint-Rémy Valois, wife of La Motte, to amende honorable, and afterward to be whipped and marked on both shoulders with the letter V, and also to imprisonment for life; Retaux de Villette to banishment for life.

Mdlle. Oliva was acquitted; so was M. de Cagliostro. As to the Cardinal, he was cleared of all charges. This judgment was received with a kind of enthusiasm. Public opinion considered it in some sort as a victory. The judges were cheered, writes De Besenval, and so warmly received by the people that they made their way through the crowd with difficulty.

It may be remarked that while the beautiful Marie Antoinette had lovers and admirers to the day when she suffered death on the guillotine at the hands of the Red Republicans in Paris, Cardinal de Rohan never paid court to her again.

THE SECRET AMOURS OF THE GREAT NAPOLEON.

LIFTING THE VEIL FROM A HERO'S FACE—NAPOLEON AS A LADY OF THE COURT SAW HIM—HIS NUMEROUS AMOURS AND HIS QUARRELS WITH JOSEPHINE—A DISPASSIONATE LOVER—HIS LAST LOVE AFFAIR—HIS LAST WIFE AND HER HORROR OF HIM—A GREAT CHANGE

EVERY intelligent person must be familiar with the public career of Napoleon Bonaparte, the first Emperor of the French.

Who has not read of his glorious campaigns in Europe and in Egypt, of his disastrous march into Russia, his defeat at Waterloo, and his death on the lone, barren island of St. Helena?

English histories, with scarcely an exception, represent Napoleon as an ambitious tyrant, as a successful adventurer for the time, and as one who wantonly sacrificed the lives of his people in his march to glory and to conquest.

If you read Sir Walter Scott's history of the great soldier, you will become impressed with the idea that he was almost a monster in human form, and that his defeat and his death should be looked upon by all mankind with feelings of profound joy and gratitude.

Some French historians criticise the actions of the emperor with great severity; but they all declare that he was the ablest general of his age, and that he introduced many just and desirable laws into the country.

Our popular American historian, Abbott, lauds Napoleon to the very skies, and he finds no words of condemnation for his hero, save and except his conduct in deserting Josephine.

Hitherto, from time to time, we have had but few glimpses into the private life of the world-renowned little Corsican, and those views were generally given us by those who had very little opportunity of looking behind the curtains that concealed the actors in their imperial domiciles.

Now, however, we are presented with the memoirs of a lady, who was for many years a resident in the palaces of the emperor, and who was a confidential friend and companion of the unhappy Josephine.

This very intelligent lady was a close observer of the foibles and failings of the emperor; she saw him in every-day life; and she expresses herself concerning him, in a manner verifying the old adage that "familiarity breeds contempt."

It may have been that Madame de Remusat was prejudiced against the great Napoleon, for causes which are not presented in her Memoirs; it may be that the lady had all her sympathies enlisted on the side of the suffering Josephine; and it may be possible that her old affiliations with the aristocrat Bourbons influenced her to look on the pet of the people with disdainful eyes; but certain it is that the most violent foreign enemy of the encroaching conqueror could not picture him with a pen more deeply dipped in gall.

Speaking of his appearance, the lady gives us a very familiar picture, indeed.

"Napoleon Bonaparte," she says, "is short in stature, and somewhat ill-proportioned; his body is too long, and thus makes the rest of his person appear short. His hair is thin and of a chestnut color; his eyes are a grayish blue, and his skin, which in his youth was yellow, became in later years a dead white. His forehead, the setting of his eye, the line of his nose, were all beautiful, and reminded me of an antique medallion. His mouth, which is thin-lipped, becomes agreeable when he laughs, and his teeth are regular. His chin is short, and his jaw heavy and square. He has well-formed hands and feet. I mention them particularly because he thought a good deal of them. He has an habitual slight stoop; his eyes are dull, which gives to his face when in repose a melancholy and thoughtful expression. When he is excited with anger his looks are fierce and menacing.

Laughter makes him look more youthful and not so formidable. It is difficult not to like him when he laughs, his countenance improves so much. He was always simple in his dress, and generally wore the uniform of his own guard. He was cleanly rather from habit than from a liking for cleanliness; he bathed often, sometimes in the middle of the night, because he thought it was healthy; the hurried manner in which he performed every action did not admit of his clothes being put on with care; and on special occasions his servants consulted as to when they might snatch a moment to dress him."

While it is evident from the above that Madame Remusat looked on Napoleon as a pleasing specimen of humanity as viewed with the eyes of a woman who was capable of appreciating manly beauty. It is very evident, from the following expressions, that she had not a very high opinion of his education and training:

"Bonaparte was deficient in education and in manners; it seemed as if he must have been destined to live in a tent where all men are equal, or upon a throne where everything is permitted. He did not know how either to enter or leave a room; he did not know how to make a bow, how to rise, or how to sit down. His manner of speech, as well as his questions, were abrupt. Italian lost all its grace and sweetness when spoken by him. Whatever language he speaks, it seems always to be a foreign tongue to him; he appears to force it to express his thoughts. And as any rule laid down becomes an insupportable annoyance to him, every liberty which he takes gives him pleasure as though it were a victory; and he would never yield even to grammar. He used to say that he loved to read novels in his youth as well as studying the exact sciences. Unfortunately, he met with the worst kind of romances, and retained such a remembrance of the pleasure they they had given him that when he married the Archduchess Marie Louise he gave her 'Hippolyte, Comte de Douglas,' and 'Les Contemporains,' so that, as he said, she might form an idea of refined feeling, and also of the customs of society."

In writing about the mental capacity of the great French lawgiver, the over-candid lady thus sums up his acquirements:

"Although remarkable for certain intellectual qualities, no man was ever less lofty of soul. There was no generosity, no true greatness in him. I have never known him to admire, I have never known him to comprehend, a fine action; he looked upon every indication of good feeling with suspicion; he did not place any value on sincerity; and he has been known to say that he recognized the superiority of a man by the greater or less degree of cleverness with which he used the art of lying; and he added, with great complacency, that when he was a child one of his uncles had predicted that he should govern the world, because he was an habitual liar. 'M. de Metternich,' he added, 'approaches to being a statesman—he lies very well.'

But as we have now to do with the love intrigues of the remarkable hero, we will proceed to present his adventures in that field; and there is not one word written by the lady on the subject which will not be read with intense interest by all those familiar with the hero's exploits on the battle-fields of Europe.

Before introducing any of the love scenes in which the great man figured, the lady thus defines his sentiments as regards woman, and gives the reasons why he was attracted to his first wife:

"Bonaparte was not entirely without experience of love, notwithstanding his habitual hardness. But, good heavens! what kind of a sentiment was it in his case? A sensitive person forgets self in love, and is changed; but to Bonaparte it only supplied an additional sort of despotism. The Emperor despised women, and contempt cannot exist together with love. He regarded their weakness as proof of their inferiority. On this account Bonaparte was under restraint in the society of women; and, as a restriction of his liberty put him out of humor, he was always awkward in their presence, and never knew how to talk to them. It is true that the women he knew were not calculated to change his views of the sex. We can imagine the nature of his experiences in youth. In Italy morals were depraved, and the general licentiousness was increased by the French army. When he returned to France society was broken up. The circle around the Directory was a corrupt one, and the Parisian women were vain and frivolous, the wives of business men and contractors. When Bonaparte was Consul and made his generals and his aids-de-camps marry, or ordered them to bring their wives to court, the only women he had about him were timid and silent girls, newly married, suddenly withdrawn from obscurity, and ill able to conform to the change in their position.

" I am inclined to believe that Bonaparte was never awakened to love except by vanity, as he was almost exclusively occupied by politics. He only looked favorably on women when they were beautiful, or at least young. He would probably agree to that doctrine that women should be killed, just as certain insects are destined by nature to a speedy death, after having accomplished the task of maternity. Yet Bonaparte had some affection for his first wife; and if ever he was really moved by any emotion, it was by her and for her. Even a Bonaparte cannot completely escape from every influence, and a man's character is composed of what he is most frequently, and not of what he is always.

" When Bonaparte made the acquaintance of Madame de Beauharnais he was young; she was greatly superior to the rest of the circle in which she moved, both by reason of the name she bore and from the elegance of her manners. She attached herself to him and flattered his pride; she procured him a step in rank; he became accustomed to associate the idea of her influence with the good fortune which befell him. This superstition, which she kept up very cleverly, had great power over him for a long time; it even induced him more than once to put off the execution of his projects of divorce. When he married Madame de Beauharnais, Bonaparte thought that he was allying himself to a very great lady, and he regarded his marriage as another conquest. When I come to speak more particularly of her, I shall give more details of the charm she exercised over him.

" Notwithstanding his preference for her, I have seen him in love two or three times, and on those occasions the full measure of the despotism of his character was exhibited. How irritated he became at the least obstacle! How roughly he put aside the jealous remonstrances of his wife! 'To submit to all my fancies,' he said, 'is your place, and you ought to regard it as quite natural that I should allow myself amusement of this kind. I have a right to answer all your complaints by an eternal *I*. I am a person apart; I will not be dictated to by any one.' But he soon desired to exercise over the object of his passing preference an authority equal to that by which he silenced his wife. Astonished that any one should have any ascendency over him, he speedily became angry with the audacious individual, and he would, in an abrupt manner, get rid of the object of his brief passion, having let the public into the transparent secret of his success."

The following story concerning one of Napoleon's intrigues was furnished the authoress by Talleyrand; and when it is remembered that Talleyrand was one of the ministers who betrayed the emperor in his hour of need, it is safe to say that the incidents are slightly colored.

" When he was traveling, or even during a campaign, he never failed to indulge in pleasantries, which he regarded as a short

respite from business or battles. His brother-in-law, Murat, and his Grand Marshal, Duroc, were charged with the task of procuring him the means of gratifying his passing fancies. On the occasion of his first entry into Poland, Murat, who had preceded him to Warsaw, was ordered to find for the Emperor, who would shortly arrive, a young and pretty mistress, and to select her from among the nobility. He acquitted himself cleverly of the commission, and induced a noble young Polish lady, who was married to an old man, to comply with the wishes of the Emperor. No one knows what means he employed, or what were his promises, but at last the lady consented to go in the evening to the castle near Warsaw, where the Emperor dwelt.

" The fair one arrived rather late at her destination. She has herself given an account of this adventure, and she admits, what we can easily believe, that she arrived agitated and trembling.

" The Emperor was in his Cabinet. The lady's arrival was announced to him; but, without disturbing himself, he ordered her to be conducted to her apartment, and offered supper and a bath, adding that afterwards she might retire to rest if she chose. Then he quietly went on writing until a late hour at night.

" When his business was finished, he proceeded to the room where he had been so long waited for, and presented himself with all the air of a master who disdains useless preliminaries. Without losing a moment, he began a singular conversation on the political situation of Poland, interrogating the young lady as if she had been a police agent, and demanding information respecting the Polish nobles who were then in Warsaw. He inquired as to their opinions and interests, and prolonged his questioning for a long time. The astonishment of a young lady of twenty years of age, who was not prepared for such an examination, may be imagined. She answered him as well as she could, and only when she could tell him no more did he seem to remember that Murat had promised, in his name, an interview of a more tender nature.

" This extraordinary wooing did not prevent the young Polish lady from becoming attached to the Emperor, for their *liaison* was prolonged during several campaigns. Afterwards the fair Pole came to Paris, where a son was born, who became the object of the hopes of Polish dreams of independence.

" I saw his mother when she was presented at the Imperial Court, where she at first excited the jealousy of Madame Bonaparte; but after the divorce she became the intimate friend of the repudiated Empress at Malmaison, whither she often came with her son. It is said that she was faithful to the Emperor in his troubles, and that she visited him more than once at the Isle of Elba. He found her again in France when he made that last and fatal appearance there. But after his second fall (I do not know when she became a widow), she married again, and died in Paris in this year (1818)."

It appears that, while Napoleon felt himself free to enjoy his amours as he pleased, he was capable of displaying great anger even on the suspicion that his wife was unfaithful to him.

While he was away in Egypt, his brother Lucien, with whom Josephine was never a favorite, sent him letters which reflected on the purity of the wife at Paris.

The scene that followed the conqueror's return is thus described by Madame Remusat:

" Suddenly there was a rumor of Bonaparte's arrival at Fréjus. He returned with his mind full of the evil reports which Lucien had written him in his letters. His wife, on hearing of his arrival, set out to join him; but, missing him, retraced her steps, and returned to the house some hours after his arrival there. She descended from her carriage in haste, followed by her son and daughter, and ran up the stairs leading to his room; but what was her surprise to find the door locked! She called to Napoleon and begged him to open it. He replied through the door that it should never again be opened for her. Then she wept, fell on her knees, and implored him in the name of herself and her two children. But all was profound silence around her, and she passed several hours of the night in this terrible anxiety. At last, overcome by her cries and her perseverance, Bonaparte opened the door at about four o'clock in the morning, and appeared, as Madame Bonaparte herself told me, with a stern countenance, which, however, betrayed that he too had been weeping. He reproached her bitterly for her conduct, her forgetfulness of him, all the real and imaginary wrongs of which Lucien had accused her, and ended by announcing an eternal separation. Then turning towards Eugène de Beauharnais, who was then about twenty years old—

"'As for you,' he said, 'you shall not bear the burden of your mother's faults. You shall always be my son; I will always keep you with me.'

"'No, General,' replied Eugène, 'I must share the sad fortunes of my mother, and from this moment I make my adieus.'

"These words shook Bonaparte's resolution. He opened his arms to Eugène, weeping; his wife and Hortense knelt at his feet and embraced his knees; and soon after all was forgiven. In the explanation which followed, Madame Bonaparte was able to justify her conduct against the accusations of her brother-in-law; and Bonaparte, then eager to avenge her, sent for Lucien at seven o'clock in the morning, and had him ushered, without any forewarning, into the room where the husband and wife, entirely reconciled, occupied the same bed."

That Josephine possessed all the jealous spirit of a passionate woman will be seen by the following incidents, and that she had good cause for her jealousy is also very evident:

"The in-door life at the château was peaceable, when suddenly the First Consul's taking a fancy to a young and beautiful actress of the Théâtre Française, distressed Madame Bonaparte, and gave rise to bitter quarrels.

"Two remarkable actresses (Mlles. Duchesnois and Georges) had made their début in tragedy almost at the same time. One was very plain, but her genius soon gained popularity; the other was not so talented, but was extremely beautiful.

"The Parisian public sided warmly with one or the other, but generally the success of talent was greater than that of beauty. Bonaparte, on the contrary, was charmed by the latter; and Madame Bonaparte soon learned through her servants that Mlle. Georges had on several occasions been introduced into a little back room in the château. This discovery distressed her greatly; she told me of it with great emotion, and shed more tears than I thought the affair called for. I represented to her that gentleness and patience were the only remedies for a grief which time would certainly cure, and it was during these conversations that she gave me a notion of her husband which I could not otherwise have formed. According to her account he had no moral principles, and only concealed his vicious habits at that time for fear that they might harm him; but when he could do so without any risk he would abandon himself to the most shameful passions. Had he not seduced his own sisters one after the other? Did he not believe that his position entitled him to gratify his inclinations? And then his brothers were taking advantage of his weakness to induce him to relinquish all relations with his wife. As the result of their schemes she foresaw the much dreaded divorce which had already been spoken of.

"'It is a great misfortune for me,' she added, 'that I cannot give Bonaparte a son. That will always be a weapon by which they can wound me.'

"'But, Madame,' I said, 'it seems to me that your daughter's child almost repairs that misfortune; the First Consul loves him, and will perhaps end by adopting him.'

"'Alas!' replied she, 'that is the object of my dearest wishes; but the sullen and jealous character of Louis Bonaparte leads him to oppose it. His family have repeated to him the insulting rumors concerning my daughter's conduct and the paternity of her son. Slander has declared the child to be Bonaparte's, and that is sufficient to make Louis refuse his consent to the adoption. You observe how he avoids us, and how guarded my daughter is obliged to be. However, independently of the good reasons I have for not enduring Bonaparte's infidelities, they always mean that I shall submit to many other annoyances.'

"This was quite true. I always noticed that when the First

Consul was attracted by another woman—whether it was that his despotic temper led him to expect that his wife should approve of his absolute independence in all things, or whether he was so constituted by nature that he was only capable of loving one thing at a time—he became harsh, violent, and pitiless to his wife when he had a mistress. He showed a sort of savage surprise because she would not approve of his indulging in pleasures which, as he would demonstrate, were both allowable and necessary for him. 'I am no ordinary man,' he would say, 'and the laws of morals and of customs were never made for me.'

"Such declarations as these aroused the anger of Madame Bonaparte, and she answered them by tears and complaints, which her husband resented with violence. After a while he would tire of his new fancy, and all his love and tenderness for his wife would revive. Then he was touched by her grief and tried to make amends by lavishing caresses upon her, and as she was very gentle, she was easily appeased.

"While the storm lasted I was placed in a very embarrassing position by the strange confidences of which I was the recipient, and at times by proceedings in which I was obliged to take part. I remember one occurrence in particular which took place during the winter of 1803, at which I have often laughed. Bonaparte was in the habit of occupying the same room with his wife; she had persuaded him that in doing so he insured his personal safety.

"'I told him,' she said, 'that as I was a very light sleeper, if any one attempted to disturb him in the night I should be there to call for help in a moment.'

"In the evening she never retired until Bonaparte had gone to bed. But when Mademoiselle Georges was in the ascendant and visited the château late at night, he did not go to his wife's room until an advanced hour of the night.

"One evening Madame Bonaparte, who was more than usually restless and jealous, kept me with her, and talked of her troubles. It was one o'clock in the morning; we were alone in her boudoir, and profound silence reigned in the Tuileries. Suddenly she rose.

"'I cannot bear it any longer,' she said, 'Mademoiselle Georges is certainly with him. I will surprise them.'

"I tried to persuade her from her purpose, but in vain.

"'Follow me,' she said. 'Let us go up together.'

"Then I represented to her that such an act, improper on her part, would not be tolerated in me, and that I would be very out of place in the scene that must ensue. She would not listen and reproached me with deserting her in her troubles, and she begged me so earnestly to accompany her that I yielded against my wishes, saying to myself that our expedition would end in nothing, as no doubt care had been taken to prevent surprise.

"Silently we mounted the back staircase leading to Bonaparte's room; Madame Bonaparte, much excited, going first, while I followed slowly, feeling very much ashamed of the part I was obliged to play. On our way we heard a slight noise; Madame Bonaparte turned to me and said:

"'It is perhaps Rustan, Bonaparte's Mameluke, who keeps the door. The wretch is quite capable of killing us both.'

"At these words I was seized with such fright, although ridiculous as it was I could not overcome it, and ran rapidly back to the boudoir, candle in hand, forgetting that I left Madame Bonaparte in utter darkness. She followed me a few minutes after, astonished at my sudden flight. When she saw how frightened I was, she began to laugh, and that made me laugh too; and we gave up our enterprise. I left her, telling her that my fright had been very useful, and I was glad that I had yielded to it.

"Jealousy altered the sweet temper of Madame Bonaparte, and she could not hide it from those around her. I was in the position of a confidante without influence, and I could not but appear to be mixed up in the quarrels which I had witnessed. Bonaparte showed some annoyance at my being made aware of the facts of his private life.

"Meanwhile, the ugly actress grew in favor with the Parisian public, and the beautiful one was often received with hisses. M. de Rémusat tried and tried to divide patronage equally between the two; but whatever he did was received with equal dissatisfaction, either by the First Consul or by the public.

"These petty affairs gave us a good deal of trouble. Bonaparte, without mentioning the actress, complained to my husband, saying he would not object to my being his wife's confidante, provided I would only give her good advice. My husband represented me as having been very carefully brought up, and too sensible to encourage Madame Bonaparte's jealous fancies. The First Consul, who was still well-disposed toward us, accepted this view of my conduct. But thence arose another annoyance. He wanted me sometimes to interfere in his conjugal quarrels, and avail himself of what he called my good sense, against the foolish jealousy of which he was tired.

"As I never could conceal my real feelings, I answered quite sincerely, when he told me how weary he was of all these scenes, that I pitied Madame Bonaparte very much, and that he ought to excuse her; but at the same time I admitted that it was undignified on her part to try and prove his unfaithfulness through her servants. He did not fail to tell her that I blamed her in this respect; and so I was involved in endless explanations between husband and wife, into which I threw all the ardor of my age, and the devotion which I felt for both of them. We went through a constant succession of scenes; Bonaparte was in turn imperious, harsh, and defiant; and at other times tender and almost gentle, atoning with a good grace the faults he confessed, but did not renounce. I remember one day, in order to avoid a *tête-à-tête* with Madame Bonaparte, he made me remain to dinner; his wife was then very angry because he had declared his intention of having a separate apartment, and he insisted that I should give my opinion on this subject. I was not prepared to answer him; and I knew that Madame Bonaparte would never forgive me if I did not agree with her. I tried to evade a reply, but Bonaparte insisted, and I said that I thought the least change in their manner of living would give rise to injurious reports, and that the least change in the arrangements of the château would surely be talked about. Bonaparte laughed, and pinching my ear, said: 'Ah! you are a woman, and you all back each other.'

"Nevertheless, he carried out his resolution, and from that time occupied a separate apartment. His manner toward his wife, however, became more affectionate, and she, on her part, was less suspicious of him. She adopted the advice I urged upon her, to treat such unworthy rivalry with disdain.

" 'It would be quite time enough to fret,' I said, 'if the Consul chose one of the women in your own society; that would be a real grief, and for me a serious annoyance.'

"Two years afterwards my prediction was fully realized, especially as regards myself."

As it was destined that the authoress of the Memoirs was to have a "little unpleasantness" with her friend Josephine, we will give her own words in describing the unhappy woman:

"She had not a remarkable intellect. A Creole, and coquettish, her education had been greatly neglected; but she knew her deficiencies, and she never compromised herself in conversation. She possessed true natural tact, and always found it easy to say pleasant things. She had a convenient memory—a very useful thing for those who are in high positions. Unfortunately she lacked depth of feeling and elevation of soul. She preferred to charm her husband by her beauty, rather than to influence him by her mind. She was excessively complaisant towards him, and kept her hold over him only by concessions, which strengthened the contempt with which women inspired him. She might have been able to teach him some useful lessons, but she feared him too much, and received, on the contrary, most of her impressions from him.

"Besides, she was fickle, impressionable, easily affected and calmed, but incapable of prolonged emotion, of sustained attention, or of serious thought. If her grandeur did not turn her head, on the other hand it did nothing towards educating her.

It was her nature to console the unhappy; but she could only look at individual troubles; she never thought about the woes of France.

"The genius of Bonaparte overpowered her; she never criticised him except in what concerned herself; but in everything else she respected what he called 'the force of his destiny.' He exercised over her an evil influence, for he inspired her with a contempt for morality, and he taught her to be suspicious, and to form a habit of falsehood, which they both used by turns.

"It has been said that she was the prize of his command of the army of Italy; she assured me that at this time Bonaparte was really in love with her. She hesitated between him, General Hoche and M. Caulaincourt, who also loved her. The ascendency of Bonaparte won her. I know that my mother, then living in retirement in the country, was very much astonished to hear, in her retreat, that the widow of M. de Beauharnais had married a man so little known.

"When I questioned her about Bonaparte's habits in his youth, she told me that he was then dreamy, silent and embarrassed when with women, but passionate and fascinating, although he was so strange a person. She attributed the change in his disposition to his journey to Egypt, which developed that petty despotism from which she had suffered so much."

The "little unpleasantness" heretofore referred to occurred soon after, and Josephine became jealous of her confidential friend.

The incidents that led to the quarrel between the friends are thus described by Madame de Rémusat:

"While at Boulogne I spent the time in conversations of this kind with the First Consul, but I soon learnt to mistrust persons among whom I was obliged to live at court. The officers of the household could not understand that a woman might remain for hours together with their master, simply talking on matters of general interest; and they drew conclusions injurious to my character. I will here say that a life-long attachment to my husband prevented my even conceiving the possibility of such a suspicion as that which was formed in the Consul's antechamber while I was conversing with him in his salon. When Bonaparte returned to Paris there was considerable talk about my long interviews with him, and Madame Bonaparte became alarmed about it. When after a month's sojourn at Pont-de-Briques, my husband was sufficiently recovered to bear the journey, we returned to Paris; but my jealous patroness received me coldly. It was the first time I had suffered injustice; my feelings revolted against such an accusation. Experience only can steel us against the unjust judgments of the world. My friend, who was really attached to me, advised me to be careful of my words. My friend's warning had, however, explained Madame Bonaparte's conduct towards me. One day I said to her with tears in my eyes:

" 'What, Madame, do you suspect me?'

"She was touched and embraced me, and from thenceforth she treated me with her former cordiality, but she did not understand my feelings. In order to justify her suspicions, she told me that the Bonaparte family had spread injurious reports against me during my absence.

" 'Do you not see,' I said, 'that political jealousy has spread suspicion broadcast everywhere, and as insignificant as I am, they want to make you quarrel with me?'

"Madame Bonaparte agreed in the truth of my observation, but she had no idea that I could feel aggrieved because it had not occurred to herself in the first instance. She admitted that she had reproached her husband about me, and he had apparently amused himself by leaving her in doubt. I began to feel that the ground which I had walked over up to that time, with all the confidence of ignorance, was not firm. I felt that from the kind of annoyance I had just undergone I should never again be free."

Very soon after Josephine was in serious trouble again, as the emperor had found a new lady-love to share his pleasures.

It appears that Madame de Rémusat became reconciled to the

jealous wife once more, and that she was again installed as her confidential adviser.

She thus describes one of the family quarrels:

"The Emperor, harassed without rest by his family, seemed to listen to these discourses, and a few words that _he let fall caused his wife great alarm. She had a habit of confiding to me all her troubles. I was very anxious to give her good advice, and I feared being compromised in such a great difficulty. An unexpected incident hastened the blow which we feared. For some time Madame Bonaparte thought she perceived an intimacy between her husband and Madame ——. In vain I implored her not to give the Emperor any pretext for a quarrel which they would use against her; too animated and anxious to listen to prudence, she watched, notwithstanding my advice, for an occasion to convince herself of what she suspected. At St. Cloud the Emperor occupied the apartment which led into the garden, and was even with it. Above this he had caused to be furnished a small private room which communicated with his own by a hidden staircase; the Empress had some reason to fear this mysterious retreat. One morning, there being several in her salon (Madame —— being established for some days at St. Cloud), the Empress, seeing her suddenly leave the apartment, got up a few moments after her departure, and taking me into the alcove of a window:

"'I am going,' said she to me, 'to confirm my suspicions presently; remain in the salon with all my circle; and if they seek to know what has become of me, you will tell them that the Emperor has sent for me.'

"I endeavored to withhold her, but she was beside herself, and would not listen to me; at the same time she retired, and I remained very uneasy at what was going to take place. At the end of half an hour's absence she entered suddenly by the door of her apartment which was opposite to that by which she had left; she seemed much moved, and could hardly contain herself; she seated herself at a work-table that was in the salon. I remained at a distance-from her, engaged with some work and avoiding her eye, but I easily perceived her trouble by the hastiness of all her movements, which were naturally so quiet.

"At length, unable as she was to keep in silence during any strong emotion, no matter what it was, she could no longer continue this constraint, and calling me in a loud voice, she ordered me to follow her. As soon as we were in her room: 'All is lost,' said she to me, 'that which I suspected is but too true. I sought the Emperor in his cabinet and he was not there; then I ascended the hidden staircase to the little apartment; I found the door shut, and through the lock I heard the voice of Bonaparte and Madame——. I knocked loudly, naming myself.

"'You may imagine the trouble that I caused them; it was long before they opened the door, and when they did so, the state in which they both were, and their disorder, left me not the slightest doubt. I know well that I ought to have restrained myself, but it was impossible; I burst out in reproaches. Madame —— began to cry. Bonaparte went into such a violent passion that I had hardly time to flee to escape his resentment. In fact, I am still trembling, for I do not know to what excess he might have been carried. No doubt he will come, and I expect a terrible scene!'

"The emotion of the Empress excited mine, as you may easily suppose.

"'Do not,' I said to her, 'make another mistake; for the Emperor will not forgive you for admitting any one, no matter whom, into your confidence. Let me leave you, Madame. You must await him; let him find you alone, and try to smooth and to repair so great an imprudence.'

"After these few words I left her, and I re-entered the salon where I found Madame —— who looked very uneasily at me. She was very pale, speaking but few words, and trying to find out if I was informed. I seated myself at my work as tranquilly as I could, but it was not difficult for Madame ——, seeing me come out of that apartment, to understand that I had just heard

something in confidence. Every one in the salon looked at each other, without knowing what was taking place.

"A few moments after we heard a great noise in the Empress's apartment, and I understood that the Emperor was there, and that a violent scene was going on. Madame —— had ordered her horses and had left for Paris. This sudden departure could not quiet the storm. I had to return to Paris in the evening, with many tears, that Bonaparte, after having insulted her in every way, and broken in his rage several articles of furniture which came under his hand, had signified to her that she must prepare to leave St. Cloud, and that, tired of a jealous watchfulness, he had decided to shake off such a yoke, and, in fact, to listen to the counsels of those politicians who were capable of giving him children. She added that she had sent orders to Eugène de Beauharnais to come to St. Cloud to regulate the arrangements for the departure of his mother, and that she saw she was lost entirely. She ordered me to go and see her daughter as soon as I should arrive in Paris, and to explain to her all that had taken place.

"I called on Madame Louis Bonaparte. She had just seen her brother, who had arrived from St. Cloud. The Emperor had signified to him his resolve to obtain a divorce, which Eugène had received with his usual submission, and refused all the personal indemnities which had been offered him as consolation, declaring that he would accept nothing when such a misfortune was about to fall upon his mother, and that he would follow her to the retreat that they would give her, were it to Martinique itself, sacrificing all, if necessary, to the sacred duty of consolation. Bonaparte seemed struck with such a generous resolve, and listened in savage silence.

"I found Madame Louis, her daughter, who was married to Napoleon's brother, less moved at this event than I had expected:

"'I cannot interfere in anything,' said she to me, 'for my husband has positively forbidden me to take any step. My mother has been very imprudent; she is about to lose a crown, but at least she will have rest. Ah! believe me, there are women more unfortunate!'

"She pronounced these words with a sadness which enabled me to guess all her thoughts; but as she never mentioned a word with regard to her private situation, I did not dare to answer in a way that would show her that I had understood her.

"'Besides,' she said to me, in conclusion, 'if there is any chance of this affair being settled, that chance lays in the power my brother may have by gentleness and tears over Bonaparte. We must leave them to themselves, avoid coming between them, and I would advise you not to go to St. Cloud, particularly as Madame—— has spoken of you and, believes that you encouraged her violent attack upon them.'

"I remained two days without sparing myself at St. Cloud, following the advice of Madame Louis Bonaparte, and the third day I went to see the Empress, about whose condition I was very uneasy.

"She had partly recovered from her anguish. Her tears and entreaties had, in fact, disarmed Bonaparte, and there was no longer any talk of his anger, or of that which had caused it. But after a tender settlement, the Emperor had caused his wife fresh pain, by showing her how necessary it was for him to be divorced.

"'I have not the courage,' said he to her, 'to make the last resolution, and if you show too much affliction, if you only obey me, I feel that I shall never be strong enough to force you to leave me; but I declare that I very much wish that you would resign yourself to my political interests, and that you would spare me the embarrassment of taking the steps necessary to this painful separation.'

"Thus speaking, the Empress added that he had shed many tears.

"While she was speaking I remember that I perceived for her

the plan of a great and generous sacrifice. Believing that the good of France was irrevocably attached to that of Napoleon, I thought that it would be an heroic action to devote oneself to all that would affirm it, and that if I had been the woman to whom such an address had been made, I should have felt tempted to abandon that position so brilliant, where they looked upon me with a sort of regret, and retired into a solitude where I could live peaceably and contented with my sacrifice. But, in seeing the shadow that the imperial words had left on the face of Madame Bonaparte, I remembered that which I had often heard my mother say, that in order to give useful counsel you must always study the character of the person to whom you give it.

"At the same time I considered the terror which the retreat would cause the Empress; of her taste for luxury and gayety, of the *ennui* which would devour her, when she had given up the world; and then, awaking from the exalted feeling which had come on me for a moment, I told her that I saw but two things for her to do: either to sacrifice herself with dignity and resolution to what they asked of her, and in that case to leave for Malmaison the next morning, from whence she could write to the Emperor to tell him that she gave him his freedom; or else, if she wished to remain, unable to decide on her course, always ready to obey; but declaring very positively that she would await direct orders to descend from the throne which they had made her ascend.

"This last advice was the one which she followed, and with a skilful and tender sweetness, taking the character of a subdued victim, she succeeded once more in weakening the shafts that the jealousy of her family cast against her. Sad, complacent, entirely subdued, but quick to profit by the power which she exercised over her husband, she put him in a state of agitation and uncertainty from which he could not escape.

"At length, harassed a little too strongly by his brothers, and perceiving the joy that the Bonapartes showed, thinking they had gained the end they wished, touched by the comparison which he made of the conduct of his wife and her children, and as far as I can remember, hurt by the triumphal air of his family, who were imprudent enough to boast of their having led him to act as they wished, feeling a secret pleasure in overthrowing the scheme that they had formed around him, after long meditation, during which time the Empress suffered terrible anxiety, all at once he informed her one evening that the Pope would arrive, and that they should both be crowned, and that she could at once commence her preparations for that great ceremony.

"One can easily imagine the joy which such an announcement gave her, and the rage of the Bonapartes, particularly of Joseph; for the Emperor, faithful to his habits, told his wife all the temptations which they had placed before him, and one may easily conceive that these revelations increased the hatred between the two parties.

"It was on this occasion that the Empress confided to me the wish she had for some time that his marriage should be strengthened by a religious ceremony, which had been neglected at the time it was concluded. She spoke of it several times to the Emperor, who showed no objection, but answered that even in bringing a priest to the palace, it could never be done secretly enough to prevent it being known that up to that time they had not been married by the church; and whether that was his real reason, or whether he wished to reserve to himself for future use a pretext with which he might annul the marriage, when he believed it really necessary, he repulsed, but with gentleness, all the efforts made by his wife in that respect. She determined to await the arrival of the Pope, flattering herself that on such an occasion he would readily accord her wishes."

Josephine carried her point. She was married to Napoleon, and she was declared Empress.

But the domestic troubles of the faithful and devoted creature were not over.

During the winter of 1807 a new rival appears on the scene, and Madame de Remusat thus describes the unhappy affair:

"I have already said that Eugène was well occupied with Madame de X——. This young woman, then twenty-four or twenty-five years of age, was fair and white, her blue eyes had all the expression she wished to give them, except that of being frank, because I believe that the habits of her character forced her to dissimulate. Her aquiline nose was rather long, her mouth charming, adorned with beautiful teeth, which she showed a great deal. Her slight figure was elegant, but wanted a little fullness; her foot was small, and she danced marvelously. She had not a remarkable wit, but still she was not without tact; she was calm, a little dry, and not easy to move, and even more difficult to trouble.

"The Empress had begun by treating her with much distinction: she praised her figure, always approved of her toilette, amused her in preference to the others on account of her son, and perhaps assisted in making her known to her husband. He occupied himself with her as soon as they returned from Fontainebleau. Madame Murat, who was the first to guess the taste of her brother, sought the confidence of this young lady, and she succeeded well enough to set her promptly in defiance of the Empress. Murat, by reason, I believe, of a private arrangement, pretended to be in love with Madame de X——, and thus gave for some time a change to the observations of the court.

"The Empress did not doubt the new preoccupation of the Emperor, but could not guess the object; at first she suspected, as I have said, the Maréchale Ney, to whom, really, he very often spoke; and during several days the unfortunate Maréchale was the object of the observation and bad humor of her mistress. I received, as usual, the confidence of this jealous uneasiness, and I could as yet see nothing to justify it.

"The Empress complained to Madame Louise Bonaparte of what she called the perfidy of the Maréchale. The latter was exhorted and questioned; and after having assured us that she only felt a kind of fear for the Emperor, she declared that he had seemed as if sometimes he paid her attentions, and that Madame de X—— had complimented her on the grand conquest that she was on the point of making.

"This recital at once enlightened the Empress. More attentive, she discovered the truth, found out that Murat only feigned to love her in order to be able to carry the declarations of the Emperor. She found, in the deference that she saw in Duroc for Madame de X——, a proof of the sentiments of his master, and in the conduct of Madame Murat a scheme very well planned against her own tranquillity. From that time, the Emperor was seen much oftener in the apartment of his wife. Nearly every evening he descended to the ground floor, and his looks and words instructed equally the Empress and the object of his preference. If his wife went to the theater and occupied a private box, for the Emperor did not like her to appear in public without him, he immediately joined her, and from day to day, less master of himself, he appeared more engaged. Madame de X—— preserved an apparent coolness, but she used all the resources of feminine coquetry. Her toilette was more and more *recherché*, her smile fiuer, her looks more intriguing, and it was soon easy enough to guess at what was passing. The Empress suspected that Madame Murat had permitted at her house secret interviews. She assured me later on that she was certain of it. Then she burst out in complaints and tears, as was her custom, and I saw myself again obliged to receive confidences which compromised me, and to recommence giving sermons which were not listened to.

"The Empress wished to attempt explanations which were very badly received. Her husband got angry, treated her harshly, reproached her with opposing him in his slightest distractions, ordered her to be silent, and while in public she, consumed by her griefs, appeared sad and broken down, he was gay, open, and more animated than we had ever seen him before—entertained us all, and lavished upon us expressions of his savage gallantry. In those assemblies in the Empress's apartment, of which I have spoken before, he seemed like a real Sultan. He placed himself at a play-table, called for his party—generally his sister Caroline, Madame de X——, and myself—and hardly holding the cards, he commenced with us dissertations, sentimental in their way, where he displayed more wit than sense, and sometimes very bad taste, but exalted enough.

"In these interviews Madame de X——, very reserved, and perhaps fearing that I should discover her, replied only in monosyllables. Madame Murat took but little interest in it, having her own end in view, and caring nothing about the details. As to myself, these conversations amused me, and I replied with all the liberty and wit of which I was capable. I had the advantage over these three other persons, who were more or less preoccupied. Sometimes, without naming any one, Bonaparte commenced a discussion on jealousy, and then it was easy to see what applications he wished to make to his wife. I understood him, and I defended her as well as I could, gayly, and avoiding to designate her, and then I clearly saw that Madame de X—— and Madame Murat were not pleased with me.

"In these soirées, Madame Bonaparte, sadly playing in another part of the salon, observed us from the distance and suffered from these interviews, which always made her uneasy. Although she had plenty of reasons to believe in me, being naturally defiant, sometimes she fancied I would sacrifice her to the desire to please the Emperor; and at least she was vexed with me at not blaming his conduct. At one time she would ask me to go and find him, and to speak to him of the harm that she pretended this new liaison did him in the eyes of the world; again, she wished to watch Madame de X—— in her own house, where she knew that Bonaparte went sometimes in the evening; or else she made me write in her presence anonymous letters full of reproaches, that I composed before her in order to please her, and in order to prevent her from getting others to do so; and that I took care to burn, after having assured her that I had sent them. Her faithful servants were employed to discover proofs of what she sought. Workmen and trades-people were in her confidence, and I suffered all the more from these imprudences, because I learnt soon after that Madame Murat blamed me for the discoveries made by the Empress, and accused me of acts of which I was incapable.

"Madame Bonaparte suffered more on account of her son, who was greatly grieved at what took place. Madame de X——, who, at first by coquetry, taste, or vanity, had listened, since her new and more splendid conquest, avoided even the slightest appearance of any relation with him. Perhaps she boasted to the Emperor of the love which she had inspired in Eugéne. One thing is certain, that is that the latter was very coldly treated by his father-in-law. The Empress was enraged; Madame Louis was grieved about it, but dissimulated her secret impressions. Eugéne suffered, and hid himself under an apparent calm, which happily took but little hold on him.

"One sees in all this the eternal hatred felt between the Bonapartists and the Beauharnais; and in which it was my destiny, however moderate I might be, to see myself always involved. I have had great experience; it is all, or nearly all, a chance in courts. Human prudence has not the strength to defend itself, and I know no means of escaping misrepresentations, unless the sovereign himself is not open to suspicion; but, far from that, the Emperor received all the reports, and even seemed to have a kind of credulity for believing all those which were unpleasant, no matter of what kind. The surest means of gaining his favor was to relate to him all the reports, to denounce all conducts; that is why M. de Rémusat, placed close to him, had never obtained it—for he had often refused to give himself up to a line of conduct which Duroc himself had often indicated to him.

"One evening the Emperor, out of patience because of a violent quarrel with his wife, and in which, driven to extremes, she had declared that she would forbid Madame de X—— to enter her apartments, he addressed himself to M. de Rémusat, and complained that I did not employ the power I had over her to moderate her imprudences. He finished by saying that he wished to see me in private, and that I had only to ask audience of him. M. de Rémusat sent me this order, and, in fact, during the next

day, I asked him for an audience, which was fixed for the following morning.

"A grand hunt had been prepared for that day. The Empress had gone in advance with the foreign princes, and waited the Emperor at the Bois de Boulogne. I arrived just as the Emperor was getting into his carriage; his suite were all assembled; he re-entered his cabinet to receive me, to the great astonishment of the Court, to whom everything was an event.

"He commenced by complaining bitterly of his private troubles; he was incensed against women in general—especially against his wife. He reproached me with having encouraged her espionage, and accused me of a thousand actions to which I was a stranger—the result of reports that had been made to him. I recognized in his recitals the bad offices of Madame Murat, and that which pained me the most was that the Empress, in order to strengthen her complaints, had sometimes named me, and had told to me what she had said or thought. This and the words of the Emperor caused me a little emotion, and tears started to my eyes. The Emperor, who perceived it, rudely apologized for the pain he had caused me, with this phrase, that was so common to him, and that I have already written: 'Women have always two means of making a scene—paint and tears.' At that moment these words, spoken in an ironical tone, and with the intention of disconcerting me, produced a contrary effect; they enraged me, and gave me the power to answer him: 'No, sire, it sometimes happens that when one is unjustly accused, one cannot help shedding tears of indignation.'

"We must do justice to the Emperor: he is never angry with you when you answer him with some firmness, whether because, not often finding it in others, he was less prepared to answer, or whether the justness of his spirit approved of that which was rightly resented.

"The feelings I showed did not displease. 'If you do not approve,' said he to me, 'of the inquisition which the Empress exercises against me, have you not sufficient power over her to restrain her? She humiliates us both by the espionage with which she surrounds me; she furnishes weapons to her enemies. Since you are in her confidence, you must be answerable for her to me, and I shall hold you responsible for all her faults.' In pronouncing these words, he brightened a little; I then represented to him that I tenderly loved the Empress, that I was incapable of leading her in a wrong way, but that it was impossible to have any power over a passionate person. I also told him that he did not act in a right way towards her, that even if she did suspect him, whether she was right or wrong, he insulted her and treated her too roughly.

"I did not dare to blame the Empress for that in which her conduct was really to be blamed, because I knew that he would not fail to repent to his wife of all that I had said. I concluded by telling him 'that for some time I would keep away from the palace, and that he would see if affairs went any better.' Then he endeavored to prove to me that, in that he neither was nor could be in love, that he had not paid more attention to Madame de X—— than ano.her; that love was intended for other characters than his. That he was wholly absorbed by politics; that he would not have his Court to be under the empire of women; that they had done great harm to Henry IV. and Louis XIV.; that his profession was a great deal more serious than that of those princes, and that the French were become too grave to forgive their sovereign published liaisons and titled mistresses.

"He spoke a little lightly of the past conduct of his wife, adding that she had no right to be so severe. I stopped him on this subject, and he did not get vexed. At length he questioned me about the persons who acted as spies for the Empress. I answered him always that I did not know. At that he approached me, and said that I was not sufficiently devoted to him. I tried to prove to him that I was more sincerely attached to him than those who reported to him so many trifling things that were not worthy to be heard. This conversation terminated better than the plan of a great and generous sacrifice. Believing that the good of France was irrevocably attached to that of Napoleon, I thought that it would be an heroic action to devote oneself to all that would affirm it, and that if I had been the woman to whom such an address had been made, I should have felt tempted to abandon that position so brilliant, where they looked upon me with a sort of regret, and retired into a solitude where I could live peaceably and contented with my sacrifice. But, in seeing the shadow that the imperial words had left on the face of Madame Bonaparte, I remembered that which I had often heard my mother say, that in order to give useful counsel you must always study the character of the person to whom you give it.

"At the same time I considered the terror which the retreat would cause the Empress; of her taste for luxury and gayety, of the *ennui* which would devour her, when she had given up the world; and then, awaking from the exalted feeling which had come on me for a moment, I told her that I saw but two things for her to do: either to sacrifice herself with dignity and resolution to what they asked of her, and in that case to leave for Malmaison the next morning, from whence she could write to the Emperor to tell him that she gave him his freedom; or else, if she wished to remain, unable to decide on her course, always ready to obey; but declaring very positively that she would await direct orders to descend from the throne which they had made her ascend.

"This last advice was the one which she followed, and with a skillful and tender sweetness, taking the character of a subdued victim, she succeeded once more in weakening the shafts that the jealousy of her family cast against her. Sad, complacent, entirely subdued, but quick to profit by the power which she exercised over her husband, she put him in a state of agitation and uncertainty from which he could not escape.

"At length, harassed a little too strongly by his brothers, and perceiving the joy that the Bonapartes showed, thinking they had gained the end they wished, touched by the comparison which he made of the conduct of his wife and her children, and as far as I can remember, hurt by the triumphal air of his family, who were imprudent enough to boast of their having led him to act as they wished, feeling a secret pleasure in overthrowing the scheme that they had formed around him, after long meditation, during which time the Empress suffered terrible anxiety, all at once he informed her one evening that the Pope would arrive, and that they should both be crowned, and that she could at once commence her preparations for that great ceremony.

"One can easily imagine the joy which such an announcement gave her, and the rage of the Bonapartes, particularly of Joseph; for the Emperor, faithful to his habits, told his wife all the temptations which they had placed before him, and one may easily conceive that these revelations increased the hatred between the two parties.

"It was on this occasion that the Empress confided to me the wish she had for some time that his marriage should be strengthened by a religious ceremony, which had been neglected at the time it was concluded. She spoke of it several times to the Emperor, who showed no objection, but answered that even in bringing a priest to the palace, it could never be done secretly enough to prevent it being known that up to that time they had not been married by the church; and whether that was his real reason, or whether he wished to reserve to himself for future use a pretext with which he might annul the marriage, when he believed it really necessary, he repulsed, but with gentleness, all the efforts made by his wife in that respect. She determined to await the arrival of the Pope, flattering herself that on such an occasion he would readily accord her wishes."

Josephine carried her point. She was married to Napoleon, and she was declared Empress.

But the domestic troubles of the faithful and devoted creature were not over.

During the winter of 1807 a new rival appears on the scene, and Madame de Remusat thus describes the unhappy affair:

"I have already said that Eugène was well occupied with

Madame de X——. This young woman, then twenty-four or twenty-five years of age, was fair and white, her blue eyes had all the expression she wished to give them, except that of being frank, because I believe that the habits of her character forced her to dissimulate. Her aquiline nose was rather long, her mouth charming, adorned with beautiful teeth, which she showed a great deal. Her slight figure was elegant, but wanted a little fullness; her foot was small, and she danced marvelously. She had not a remarkable wit, but still she was not without tact; she was calm, a little dry, and not easy to move, and even more difficult to trouble.

"The Empress had begun by treating her with much distinction: she praised her figure, always approved of her toilette, amused her in preference to the others on account of her son, and perhaps assisted in making her known to her husband. He occupied himself with her as soon as they returned from Fontainebleau. Madame Murat, who was the first to guess the taste of her brother, sought the confidence of this young lady, and she succeeded well enough to set her promptly in defiance of the Empress. Murat, by reason, I believe, of a private arrangement, pretended to be in love with Madame de X——, and thus gave for some time a change to the observations of the court.

"The Empress did not doubt the new preoccupation of the Emperor, but could not guess the object; at first she suspected, as I have said, the Maréchale Ney, to whom, really, he very often spoke; and during several days the unfortunate Maréchale was the object of the observation and bad humor of her mistress. I received, as usual, the confidence of this jealous uneasiness, and I could as yet see nothing to justify it.

"The Empress complained to Madame Louise Bonaparte of what she called the perfidy of the Maréchale. The latter was exhorted and questioned; and after having assured us that she only felt a kind of fear for the Emperor, she declared that he had seemed as if sometimes he paid her attentions, and that Madame de X—— had complimented her on the grand conquest that she was on the point of making.

"This recital at once enlightened the Empress. More attentive, she discovered the truth, found out that Murat only feigned to love her in order to be able to carry the declarations of the Emperor. She found, in the deference that she saw in Duroc for Madame de X——, a proof of the sentiments of his master, and in the conduct of Madame Murat a scheme very well planned against her own tranquillity. From that time, the Emperor was seen much oftener in the apartment of his wife. Nearly every evening he descended to the ground floor, and his looks and words instructed equally the Empress and the object of his preference. If his wife went to the theater and occupied a private box, for the Emperor did not like her to appear in public without him, he immediately joined her, and from day to day, less master of himself, he appeared more engaged. Madame de X—— preserved an apparent coolness, but she used all the resources of feminine coquetry. Her toilette was more and more *recherché*, her smile finer, her looks more intriguing, and it was soon easy enough to guess at what was passing. The Empress suspected that Madame Murat had permitted at her house secret interviews. She assured me later on that she was certain of it. Then she burst out in complaints and tears, as was her custom, and I saw myself again obliged to receive confidences which compromised me, and to recommence giving sermons which were not listened to.

"The Empress wished to attempt explanations which were very badly received. Her husband got angry, treated her harshly, reproached her with opposing him in his slightest distractions, ordered her to be silent, and while in public she, consumed by her griefs, appeared sad and broken down, he was gay, open, and more animated than we had ever seen him before—entertained us all, and lavished upon us expressions of his savage gallantry. In those assemblies in the Empress's apartment, of which I have spoken before, he seemed like a real Sultan. He placed himself at a play-table, called for his party—generally his sister Caroline, Madame de X——, and myself—and hardly hold-

...ing the cards, he commenced with us dissertations, sentimental in their way, where he displayed more wit than sense, and sometimes very bad taste, but exalted enough.

"In these interviews Madame de X——, very reserved, and perhaps fearing that I should discover her, replied only in monosyllables. Madame Murat took but little interest in it, having her own end in view, and caring nothing about the details. As to myself, these conversations amused me, and I replied with all the liberty and wit of which I was capable. I had the advantage over these three other persons, who were more or less preoccupied. Sometimes, without naming any one, Bonaparte commenced a discussion on jealousy, and then it was easy to see what applications he wished to make to his wife. I understood him, and I defended her as well as I could, gayly, and avoiding to designate her, and then I clearly saw that Madame de X—— and Madame Murat were not pleased with me.

"In these soirées, Madame Bonaparte, sadly playing in another part of the salon, observed us from the distance and suffered from these interviews, which always made her uneasy. Although she had plenty of reasons to believe in me, being naturally defiant, sometimes she fancied I would sacrifice her to the desire to please the Emperor; and at least she was vexed with me at not blaming his conduct. At one time she would ask me to go and find him, and to speak to him of the harm that she pretended this new liaison did him in the eyes of the world; again, she wished me to watch Madame de X—— in her own house where she knew that Bonaparte went sometimes in the evening; or else she made me write in her presence anonymous letters full of reproaches, that I composed before her in order to please her, and in order to prevent her from getting others to do so; and that I took care to burn, after having assured her that I had sent them. Her faithful servants were employed to discover proofs of what she sought. Workmen of her favorite trades-people were in her confidence, and I suffered all the more from these imprudences, because I learnt soon after that Madame Murat blamed me for the discoveries made by the Empress, and accused me of acts of which I was incapable.

"Madame Bonaparte suffered more on account of her son, who was greatly grieved at what took place. Madame de X——, who, at first by coquetry, taste, or vanity, had listened, since her new and more splendid conquest, avoided even the slightest appearance of any relation with him. Perhaps she boasted to the Emperor of the love which she had inspired in Eugène. One thing is certain, that is that the latter was very coldly treated by his father-in-law. The Empress was enraged; Madame Louis was grieved about it, but dissimulated her secret impressions. Eugène suffered, and hid himself under an apparent calm, which happily took but little hold on him.

"One sees in all this the eternal hatred felt between the Bonapartists and the Beauharnais; and in which it was my destiny, however moderate I might be, to see myself always involved. I have had great experience; it is all, or nearly all, a chance in courts. Human prudence has not the strength to defend itself, and I know no means of escaping misrepresentations, unless the sovereign himself is not open to suspicion; but, far from that, the Emperor received all the reports, and even seemed to have a kind of credulity for believing all those which were unpleasant, no matter of what kind. The surest means of gaining his favor was to relate to him all the reports, to denounce all conducts; that is why M. de Rémusat, placed close to him, never obtained it—for he had often refused to give himself up to a line of conduct which Duroc himself had often indicated to him.

"One evening the Emperor, out of patience because of a violent quarrel with his wife, and in which, driven to extremes, she had declared that she would forbid Madame de X—— to enter her apartments, he addressed himself to M. de Rémusat, and complained that I did not employ the power I had over her to moderate her imprudences. He finished by saying that he wished to see me in private, and that I had only to ask audience of him. M. de Rémusat sent me this order, and, in fact, during the next

day, I asked him for an audience, which was fixed for the following morning.

"A grand hunt had been prepared for that day. The Empress had gone in advance with the foreign princes, and waited the Emperor at the Bois de Boulogne. I arrived just as the Emperor was getting into his carriage; his suite were all assembled; he re-entered his cabinet to receive me, to the great astonishment of the Court, to whom everything was an event.

"He commenced by complaining bitterly of his private troubles; he was incensed against women in general—especially against his wife. He reproached me with having encouraged her espionage, and accused me of a thousand actions to which I was a stranger—the result of reports that had been made to him. I recognized in his recitals the bad offices of Madame Murat, and that which pained me the most was that the Empress, in order to strengthen her complaints, had sometimes named me, and had told to me what she had said or thought. This and the words of the Emperor caused me a little emotion, and tears started to my eyes. The Emperor, who perceived it, rudely apologized for the pain he had caused me, with this phrase, that was so common to him, and that I have already written: 'Women have always two means of making a scene—paint and tears.' At that moment these words, spoken in an ironical tone, and with the intention of disconcerting me, produced a contrary effect; they enraged me, and gave me the power to answer him: 'No, sire, it sometimes happens that when one is unjustly accused, one cannot help shedding tears of indignation.'

"We must do justice to the Emperor; he is never angry with you when you answer him with some firmness, whether because, not often finding it in others, he was less prepared to answer, or whether the justness of his spirit approved of that which was rightly resented.

"The feelings I showed did not displease. 'If you do not approve,' said he to me, 'of the inquisition which the Empress exercises against me, have you not sufficient power over her to restrain her? She humiliates us both by the espionage with which she surrounds me; she furnishes weapons to her enemies. Since you are in her confidence, you must be answerable for her to me, and I shall hold you responsible for all her faults.' In pronouncing these words, he brightened a little; I then represented to him that I tenderly loved the Empress, that I was incapable of leading her in a wrong way, but that it was impossible to have any power over a passionate person. I also told him that he did not act in a right way towards her, that even if she did suspect him, whether she was right or wrong, he insulted her and treated her too roughly.

"I did not dare to blame the Empress for that in which her conduct was really to be blamed, because I knew that he would not fail to repeat to his wife all that I had said. I concluded by telling him 'that for some time I would keep away from the palace, and that he would see if affairs went any better.' Then he endeavored to prove to me that, in that he neither was nor could be in love, that he had not paid more attention to Madame de X—— than ano.her; that love was intended for other characters than his. That he was wholly absorbed by politics; that he would not have his Court to be under the empire of women; that they had done great harm to Henry IV. and Louis XIV.; that his profession was a great deal more serious than that of those princes, and that the French were become too grave to forgive their sovereign published liaisons and titled mistresses.

"He spoke a little lightly of the past conduct of his wife, adding that she had no right to be so severe. I stopped him on this subject, and he did not get vexed. At length he questioned me about the persons who acted as spies for the Empress. I answered him always that I did not know. At that he approached me, and said that I was not sufficiently devoted to him. I tried to prove to him that I was more sincerely attached to him than those who reported to him so many trifling things that were not worthy to be heard. This conversation terminated better th...

had commenced. I fancied that I had left him with a pretty good impression of me.

"The interview had been very long. The Empress, tired of waiting at the Bois de Boulogne, had sent a mounted footman to know what kept her husband. Word was taken back to her, that he was closeted with me. Her uneasiness became very great; she returned to the Tuileries, and as she did not find me there, she sent after me Madame de Talhouet, charged to find out what had taken place. In order to obey the Emperor's orders, I answered that he had only asked a question in relation to M. de Rémusat.

"In the evening the General Savary gave a small ball, at which the Emperor had promised to assist. During that winter he sought all the occasions of reunions; he was gay, and even danced a little, and rather badly. I arrived at Madame Savary's a little before the Court; I saw coming towards me the Grand Marshal Duroc, who gave me his arm as far as my place; the master of the house was very polite. The long audience I had had in the morning, gave me plenty to think about; they cared for me as if I was a favored person, or in the grand confidences. I laughed to myself at these precautions of courtiers. The Emperor arrived with his wife; in walking through the assembly, he stopped before me, and spoke to me in an obliging manner. The Empress had her eyes fixed on us, and was dying with uneasiness. Madame Murat appeared surprised, Madame de X——, slightly troubled. All this amused me; I did not foresee that which was about to result from it.

"The next day the Empress asked me a thousand questions, to which I replied with caution; she was hurt, and pretended that I was sacrificing her to the Emperor, that I went on the safe side, that I did not love her more than another; she greatly afflicted me. I reported to my excellent mother all my secret griefs. I was acquiring a painful experience, and I was yet young enough for it to cause my tears to flow. My mother consoled me, and advised me to remain aloof, which I did; but that did not aid me any. The Emperor did not fail to make me speak, and to back himself with the opinions that he had given me, in reproaching his wife, for her imprudences; the Empress treated me coldly; I saw that she avoided speaking to me, and on many accounts I thought it best not to seek her confidences.

"The Emperor, who liked to be at variance, seeing our coldness, treated me better; but Madame de X——, whom they had persuaded to dislike me, was uneasy at the little favor which I seemed to be enjoying, and, perhaps, doing me the honor of being jealous, sought for the means to injure me, and as the things of the world when evil is intended always arrange themselves only too well, she soon found an opportunity which succeeded perfectly.

"On the other side, Eugène and Madame Louis were persuaded that I had betrayed their mother in denouncing her, and that on account of the ambition of my husband, who preferred the favor of the minster to that of the mistress. M. de Rémusat was entirely a stranger to all these manœuvres; but as to ambition among the inhabitants of courts, that which is probable is always true. Eugène, who had some friendship for my husband, kept away from him.

"As courtiers our situation would not have been bad; but we were honest people, and we were both grieved, and we would not make any shameful profit out of our position."

One of the last of Napoleon's love affairs of which Madame de Rémusat gives us an account, was rather tame as compared with the others, and it is described in a few words:

"When the Emperor found himself at Munich, the thought passed through his head to gratify a certain fancy, half gallant, half political, with regard to the Queen of Bavaria. This Princess, second wife of the King, without being beautiful, had an elegant figure, and agreeable manners, which added to her dignity. The Emperor pretended, I think, he was in love with her. Those who assisted at this scene said it was curious enough to see him, with his weak character, and his somewhat common manners, endeavoring to succeed with a Princess accustomed to the kind of etiquette from which they never depart in Germany, no matter what the occasion may be. The Queen of Bavaria held in respect her strange admirer, and yet seemed to be amused with his homage. The Empress found her a little more of a coquette than she wished, and this inspired her with the wish to quickly quit the Court of Bavaria, and spoilt the pleasure which the marriage of her son had caused her."

The last amour of all which she had any knowledge of depicts Napoleon in the character of a sensual man, who was not in the least inspired by emotions that would serve to inspire even the guilty love of a weak woman:

"During that sojourn at Fontainebleau, there appeared among us a very pretty personage, in whom the Emperor was somewhat interested. This was an Italian lady, whom Monsieur de Talleyrand had seen in Italy, and had persuaded the Emperor to place her near the person of the Empress in the quality of reader. Her husband was made Receiver General. The Empress, at first considerably startled by this apparition of this beautiful one, soon decided that it were best to lend herself complacently to those amusements, which it was impossible to oppose for any length of time, and she consequently closed her eyes on this occasion to what was going on. The Italian was a gentle creature, submissive, and by no means elated by her success. She yielded to her master from a sort of conviction that she had no right to resist him, she felt a great attachment to Madame Bonaparte for her complaisance in not opposing the Emperor's fancy. Consequently the whole affair blew over without any noise and scandal. The lady was by far the most beautiful of a court which numbered many fair faces. I have never seen finer eyes, nor more lovely features. She was tall and elegantly made; she needed only a little more *embonpoint*.

"The Emperor had no great passion for her—he confided this fact to his wife, and reassured her, as, without any reserve, he told her the secret of that cold *liaison*. He had established her at Fontainebleau in such a way that he could see her whenever he pleased. It was whispered that she went to him in the evening, or that he ascended to her rooms; but in society he spoke to her no more frequently than he did to others, and our Court soon ceased to notice the affair, finding that it brought no changes in its train. M. de Talleyrand, who had first suggested to Bonaparte that he should take the Italian as his mistress, received the confidence as to the amount of pleasure she gave him, and this was all."

Madame de Rémusat retired from the court when Napoleon put the loving Josephine aside to marry the daughter of the Austrian.

AN AMOROUS KING OF SPAIN GETTING INTO A DROLL SCRAPE.

VISITING A FAIR LADY IN THE DARK—THE KING AND HIS FRIEND TREATED AS THIEVES.

THE sons and daughters of sunny Spain were always noted for the order in which they carried on their love intrigues at home and abroad ; and the historians inform us that King Philip IX. was not an exception to the general rule prevailing in that country.

Philip had a fair wife of his own, but that fact did not hinder him from casting lascivious eyes on a certain fair duchess who was attached to the court.

The duchess had a husband, however, who was powerful, jealous, and watchful, and he managed to keep a strict watch upon his tempting wife.

King Philip attempted several stratagems in order to send the watchful duke away from his wife, but the husband baffled him on every occasion; and when he was compelled to travel on warlike missions, he was always accompanied by the bewitching duchess.

Yet the king did not despair; and the more he waited and plotted, the more resolved did he become in his unholy love for the fair princess, while at the same time he feigned an indifference for the object of his passion.

At length Philip became convinced that the lady would receive him with smiles and caresses if it was only possible for him to elude the vigilance of the jealous husband and gain admittance to her private apartments at an hour when her lord would be engaged elsewhere.

One night when the king was playing a very close game of cards, he feigned to recollect that he had a letter to write of the utmost importance, and requested the duke to take his cards. Soon after the king went to his closet, put on a cloak, and accompanied by his favorite the Count of Olivarez, left the palace by a private staircase and repaired to the fair duchess.

The jealous duke, thinking more of his domestic interests than a game of cards, concluded that he had some particular design in giving him this charge. He began to complain of sudden and violent illness, and throwing his cards to another ran in haste to his house.

The king was in a dark room with the lady, and they were engaged in a very agreeable conversation, when the watchful husband rushed into the house, crying to his servants:

"The place is beset with thieves. The watchman outside tells me that he saw the rascals stealing in over the garden wall. Get sticks and we will beat the life out of the miscreants."

The lady appeared to be in a great terror when she heard her husband's voice, and she turned to the king crying:

"I am undone, sir. You must hide under the bed, or I am lost."

"Under the bed," returned the king. "I will hide where you will, fair lady. But what will become of my friend the count, who awaits me outside in the arbor?"

"He has fled, I trust, sire. Hasten under, or I am undone."

"But when can I escape?" asked the king, as he crawled under the bed.

"When my husband sleeps, I will lead you out by the garden gate. He comes this way now. Silence, or I am lost! He is so violent that I fear he will murder you."

"Thieves!—thieves!" yelled the husband, as he ran from room to room. "They are in the house, the knaves. Where is the duchess?"

"What is all this uproar about, my lord?" cried the duchess, as the jealous man rushed into the dark bedroom. "I thought the house was on fire when you aroused me from my sleep."

"There are thieves in the house, my dear. We have searched every apartment in the house save this. They must be hiding here."

"Mercy on me, my lord! Thieves in my apartment! It is impossible, I'm sure."

"There's one of the rascals," cried the husband, as he dragged the king from under the bed, and commenced to beat him with all his might.

"Here's the other," cried some of the servants, who had seized the king's friend in the garden below.

"Beat the rascal as I belabor this fellow," cried the duke, who kept striking the king in the dark room.

The count, who was not better treated, fearing the worst, cried out several times that it was the king; but the duke only redoubled his blows upon the prince and minister, assuring him that this was a great stroke of insolence, to make use of his majesty's name upon that occasion, and that he had a great mind to have him carried to the palace, and that the king would surely have him hung.

The king was silent during this uproar; he at length escaped, much mortified at receiving so many blows, without being consoled with any of the favors that he had anticipated.

On the following day the duke appeared at court with his fair wife; and they told the courtiers about the two robbers who had entered the house on the previous night.

"Just imagine their insolence," said the duke. "One of them asserted that the other was the king. If the rascals had not escaped through the window I would have dragged them here to the palace, so that his majesty could have them put to death."

This adventure did not terminate to the prejudice of the Duke of Albuquerque; on the contrary, the passion of the king for the duchess having subsided, he laughed at it himself.

THE STORY OF AN INFAMOUS SOCIETY IN ANCIENT ROME

THE REFORMED MISTRESS—EXPOSING THE CRIMES OF THE SECRET ORDER.

THE Roman historians furnish us with the following startling account of a terrible order which flourished in Rome in ancient days, and of the manner in which the members were exposed.

A young man, the son of a Roman knight, and whose name was Æbutius, lost his father at a very tender age, and also lost too soon the tutors who had been given him. By these means Titus Sempronius Rutilus, his step-father, had the whole control of his large estate. He misused the trust, and when the time came to render his accounts, he, in concert with the mother of Æbutius, took the resolution of destroying the son-in-law. Durania, his mother, reminded her husband that during her last illness she promised to initiate him into the mysteries of Bacchus, and that in the course of two days she would take him to the Bacchanals.

Æbutius was in love with a beautiful woman, called Hispala Fiscennia, who having acquired much wealth by her crimes, had entirely renounced her wicked life. As she was sincerely attached to the young Æbutius, it afforded her much pleasure to contribute to his wants, which were often pressing. Æbutius soon imparted to his mistress the project of his mother. What was his surprise when he saw Hispala employ all her prayers and tears to dissuade him from being initiated into the mysteries of Bacchus.

However, as he seemed averse to yield to her prayers, she confessed to him that during her servitude she had accompanied her mistress to the assembly of Bacchanalians, and that it was the sanctuary of the most scandalous crimes, that almost all the young men who were admitted died before the age of twenty, in a most strange manner. This recital, accompanied with many tears, made a deep impression upon the mind of Æbutius.

On his return to his home he informed his mother that he would not go to the Bacchanalian assembly; but did not disclose his reason. Durania then threw aside the mask, and turned her son from the paternal home. He took refuge with an aunt, and related to her the cause of his disgrace. She advised her nephew to inform the consul what he had heard of the murders and infamies committed in the nocturnal assembly, which were held in the forest of Stimula.

The consul, whose name was Spurius Posthumius Albinus, was seized with horror at this disclosure, and being desirous of finding out all the particulars, he sent for Hispala, at the house of Sulpicia, his mother-in-law. There it was that he learned all the minutiæ of those infamous meetings, where all modesty was thrown aside, and where the most decent were sure to lose their lives. Hispala concluded her account by naming several men and women of the highest distinction who were members.

After taking proper measures to prevent harm to Hispala and Æbutius, the consul reported to the Senate all that he had heard of those criminal meetings.

Pudicity had always been a cherished virtue by the Romans, and those venerable "patres conscripti" heard with horror the news of the disorders which reigned in the republic. By order of the Senate and people, the most exact inquiry was made to find out the guilty. Most of them were put to death, and this abominable set were entirely destroyed both in Rome and its environs.

Hispala and Æbutius both received one hundred thousand brass asses as a reward. Hispala received all the privileges of a free woman, while her two sisters stood by her side in threatening attitudes, as they bent flashing glances at the insulting stranger.

Hispala and Æbutius both received one hundred thousand brass asses as a reward. Hispala received all the privileges of a free woman, with the permission of choosing a husband from any rank she pleased. History does not inform us whether Æbutius married his mistress.

SOME OF THE PRIVATE AMOURS OF EMPEROR NICHOLAS OF RUSSIA.

THE DARING TRAVELER AND THE PRETTY JEWESS—KISSES FOR ONE AND ALL—THE OLD NURSE'S DISCOVERY—A ROMANTIC COURTSHIP—A DUTIFUL WIFE SHUTS HER EYES.

ONE stormy evening in the month of December three young Jewish girls were seated in the public-room of an inn on the outskirts of St. Petersburgh, when a tall traveler entered the place and advanced to the stove, crying in very abrupt tones, addressing the oldest-looking:

"A bottle of your best wine on the instant, girl, and some bread and ham."

"I am not a girl, sir," replied the person addressed. "I am a married woman. Rachel, you will wait on the gentleman. I will order the bread and ham for you, sir."

"Stay a moment," cried the stranger, as he fixed his eyes on the beautiful Jewess. "You say you are a married woman?"

"I am, sir. My husband is the owner of this inn, and those young girls are my sisters."

"You are all very pretty, I swear," said the abrupt traveler, as he cast a glance at the girls; "but you are surprisingly handsome, madam. I envy your husband."

"You are very free in your remarks, sir," said the beautiful Jewess. "If my husband were present he would resent a——"

"I would fling him out of that window if he did, madam. Pray what is your name?"

The man spoke with an air of authority; he wore a sword at his side, and he held a brace of pistols in his belt; while he was evidently very strong and active.

The woman, who was one of a race accustomed to bow the knee in despotic Russia, fearing that her visitor was some powerful nobleman in disguise, answered in humble tones:

"My name is Rebecca Leman, sir."

"Where is your husband?"

"He is in Poland on business, sir."

"Ha!—in Poland. He is a Jew and a Pole, I could swear. Is he not?"

"He is, sir."

"And a rebel. He is up in arms now with his countrymen, I'll warrant you, madam."

"My husband is a traveling merchant, sir," replied the cautious Jewess.

"Have you any children, madam?"

"I have none, sir."

"How long has your husband been absent from you, my sweet dame?"

"Over six months, sir."

"You have a lover in his absence, of course?"

"You would insult me, sir. The daughters of our race, I would have you know——"

"Are like all the other daughters of Eve in this wide world, madam," cried the rough stranger, with a meaning smile. "I will remain in this house to-night. I will sup with you in your private room. I will take your husband's place for the time, and I——"

"You will leave this house on the instant, sir, or I will summon the officers of the law and have you expelled," said the indignant Jewess, while her two sisters stood by her side in threatening attitudes, as they bent flashing glances at the insulting stranger.

"Leave this house on the instant," cried the stranger. "No, on my oath. Summon the police, if you will; but I will have one kiss ere they can come."

As the man spoke he seized the fair Jewess in his powerful arms, lifted her up as he would a child, and pressed his mouth to her red lips with all the ardor of a returned sailor kissing his sweetheart.

The two sisters attempted to seize the male stranger, but he flung them aside impatiently, as he cried in merry tones:

"Your turn some other time, girls. On my oath, but that was the sweetest kiss I ever had, madam, and you will be well paid for it."

"If I had had a dagger I would have stabbed you to the heart, wretch," cried the indignant Jewess, as she tore herself away from the man's passionate embrace.

"Nay, madam, you will bless me for it on the morrow. Come and join me in the good wine, and then I will sup with you. I am not a brute. Look at me well. Is your husband half as comely as I am?"

"On my word but he is not," cried one of the girls, as she burst out laughing at the contrast. "He is not half your size, he is deformed, and Rebecca knows she hates him."

"Hush, Rachel," cried the pretty madam, as she saw the heavy purse in the stranger's hands. "My husband is a good man, if he is a little crooked in the back."

"I'll wager the contents of this purse, my fair dame," cried the stranger, "that you never enjoyed a kiss from him half as much as you did the one I have given you."

"Why he has no teeth," cried Rachel; "and he snarls like an old hound."

"She hates him," cried the other girls. "We all hate him, for he is a stingy old rogue."

"And you all love me, as I am young, handsome, and liberal," cried the stranger, flinging his purse on the table. "There's something to buy you all new dresses, girls. One kiss apiece, and the madam here will not be jealous."

Quick as thought, the forward stranger seized the girls, passing one of his strong arms round each of their waists, and raising them up, he pressed his mouth to their pouting lips, as he continued to cry:

"On my faith, but you Jewish dames are the most charming

damsels I ever met; but the matron here tastes sweetest of all. You must each wed an old toothless miser, girls, and then you will know how pleasant it is to kiss a young man."

"You act as one accustomed to kiss whom you please, sir," said the young woman of the house, who was becoming very much interested in the handsome stranger.

"Well, yes, my sweet maidain. I have kissed some of the noblest ladies in the land ere now."

"What impudence," cried Rachel. "I presume you will tell us that you have kissed the empress herself."

"I have kissed the empress, fair damsel, and before she was an empress at all."

"Treason," cried Rachel. "That is, if you are not her brother?"

"Indeed, and I am not a brother of the empress, pert damsel. But a truce to this folly. I will sup with you, dame."

"You are pressing too far, sir," replied the blushing woman. "You will not sup with me."

"I will sup with you, sweet dame. Come, come, and be not so bashful. Forget that snarling old husband of yours, and imagine that I am your lord and master. Ha!—you would fly from me, but you cannot. See! I am very strong and active. Stand aside, girls, your sister will be my companion to-night."

The strong stranger lifted the young woman in his arms and bore her into an inner apartment, despite her cries and struggles.

The two young girls, being somewhat alarmed at the bearing of the young stranger, ran to the door and called aloud for help.

"What is the matter?" cried an agent of the police, who appeared at the door on the instant.

"Our sister has been insulted by a rude stranger, officer. He is now in there."

"Your sister makes no outcry, girl," said the man, with a peculiar smile. "Trust me the young stranger will be more welcome than the old husband. Perchance, when the old Jew comes back from Poland he will find another young stranger here before him."

The two girls were impressed with the policeman's remarks, and they stepped back to listen.

"Rachel," cried their married sister from the inner apartment, "see that you order a splendid repast at once. The young stranger will sup with me to-night. Do not raise an outcry. The gentleman will not injure any of us. We will not be disturbed by other guests."

"Who can it be, Rachel?" inquired the youngest sister, as the police agent turned to leave the door.

"I cannot say, Ruth. I trust he will not remain here all night, for our sister's sake."

"He is very handsome, Rachel. I could love him myself, if he were of our race."

"I would give the world to see the old miser walk in soon, and find Rebecca supping with the young man in the private room."

"And so would I, sister. Let us hasten the supper, and perchance the stranger will invite us to share it with him."

"No danger of that, young one. He is taken with Rebecca to-night. You heard what he said about our wedding old men. Sister, sister! I know who he is!"

"Who is he, girl?"

"The Emperor Nicholas! Oh, our sister is a lost woman! She will become his mistress!"

The daring stranger was Nicholas, Emperor of all the Russias, and the handsome Jewish woman did become his mistress.

When the old Jew returned from Poland, after a year's absence from his home, he found his young wife surrounded by many luxuries, and in a fair way to become a mother.

When the old man commenced to upbraid the handsome woman, he was arrested by a police agent and taken back to Poland.

Two years after his banishment, he stole back to St. Petersburgh, for the purpose of reclaiming some gold and jewels that he had buried in the yard back of the river. On making secret inquiries about his young wife and her sisters, he learned that they were all living together in a grand mansion; that the emperor often visited them in disguise; and that each of the fair women had two children, without being at all troubled by snarling old husbands.

While Nicholas of Russia carried on his secret amours in the manner described, he would play the gallant with his equals in another fashion.

His marriage with the charming princess of Prussia had a pleasant piece of gallantry in it. It is customary, when a monarch is to be married, to have the whole affair arranged by the courts of the marrying parties. But not so with Nicholas.

He determined to pick out his own wife, and he went rambling about among the courts of Europe in search of a woman who had those peculiar personal charms which could captivate his heart. At last he found such a one in the person of the young and beautiful princess of Prussia.

At her father's court he tarried long enough to become well acquainted with her qualities of mind and heart; and one day at dinner he rolled a small ring in a piece of bread, and handed it to the princess, saying to her in an under tone:

"If you will accept my hand, put this ring on your finger."

And what do you think she did? She popped the question.

She took no time to deliberate, in the fashion of cunning prudes, but suffered her heart to tell the truth at once, and instantly put the ring on her finger.

Nicholas was one of the finest-looking men in Europe; and, at the time of his marriage, he and his spouse were considered the handsomest couple in Europe.

Notwithstanding the innumerable little gallantries of Nicholas, he was always kind, attentive and affectionate to his wife; and she had the wisdom and amiability never to annoy him with any of the reproaches of jealousy.

In 1830 she lost her beauty by a most singular freak of nature, occasioned by a fright she received at the moment when the emperor rushed into the presence of the infuriated mob that sought his life, and commanded them to "down on their knees" before him.

It was after this that Nicholas fell in love with the young and beautiful Nellydoff, one of the maids of honor to the empress.

The empress, though perfectly aware of this affair, always treated Nellydoff with the greatest respect in public.

This love affair was terminated only by the death of Nicholas, but it did not prevent him from numerous other intrigues.

THE LOVE INTRIGUE OF A GERMAN ARCHBISHOP.

LOVING AND WEDDING IN SECRET—THE JEALOUSY OF A FAMOUS QUEEN.

At a time when the world was agitated by religious discussions a noble German archbishop became involved in a lively love intrigue.

Gebhar Truchess, baron of Walbourg, was the son of William, and nephew of Otho, Cardinal of Ausbourgh, who died in 1573.

He was ordained Archbishop and Elector of Cologne, in 1577, at the age of thirty; and appeared in character of Deputy to the Emperor, at the famous assembly of Cologne, for the purpose of trying to effect a peace between the emperor and the United Provinces.

There it was that the prelate became acquainted with Agnes, the daughter of John Georges, Count of Mansfeld, and Caноness of Gurisheim, with whom he became passionately in love.

This passion was so publicly talked of, that the brothers of Agnes, irritated by the scandalous assiduities of the Elector toward their sister, threatened to wash away in his blood, and in that of their sister, the injury done to their house.

Truchses was too much enamored to hesitate an instant; he promised to renounce all ecclesiastic dignities, to marry Agnes. Nevertheless, the Archbishopric de Cologne was an object of sufficient importance to occasion his regret; the prelate would willingly have retained the one and possessed the other.

They persuaded him that this was not difficult, and that by embracing Lutheranism, he could marry his mistress and remain Archbishop de Cologne. Love decided it, he espoused Agnes, and carried her to the Episcopal Palace.

This marriage was for some time kept secret, but strong suspicions of it arising, the Chapter of Cologne resolved to bring the prelate to an explanation, and took up arms against him.

In this critical situation, Truchses threw aside the mask, and publicly declared his marriage and his imprudent step hastened on his ruin. The Emperor Rodolphus declared himself for the Chapter, and the Pope after having for some time debated upon the punishment he should inflict, issued excommunication against Gebhar.

The Canons, on their side, proceeded to an election, and the choice fell upon Ernestus, of Bavaria, already Bishop of Thesingue, of Hildesheim, and of Liege—war must of necessity decide the difference. The Protestant princes of Germany took up arms in favor of Gebhar. The electors and princes, being assembled at Frankfort, proposed a means of accommodation to put an end to the miseries inseparable from war.

Their proposal was, that Gebhar should resign his dignity of elector and archbishop, in favor of Ernest; reserving to himself a pension sufficient to support him honorably. Gebhar consented to give up the title of archbishop, but insisted upon retaining the dignity of elector with Westphalia; this irritated the princes, and they resolved vigorously to prosecute the war.

The siege of Bonn, where Charles Truchses, brother of the prelate, was shut up, concluded the war. Charles was delivered to the enemy by his own troops, who seized upon the city. Gebhar, deprived of every resource, retired with his wife (the only comfort left him) to Delf, in Holland, to the court of the Prince of Orange.

It was not long before this prince received a mortification very humiliating. He had always relied upon the protection of Queen Elizabeth; and on his arrival at Holland, wrote to that princess to ask succors and leave to retire into England.

The queen sent him two thousand crowns, but refused to grant the permission he requested. Truchses thinking that his wife, through her beauty and address, would obtain more than he had by his letters, sent her into England.

Madame Truchses thought she could not do better than to solicit the Earl of Essex to speak in her favor to Elizabeth, which he accordingly did. The earl, either from gallantry or compassion, gave Madame Truchses apartments in his house, and loaded her with civilities, waiting for the return of the queen, to speak in her behalf. That princess, informed of all that had passed, conceived the most violent jealousy; she sent a message to this unfortunate lady to leave England immediately, and forbade the earl to appear before her till Madame Truchses had quitted London. She soon after rejoined her unfortunate husband, who finished his life in poverty and grief.

THE VENGEANCE OF AN OUTRAGED HUNGARIAN PRINCE.

THE PALATINE'S FAIR WIFE—A PASSIONATE PRINCE—THE VILE OUTRAGE AND THE VENGEANCE.

AMONG the gallant warriors who went to fight the infidels in the Holy Land was Andrew, King of Hungary. When the king left his kingdom he trusted the administration of it to the palatine of Hungary, whose name was Banchanus, and recommended him, above all things, to do strict justice to every one, without any regard to either rank or fortune.

Banchanus's wife, a woman of the greatest beauty, anxious to soothe the melancholy of the queen, bestowed upon her the greatest attention.

The Count of Moravia, who was the queen's own brother, coming to Hungary under these circumstances, was received with all possible marks of distinction, and it was the endeavor of every one to amuse him with balls and assemblies.

It was amidst those entertainments that the prince fell in love with the regent's wife. It was not long before he made a confession of his passion, and employed all the means which the most ardent love can inspire to win the heart of that lady.

All his attempts were vain, and Banchanus's wife, followed with so close a pursuit, pretended indisposition for some time, that she might keep away from court. This obstinate repulse only increased and irritated the prince's desires.

A gloomy melancholy, the usual effect of a great passion, took possession of his mind, and, to ease his soul, he was obliged to intrust it to the queen, his sister. This princess took rather too much interest in her brother's distress of heart, and was weak enough to favor his criminal intentions.

In order to succeed better, the count affected a more respectful behavior towards his mistress; and her fears being removed by the alteration of his conduct, she took less precaution; and one day, having accompanied the queen to a remote place of her apartment, she was abandoned to the count, who was there, and who cruelly abused the opportunity.

Although the regent's wife was enraged in her soul, she kept the secret of this adventure for some time. But one day, seeing her husband disposed to caress her with his usual tenderness, she exclaimed:

"Approach me not," at the same time pouring out a flood of tears, "and leave a woman who is no longer worthy of your pure embraces! A villain, full of boldness, has been rash enough to abuse me; and the queen, his sister, herself delivered me into his power. I should have punished myself for this crime, did not my religion forbid my attempting to take my life. I am but too guilty since I have lost my honor, and I beg of you my death, that I may no longer survive my shame and disgrace."

Banchanus, after having consoled his wife, considered how it was best to avenge this affront. The first victim should have been the Count of Moravia, but he had prudently left the kingdom.

Banchanus then repaired to the palace of the queen, and asked her to retire to a closet with him, in order to read some letters he had just received. When alone with her, he reproached her with great bitterness of her crime, and stabbed her. He himself informed the court of what he had done. Then, taking the road to Constantinople, he met there the king, Andrew, and said to him—

"Mighty Lord, in giving me your last commands, as you were starting for Hungary, you charged me to administer justice with the strictest rigors to your subjects, without any regard to rank or fortune. That I have done. I have killed the queen, your wife, who had ruined mine; and far from seeking my own safety by a shameful flight, I bring you my head. Dispose as you like of my life; but remember, that by my life or my death, your people will judge of your equity, and whether I am innocent or guilty."

The example of bravery was without parallel. The king thus replied:

"If you have spoken truly, go back to Hungary, continue to administer justice to my subjects with the same severity as you did to yourself. My stay in the Holy Land will not be long, and on my return, I shall judge for myself whether your action is worthy of praise or punishment."

The prince did not remain long in Palestine, much to the detriment of the Christians, to whose aid he had come. The action of Danchanus had made on him a terrible impression, and immediately on his return home, he examined for himself all the circumstances, and was equitable enough to acquit Danchanus.

CURIOUS ANECDOTES OF TRUE LOVE, AND A BASE INTRIGUE.

THE FAIR INFIDEL AND THE PRISONER—THE WILLING WIVES—AN AMOROUS MINISTER—HIS VILE ACTS AND HIS PUNISHMENT.

During one of the wars waged by Poland against Turkey, a brave German count was taken prisoner by the infidels. He was taken to one of the Turkish provinces, where he was sold as a slave to the king.

His employment, among other servile occupations, was that of cultivating the earth. As he was one day thus employed, he was accosted, and much interrogated, by the daughter of the king, his master, as she took the air. His good mien and genteel address wrought so powerfully upon the princess that she promised to break his chains, and at the same time to follow him to him to his own country, provided he would marry her.

"But I have a wife and children," replied the count.

"That," answered the princess, "will not be an impediment; it is the custom in Turkey to have several wives."

Considering liberty as the most precious of all human possessions, the count did not make any further objections, but expressed his gratitude and engaged his word to the princess. She employed herself to such advantage that the count soon after found himself at liberty, and embarked with her.

They arrived without interruption at Venice, where the count found one of his gentlemen, who informed him of all that had happened during his captivity.

From this domestic he learned that his wife and children were well; and before he allowed himself the pleasure of embracing them, he went to Rome; and after having related the whole of his singular case to the Pope, the pontiff gave him permission to keep his two wives.

If the Court of Rome had shown complaisance upon this occasion, the wife of the count could not do less. She loaded the Turkish princess, to whom she was indebted for the return of her beloved husband, with caresses and marks of friendship. The princess was sensible of, and returned all these civilities; she had no children, but was not the less attached to the children of the other.

The above anecdote demonstrates the truth of the assertion that the spirit of gratitude will always be found predominant in the noble breast.

The next incident will serve to show that a base mind will never rise above the follies and mistrusts of early youth.

Louis XI. of France was one of the most crafty monarchs in the world, and he gathered around him, as his instruments, the vilest wretches in the kingdom. This monarch's prime minister was a licentious villain who had once been his boarder, and who arose to great power by his cunning intrigues.

The vile minister's name was Oliver le Dain; and the following story will serve us an example of his many acts of treachery:

A gentleman, arrested by the order of the king, was in great danger of his life. His wife, who was tenderly attached to him, ardently solicited his pardon; and thought she could not apply to a more powerful protector than Oliver le Dain. She was young and handsome, and her tears and grief increased and embellished her charms. She made an impression upon the favorite, who was not ashamed to promise this unhappy woman the pardon of her husband, on condition that she would make him a sacrifice of her honor. The alternative was cruel, but honor carried it. This virtuous woman had the liberty of seeing her husband, and she imparted to him the proposition of Le Dain. The unfortunate prisoner conjured his wife to save him, and such was his control over her that he succeeded in persuading her to accept the terrible terms. And when this unfortunate victim of conjugal love sought to dry her tears in the arms of her husband, she had the horror to learn that he had been put to death.

The barbarous Oliver, to have longer possession of a woman he loved, ordered her husband to be put into a sack and thrown into the river. The corpse was discovered by some fishermen who acquainted the wife with her misfortune. She remained silent during the reign of Louis XI. Her tears and groans would not have reached his throne. But after the death of that prince, and under the reign of Charles VIII., she became the accuser of Le Dain, who was hanged, together with the accomplice in his guilt.

SOME OF THE STRANGE ADVENTURES OF TWO AMOROUS NOBLES AND ONE OF RICHELIEU'S FAVORITES.

SELECTING LADY-LOVES—A QUARREL AND ITS CONSEQUENCES—FOOLING A RIVAL.

The celebrated Marion de Lorme, who had bewitched Cardinal Richelieu, was one of the most remarkable coquettes of her time, and many strange stories are told of her intrigues with the noted men of France.

Count de Gramont, after the siege of Turin, passed some time in that city with his friend the Chevalier de Malta. They were not long before they each chose a lady-love. Count de Gramont addressed his vows to Mademoiselle de Saint-Germain, and recommended to his friend Madame de Senantes.

The count made an early impression on the heart of his favorite, but in spite of his vivacity and insinuating address, was not able to bring his passion to the conclusion he wished. In the mean-

Miss Howard was saluted by General F—— and M. P——, a banker, by the title of the Countess de Beauregard.

They presented her as an acknowledgement of the debt of Louis Napoleon the title-deeds of an estate which bore the name of Beauregard, and was situated near Versailles.

For a time the new-made Countess was satisfied.

After a time, however, the Englishwoman again made herself conspicuous. She was eager to annoy the Spaniard who had "robbed her children of their bread," as she expressed it.

She showed herself at the Bois in her caleche with the Imperial livery, and for some time all Paris enjoyed at the races the presence of "the two Empresses."

For this performance Miss Howard paid dearly. She was taken off in the night and carried over the frontier. She was never heard of again, though rumor had it that she was stilled in her bed.

Although Louis Napoleon was well advanced in years when he took the beautiful young Spanish lady for his wife, he was not satisfied with the pleasures of his married life, and he very often gave the Empress proofs of his inconstancy.

While his foreign enemies sent beautiful women to Paris to entrap him, Louis employed his own fair creatures as spies.

Monsieur Claude gives us a very interesting account of an adventure in which one of these spy-mistresses played a disagreeable part:

A woman unconscious and entirely nude had been found by the police within an inclosure, surrounded by the materials of a house that was rapidly being erected.

The inspector who made the discovery had hastened to tell me of it, leaving two of his men mounting guard over the unconscious woman.

I went at once with the inspector to the place, which was one of the most obscure, and of the worst repute in the whole vicinity.

The immense Parc Monceau at this time was like a huge black spot in the outer boulevards. It was entirely unlighted, and its darkness insured impunity to the most daring villains.

Odious tumble-down buildings, with grimy windows and barred doors, stood not far from the thick shadows of the park. The places were mostly occupied as wine shops. They overlooked an enormous plain, as rough and uneven as a sea in a heavy gale. The whole plain was redolent of crime and poverty.

The inspector led me to the corner of a road crossing the Plaine Monceau, and then took me within the walls of a house that was being built. These walls were only a few feet above the ground, but they were high enough to conceal what was going on inside.

I entered the hollow square, which was lighted by the sky. In the center I saw a group of men holding lanterns. I saw the nude form of a woman lying on the ground. She looked like a statue on a granite base. Hardly had my eyes fallen on this woman than I uttered an exclamation of pained surprise. I signed to the men to raise their lanterns and mass them above the face of the poor creature, that I might be sure that I was not mistaken.

When the light fell full on the beautiful face and form of this woman, I saw that my first supposition was correct.

"Madame X——!" I cried. "It is certainly she!"

I had recognized the Mme. X—— whom, when in the companionship of my old friend, I had been fortunate enough to rescue from great peril. How this woman, whose conduct, it is true, was less to be admired than her beauty, came in this place and in this condition, was a thing which seemed to me absolutely incredible.

Who had carried her there?

Of course it could only be a man animated by motives of the basest revenge.

But this man could never have carried her to this place alone: he had accomplices. And that a man could find any one to assist him in such a dastardly revenge, it must be that Mme. X—— was on her side very guilty, or she must, at all events, have

given to her persecutors some most powerful reasons for hatred and vengeance. Yes, it was plain; for not only was Mme. X—— as nude as Eve, but while under the influence of a powerful narcotic her magnificent hair had been shaved close to her head!

I remembered that she was more proud of her hair than of all her other natural advantages.

The loss of the lady's hair convinced me that her enemy was a jealous lover!

And I reflected that only a lover who had been deceived could be guilty of such villainy.

I also felt certain that he must consider his wrongs something beyond parallel.

I recalled the incidents of a few years before, when Madame X—— so nearly fell a victim to the bandits of the Trocadéro, when I had said to myself that some day—her imprudence was so great—she would not escape so readily.

That day had come.

By a singular accident I was summoned at Monceau, as at Passy, to save her if possible.

I suddenly asked myself if Madame X—— was not a spy?

That I was on the track of the mysterious crime of which this unfortunate woman was the victim, I felt certain.

It must be that persons whom she had denounced had humiliated her after this cruel fashion.

I did not linger at this time to verify my conjectures. I simply assured myself that the woman was living and that she had sustained no fracture of any limb, and then I called up the inspector. I said a few words to him in a low voice. He went back to his agents and in formal terms repeated to them what I had said in less formal words.

Presently one of the agents offered his cloak to the inspector, which he himself wrapped around Madame X——. He bore her then, assisted by one of his men, to the carriage, which had been sent for and which stood not far away.

Five minutes later the inspector and Madame X—— were driving rapidly toward the residence of the latter.

The agent had done this at my orders, I having told him of my suspicions, and assured him I felt perfectly sure that Madame X—— was the secret agent of the Chief of the Division of Police, M. Lagrange. I told him, moreover, that the whole affair must be kept as quiet as possible, because were it known it would occasion great joy to the enemies of the Empire, and if this scandal got into the journals it would be especially disagreeable to the château.

After this I, of course, set to work to know the cause of this still inexplicable catastrophe.

I ordered the two agents who remained on the place where the unfortunate woman had been found to go forward with their lanterns.

I threw myself on my knees near the spot where Madame X—— had lain. Crawling slowly over the ground, I soon discovered the footprints of the men who had deposited their victim within the walls. After a long and close examination of these footprints, I exclaimed:

"There were two. By the shape of their boots I am convinced that one is a civilian and the other a military man. We will follow these indications, and in that way can at least discover from what direction they entered this place. It has rained, the ground is very soft, and I think we hold the clew in our possession."

The police of the Empire had created a new class of secret agents. They were under the absolute orders of M. Lagrange. They were called "indicators," and were in no way to be confounded with the policemen whose duty it was to maintain order in the streets, nor with the inspectors, who were charged with the responsibility of carrying on investigations which affected the welfare of the public.

These "indicators" were distributed through every class of society. They wrote to M. Lagrange under fictitious names. They sent to him detailed accounts of their most intimate conversations with their friends. Mme. X—— was one of these "indicators" in the pay of the government. At this time women played a most important part in the police of the Empire.

Unfortunately, it was not the women about the Emperor's household who alone exercised this degrading but lucrative profession.

The police of other lands, more especially of Italy and Germany, imitated the policy of the Emperor. Italian and German princesses appeared in Paris, being intrusted by their governments with the mission of dragging his Majesty, through the magic of their beauty, into some trap, laid by his mysterious enemies.

It was through one of these foreign women that Pieri, the Italian refugee and former cavalry officer, learned that he had been denounced by Mme. X——. This was in 1852. Pieri, attached to a secret society, known as "Young Italy," came to France under a false name, hoping to awaken among the noncommissioned officers in the army a feeling of indignation against the *coup d'état*. Before reaching London and entering into communication with Ledru-Rollin, Pieri had renewed his acquaintance with a second lieutenant, a former companion in arms in Africa.

The young man was a fascinating fellow; he had all the prestige imparted by epaulettes, as well as manly beauty and a perfect education.

Mme. X—— did not serve Napoleon with impunity like the mother of our Sovereign. She had some of the blood of Messalina in her veins.

As soon as she saw the young lieutenant—as soon as she talked with him—she fell madly in love with him, and Circe-like, employed all her witchery to entice him.

As the young man met her half way, their relations were soon of the most passionate nature.

Mme. X—— speedily informed the lieutenant that she was very intimate with the Minister of War, and that he had been a friend from childhood of her father, who was a page to Charles X. at the same time as the Marshal.

The lieutenant was delighted at his conquest, and felt sure that fortune had begun to smile upon him, and that this fair creature would soften the heart of the Marshal in his behalf. Mme. X——, who was amiably disposed toward all the world, did not long delay in pleading the cause of her lover before the illustrious friend of her father.

The Marshal replied sharply:

"You are a simpleton, my dear. You do not know in the least to whom you have given your heart. This man is an enemy of the empire. I have most explicit information in regard to him as an Orientist. At this very moment, when you are pleading his cause, he is in correspondence with the London Socialists. Far from promoting him, we intend to seize the first opportunity of cashiering him. If you wish to be acceptable at the château you, instead of protecting him, will assist us in getting rid of him."

Mme. X—— was greatly perplexed. She had not in the least anticipated such an outbreak as this from the Marshal.

As at this time the wishes of the château were looked upon as orders, she did not hesitate to follow the advice of her father's powerful friend.

This spy, Mme. X——, enjoyed the friendship of a certain princess, who was a spy like herself. Only this princess, who ostensibly worked with Mme. X—— for the château, in reality managed to possess herself of the secrets of her companions, only to hand them over to foreign courts.

The spy of the Tuileries told the foreign spy everything that took place.

Entirely *au courant* with each act of the society known as "Young Italy," the foreign princess discovered and informed Mme. X—— that the handsome young lieutenant, furious against the Empire, had put himself into communication with Pieri, Mazzini's agent, and had agreed to work against Napoleon III. and for his downfall.

"Now my dear," said the Princess in conclusion, "use my in-

formation as you will, make such profit out of it as you can. Were I in your place I would see Pieri and pretend that I was with him and wished to be of use. In that way you would have it in your power to deliver one, if not both of these conspirators, over to justice."

Mme. X—— did just what this perfidious foreigner advised. It was not difficult, through her lover, to make Pieri's acquaintance.

At first the unsuspicious young lieutenant, who had never spoken of this Italian to his fair friend, appeared very much surprised, but was entirely unsuspicious.

Mme. X—— made him believe that the Marshal Saint-Arnaud was out of temper with the Emperor because he had alienated the estates of the Orleans family, and was quite ready to take a stand with the disaffected, and that he only waited for an opportunity to promote the officers of his old regiment, thus strengthening the adversaries of the Empire.

"Appoint a time when I can see your friend Pieri," she said, "and I will tell him all the thoughts of the Marshal, who, let me assure you, is so far from being an enemy of yours, that he only awaits the opportunity of becoming your ally."

The young man who would not have yielded so ready a credence to Mme. X—— had he not been in love with her, went at once to Pieri, who was just about to embark for Havre, and told him all that had been said.

Pieri, however, was far less confident, and warned by the Princess, told the lieutenant that he was deceived and was in mortal danger.

The lieutenant, at last convinced, swore to be avenged.

"No; let me attend to that," answered the fierce Pieri. "As your fair friend desires to make my acquaintance, I prefer to satisfy her and make her pay very dearly for having had the presumption to suppose that she could dupe us."

On this the horrible revenge, and the details of the plot into which Mme. X—— fell, were concerted between Pieri and the young lieutenant of the 47th.

How was it all managed?

It was Mme. X——, who, later, explained all this to me, when, less than a week after, I called at her house, by special invitation.

Hardly had I entered the presence of Mme. X—— than the Marshal Saint-Arnaud walked in. This old friend, by reason of the warm affection he had felt for this lady ever since she had sent for me, had been summoned for the same reason she had sent for me. A young lieutenant was also there, whom I did not know, but when he saw me the young officer turned deadly pale.

My appearance was certainly not calculated to re-assure him, notwithstanding the cordial manner in which the Marshal treated the *protégé* of his fair friend.

My appearance produced on this man, however, a most chilling effect.

He was a youth of twenty-five. His heavy, sulky face was not interesting; his forehead was low, and his mouth sensual.

I made up my mind that he was a hypocrite, whose epaulets and uniform covered a vulgar, covetous nature.

It was difficult for me to understand how a woman, refined in spite of all her mad follies, like Mme. X——, could possibly be interested in such a person.

I felt sure that she would never forgive herself for having been in the power of a man like this, and began to be a little uneasy for him, as I well knew the courage and determination of Mme. X——.

That lady wore, for some reason which I could not comprehend, a riding costume.

She invited us, however, after breakfast, to ride to the Bois, out of compliment to the Marshal, who was a great admirer of English horses.

"She wished," she said, "to show her new ponies, which had just come from the stables of her Majesty, to the Marshal, who knew a good horse when he saw it."

The conversation at the breakfast-table turned on the Duchess of Berri, which could hardly be agreeable to him who looked back on a past of treachery.

"My dear child," exclaimed the Marshal, anxious to turn the conversation, and addressing Mme. X——, "we have talked enough of the past, suppose we confine ourselves now to the present. Have you any clew to the rascals who played such a foul trick on you recently—a trick which I thirst to avenge?"

"Yes, Marshal," responded our hostess, turning toward me as she spoke; "thanks to Monsieur Claude, who has the eyes of a lynx and the scent of a bloodhound, we have a clew."

"Good!" cried Saint-Arnaud, clapping his hands joyously; "I pray Heaven that, with the aid of Monsieur Claude, we may punish the scoundrels as they deserve, though I hear that one of them has got off to England!"

While the Marshal uttered these words without seeming to suspect the lieutenant, I never took my eyes from the young man. I saw him change color, become perfectly livid, and then deep crimson. He coughed violently, and passed his handkerchief over his face to hide his confusion and mortal anxiety. Mme. X—— did not seem to notice the embarrassment of her unhappy guest, but continued to converse with the Marshal.

"My dear friend," she said, "your wishes and my own will be thoroughly gratified. The wretch who aided this Italian to betray his Majesty and assisted him in this deadly insult to me is in Paris. We think, Monsieur Claude and I, that we have him in our power."

At these words, the young officer made a movement as if to rise. He stammered a word or two and sunk back in his chair, paralyzed with terror.

In this movement he knocked over a glass of champagne which had been standing by his side, and which he absolutely had not the courage to lift to his lips.

"What is the matter?" said Mme. X——, as she hastily drew her dress aside to save it from the wine.

"I beg ten thousand pardons," stammered the young officer, summoning all his self-control. "I feel such deep interest in all that concerns you, madame, that I can never hear an allusion made to that terrible affair without becoming excited."

Mme. X—— was utterly amazed at the audacity of this accomplice of the Socialist. She turned her eyes full upon him; they were blazing with contempt.

He felt it and again turned pale.

Then Mme. X—— rose from her chair, and in a clear, ringing voice said:

"You are quite right, sir, in expressing yourself with such scorn. I feel quite sure that your indignation will be shared by my friends, when they learn that this man who aided his accomplice in his plan of degrading and humiliating me, whom they learn, I say, that this man enjoyed my confidence, that he owed everything to me, even his honor—for my purse was emptied for him at a moment when, but for me, he was friendless. The time he selected for this outrage was when I had just discharged his debts of honor and saved his being dismissed from his regiment."

"Madame! Madame!" stammered the lieutenant, with his hands extended to his hostess, "it was not I who did this. I have been calumniated—I swear that it was not I."

"Calumniated!" replied Mme. X——, with her arms folded on her breast, and her eyes blazing. "Calumniated I suppose by the woman who favored you with her advice—by this Princesse C——, by this Italian, this worthy accomplice of your Mazzinists. Pshaw! It is useless to add falsehood to your baseness."

"But," added the officer, whose self-possession was now gone, "I was not with the Italian when the assault was committed upon you."

"You were there!" she cried, as she showed him a button which I had found in the Parc Monceau.

At the sight of this button, bearing the number of the 47th regiment, the lieutenant blanched as he uttered a terrified exclamation, followed immediately by a cry of pain.

Just as he had leaned over to look at the button, Mme. X——

struck him across the face with her riding whip, which she had snatched from a table at her side.

Neither the Marshal nor I had time to interfere, and the face of the young officer was nearly cut in two by the lash.

The revengeful spy had kept her word. She had returned insult for insult to the wretch who had treated her in such a dastardly fashion. I considered it expedient to bring the scene to a close. It was neither in the interest of the amazon nor for the dignity of the Marshal that it should continue.

I thought, too, that the officer had been sufficiently punished by his mistress, and that it was time for the law to interfere.

I drew my scarf from my pocket, and tying it around my waist, I went up to the young man, who had dropped into a chair and was wiping the drops of blood from his face.

I said to him:

"I command you in the name of the Law to follow me."

The Marshal and Mme. X—— vanished; they did not choose to figure with the guard and policemen in the scene which this impetuous amazon had prepared.

When I opened the door two sergeants came in; this made me believe that the fair spy with the Marshal had prepared the whole plan, in which I was a necessary assistant.

The lieutenant was at once taken to the station-house, and shortly afterward, on an order from the Minister of War, was transferred to the prison of Cherche-Midi.

The accomplice of Mazzinists realized that his career was ruined, and I felt sure that he would never be heard of again; but I was mistaken. I under-estimated the vengeance of Mme. X——, and later I learned the mysterious and tragical fate of the lieutenant.

Once degraded, once imprisoned, the officer believed that Mme. X—— would be satisfied. But a woman's hatred is implacable.

On the eve of being taken to Lambessa to suffer his punishment there, as the accomplice of Mazzini, our lieutenant received a letter full of repentance from Mme. X——.

She implored his forgiveness in most touching phrases for having so cruelly avenged herself. She explained the excess of her passion by saying she was madly jealous. She promised that she would have him restored to his rank, and to insure him a future if he would swear never to see the princess again. She solicited him to grant her a last interview in his prison, in order that she might receive pardon from his lips.

Men are foolish at times. This one fully believed in the penitence of this Circe. The hope of regaining her favor, and through her the favors of the château, where she was all powerful, induced him to commit the imprudence of receiving in his prison her whose vengeance was far from being assuaged.

Mme. X—— ordered an excellent breakfast to be served to the prisoner in his cell, and the two sat down at table together.

The credulous youth drank a glass of wine, and as he replaced the glass on the table, he said to this woman, whom he fancied himself deceiving:

"The Empire will not last, and the Republic will remember my services."

Mme. X——, lifting her glass to her lips, replied:

"You speak as confidently of the future as if your hours were not numbered. You forget that you have received me here and are breakfasting with me!"

Mme. X—— then went on to inform him coolly that she had given him poison.

The next morning the officer was found dead in his prison.

It was whispered about Paris that the young man was poisoned at a farewell breakfast with his mistress.

Such crimes were by no means rare at the court of this Emperor.

The vengeful woman was not satisfied with the death of her young lover, as she was determined that Pieri, the Italian, should also suffer for his cruel act against her.

Some time after the death of the young officer, Napoleon became infatuated with an Italian princess, who was the mistress of Orsini, the great conspirator. This charming creature invited the Emperor to sup with her in private at her house in the suburbs of Paris.

Louis Napoleon drove to the house disguised as a servant, and accompanied by a faithful Corsican named Griscelli, who acted as coachman.

Griscelli had notified Mme. X——, the owner of the house, of what was to take place that evening. He had told her that the Emperor was to sup with the Princess that night.

When the Emperor reached the house he was in the best of spirits, and was greatly amused because the gardener, taking him for a lackey, had said that he could not enter the vestibule. This colloquy went on for some time to the great delight of his Majesty, who enjoyed practical jokes. But the Princess appeared; and on seeing Napoleon III. in her livery, began to laugh, declaring that it was the best thing she had ever seen. The Emperor had never thought the Princess half as lovely before.

Her manner was usually reserved and dignified, and her costume usually black—her mourning, as she said, for her country. But to-night she was altogether transformed. She was radiant, and the bright colors of her costume corresponded with her eyes and her bright color. Napoleon III. attributed the gayety of the Princess to very different causes from the real ones—it was inspired by the hope of the liberation of her beloved Italy.

They went to the table. The repast was a gay one. The Italian, usually so quiet and melancholy, was now wit itself, astonishing the Emperor more and more.

He did not notice the movements of her *soubrette*. This woman had been in the room all the time, coming and going, and speaking occasionally in a low voice to her mistress, all this to the great annoyance of the Emperor, who was burning to be alone with the lady; and yet he did not think it at all strange that this woman should be obliged to come to her mistress for orders so often, more particularly as the man-servant who usually officiated in the dining-room had been dismissed for the evening.

If Griscelli had still been there, he, however, would have been greatly disturbed by seeing this woman go so often to the *buffet*, where the dessert was laid ready.

Griscelli, however, was in an adjoining room, waiting until the *soubrette*, having finished her duties, should join him there.

At last she left her mistress alone with the Emperor. His Majesty was by this time embarked in a long conversation with the Princess on the subject of Italy and its independence, of Victor Emanuel, Cavour, and Mazzini, all supporting, under different titles, the Democratic cause. But at dessert, under the influence of champagne, politics were laid aside and the Emperor was only the lover.

At this moment they were dining in the two rooms—Griscelli and the *soubrette* in the anteroom being also seated at table.

Napoleon rose from the chair; but when he fell on his knees before the Princess, it was as if a mantle of lead had fallen on his shoulders and weighed him down.

The champagne, instead of exhilarating him, had made him deadly sleepy; his eyelids drooped, he found his ideas confused, and his tongue heavy.

He was on his knees and couldn't rise; he was as if touched by a magic wand. By a last effort he lifted his eyes and looked at the Princess. He fancied that he detected an expression of hate and triumph in her face; her lovely lips were parted with a smile of scorn.

Then Napoleon, gasping for breath, stretched out his arm, which seemed almost paralyzed, and taking, with a feeble grasp, a glass from the table, he threw it with all the strength he had against the door opposite, behind which Griscelli was supping with the maid.

At this moment the door was thrown open with a crash, and Griscelli appeared with a dagger in his hand. He leaped over the table, but the Princess sat motionless but perfectly mistress of all her acts.

A new prodigy now took place. Hardly had Griscelli executed this perilous feat, than he fell like the Emperor an inert mass upon the floor.

The Princess, who had quietly raised a revolver, now leaned over and placed it against Griscelli's forehead, when the *soubrette*, with a wild shriek, caught the arm of her mistress, crying:

"Do not kill him! Ah! do not kill him!"

As if the agent had been awakened by this despairing shriek, he started to his feet with one bound, but only to fall again by the side of Napoleon, who lay without the smallest sign of life.

"Then," said the Princess, coldly, handing her woman the revolver, "Then kill him yourself!"

As the woman made no movement to take the revolver, the lady said, as she drew a dagger from her belt:

"No—this is better, for it will make less noise."

The *soubrette* took the dagger with some hesitation.

She finally dashed it away, crying aloud:

"No—I cannot! I cannot!"

"Coward!" exclaimed her mistress, "you love him! And your guilty love for the assassin of our fathers and brothers will be our ruin!"

While she was speaking, the door was thrown open. The Italian recoiled; she recognized Mme. X——, who, warned by Griscelli, had secreted herself in the vicinity of the house. She crossed the room, and, standing before the Princess, said, quietly:

"No, madame, you shall not carry the Emperor away. You shall not take him across the frontier. You shall not kill Griscelli. I have watched you, and, in spite of your putting all the servants in this house to sleep, you will find that other agents than yours have also watched the Avenue d'Auteuil."

"Oh! that woman! She is here again!" cried the Princess, tearing her hair with rage. She had just recognized Mme. X——, who had known her only too well and too long.

"Yes, madame," added the avenger, "you are right, I am 'that woman!'—a woman whom you can deceive no more, as you did, when you alienated my lover's affections and inspired him with your diabolical ideas. He is dead; his death lies at your door, for you brought him into communion with one of your Mazzinists, a certain Pieri, who has not long to live. Yes, madame, you triumphed over me once; it is my turn to triumph over you. You have played a most daring game to-day; but wait until I kill your lover, your Orsini, as you killed mine. In the meantime, learn that I kill you because you have tried to kill my Emperor!"

As she said these words, Mme. X—— went nearer to the Princess, whom she ordered to leave the room.

The Princess hesitated, and then glided away like a serpent. On the threshold of the door she turned and cried to her maid:

"Léona, if you love me, if you are faithful, come with me, leave this woman here with these men. It must be that all my people are asleep or Mme. X—— could not have been allowed to enter."

The door closed. The spy, Mme. X——, uttered a cry of rage when she heard the *soubrette* lock the door, and knew that she was left alone with her unconscious Sovereign and with Griscelli, who had fainted.

Then Léona followed the Princess. They went all through the house and found that every one was as sound asleep as in the château of the Sleeping Beauty.

As soon as the servants in the house were put to sleep by the same process which had reduced the Emperor and his improvised coachman to unconsciousness, the Mazzinists had quietly placed the horses again in the coach to which the Emperor had arrived.

When the Princess and Léona drove away in this carriage, driven by a coachman who was a Mazzinist in the livery of the Princess, the guard that had been stationed around the house never dreamed of arresting the calèche, because they recognized it as the same in which they knew the Emperor had gone to the cottage.

The calèche, therefore, went on unquestioned, as far as the

Rue de Chaillot, but the Mazzinist who drove knew little about horses, and a catastrophe was imminent.

Orsini, who was watching, beheld this carriage coming like the wind, and also saw that the coachman had lost all control over the animals. He, without the smallest hesitation, shot one of the horses through the leg, for cost what it would, the persons in that carriage must not be detained by any accident.

Around Orsini there were only Italians in disguise; the square was then only a vast extent of open ground. Orsini had hoped that no police agent would arrive before he could remove the Emperor from the carriage.

What then was his disappointment when Orsini beheld only the Princess and her maid. In a few hurried words, the Italian told him that the abduction of the Emperor had been prevented by the sudden appearance of Mme. X——.

The Princess told Orsini that she would not have hesitated to administer a dose of cold poison to this lady had she suspected her vicinity.

As the climax of misfortune, the police now appeared on the scene, having heard the report of the pistol.

One of Orsini's accomplices answered the agents who questioned him. He said to them:

"It is Sir Henry Backett's carriage; he is an eccentric, orginal person, sir—an Englishman. When his horses are troublesome, he always shoots them. This is the fourth animal he has shot in the year that I have been in his service."

The carriage drove on with the wounded horse. But Orsini was not in a happy frame of mind, for his plan had failed.

During all this time, Mme. X—— was in a state of utter desperation. It was not until the next morning that she was able to summon any one to her assistance. Then the gardener heard her, he having been less heavily drugged than the others. When this man entered the room, he cried:

"The Emperor! He and his agent are both poisoned!"

Mme. X—— bade him hold his tongue, and persuaded him that this man in the costume of a chasseur was not Napoleon III.

The gardener knew better, however, the soubrette having made him notice the chasseur the evening before, and laughed at him for not recognizing the Emperor. His silence, therefore, was purchased by Mme. X—— only with gold. This lady at once dispatched to the Prefecture the details of this nocturnal adventure. A carriage and guard were at once sent to the cottage.

It was not until six o'clock in the evening that the Emperor recovered his senses, long after Grescelli had recovered. The Sovereign, already debilitated, needed violent remedies to rouse him from his lethargy.

When the Emperor was finally able to enter the carriage sent from the Prefecture, he begged Mme. X—— to precede him to the château, and relate there the terrible experiences of the night.

The Empress, at this intelligence, fell into a rage, which Mme. X—— found it impossible to soothe. She sent for the Duc de Morny, who succeeded, not without difficulty, in reconciling the Emperor with the Empress, who had been so cruelly humiliated.

The story was soon told abroad by the Princess and by Orsini. They both said:

"We could not carry out our plans of abducting the Emperor, but we can kill him."

Orsini went back to London, after the failure of this scheme, there to mature the infernal plan which led to the catastrophe of the 14th of January.

The details of this adventure, which were as ridiculous as they were extraordinary, appeared in all the foreign papers. The Emperor and his agents, found unconscious in the livery of servants in a cottage at Auteuil, became the subject of a story in verse, called, "The Sleeping Beauty; or, the New Mysteries of the Tour de Nesle."

Orsini and Pieri were arrested in Paris soon after, while engaged in an attempt to assassinate Napoleon by means of bombs. Mme. X—— witnessed the execution of her enemy, after she had paid him a visit in his prison cell.

The affair with the fair Italian did not seem to quell the ardor of Louis Napoleon for love intrigues.

He soon had a new mistress, Marguerite Bellanger, who deceived him, and made him believe that her child was his. She hoped by this falsehood that Napoleon III. would do for his son what Louis XIV. did for his bastards.

She did not take into account either the jealousy of the Empress or the weakness of the Emperor, whose faculties were rapidly failing.

It was the first president of the court, M. Devienne, who made himself ridiculous, if nothing worse, by condescending, at the mandate of the Emperor, to perform a mission most unworthy of his position.

After a violent scene between Louis Napoleon and the Empress, who unquestionably feared some rivalry between the child of this Marguerite Bellanger and the "Child of France"—the Emperor compelled his mistress to write to M. Devienne, president of the court, the following curious and disgraceful letter:

"SIR.—You have asked an account of my relations with the Emperor. However much it may cost me, I feel that I must tell the entire truth. It is terrible to confess that I have deceived him to whom I owe everything, but he has done so much for me that I must tell all. I will only say that he is not the father of my child. Tell him that I ask his forgiveness. I have your promise, sir, that you will keep this letter.

"Accept, sir, the assurance of my distinguished consideration.

"MARGUERITE BELLANGER."

For this amende honorable, sent through the hands of a president of the court, the estate of Mouchy was presented to Marguerite Bellanger, while for the honorable president of the court there was only ridicule and contempt.

THE LOVE INTRIGUES OF JULIUS CÆSAR AND OTHER FAMOUS ROMANS.

CÆSAR'S THIRD WIFE AND HER ERROR—THE SAD STORY OF LUCRETIA—HER TRAGIC DEATH—THE GUILTY LOVES OF NERO—THE LOVE INTRIGUES OF CATILINE.

ALL those who have read about the loves and crimes of the infamous Cleopatra, Queen of Egypt, will remember that the renowned Roman general, Julius Cæsar, was her favored lover before Marc Antony was enslaved by the wicked charmer.

When the great Roman first met the Egyptian queen he was somewhat advanced in years, and he was at the zenith of his fame. During his early life, Cæsar was a great admirer of female beauty; he was unscrupulous in the pursuit of the objects of his love; and he was more than severe on one of his own wives, under circumstances where doubt existed as to her guilt.

Having disposed of two wives, Cæsar selected a fair creature as his bride. Some historians maintain that this woman, who was named Pompeia, was pure and virtuous, while others maintain that she had been seduced by one Clodius, a young Roman gentleman of fortune, who had the reputation of being a vile libertine.

One writer, in his account of Cæsar's quarrel with his third wife, gives us a peculiar account of the intrigue.

He states, in positive terms, that Pompeia had been seduced by the celebrated Clodius; but as she was so closely watched by

Cæsar and her mother-in-law, she could not obtain a favorable opportunity of seeing her lover. She thought, however, to accomplish this by a trick. The day on which they celebrated the rights of Venus at her house, Clodius, disguised in woman's clothes, passed for a singer, and was introduced among the rest. Unfortunately he was discovered, and Pompeia divorced. †

"It is not enough for the wife of Cæsar that she should be innocent, she must also be above suspicion," said Cæsar.

Not content with divorcing his wife, Cæsar resolved to pursue Clodius. The prosecution was at first suspended, on account of the triumph of Pompey, who returned from Asia; but afterwards, Cæsar pursued it with great spirit against Clodius. Happy for the latter, all were venal at Rome; money and love saved him. Of his judges, some were gained by money, others by their mistresses. The great Cicero, so formidable to Catiline, took the part of Clodius, because he was passionately in love with Clodia, his sister. This connection was so public, that they jested upon it at Rome; but Terentia, the wife of Cicero, who had the ascendency over her husband, and who feared that his attachment to Clodia might induce him to divorce her, obliged him to depose against Clodius. The young lover was acquitted, however; but he was killed soon after in a private quarrel.

Another thrilling story of love intrigues in ancient Rome is presented to us in the sad story of Lucretia, which Shakespeare has given us in glowing verse.

Tarquin, surnamed the Proud, having ascended the throne of the Romans, sought to support himself on it by the fear with which he inspired his subjects. His victories did not a little contribute to obliterate the memory of his injustice and cruelty. He had attained to an advanced age when the people of Rutuli obliged him to turn his arms against them; his first efforts were carried against Ardea, the capital of the enemy, the riches of which excited the avarice of Tarquin. He found more resistance than he expected, being obliged to besiege it in form. During this siege a singular revolution broke out at Rome.

The young nobility sought to forget their fatigues in the pleasures of the table, at a repast given by Sextus Tarquinus. The king's son being a little elevated, and the conversation turning upon the merit of their wives, every guest made the eulogium upon his own, but none with so much ardor and tenderness as Collatinus, cousin of Sextus. He was descended from Ægirus, nephew of the ancient Tarquin, and enjoyed, as his own inheritance, the city of Collatia, which had been given him by his grandmother.

It was there he passed the most happy days with Lucretia his wife. Her beauty, her birth, her virtue and the gentleness of her disposition, all united to render her extremely amiable.

Collatinus loved her to adoration, and was sensible of no greater pleasure than an opportunity to boast of his good fortune. The portrait which he drew of Lucretia at the entertainment of Sextus excited the curiosity of the guests, who proposed to go and surprise their wives, and immediately every young noble mounted his horse, and when they had arrived at Rome they found the three wives of Tarquin's sons engaged in their pleasures; and from them they proceeded to Collatia, where the scene was very different, for Lucretia was tranquilly seated in the midst of her women at work.

This interview made the deepest impression on the heart of Sextus Tarquin; he conceived for Lucretia the most violent passion, and thought only of the means to accomplish his wishes.

A few days after he introduced himself, towards night, into the house of Collatinus, under pretense of giving some orders concerning the siege. Lucretia received him with all the civility due to the son of a king, and to her husband's relation.

Scarcely had this young prince retired to his apartment, and when thinking every one in the house to be asleep, he repaired to the chamber of Lucretia. His first words were a threat to kill her if she attempted to make the least noise; he then declared his passion in the most ardent expressions.

Finding the virtue of Lucretia immovable, he again renewed his threats to kill her, adding that he would convey a slave into her bed, whom he would also kill, and publish that he had, by these murders, avenged the honor of Collatinus.

Death appeared but trifling in the eyes of the chaste Lucretia, but to die dishonored in the opinion of her husband, his family, and the public! she could not support the idea, and yielded.

The following day Lucretia desired her husband to meet her at the house of her father-in-law, at Rome, where she repaired attired in deep mourning. This appearance surprised her father and her husband, but she refused to satisfy their curiosity till they had assembled her family.

It was then she informed Collatinus of the crime of Sextus Tarquinus.

This recital excited the indignation of all present, but the sight of Lucretia, who plunged a dagger into her own bosom, inspired the whole assembly with the greatest horror and fury.

Junius Brutus, the son of a respectable senator, whom this prince had put to death on account of his virtue and riches, being present at this affecting scene, drew near the expiring Lucretia, and tearing out the dagger stained with her blood, held it up, and said:

"By this blood once so pure, and which had never been contaminated but for the detestable Tarquin, I swear that I will pursue with sword and fire, the king, the queen, and their children, and will exterminate from these places a guilty race, which infects the throne of the Romans; Gods, I call you to witness my oath!"

These words, pronounced with firmness by a man, who, till this moment, had been considered an idiot, made the deepest impression, and all present took the same oath.

Without losing a moment, Lucretius, who was governor of Rome in the king's absence, caused the gates of the city to be shut, to hinder any from going out.

Brutus then assembled the people, and after exposing the bloody corpse of Lucretia, he painted in the most energetic terms the unjust, tyrannic and violent conduct of Tarquin, and what they had to expect on the part of his sons, and concluded with offering liberty to the Romans if they would join with and support him.

Repeated acclamations convinced Brutus that they applauded his views. The senate issued an edict, which perpetually condemned the Tarquins and their posterity to banishment, and deprived them of the rights and honors of royalty. They then confided the authority to Spurius Lucretius, and the resolution was taken to destroy the monarchy, and to create two consuls.

Brutus and Collatinus were immediately chosen to fill their places. Without suffering the ardor of the Romans to cool, they departed for the army which lay before Ardea, the chiefs who had been informed of the revolution, had gained the troops, who declared in favor of the new government.

Tarquin attempted to enter Rome, but having found the gates shut against him, was obliged to retire with his family to Ceri, the city of the Etrurians.

Sextus, author of the king's misfortune, retired to the Gabians whom he had once deceived in the most unworthy manner; and as he was in a situation no longer to be feared, they deprived him of his life to punish his perfidy.

The criminal love intrigues of the famous Nero also form a very interesting chapter in Roman history. This prince attained the throne through the crimes of Agrippa, his mother, and he began his reign with great moderation. He became deeply in love with a girl named Acta, but the fear which he felt for his mother made him take all possible precautions to conceal this intrigue.

Agrippina, who employed vigilant spies, was soon informed of all. Desirous of reigning under the name of her son, she feared that Acta might prove a dangerous rival. She broke out into the most violent reproaches against her son, and those who assisted him in his amours.

Afterwards, she endeavored to overcome him by her caresses and prayers, but she clearly perceived that Nero had more respect than affection for her.

Nero had married Octavia, who, by her birth, her graces, and her virtues, merited all his attachment. But becoming enamored of Poppia Sabina, the wife of Otho, he evinced even disgust for the virtuous Octavia.

Poppia, who had made herself sole mistress of his heart, soon succeeded, by her caresses and tears, in making him divorce his wife. But he still feared Agrippina. Already familiar with crime, and vanquished by the endearments of the woman he adored, he at last resolved upon the ruin of his mother.

Having reflected upon the means he should use, he determined that she should perish in a storm. This plot did not succeed, and Agrippina being only slightly wounded, Nero resolved to throw off the mask. Without giving his mother time to recover herself, he sent a band of soldiers to put her to death.

It appears almost incredible that Burrhus and Seneca, two wise men of Rome, were accomplices in this most horrid crime; and that the Romans offered up thanks to the gods for Aggripina's death, on pretense that she would have attempted the life of her son.

Nero, however, did not dare to divorce Octavia; but some two years after he exiled her, after having put her slaves to the torture to prove that she had been untrue.

The people, who were extremely attached to the princess, made their displeasure known to the emperor, and he was obliged to recall her.

Poppia then fearing for her life, threw herself with tears at the feet of the emperor, and made him determine upon the death of Octavia. To justify this new crime, they had recourse to a vile freed-man, who publicly declared that he had recently received favors from the princess.

No one believed it; but still this unfortunate lady—the daughter, the sister, and the wife of an emperor—was exiled to the isle of Pandataria, where she soon after received the barbarous order of renouncing her life. It was said to die at the age of twenty; but they opened her veins in spite of her cries and tears, and, as the blood did not flow quickly enough, they stifled her in a hot bath.

The Roman senate ordained that thanks should be offered to the gods for this event.

Poppia, after the many crimes she had caused him to commit, at last married Nero. Her happiness was not of long duration. Having made some remonstrance to the emperor, he gave her a kick with his foot, of which she died.

Nero then became enamored of Antonia, daughter of Claudius, and because she refused to marry him, he had her put to death, under pretense of a crime against the state.

The love intrigues of the famous Catiline form another interesting chapter in the history of the great Roman empire. This man was of illustrious descent, and while he was minister of the cruelties of Sylla, he had acquired great riches, which he soon dissipated in licentiousness. Given up from the most tender age to his passions, he ruined a young person of high birth who afterwards became his mother-in-law.

He had the presumption to offer his vows to the vestal Sabina Terentia, and he did not meet a refusal. It is known how severe the Romans were upon the faults of their vestals; it required all the credit of Catilina to save Terentia and her lover.

Catiline became afterwards desperately in love with Aurelia Orestilla, an illustrious Roman, then a widow, who had a child by her first husband. Catiline ardently desired her to marry him, but the affection Orestilla entertained for her child prevented her yielding to the wishes of her lover.

Catiline stopped at no crime when it tended to gratify his passions. He poisoned the child which was the obstacle to his marriage, and espoused the mother.

Soon after this his licentiousness and prodigality reduced him to misery; this wretched situation threw him into despair, to escape which he abandoned himself to the delirium of his imagination. Connected with a number of debauchees as ruined as himself, Catiline thought he must overthrow his country to retrieve his shattered fortunes.

His connections with the most illustrious young men of Rome, and likewise with several Roman colonies of Italy, made him hope his projects would be crowned with the greatest success. What still increased the number of the conspirators was a society of licentious young women, loathers of their husbands, and given up to crime. In this number, Sempronia, the wife of Junius Brutus, was above all distinguished.

Never had woman more talents than she to captivate hearts. To an uncommon share of beauty she joined a charming voice and all the allurements of wit. It was from her school that Catiline drew several of his associates. Nothing less was attempted than to assassinate the consuls, and above all Cicero, one of them; to set fire to the four corners of Rome; to massacre a great part of the Patricians; to seize upon their riches and the government of the republic.

The conspirators several times fixed the day and hour to execute their projects, but they always observed that precautions were taken against their enterprises. The conspiracy was at length discovered; Cicero told it to Catiline in the senate.

It was then this prince of orators made one of those orations which will be the admiration of all ages. Catiline, although discovered, did not lose all hope; he left Rome, and put himself at the head of the troops which he had raised in Italy, relying on those friends he left at Rome who were not yet discovered to execute what they had agreed to, and facilitate his entrance into the city.

This hope was vain. Cicero having obtained the most unequivocal proofs of the conspiracy, four of the principal conspirators were put to death. Catiline, pursued by the Roman legions, gave them battle; and feeling his army give way, listened only to his despair, threw himself into the midst of the enemy and was killed. Thus ended, with its chief, this famous conspiracy.

Among the number of the conspirators was one named Quintus Curius, who had been expelled the senate for the number of his crimes. Passionately enamored of a woman named Fulvia, he had dissipated all his property with her, and was reduced to the most extreme indigence; Fulvia had not then the same attention and affection for her lover as before.

Curius, enchanted with the project of Catiline, which he hoped would soon put him in a situation to regain the affections of Fulvia, whom he adored, had the weakness to intimate to this woman the greatness of his expectations; but he affected the utmost secrecy upon all the rest. Fulvia was soon informed of all she wished to know. Either through inadvertency, or what is more probable, from disgust of Curius, she divulged the secret.

Cicero, then consul, was apprised of it. He sent privately for Fulvia, to draw from her all the necessary information, and likewise engaged her to obtain from Curius a particular detail and plan of the whole conspiracy. It was by this means that Cicero, who distinguished himself so greatly on that account during his consulship, frustrated the fatal machinations of Catiline, and saved his country.

THE TRAGIC INTRIGUES OF A FAMOUS MOTHER AND HER SON.

KILLING A RIVAL—THE DOUBT OF THE GREAT SON'S LEGITIMACY—ALEXANDER'S LOVE INTRIGUE.

The world has heard of Alexander of Macedon, as a great conqueror, and as a founder of noted cities; but it is not so generally known that his mother was one of the most infamous characters of ancient times.

Olympia, the mother of the great general, was divorced by Philip, King of Macedonia, in consequence of her bad conduct. It is in fact believed that this prince was not the father of Alexander, and Olympia did not strongly affirm that he was. After the divorce, Philip married Cleopatra, daughter of Attalus.

Olympia conceived a jealousy so violent that she was determined to revenge herself. It was she who engaged Pausanias, her lover, to assassinate the king.

After this murder she took no measures to conceal her guilt, and caused the greatest honors to be paid to the memory of Pausanias, who had been punished with death. Cleopatra, the principal cause, was not forgotten. Olympia first murdered Philip's child, and then hung the mother.

This wicked woman then cons . . to Apollo the poniard that had devolved her h■■■■■ ■f the | fe

At the f .■t of the p■■t■■l■ of the p■ ■re Cleopatra, At-■l ■ ■a ■ng ni■shed to m ■h v h ■ ■ ■ Macedonians ■ ■ ■■■ the ■ ■t ■ ■r ■ ■a ■f ■ p■■■ might give Philip a legitimate ■■r ■ ■' ■ingdom.

Alexander, who was present, exclaimed with rage:
" How, rascal, dost thou take me for a bastard?" He threw his cup at his head at the same moment.

The king, who was at another table, rose in fury, and advanced, sword in hand, towards his son. Happily, his anger and

the fumes of the wine, caused him to fall, which gave the spectators time to prevent any serious consequences.

The celebrated conqueror also became involved in a tragic love intrigue.

After the celebrated battle of Arbelles, which decided the fate of Darius and that of his vast empire, Alexander marched towards Persepolis, the capital of Persia, the gates of which he found open.

The conqueror gave the plundering of the town to his soldiers, and reserved for himself the treasures of a king. The palace of Darius was reckoned a superb edifice.

One evening Alexander gave himself up to the company of a beauty named Thais, who begged of him to have that place set on fire. The prince, whose reason was drowned in wine, and who felt himself incited by the caresses and prayers of a pretty woman, took upon himself the trouble of setting fire to that splendid building; the flames soon reached the town, and all was reduced to ashes.

Thais, according to Plutarch, was the favorite of Ptolemy, who was king of Egypt. She solicited the ruin of Persepolis for no other reason but to make up for the conflagration of Athens, and that it might be said that a woman had more contributed to avenge Greece than the greatest soldiers had been able to accomplish.

THE FATAL LOVE INTRIGUE OF A BEAUTIFUL COUNTESS.

[THE JEALOUS HUSBAND AND THE KING LOVER—THE VIRTUOUS WOMAN FALLS—THE REVENGE OF A TYRANT HUSBAND.

ONE of the most beautiful women in France during the reign of Francis I. was the daughter of Madame de Grailly, of the once powerful but impoverished house of Froix.

This unfortunate woman was celebrated for her beauty before she had attained her thirteenth year; and it was at that period that the wealthy Count de Chateaubriant sought her in marriage. She being without portion, his proposition was readily accepted; and this young beauty was delivered into the arms of a man she did not love. His conduct was not such as to gain the heart of his wife. Jealous to excess, he confined her in a castle, where he permitted her to see no one but himself—a certain way to inspire her with the desire of seeing others. Chance at length wrested from this jealous man the treasure he guarded with so much care.

He was obliged to repair to the court of Francis I. to defend a lawsuit of the greatest consequence, upon which his whole fortune depended, and the king asked the Count de Chateaubriant why he had not brought his wife with him, adding she was young and handsome, and with those qualities was sure to be an ornament to his court.

The count replied that his wife hated the great world, and only delighted in solitude. But the king pressed him so often that to at length promised that he would write to his wife to come to him.

The count well knew that this letter would not produce the expected effect, as he had agreed with the countess that she should not leave the castle without a bracelet of hair, which she had presented to him, and this bracelet did not accompany the letter; at least he believed so.

But M. de Lautrec, brother of the countess, entertained a passion for one of her ladies, and greatly desired that his sister should come to court, that he might see his mistress; the young lady, who anxiously desired it, informed by him of all that had passed, sent him a bracelet worked with her mistress's hair, and exactly resembling that which she had given to her husband.

The bracelet being sent to the countess, with a letter from the count, she instantly began her journey with her attendants. On her arrival, she easily proved to her jealous husband that she had been deceived.

Then the Count de Chateaubriant grew frantic; and, regarding

himself as already dishonored, he abandoned his wife and his lawsuit, and retired to his castle in Brittany.

A young and beautiful woman, yet inexperienced, and admired by a king as amiable and gallant as Francis I., was in great danger of forgetting herself. This was the case in which we find the Countess de Chateaubriant. Her beauty made the most lively impression upon the heart of the king, and it was not long before he acquainted her with it.

The countess was proud of her virtue, and relied too much upon it. The resistance she at first opposed inflamed the king fear that his cause was hopeless. But the match was unequal. The little god conquered, and the Count de Chateaubriant, in his retirement, was soon informed that his wife had become the mistress of the king, and that she was the distributress of favors and rewards.

The brothers of the countess thought they ought to profit by this circumstance; but the incensed husband refused all their entreaties, and inwardly swore that he would in a signal manner avenge his honor.

Francis I., being called to Italy, left the countess at court. The battle of Pavia, where he was made prisoner, retarded his return. During his absence, the Duchess d'Angoulême, mother to the king, inflicted so many mortifications upon the countess, that she preferred to return to her husband.

In vain this faulty but charming woman wrote a letter, in the most submissive terms, to her husband. He was inflexible; and if he did not take her life upon the spot, it was because he had some remains of affection, which, in spite of her conduct, he still felt for her.

When the king had regained his liberty, the Count de Chateaubriant, fearing that he would exert his authority to take his wife from him, entered the apartment of the countess, accompanied by several masked ruffians, and told her that she must die. She made little or no resistance; they opened her veins, and her barbarous husband found the cruelty to stay till she breathed her last sigh. After this severe vengeance, he escaped into England, and never returned to France, till after having given the house that bore his name to the High Constable de Montmorency, to shelter himself from the pursuit of the parents of his wife.

[THE END.]